LAST
CONNECTION

SUZANNE HILLIER

LAST
CONNECTION

SUZANNE HILLIER

AquaZebra™
Book Publishing

Cathedral City, California
2025

First paperback edition September 2025
Library of Congress Control Number: 2025911236
ISBN: 978-1-954604-19-3 (paperback)

Book design by AquaZebra.com

AquaZebra™
Web, Book & Print Design

DEDICATION

To J. Thomas Wiley, always my first and favourite reader.

"Come to me, my melancholy baby,
Cuddle up and don't be blue;
All your fears are foolish fancy, may be,
You know, dear, that I'm in love with you".

—*My Melancholy Baby*, lyrics by George A. Norton

Prologue

Chesapeake Park was packed with claws of arthritic ice, clinging to the bare branches of its maple and walnut trees half hidden by clumps of pines and spruce, their thick branches heavy with snow. Then the shadows started. Needles of sleet came, peppering the faces of the search party, causing the fur-trimmed hoods of some of the group to bristle like the fur of wolves hungry for food. The park was filled with crags overlooking plunging sunken gullies.

They knew who they were looking for but feared finding them. The car, covered with snow, had been parked outside the entrance. It was getting darker and soon it would be harder to see through the needles, needles that put you to sleep, sometimes forever.

PART 1

CHAPTER 1

1978

Lawrence Park in North Toronto, bordered by Yonge, Lawrence and Bayview, was one of the city's most desirable neighborhoods. The northern Yonge-Lawrence area had swings and a children's playground built on a rich green lawn, and south of this were flower gardens and more sunken lawns. The intervening avenues that stretched into Bayview were lined with large maples and sedate stone or brick houses occupied by "professionals," most often doctors and lawyers, and on occasion a corporate tycoon. Less often, there were more modest homes where salesmen and teachers, who had purchased when property values were much lower, resided.

The MacKenzies had the cheapest home on one of the best avenues. Douglas MacKenzie was a salesman for a well-known drug company. His wife Margaret, formerly Peggy Hearn of Belfast, who'd met Doug during one of his Irish promotional trips, was a stay-at-home housewife. They had two daughters, Della and Rosemary, known as Del and Rosie, who were born three years apart. Rosie was three years old in 1978.

Mid-summer days are hot in Toronto, and in Lawrence Park during the late '70s, only a handful of wives worked outside the home. In the afternoons, many of them sat by their glistening new pools sipping long coolers spiked with gin, while others, the church goers, poured pink lemonade from chunky crystal jugs where fast dissolving grey ice cubes floated. They lay on their stuffed lounge chairs and watched, with half-closed eyes behind fashionably slanted dark shades, while their tanned children and playmates screamed at each other as they paddled in their brightly colored tubes. Some of the visiting children were on play dates, their mothers having gone to shop at the supermarkets on Eglinton, or to get their hair cut and curled—or permed—in the salons of Yonge, to enhance the current feathered look.

Since the MacKenzies had no pool or garage, Rosie usually played in the driveway of their home. She was a pretty, slight, dark-haired child with eyes the color of green glass and a mop of curls that streamed down her back in a tangled ponytail. She was playing as usual with Jessica and Mathew Langdon, whose mother, Joan Langdon, worked part-time as a secretary at her husband's law office. The Langdon children, whose family had a garage, two cars and a swimming pool, still favored the MacKenzie's driveway. This was probably because of the pink lemonade and chocolate chip cookies Rosie's mother served at three each afternoon. Rosie's mother fluttered, which the Langdon children found interesting, constantly anointing Rosie's face and arms with sunblock, even rubbing her back with a soft towel and Johnson's baby powder to get rid of possible perspiration. That afternoon Margaret had produced six freshly baked chocolate chip cookies, and three glasses of pink lemonade. She had placed them on the front wooden steps near the playing children.

While the MacKenzies' home was the most modest on the street, the Bishop-Dunlops', directly across from it, was the most majestic. There were even two columns at the entrance to give it a slight southern plantation look. Jim Bishop-Dunlop managed highly successful stock portfolios at one of Toronto's largest brokerages and his wife Lucille, whose father had been in steel, was active in several of Toronto's charities: work so demanding, she often complained, it was like having ten jobs.

The Bishop-Dunlops had two teenagers: Alma-Louise, or Alley-Lou, who had been accepted for first-year arts that coming September at McGill University; and Alexander, known as Sandy, aged sixteen, who was still in high school. Sandy's father had promised he could take driving lessons the next year and be the owner of a secondhand convertible at eighteen. Sandy yearned for the day. He was always referred to by his father at the brokerage as "a really good kid," and they played golf together every weekend during the summer. He was also a reasonable hockey and tennis player. In the summer of August 1978, he was without a summer job and unusually restless.

Alley-Lou's friend, Denise, aged eighteen, was sitting on the diving board. She was wearing a black bikini and its top barely covered the nipples of her high cone-like breasts. One of her legs was folded, and visible on the inside of her thigh, as she sat swinging the other leg, was the tattoo of a navy-colored dragon, its nose pointed at what Sandy envisaged as her soft pink pussy. He thought of it like a cluster of warm moist rose petals and of the joy of penetrating it on a morning and nightly basis. Denise followed his eyes, smiled, and getting up and standing straight on the diving board sliced into the sun-silvered pool. He felt her arm brush against his as he stood in the water and felt a familiar tightening under his soaked trunks.

"Too bad Sandy's only sixteen," he heard her say to Alley-Lou in a loud whisper before their giggles became muffled under the soft warm water. He left the pool and went into the garage on his way to the house. His mother's Porsche was there, shining silver like the pool's water. She was home, unusual in mid-afternoon. He placed his hand on the car's silver flank and the warmth coursed up his arm. He opened the car door. The keys were in the ignition, again unusual. They were always placed in the gold bowl on the mahogany table in the front hall. He got in and pressed the garage door opener. Then he turned the ignition key. The engine purred like a metal cat. He pressed the pedal with his bare foot and it leapt forward. He pressed his foot on the brake but it was the accelerator, and the silver cat, now a tiger, leapt across the street, over the curb, and into Rosie and the Langdon children.

The Langdon children were killed instantly, their small broken bodies soaked with blood: Jessica still with a half-eaten chocolate chip cookie in her lifeless hand. Rosie called out to them and tried to hobble over but her leg gave away. Now out of the car, Sandy stood looking at them. He wished he was dead.

Joan Langdon spent two months at the Clarke Psychiatric, following which she and Gerald Langdon successfully sued the Bishop-Dunlops for negligence causing the deaths of Jessica and Mathew. Both families moved from the Avenue. Sandy Bishop-Dunlop, in spite of two years of therapy, died of an accidental drug overdose at nineteen. And Rosemary MacKenzie moved into her parent's bed and stayed there, tightly pressed against her mother, while her father thought, quite correctly, that she might never leave.

The childhood post-traumatic stress disorder, Rosemary's diagnosis at age six, lingered. She had friends, but not close ones. Her mother invited members of her class on play dates, but she would not play with them. "Why?" asked her mother. "They're sweet little souls and they like you." Rosemary would look at her mother, her small pale face solemn, and reply, "They might get hurt like Mattie and Jessie." Nothing could ever persuade her otherwise.

Rosemary's sister Della—with her thick ginger hair that she'd never let her mother secure in a pony-tail, her up-tilted nose with its dusting of freckles, and her quick giggle—surveyed it all as if sitting before a large screen watching a Disney Production. Her mother, who in the past had shared her time between them, was now fully focused on Rosie. Del had resented it at first, but then flourished under her mother's benign neglect. She became independent early, usually surrounded by friends who shared her quick giggle. And she became close to her father, whose concern for Rosie had turned from worry and perplexity to irritation. Del and her dad had breakfast at a pancake house on Eglinton on Saturdays, and then they shopped at various stores on Yonge where she picked out her choices of clothes for school—and later, parties. Although there were money concerns, she knew she could always count on her dad, even after he started to spend every Saturday overnight with his secretary, Alice Dion. Alice, who had loved Doug from a distance for years, had benefited from Rosie and her mother's unusual closeness.

"We have a brother-sister relationship," he had sighed to Alice, just before they started having sex. "Not that my wife was ever into sex that much, but now you can forget it. Everything's poor wee Rosie and her hang-ups."

Their mom and dad had gone out together—a rare happening—to a neighborhood cocktail party. Del, aged fifteen and in grade eleven, had been reprimanded by her mother, who had watched that afternoon from the living room window as she'd necked with Eddie Gushue on the front porch. When she came in, her mother had told her she was "cheapening herself," and well on the way to becoming "a rag on every bush." As well, her mother had reported her conduct to her much-loved daddy, who had given her a conspiratorial wink. But none of this had improved Del's mood.

"You've ruined Mom and Dad's sex life," she told twelve-year-old Rose as they washed dishes together. Rose went weak with shock at this information. "How?" she whispered.

Del felt a twinge of satisfaction at seeing her mother's little princess so upset. "They can't make out," she told her. "That's when they do it, married people, in bed at night. But you're always there—like a little log. And that's why Daddy makes out with Alice and not Mom."

Rose sat slowly down on a kitchen chair, bent over the kitchen table, placed her hands over her face and shook with sobs. Del, outspoken but good-hearted, walked over and rubbed Rose's thin convulsing shoulders with warm, firm hands. "Not your fault, Rosie—it's all Mom. It started with that awful Langdon accident when you were three—instead of helping you get over it, she made it worse."

The way Del said it convinced Rose that she had discussed the situation with her father, and when she continued, she was sure of it. *"An avoidant personality disorder, over-sensitive, easily hurt, reluctant to be involved,"* Del parroted. "Such crap. That's in the report that the psychologist wrote, and Mom's made it worse, treating you like a piece of china and ignoring the rest of us, not that I care. I'd hate to have her poke her Irish nose into everything I do." But Rose kept sobbing.

The next day, as she watched her mother peel vegetables for dinner, Rose spoke up: "Mommy, I'm getting too old now to be sleeping in your bed. I need my own room."

Her mother did not answer, but gathered the carrot and potato peels, wrapped them in a newspaper, and placed them in the garbage can under the sink. When she spoke her voice was heavy with hurt. "Of course you do. I only did it for you—you needed me so much . . ."

Rosie escaped into her novels: she would select an author from the North Toronto Public Library and then plow through all of his or her work. By grade ten, she'd conquered Jane Austen, the Brontes, Dickens, and Flaubert's *Madame Bovary*. She even read Judy Blume for general information. "A true academic," her teacher had written on her grade ten report card. This was the same year that Del, in grade twelve, had stayed out all night and her sobbing mother had blamed her father for creating "an immoral family atmosphere."

Rose had friends, even a circle she had lunch with, and they liked her—or appeared to—but there was no best friend—and no boys.

"Treat boys like girls except for the plumbing," instructed Del one afternoon, as they sat together on the back steps, not noticing their mother standing near the screen door listening.

"And perhaps you'd like to tell us how you acquired your knowledge of male plumbing."

Del stifled a laugh, and Rose turned her head away quickly so her mother would not notice her smile. She had not been asked to the prom, but she was not unduly concerned, although an invitation would have been nice. She had no doubt that eventually in her life an academic Darcy would step forward, right out of the pages of *Pride and Prejudice*, and they would have wonderful lovemaking, children, and literary discussions. And besides, her mother, to whom Del had broken the prom news, was taking her to the Royal York that night for dinner and an appearance by the singer Lena Horne.

Then everything changed. Douglas MacKenzie had spent the weekend having sex and drinking Johnnie Walker with Alice Dion, who had become like a second wife—and a much more responsive one. As he left her small bungalow in Etobicoke at nine o'clock that Sunday night in 1992, he crumbled on her wooden steps and suffered a sudden and fatal heart attack. An hysterical Alice had phoned 911, but the next time Rose saw her father, he was dressed in his best dark suit, looking quite healthy at Stafford's Funeral home the night before the funeral—a funeral from which Alice Dion had been banned.

Del's grief was loud and uncontrolled. She threw herself on her bed and sobbed her heart out. She had loved her father. They had been co-conspirators against the duo of her mother and the fragile Rosie. They had laughed at them—together—in guilty and muffled mirth. What she did not understand, until later, was that Rose had also mourned. Rose was uneasy in her father's presence—knowing he was also uneasy—but never unkind: just sort of tentative, as if she were made of fine crystal where too quick a move would cause breakage. But she'd hoped that would go and later on they might have a relationship like he and Del had. Now it would never happen. Daddy was gone and they'd never laugh together.

"I'd hoped," she said to the shaking, howling Del, whose face was pressed against her soaked bedroom pillow, "that someday I'd be close to Dad like you were, but now it's too late." Then she also started to cry, not in Del's howling rasp of sorrow, but in a broken and hopeless way. Del sat up, suddenly pressed her burning swollen face against Rose's cool damp one and hugged her, rocking with her on the bed. And from then on Rose realized that Del loved her, and that any problems Rose faced were attributed to her mother, who Del held responsible not only for Rose's "piss-poor" teen years, but her father's untimely death.

Douglas MacKenzie's estate was disappointing. There was $200,000 in insurance and a battered stock portfolio, which fortunately recovered due to his widow's fear of selling. Del was in the final year of her legal clerical course so it was decided she would finish. But for Rose to attend the four-year Honours English course at the University of Toronto she'd applied for was thought to be impractical. With this decision, Rose saw the academic Darcy step back into the Austen novel.

"We've gotta be sensible, lovey dove," murmured her mother. "You've gotta go the practical route—too bad your father didn't think more of us." So Rose considered applying for the dental hygienist course at a community college. Her father's death had made her mother even more demanding in her desire for closeness and Rose felt obliged to reciprocate.

In grade twelve, Donny Lewis had started to walk her home after school. He was in her class at North Toronto Collegiate, a quiet and rather shy boy with dark hair, a bit of a loner like herself and not into sports. He lived on Mount Pleasant Road, south of Lawrence Park, so she knew he must like her as walking her home was out of his way. They talked mostly of books. He'd read the Russians—*Crime and Punishment* and even most of *War and Peace*—and this impressed her.

"Way to go Rosie," Del had said at the table that night, after she had spied them walking home together. Rose saw her mother frown and noticed that she got up from the dinner table abruptly. Since her father's death they had gone everywhere together.

Donny's father was a mechanic and his mother packed food for one of the large commercial food operations. He'd told her this with some hesitation, as if such occupations might be looked down on by a Lawrence Park resident. "My dad just sold drugs—legal ones," she'd said reassuringly and they'd both laughed. He appeared relieved.

One Wednesday afternoon in April, he'd asked her to go to a movie with him that Saturday night. There was a small movie house on Mount Pleasant, south of Eglinton. "It's *The Bodyguard*, really cool—John Dino was talking about it." John Dino was the school's quarterback and he had a future scholarship from an American University. His opinion meant something.

"That'd be great," Rose said. He had been looking at the sidewalk when he asked her, but when she agreed, he looked up and their eyes had met. She mentioned it at dinner that night, and saw her mother compress her lips. And she'd said to her as they were doing the dishes, "I'll be all alone and I'd hoped we'd see it together." Rose felt Del, who was not helping with the dishes, give her a swift shin kick in passing. But Rose had a flush of guilt. She'd not only ruined her mother's sex life, but she was deserting her on a Saturday night.

That Thursday, as Donny walked slowly home with her after school, Rose told him she couldn't go. He stopped walking, "Why not?"

She could see he saw it as a rejection and remembered how difficult it had been for him to ask her. She thought afterwards she should have said, "I ruined my parents' sex life and my father died. Now I can't leave my mother. She needs me and I'd die of guilt." But she didn't. She merely said, "I can't go—something else came up."

He stopped walking, turned abruptly and walked away head-down, again looking at the sidewalk. She knew she should have called after him. She had hurt his feelings—made him feel unworthy. She remembered Del and the plumbing remark.

"It's all Mom's fault," Del said, that night when she told her. "But you never stand up to her—she plays you on her Belfast fiddle. There goes your date for the prom. You can keep the one with Mom and Lena Horne at the Royal York."

She was right: neither Rose nor Donny attended. In fact, Donny never looked at Rose again.

Upon her acceptance as a dental hygienist trainee at George Brown College, Rose had reluctantly withdrawn her application for Honours English. Her mother had informed both daughters that, as a woman in her fifties, she had no intention of starting a career. She had passed on this information as she sat at the table before a plate of meat loaf and mashed potatoes, with carrots and canned peas, that she seemed to serve every night.

"I'm gone," Del said. "I'll be free to live it up at twenty-one."

Her mother sniffed and took a small bite of meat loaf which she'd munched and swallowed before answering. "I've never known you not to be free to live it up," she said. "I've certainly not held you back." She'd been looking forward to Del's staying and contributing to household expenses and found it difficult to hide her annoyance.

"You've heard your selfish sister," she said to Rose, as they did the dishes together. Her mother refused to use the dishwasher, which she said would ruin her china, a wedding gift collected in a far happier time. "It looks as if you've little choice: you'll stay with me and help with expenses."

So Rose started her two-year course, having passed the aptitude test for manual dexterity. There were no boys in the dental hygienist class, but several in other courses, and they were interested. She was, after all, an attractive girl—at times almost beautiful. She refused all requests for dates, telling them she was "attached." Not adding that the attachment was to her mother.

CHAPTER 2

Elsewhere in 1978

The belt hung by its buckle from a nail next to the kitchen stove. It was worn and battered, as it had been used on a daily basis for everything Ricardo did from wetting his bed to stealing food from the refrigerator. At the very beginning when he was starting to walk, he cried, but then when he was about three, he stopped. And no matter how hard she did it, he wouldn't make a sound. "Stop beatin' up on him," his father would yell from the next room. But then she'd do it harder, erupting in a cascade of Spanish he refused to speak, although he understood every word. He was a good-looking kid with dark hair and eyes like her, but with a large frame like his old man.

Dolores Diaz's parents had arrived at Nova Scotia from Honduras in the '50s. They were heading for Toronto, but by some navigation error had landed in Halifax and decided to stay. Her father had gotten a job as a waiter in a fish restaurant, and her mother cleaned rooms at the Lord Nelson Hotel. They lived in a rented flat on Ingles Street. Dolores was a tiny girl, who later wore tottering high heels to compensate, showing off her bird-like ankles and high-muscled calves. In high school she had been famous for her breasts, and behind her back was known as "Tittie Diaz" by the male students. She always covered her full lips with dark red lipstick and wore her black hair in a high pompadour in front, while the back swung in a long curly ponytail.

When Vince McCready had first seen her in grade eleven he knew he had to have her, and on their second date he did, right on the front seat of his father's battered Ford pick-up he'd borrowed for the occasion. And on the fifth date, she got pregnant. He was a big, blond, broad-shouldered boy whose father had once owned a trawler, but who was done in by competition and drink. After she found out about her pregnancy, they'd both quit school. He'd been an indifferent student but she'd always done well. "A waste," her teacher had said when she'd told her, "And what are you going to do now with no education, a baby, and Vince McCready?" They moved into her parents flat but only briefly. She had disgraced them, her mother had wailed in Spanish, after the wedding dress she'd bought her failed to conceal her swollen belly.

"Don't want to stay here," she kept complaining to Vince. "*Nada* for me here."

Vince did not want to leave. He liked working on the trawler his father had lost to Skipper O'Neil, who, feeling sorry for him, had let him join the crew. He drank at the local tavern with his buddies in the evenings when they'd finished emptying their haul of glistening cod. But Dolores kept on about moving to Toronto.

"Don't know what the fuck I'd do there," he grumbled.

"Plenty of jobs," she insisted, "Work for us both—more money than here."

The baby was large and forceps were needed, so for the first few weeks after birth one side of his face had been paralyzed. But it disappeared over time. She did not nurse, using the facial paralysis as an excuse. He cried a lot and spit up his formula. He had, she thought, looking at him, ruined her life. In Toronto she would put him in daycare. To her surprise, Vince walked the baby at night, even if half-cut from his nightly booze.

In the early '60s, Regent Park was a public housing project of about sixty acres. Parts of it had been called Cabbagetown, because the Irish, when they moved in, had planted cabbages in their small front gardens. Now there was gentrification, and there were musicians and artists in the neighborhood. In the main however, Regent Park was an area in the bowels of Toronto bordered by Gerrard, River, Shuter and Parliament Streets, all made up of social housing. There were row houses full of Irish people who squatted there temporarily, and then Calabrians, whose stay for the most part was brief. In the '70s, the Chinese and Caribbean immigrants started to arrive. They lived in some of the row houses on Parliament or in the five high-rise apartment towers on the south side of Dundas. At that time, the McCreadys rented the first floor of one of the Dundas Street brick row houses on the east side, using money borrowed from the Diazes. The Canarellas lived on the second floor.

When Rick looked back he thought of the smells, the tomato sauce full of basil and oregano from Mrs. Canarella's flat, his father's cigarette smoke drenched with rum and his mother's biting cologne. There were good things about it: Cherry and Sugar Beach bordering the lake, and the publicly funded pool at the community center where he swam at every opportunity. And if you were really starving, and didn't mind the smell, there was always the Sally Ann or the Mission where they'd feed you—but no self-respecting resident of Regent Park would be caught dead there.

The first week they arrived, Vince got a job in construction. At that time buildings were going up all over Toronto, and he was strong and knew some carpentry work. But he lost the job. He drank at night, this time at home, smoking one cigarette after the other and wanting to leave. He thought of the Atlantic, the glistening silver of the fish, and his buddies at the tavern.

"You always late," snarled the foreman from Calabria. "Ona more time an' you go."

There was always one more time and soon there were no more jobs. They knew about him in construction. When his bottle was finished, he'd crawl in bed with Ricky, who'd say in the morning, "Pa, you gotta get up." But he never did.

Dolores got a job at Roberto's on Bloor as a shampoo girl. There were good prospects: she would become an assistant to a stylist, and in time become one, even though she lacked the usual courses. She was good with her hands. "It was," she told Vince, when he insisted he wanted to leave, "just a matter of time." At night, after the last customer left, there were cocaine parties. She liked Rocco, the top stylist, and they'd go to his car. His wife found out and told Roberto that Dolores had to go or "no more Rocco." She left, but the beauty salon community was small, and there were no more jobs. But by then she had found other ways to make money.

Vince knew he was lucky to get the roofer job. He liked the crew, some from Cape Breton and some from Newfoundland, who he could go to the bar with after work. The pay wasn't bad, although nothing like construction. He stopped being late, as Dolores and Rick forced him out of bed, always hung-over, but after three cups of coffee and two bottles of Coke, mobile. Rick would bring him the first icy bottle of Coke at six-thirty, and he would gulp it down, still stoned. Rick would even lay his clothes on the bed, taking them from the floor where he'd dropped them the night before.

"You're my little buddy," Vince would say, and rumple his hair with his large rough hand that stank of tar and smoke. He had a thermos and he filled it with rum. It got him through the day. Until the day it happened.

It was only a two-story building, but he had fallen off the roof and cracked his back—his first and second lumbars. He couldn't move—not without crying out—so he was taken to St. Mike's where he was given morphine, cortisone shots and Percodan pills. He got Workers' Compensation for four months: then their doctors said his back was healed and he could work. But his back was still killing him, and he still got the percs, thank God—eventually from two doctors. He took them with his rum, cracking them between his back teeth so he'd feel a rush. Then all of a sudden he'd be back on the trawler, laughing with his mates and seeing the sea glittering silver or grey and nasty with the wind pushing the waves against the sides of the ship. And drinking in air so clean it cut through him like a knife. During this period sometimes he'd imagine taking off, just him and the kid.

Money was scarce, so at times he'd sell a few percs to Marty—who'd buy anything—and who lived in one of the high-rises on the south side of Dundas, complaining that he knew he'd do a double mark-up. But then he couldn't sell the pills because he needed them so bad. He'd ask her for money. "Get your *dinero* from Workers' Comp," she'd say, or "Sue the friggin' company." But the lawyer told him he couldn't sue—he'd already tapped Workers' Comp and they'd found his thermos stinking of rum. "But my back still fuckin' kills me," he protested. That's when he got that second doctor for more pills, knowing that when he chewed them with his rum the pain would lessen and he'd leave Toronto—at least in his mind.

It was July 1978, and Ricardo would be turning nine that fall. "Can we go to Centre Island?" he asked. "You been promisin' me all week." He brought Pa an icy Coke from the fridge, and watched as he took the two yellow pills from the bottle and crunched them between his back teeth. He knew the coke made them sizzle through his body, not as good as the rum, but enough to get him up.

"She gone?" It was ten on a Saturday morning.

"Never saw her. Don't think she came back."

She'd made them beans and rice the night before and then Ricky, through the half-opened bedroom door, watched her get ready. She made up her face like an artist, drawing a navy pencil around her eyes, brushing paint on her lashes and scrutinizing her black plucked brows for stray hairs. She applied beige liquid to her face and then outlined her lips—again using a pencil—this time a brazen scarlet and filling in the void with lipstick, like he used to do in his coloring books.

But she'd spotted him.

"Who do yuh think yer lookin' at?" Then the door would slam shut.

When she appeared again she'd have on shorts if it was summer or tight jeans if it was spring or fall, and always the snug cotton shirt that showed inches of her breasts and the sandals or pumps with the towering spike heels. If it was cold, she'd have her black leather jacket over her shoulders. Sometimes she'd give him a ten and say, "Jus' in case I can't make it home you can get some grub for you and the asshole."

"We'll need bucks—for the ferry an' your rides an' dogs," Pa said.

"She gave me a saw-buck."

"Not enough. See what she got in her room, taped under the bureau or mattress. I know she got money stashed." His father slept with him. She kept her own room, which was banned to them both. But not locked.

"She'll beat the livin' crap outta me."

"I'll tell her I done it."

His mother's room pulsed with a mixture of hairspray and piercing floral cologne that he'd watched her spray on her neck and half-exposed breasts. He felt his heart beat against his ribs knowing he'd be finished if she caught him. Then his father was at the bedroom door. "Look under the mattress." He found it: a thick roll of bills held together by a rubber band. "Take three twenties"

"I'll take two twenties, she gave me ten."

Anger pushed through the golden nugget of love he always carried for Pa. He knew Pa wouldn't save him from her belt if she found out it was him.

"Ferry for two to Centre Island and back, rides, an' you gonna go without your dogs an' chips?"

Rick thought of the dogs, felt their rubbery spice mixed with mustard and relish against his tongue and the roof of his mouth, and the bite of the Coke to wash them down. He took another ten. But he knew she'd count every bill.

He watched as his father tried to make him toast, but he was too clumsy and his fingers shook so he couldn't put the slices in the toaster. Rick took over. "Don't need it, Pa, but you should have somethin.' I'll just have a few cornflakes an' make you coffee."

His father sat down carefully on the kitchen chair and gave him a tobacco-stained half smile. "No one got a boy like mine," he said. "Eight years old and he's makin' his ol' man breakfast." Rick felt a surge of love and pride.

Later they walked together to where the ferry docked. His father took his hand and he felt the love like electricity go up his arm and spread through his body. He looked at his father's arm, with the sprinkling of golden hairs and the blue tattoo of an anchor. If he'd seen another kid holding his old man's hand he'd label him a suck. But he didn't care. He squeezed the large coarse fingers just so he could feel a repeat of the electric love charge.

They lined up for the tickets and then waited for the ferry. Because it was Saturday there was a crowd, families all speaking in different accents and tongues: Caribbeans, Chinese, Italians, and some Indians and Pakistanis. Once on board, a lot of the crowd stood at the railing looking at the gold dappled lake. Rick and Pa sat together on the lower deck, Rick nuzzling close. His father took a swig of the mickey of rum he carried and looked at the lake with half closed eyes. "Look at what they're watchin'— nothin' but a fuckin' pond. Nothin' like the ocean, but they think they died an' went to heaven just lookin' at it. When you an' me go back to Nova Scotia an' we go out on a schooner together, you'll see what real water's like."

Pa got the day pass so Rick went on every ride, except those for really little kids. His father lay on the grass watching him with a smile. He was such a big good-looking kid and very agile. He laughed when some of the other kids squealed on the rougher rides. No pussy, thought Pa proudly; he'd take on anything. He started to doze, lying there on the grass in the sun, and when he woke Rick was standing there. "You gotta eat somethin' Pa."

"Not hungry. Get yerself a dog an' some chips."

When Rick came back he had a dog, a carton of warm chips sprinkled with salt and vinegar, and a Coke. "We'll share," he said. He sat down next to his father and ordered "eat." His father picked up a long golden fry and swung it into his mouth, then he took a swig of Coke and felt the burn. The kid was right, he felt better. Rick took his dog, tore it gently in two, and placed one half in Pa's hand. "Eat."

"What am I? Yer fuckin' baby?" Pa reached over and pushed the thick dark hair away from his forehead and Rick felt his love, like the icy burn of the Coke that filled his throat. He bit into his dog and felt the sweet sting of the ketchup and the burn of the mustard. He chewed it slowly, grinding his teeth against the rubbery pink texture. He could have eaten another, but he knew they might be short of money and he wanted an ice cream, cold and creamy, to replace the burning sweet spice.

"Go back to the rides," Pa ordered. "We paid for a day of rides, might as well take 'em." Rick knew his father wanted to nap some more cause he'd been nipping at his mickey and taking his percs. "Go easy on booze and pills," Rick ordered, "we gotta make the ride back."

"Bossy little bastard," Pa said, but with such affection the words were like a kiss.

He did the rides again, this time with a young Black boy about his age, who, when he laughed, showed such perfect white teeth that Rick couldn't stop looking at them. "Where you go to school?" Rick asked. "Nelson Mandela," the boy replied. They both laughed and exchanged glances of comfort. It meant they were from the same area and had a shared knowledge that no one not experiencing it would understand. His name was Chester.

"Back's killin' me," said Pa, "Gotta walk a bit. Let's get you another ice cream."

Rick bought the ice cream and another carton of chips for Pa, although he said he didn't want them. Then they started to walk. Rick wrapped his tongue around the vanilla scoop and sucked the creamy coolness down his throat. "Want a lick?" he asked Pa. Pa only shook his head. Rick feared he was sinking into what he thought of as "black" when nothing, not even percs or rum, could reach him. This happened every few weeks and it worried him. They kept walking, slow and silent until the air became grey, and they could see the lights from Toronto winking at them from across the lake.

"Last ferry's at nine," Rick said. Pa did not answer. He just kept walking, his head down, his breathing heavy. Then he sat down on a grassy patch, his movements slow as if he was hurting. The air was growing cool and Rick smelled lilacs from the garden of a nearby cottage, a sad sweet aching smell, so unlike his mother's harsh cologne.

He sat down beside his father. In the background he heard the drowsy throb of the doves that had returned to their nests. Then Pa spoke, his voice coming out of the grey where only the doves and a handful of crickets pierced the silence.

"Yuh know how yer mother makes her money?"

Rick did not answer. He did not want to think of his mother, perhaps fuming at home because of the theft from her money wad.

"She does hand and blow jobs, gets forty for hand and eighty for blows."

"How do y'know?" He was not sure what his father was describing but it sounded bad.

"She tol' me. An' she gets a hundred for straight fucks. She blames me. Says I turned her into a *hoar*. Her all-nighters: they're straight fucks."

"She does it with guys?" Rick felt like throwing up. He hated and feared his mother but he didn't want to hear this. "Where?"

"Mostly in their cars: underground parking fer the hand an' mouth."

"She does it to their dicky birds?"

"Yup," said Pa, "a lot of blows, that's why you always see them little bottles of Scope around . . . she rinses her mouth after." He paused, as if suddenly realizing he'd just confided his mother's source of income to an eight-year-old. Then he rolled over and passed out.

"Pa, we're gonna miss the ferry back." The grey had turned dark, and in the distance he could hear the crowd waiting for the ferry's last trip. He shivered from both the suddenly cool air and his father's information, which he tried not to think about. It gave his mother's dressing-up a whole new meaning.

He could not wake Pa up so he coiled around him, warmed by the heat of his body. The warmth and the smell of the grass and lilacs made him want to sleep, but his thoughts darted around. Now he saw things differently. He saw his mother with her painted face and short white legs in her tottering heels. And her full red mouth, a mouth that would be used in underground parking garages on a variety of unknown dicks and later rinsed with Scope. He would, he decided, tell Pa they must go back to Nova Scotia. Then his mother would stop. He no longer wanted her money.

Rick watched the sun rise, pink against the jagged Toronto skyline. He had hardly slept but he knew they had to leave. Pa lay leaden, his mouth slightly open, obviously wanting to sleep for hours. He thought of getting Coke or coffee, but they were too far from the amusement center and the concession stands weren't open yet. And there was little money left. The sun was out and he could hear the arrival of the ferry before he could wake up Pa.

"Yuh gotta get up," he begged. "It'll be an hour before another one comes." Pa looked at him vacantly, eyes encrusted and mottled red. He dug his hands into his father's jeans pocket and pulled out the remaining damp bills—enough for Coke and coffee to go. He took the bottle of percs and placed it in his jeans pocket. There was nothing left to steal. Then he remembered the return tickets and took them from Pa's other pocket.

As he headed towards the stands, his thoughts started again. He decided the next time Pa started on his Nova Scotia dream he would call him on it: pin him down. Being beat up with a leather belt for sweet fuck-all was one thing, but living off a hooker mother was another. And perhaps if Pa went back he'd stop the booze and percs and be happy. Every part of him wanted Pa happy.

He walked fast, the coffee with its four teaspoons of sugar burning his hand through its cardboard container and the bottle of icy coke, from which he'd already taken a gulp, in the other. Pa was still lying there, sodden and motionless, his arm with the navy anchor and golden hairs stretched over his eyes.

"Yuh gotta drink this an' take the percs," he ordered. Pa groaned, swore, and took a long swig of coke and then belched. Ricky took two pills from the bottle and pushed them into his mouth. Pa ground them against his teeth and then took another gulp of coke, perhaps waiting for his usual rush. And he was awake. They got to the pier in time to see the ferry taking off with the island's commuters. It would be good to live here, Rick thought, away from everyone. But now they would be forced to wait and the money was gone. No dog or ice cream. But the heat would not start for a few hours, and on the ferry there would be a breeze, even on the lower deck.

They sat on the edge of the pier, Rick's feet dangling, Pa hunched over, eyes half-shut. "No money for more coffee," said Rick, "not even for a Coke, an' she'll be pissed bout the money, she always counts it."

"I tol' yuh I'd take care of it," mumbled Pa. Rick glanced at him, sitting bowed over on the edge of the pier, sun-bleached hair falling over his blurred eyes. He couldn't take care of anything, not even his next drink. "Gotta have a butt," he muttered. At the other side of the pier a crowd had gathered waiting for the next ferry. "How 'bout you go bum a fag from someone in the crowd, tell 'em your ol' man got robbed."

Rick hated this, having to go up to some stranger to bum a fag. "Why don't you do it?"

"Not up to it. C'mon, do it for yer ol' man."

Rick walked slowly towards the group. The crowd landing on this and the last ferry were from Toronto, parents with their kids enjoying their summer vacation. A man was standing away from the crowd, smoking, wearing a jacket and trousers. He looked like he was heading for work—a Sunday office job perhaps. "'Scuse me, but my ol' man got beat up last night an' they even took his butts. Could you spare me one of yours?"

"Any reason he can't ask himself?"

"He's in bad shape. They done it while I was at the concession stand."

The man smiled, obviously amused that this kid—not even a teen-ager—thought he could rescue his father from a gang attack . . . if such ever existed. He took a package of DuMauriers from his pocket and handed Rick two and then took out his wallet and handed him a deuce. "That's for you, for being a good kid."

Rick felt a gush of relief. It meant they could take the streetcar home, rather than him dragging Pa, with him complaining all the way about his back. "Really good of you sir," he said. The guy must have bucks—even if he was living on Centre Island.

He and Pa sat in the lower deck as usual. Pa put his arm around him and Rick melted into him. "Such a good kid, my best buddy," he said. Rick pressed into him harder. He wished his father's back was better and he didn't need his booze and pills, then perhaps they could go back to Nova Scotia and go on a schooner together. But best, they could get away from his mother. He wondered if Pa remembered telling him about her; he was pretty juiced last night. He knew it was true, a lot of things made sense. His dislike and fear of her had turned to disgust. He thought of the unspeakable things she did in dark underground parking lots and he wanted to puke. He wished Pa hadn't told him.

Rick looked at the water as they neared Toronto: it was an amber sheet of silk and the smell of Pa, of rum, butts and sweat, gave him comfort. Pa smoked his second cigarette and looked out at the lake with narrowed eyes, "It's no Atlantic, but pretty when the sun shines on it." Pa needed a drink, his hands were shaking, and even the Coke and two more percs didn't help. He was weak on his feet after they got off the streetcar and started to head for home.

It was after twelve, and she was dressed in her shorts ready to leave. Going to meet and greet the lunch crowd, Rick thought, then he remembered it was Sunday. When they came in, she came at them, but mostly Pa, her short pale arms and small fists pounding with fury against his chest. But for her anger and Pa's weakened state, it would have been funny. But it wasn't. Pa didn't fight back, just stood there while this dwarf-like piece of frenzy tried to hurt him. Then as a final gesture, she kicked him hard. She was screaming in Spanish, the only English words being "son of a beetch." Rick knew she could speak perfect English, but when incensed she lapsed into Spanish, the sole language she'd heard until she'd attended kindergarten in Halifax.

"Stop it, Ma," Rick said. He felt a sharp slap across his face but he did not even flinch. "You help him steal my money." Then he said it, knowing he shouldn't, knowing it would make everything much worse, "I know how yuh make yer money."

She stopped. Then she marched into her bedroom and slammed the door shut.

"You shouldna said that," said Pa. Pa lay on their bed and he was starting to shake again. He moved restlessly and Rick knew his back was killing him because of the walking from the ferry and the streetcar. His last perc was two hours ago.

She came in with one of her spike-heeled shoes in her hand. She started to hit Pa with it and got him right on his temple. He started to bleed and pulled a pillow over his head. "Stop," said Rick, "or I'll call 911." It was an empty threat: no one in Regent Park ever called the police unless there was a murder—and sometimes not even then. She smacked him again and he wanted to spit at her but instead threw himself on Pa.

"*Dos malditos bastardos*," she yelled, and then said, "Why you think I have to make money? Your *padre* he makes *nada*, all he likes is pills and rum." He heard her heels on the wooden hall floor and then the banging of the front door. From upstairs he smelled Mrs. Canarella's tomato sauce. She had been yelling at her kids but she liked him, perhaps because she hated his mother.

When his father pulled the pillow away he could see there was blood on it, and more blood oozing from the side of his forehead. He went to the kitchen, pulled a dishtowel from the drawer and ran the cold water. When he came back with the wet towel, he noticed there was a flap of skin and blood was leaking from under it. "Pa, perhaps we go to the Centre for stitches." His father merely groaned so he pressed the cold cloth against his forehead. He would, he decided, see Mrs. Canarella and get Pa a half glass of red vino. The Italians always had vino. He trudged up the wooden stairs to the second floor and knocked. "Come in," she called.

"Pa got his head cut. Yuh got a half glass of vino and a band-aid?"

"Your Mama go?" He nodded, knowing Mrs. Canarella had heard the fight.

"I give you vino and spaghet."

Rick sat at Mrs. Canarella's oil cloth–covered table and sucked down the long strands of rubbery spaghetti soaked with tomato sauce. The Canarella boys kept watching him from across the table, mute and wide-eyed. "Can I have some for my father?"

She filled a bowl with long worms of pasta, and then poured a cup of the sauce from the top of the stove pot over it. She half-filled a tumbler with red vino. "I donna want to go to your place. You take it and bring back bowl and glass."

He thanked her, and she smiled and ruffled his thick dark hair. Women liked him, which was good. His mother was the only one who didn't.

His father was lying there, dark blood still leaking from under the flap of skin, his hands shaking. Rick took two percs from the bottle and pushed them between his father's stiff lips and Pa started his grinding routine. Then Rick held the glass with the vino to his mouth and he gulped it down. It was obvious it was not his choice of drink but the shaking stopped.

"Mrs. Canarella sent spaghet. Yuh gotta eat." His father rolled to his side and groaned. The blood kept leaking on the pillow. The nurse at school had sometimes treated his cuts, some from the belt buckle, with strong smelling liquid. "For germs," she'd said. Now he needed something for Pa's cut.

The small bottles of Scope were lined up in his mother's bathroom cabinet. He took a bottle, soaked some toilet paper with the green liquid and returned to the bedroom with the wet wad. "Hold it against it Pa," he said. When his father just lay there, Rick held the wad firmly against the still seeping cut. His father shuddered. Rick felt guilty. He had caused this by telling her he knew.

"Gotta eat some spaghet," he ordered, taking a teaspoon of now-cold pasta and attempting to force it into his father's mouth. His father turned his head away. There was no booze or butts, just a few pills left from a bottle of Percodan. In two months, he'd be nine. He had to make money, real money, not just the crap he earned as a paper boy.

He lay down beside his father. His gut was filled with Mrs. Canarella's spaghetti and he hadn't slept much during the night on the island. He placed his arm around Pa's sleeping body. When Pa woke up there'd be no butts or booze, just Mrs. Canarella's cold spaghetti in a bowl that he had to return before his mother came home.

Chapter 3

Rick's paper route was in that part of town known as the Annex, north of Bloor Street and south of Davenport. There were many pensioners there, living in duplexes, and they carried bills in their stained wallets. Only a few tipped and he wouldn't bother them. Just the ones who wouldn't part with one lousy nickel. He thought of Mr. Hennessey on Huron Street.

The air was thick and silent at nine that night, but on Bloor everything was alive. Rochdale, a former hippie commune for university and college students, was being renovated, and groups of chatting young people crowded the sidewalk in front as if it were still open. But Huron Street was quiet, its rows of two- or three-story duplexes with lights showing behind closed blinds. Old Hennessey lived in a duplex with Banjo, his Doberman. Rick liked Banjo; he liked all dogs, really. He knew Banjo would give him a quiet and friendly reception—not even a bark. He tried the door. It was unlocked. He crept up the stairs. Banjo greeted him, tail wagging his love, and he rubbed his ears. Hennessey was in a chair sleeping, mouth open, with what looked like a half tumbler of booze on the table beside him. The TV was on really loud: *The Price Is Right*. These old guys went in for money shows.

The wallet lay beside a package of Camels. He picked it up carefully. There was a thick wad of bills inside. He took two-thirds of them. It was a trick that would work well in the future and one of the reasons they didn't catch him. Hennessey would think he'd lost or mislaid his cash—might not even report it.

The moon was out as he sauntered down Huron, a fat silver-dollar of a moon, like the silver on the lake when he and Pa had taken the ferry from Centre Island that day. He fingered the bills in his jeans pocket and rubbed them between his fingers. But he would not count them on the street. Under his ribs he hummed with satisfaction.

She was still gone when he got back, but Pa was up, sitting at the kitchen table shaking, the band-aid hanging from the cut on his temple, which was no longer bleeding. It was almost ten. "Made a score," Rick said, "Picked up a wallet an' we got scratch."

Pa looked at him hard. "You steal it?"

"Nah, checkin' on my paper route an' there it was, jus' lyin' there, waitin' to be picked up." He sat at the table and started counting: two-hundred and sixty-seven bucks. "We'll go to the Adda, an' yuh can have a double rum, even a double-double, an' some butts, an' we'll have some burgers and fries. He put down two twenties on the table for her—another thing he was to learn: the power of sharing.

Pa was smiling. "Don't know how I got you, little buddy, but I musta done somethin' right."

They headed for Adda. He felt his father's large rough hand rub his head and felt full of pride. And a lot less guilty about telling her he knew what she did.

***

Miss Swinton, Ricardo's grade six teacher at Nelson Mandela, liked him. He knew it because she always smiled before asking him a question. He did not do homework but listened in class, not acting up stupid like a lot of them. "You know, Ricardo, you could go far if you did your homework, and put your mind on your studies," she'd said to him one afternoon after class. He smiled and looked at the floor, not meeting her eyes. Since July there'd been a series of successful break and enters. He'd always left a few bucks on the table for his mother, and she'd never asked where they'd come from. But she'd stopped hitting him.

Rick kept Pa in booze and butts and both his doctors kept supplying him with Percodan. But Pa was restless, twisting and turning at night and muttering in his sleep. "Why don't we just leave?" he asked him one night. "Jus' go back to Nova Scotia. She won't care—happy to see us go." In a rare rush of candor Pa replied, "Can't get my percs back there, got a sure source here." Rick felt a pang of disappointment and then a rush of anger. So his father had no intention of going back—it was just some dream. Going back would interfere with his drug supply.

That October afternoon was not the kind of fall afternoon Rick liked, with a hard blue sky, cotton wool clouds, sun and a tough breeze.

It was a dull grey afternoon with a fine mist in the air, and he refused his gang's request to play basketball on the asphalt square in the schoolyard. He gave Chester, the kid he'd met at the island, a brief wave, which Chester returned with a show of his dazzling teeth. That day, Miss Swinton had written "Excellent!" on his paper when he'd got perfect on his math test, and said to him when the others had left, "Think of how you could lead the class with just a little effort." He did not want to lead the class. He was not a geek but their leader—so far for some pretty mild things—but they all knew.

The Chevy was gone, which meant she was gone: his father's license lost and long expired. The door was unlocked as usual. Nobody locked their doors in Regent Park—nothing to steal but stolen goods—and they didn't stay long. There was a tired stale smell as if nobody lived there, and no cooking had started from upstairs.

"Pa," he called softly. The house sat silent. He went to the bedroom: the bed had its usual tangle of cotton blankets, and beside it there was an empty rum mickey on the scarred wooden table. An ache started in the pit of his stomach and he had problems breathing. He went to the kitchen where no belt was hanging by the stove. The basement door was closed. He opened it and walked down the wooden stairs slowly. The musty air became heavier and the small square basement window covered with dust and spider webs gave only a dim lemon light. But he could see Pa swinging from the ceiling pipe, the belt a noose around his neck, his mouth open, eyes bulging and unseeing. The small stool he'd used had been kicked away. So, Rick thought later, he couldn't change his mind.

Rick took the stool, moved it over to where Pa was hanging, sat on it and gripped Pa's lower legs. He reached up and touched Pa's hands. They were cold. He could see the navy anchor on his white arm and the light hairs. He did not cry, just sat there gripping Pa's legs, waiting for him to start to talk and tell him what a great little buddy he was. Gradually, the window's lemon light faded and the basement was heavy with grey mist. Rick kept seeing him and Pa on the lower deck of the ferry, with Pa rubbing his head with his large rough hands, telling him how they'd leave and go to Nova Scotia. And then he saw the silver of the water.

It was hours before she came. The basement was dark, with only the faint glimmer of the street light showing through the window. He heard her from upstairs calling and then the bulb came on. He heard her heels sharp on the wooden steps. And the cry of 'Jesus.' And her voice, softer than he'd ever heard it, say, "Ricardo, you can't stay with him. They have to come an' take him away. He's gone an' you can't bring him back."

But he only gripped Pa's legs harder, and when they came, the morgue people, they had to pry him away because he wouldn't let go. "He and his *padre* was close," she told them, and they shook their heads and one said, "poor kid." And all the time he did not cry. He said to her, "I want 'em to send him back to Nova Scotia."

But she said, "Too much *dinero*. They burn him up, an' someday you have a little box of ashes an' you take 'em back."

"I don't want 'em to burn him up. I'll pay. How much to send him back?

"Hundreds," she said. "No money for that."

All that night he couldn't sleep, just kept reaching for Pa, for his warmth and for his smell of rum and smoke. But he still did not cry. Then the next day she said, "Ricardo you have to go to *escuela*, you canna just mope here alone in the *casa*."

He heard her talking to Miss Swinton. He did not hear what was said but Miss Swinton had him sit next to her desk, and he sat there for the rest of the week, his head in his arms. And Wednesday and Thursday passed and Friday came, and he just kept sitting there, his head still in his arms. And the other students, his friends, did not bother him or try to speak to him as he was their leader. The only one was Chester. He touched his shoulder and softly said, "Sorry."

Then on Friday afternoon, after three days of little food or sleep, just sitting there at his desk with his head in his arms, something happened. Miss Swinton waited until everyone had left, and she came and sat by him. He felt her arm around his shoulders and smelled her scent, not harsh like Ma's, but sweet, like funeral flowers. She said, "Ricardo, he's gone, and you can't bring him back. But maybe you'll see him again someday in heaven."

Although he didn't believe her, it was then he started to cry for the first time. She held him and he shook and cried right into the softness of her silky white blouse. And she held and rocked him for what seemed like hours. From then on he started to get better. He loved Miss Swinton, and for the first and only time in grade six he led the class.

CHAPTER 4

His friends in grade eight knew he had money, and that he did break-ins—with success. They wanted to be part of it: Chester, Iggy, Diego, Brendon, and sometimes Tomas. "Only if," he said, "Yuh do like I say. I can't take a chance on yuh fuckin' up and landin' us all in some reform school." He'd toughened up his language now that Pa was gone, to fit his image as a tough guy and leader. They nodded solemnly. They knew he was smart. "Yuh take what I say an' I'll get rid of it, and we divvy up the cash, with me gettin' extra for the plannin' and gettin' us the cash for the goods."

They stood and nodded nervously meeting his stern look, and then looking down at the asphalt at the back of Nelson Mandela School. Rick continued, his voice low and firm. "There are rules: yuh don't fink—if yer caught you never tell names. Yuh say you were alone. Understand? An' you don't rob crap. Nothin' but cash or jewelry, or somethin' I can turn into cash. Make like it's a business." The boys stood hunched over and tense, heavy with the responsibility of being part of such an enterprise.

Their first target was Casa Loma, a magnificent castle in the middle of town that had bankrupted its owner some fifty years before and was now a semi-museum tourist attraction and a site for large wedding parties. It was December 1982, and they all wore thick jackets with wool caps pulled down over their foreheads, running shoes, and breathed white into the chilled air. Admittance was easy. They jimmied open a window and they all crawled in. There was no alarm. Then chaos broke loose. They rushed around picking up goblets from what was obviously to be a planned wedding dinner, fake gold cutlery, small pictures, and even an ancient sword. Rick watched in disgust. "We're outta here," he yelled, "Jus' put everything back."

They stood shocked and then they all trooped out, after they'd removed the bolt from the front entrance. Later in the booth at Adda's, a place that always gave Rick a little ache in his gut because of Pa, he spoke to them kindly but firmly: "Look, was I speakin' to air when I tol' you guys to take nothin' but cash—or somethin' yuh can turn into it? Do you really think I'd take the crap you was collecting into my contact? He'd laugh me out of his place."

The boys gulped their Cokes and gnawed at their fries, embarrassed and ashamed.

The next venture in the early months of 1983 was more successful—for a time. Diego and Iggy were, at their parent's insistence, altar boys at St. Thomas Aquinas Catholic Church. There was, they told Rick, a whole piss-pot of money in the collection plates that were placed on a table in a special room that could be accessed from the stairs leading from the outside back entrance. Rick could get into the room this way and help himself to the monies while the Mass was continuing, and then share it with the boys later.

"Easy for you," said Iggy, "Yer not a Catholic. We can be lookouts."

It crossed Rick's mind that being Catholic wasn't stopping them from sharing in the collection money, and that altar boys may not be the best lookouts, but the scheme in general was good. For the first few months it worked. Rick did his usual, taking about one-third of the money so that the theft was not even detected. "You takin' extra?" asked Diego, pocketing his fifty.

Rick felt himself flushing with anger. "What I do is skim a third off the top, then they won't know about it and we can keep goin'—if you get fuckin' greedy, game's over." He always gave his mother a share, placing bills on the kitchen table, which she always took without comment. And she kept doing what she'd always been doing. But she no longer hit him. Never. Instead she brought guys home and he'd have to leave. It bothered him.

St. Thomas Aquinas was packed full on Easter Sunday of 1983. The choir sang "Christ the Lord has risen today" with lusty enthusiasm, and the collection plates were overflowing with bills. Even if, Rick thought, eyeing it all, he just took his usual third, they'd be making the haul of a lifetime. But just when he was about finished, his pockets stuffed with bills, in walked Diego and Iggy—still in their altar boy gowns—who started stuffing their pockets with bills from the plates.

Even before he could say 'what the fuck,' the rector walked in. Diego and Iggy stood stricken, Rick dived under the table, and the rector asked,

"What are you boys doing here?" At that moment, a twenty-dollar bill floated from underneath Diego's altar-boy gown to the floor. There were months of penance, hundreds of Hail Marys and Our Fathers, but Rick, who'd made it to the door in the general uproar, got away while the boys were being searched.

"Better we'd been charged," wailed Iggy. "The ol' man almost killed me an' we'll be doin' penance till July." Rick had given them one-fifty each from his eight hundred. They didn't deserve it, but at least they hadn't squealed.

***

Chester was different from his other partners. Smart and soft-spoken, he listened carefully and made suggestions—good ones. They were fifteen, and in grade ten at Lord Dufferin on Parliament. Chester was also a part-time bellboy at The Four Seasons, where many of the actors stayed while attending The Toronto Film Festival. There were dozens of showings and dinners, and on those nights there was always a chance that jewelry would be left scattered on dressing tables—safety deposit boxes ignored.

Some of the jewelry had been loaned by Tiffany's and Birk's for the occasion: beautiful glittering earrings and necklaces, embedded with diamonds, rubies and emeralds. And there was cash—from people who made so much of it they left it lying around. The haul in 1984 had been phenomenal: Chester had let him into three of the suites with his pass key, and Rick had cased the rooms, surfacing with jewelry Marty had paid him four thousand for—about one-tenth of its value. He'd also found two thousand in cash, which from the remains of lines of powder on one of the walnut tables had been to pay drug dealers.

They divided the money between them in the back row of a darkened movie house late one night. "If," confided Chester, "my ol' lady found out—game's over. She'd kill me, right there where I was standin'—I'm like gone." Rick smiled. Not his worry. The papers mentioned the robbery but the publicity was sparse. Everything, he concluded, was covered by insurance.

Rick purchased a bike, a black leather bomber jacket, jeans and running shoes. He saw his mother looking at him hard, but she said nothing. He had, after all, given her five hundred. And he and Chester took the gang to Adda's, including the greedy Diego and Iggy, who had finally finished their penance and were formally absolved.

"A big oil man's convention," said Chester. "Rich Texans, money comin' out of their wazoos. There'll be banquets and cocktail parties all sponsored by the big drillin' companies an' pipelines. At least three hundred comin'. We'll do the suites man, that's where the big money be. An' jewelry. No way these rich wives gonna use the boxes, there be jewels scattered all over, jus' wait an' see."

Rick nodded his agreement—and excitement, remembering their last six thousand dollar haul. They agreed that on the night of the opening banquet everyone would attend. There was a cocktail party at seven and dinner at eight. There would be welcoming and opening speeches before the sit-down five-course dinner. They were safe until eleven.

Rick struck gold in the first suite. The wife had not even unpacked, and there was a small velvet case packed with jewelry and various earrings on the dressing table that had obviously been tried on and discarded. Even better there was a woman's purse, obviously carried on the plane, containing a wallet with over a thousand in American bills.

"Shit, we made a score," Rick told the nervous Chester, standing guard outside the door. Chester opened the second suite and Rick turned on the light. A naked woman, obviously not banquet-bound, screamed from the bed and immediately called the desk. The hall was suddenly flooded with security. Rick made for the fire stairs, but he was barricaded there as well. The police came and handcuffed them. Rick's teeth chattered with fear and Chester appeared frozen.

They were given legal aid and separate defense counsel, who advised them that it was useless to have a trial, and that a plea would be best—provided they had witnesses to speak to sentence. As first offenders, they were released into their mothers' custodies on condition they go nowhere but home and school.

Chester's mother was a mountainous woman, built like a prize fighter. She had, Rick suspected, given Chester the shiner that had completely closed his left eye. And she was loudly vocal in telling everyone in sight, including the judge—much to Chester's obvious embarrassment—that all of her son's problems had been caused by Ricardo McCready, a well-known gang leader, who had been leading his fellow students astray—without detection—for years.

Rick asked his duty counsel, a guy named Martin Springer, not to contact his mother. But Martin insisted on it. "Got to get a witness who'll say you're a good kid—like a hockey or basketball coach, or even a teacher . . . or whoever." Rick knew right away who his mother would call—and he hated it. It was the worst. The one woman in the world who he really cared about: Miss Swinton.

She stood in the witness box, slim, in her soft white blouse with the bow in front—a blouse similar to the one he'd buried his face in and sobbed his despair after Pa had hanged himself. She had let him mess it up with his tears and snot. On the witness stand she'd looked at him with such affection that he'd almost passed out right there in the courtroom.

"Ricardo," she'd almost whispered, "is a wonderful boy, a bright boy, who didn't even need to study—he led my class in grade six." She looked at him with such love and compassion and smiled, just like she'd always done before asking him a question, and he'd almost collapsed.

"When his father died in that truly horrible way Ricardo found him, and he stopped speaking to the other students, but after three days he finally cried, so hard I thought he'd never stop. I find it impossible to believe that he'd do anything wrong, anything to hurt anyone else. Inside I always knew he was such a loving boy." Miss Swinton's voice broke and she removed a Kleenex from her purse and gently wiped her nose.

Chester's mother, who'd referred to Rick both inside and outside the courtroom as "the reprobate who ruined my Chester," sniffed her utter disbelief and even Rick's mother pursed her cherubic dark red mouth. But Judge Carter was impressed—and even more so when his mother reached up and gave Rick one of her stinging doozies on the cheek. And he didn't so much as blink. A vicious woman, Judge Carter concluded, and the boy had shown by his response that such attacks were a common occurrence. Similarly, he had wondered about Chester's swollen eye that he had attributed to some racist police officer—but now suspected that this soft-spoken lad had been clobbered by his own mother, and that living with her would impose its own punishment.

"You have expressed remorse," he said, in a kind but firm voice, "and I have reason to suspect that your mothers have meted out punishment, and that a major crime such as theft over was out of character for you both. There was no violence, although Chester has badly betrayed his employer. Because of this, I won't impose a period of juvenile detention.

Instead, I will give you both a conditional discharge, with probation for a period of one year. You'll report to your probation officer on a monthly basis and not associate with anyone with a criminal record. But there is one thing I want you both to remember: you are now fifteen. Once you are eighteen and no longer minors, everything will change. At that time should you break the law, you'll be sent to a penitentiary for what could be a long period, and have a criminal record that will follow you through your lives. Learn from this, Ricardo and Chester. Never permit yourselves to break the law again."

Chester fixed Rick with his one good eye and Rick rolled both of his. Neither had attempted to blame the other, except for Chester's mother. They would remain friends.

Rick however, took up gambling with great dedication, and avoided robberies unless a declining stash for his poker made it necessary. He was a good player and counted cards and cheated with great deftness. But gambling was not as reliable a source of funds as his successful robberies and other exploits, and he saw his mother sniff around the empty table with disgust.

CHAPTER 5

Rick's sex life started at twelve, the same time his mother's friend, Marlene Drover, gave him what he considered his most important sex lesson. He knew about sex—it was hard to avoid if your mother was a prostitute, but what Marlene taught went beyond basics. Marlene often walked Church, Wellesley and Jarvis Streets with his mother. She was a big, heavy woman with pale, lightly freckled skin, ginger hair and an enormous bosom displayed by her low-necked blouses, while the rest of her was covered by long loose skirts. She was, she used to joke, "the Rita Hayworth of the chubby chaser."

"She's so *grande* she makes me look *pequena*," said his mother in one of her rare confidences.

On the night in question there was to be a threesome, but the rather fastidious-looking man in a pin-striped suit and glasses had looked at Marlene long and hard and decided against it. He disappeared into the bedroom with Rick's mother, after giving Marlene $100 for what she'd complained was "wasting my time."

Marlene sat watching Rick with half-closed eyes. She'd been taking pills and smoking up. She seemed stoned.

"I'm gonna give you a sex lesson tonight, Ricky," she said. "You may not 'preciate it now, but later on you'll say 'that Marlene, I owe her one big time.'" She patted the seat next to her on the leather sofa. Rick did not want to fuck Marlene. She was too big. She would drown him with her flesh. And his dick, which he massaged at night with enthusiastic regularity, would be lost in what he envisaged as a huge loose series of greasy pink cushions. But Marlene was not having sex with him. She was into demonstration.

She pulled up her skirt, exposing her full white thighs and the auburn bird's nest in her crotch. She smelled of raw fish, the kind Pa used to complain about at St. Lawrence market. Then she pulled the bird's nest apart and displayed a fleshy beak, above the pink opening. She took the beak between her finger and thumb. "See this, it's my clit—or joy button, it's where yuh can get a woman off—not jus' by pumpin' away with your cock." She reached over, took his hand, and rubbed his fingers against the beak. She appeared to like it and lay back with half-closed eyes. "If yuh want to make it special then yuh take it, suck it, an' roll it around in yor mouth, like yuh got a grape there." He knew she wanted him to do it—but he couldn't. The smell was too harsh. He would be sick. She laughed, seeing his reluctance. "Yuh can get away with yor hand—I'm jus' tellin' yuh the special goodies."

At that point his mother came out with the man in the pin-striped suit, who left quickly. "He could hardly do me, let alone a threesome," she laughed. They got ready to go out together.

"What's Marlene up to?"

"Teachin' him how to make a girl happy: he owes me one." His mother laughed again.

Elsa Gruber, the neighbourhood lay, was blonde and fourteen, and would often take on three or four of the local boys in turn. They paid her two dollars each and she insisted they either wear a "cock jacket," or "spit in the bush." Rick did not want to be part of a line-up. "Don't want your sloppy seconds," he'd said. Then Elsa told him one day—she lived in the same apartment house as Barry the Fence and attended Lord Dufferin—"If you want it to be jus' you, fine, but it'll cost more." He gave her a double deuce, but before he went into her, he tried the Marlene rub. She moaned her appreciation, and sometimes after that she didn't charge him at all.

Chapter 6

1986

Rick was sixteen and in grade eleven when he left home and never went back. His mother had brought a big Slovak man, who drove a huge transport truck, home for an all-nighter. He'd had a poker game that night with a group of older guys, and although he'd seen the truck parked outside, everything was quiet when he got home. He'd been lucky, five hundred ahead, and he'd left a hundred on the table for her.

In the morning, the guy was still there. He was a swollen hairy man with a roll of fat under his chin, and a gut that rolled dough-like over his worn jeans. He picked up the hundred from the kitchen table and held it up gingerly, "What the hell's this?"

"It's from Ricardo's poker. He shares it."

"You mean this kid wins at cards—give me a break. I bet he stole the cash."

Rick was shoveling down corn flakes, and his anger that this hairy character was invading his house at breakfast, and now insulting him, got the better of him. "Who the fuck you think yer talkin'about?" The next thing he saw was a black sky with a sprinkle of yellow stars, and he heard an ambulance siren, but it was far away. And then they were shining a bright light in his eyes and he had a lot of strange sticky things attached to his scalp.

"You've had a severe concussion, son," the examining doctor at Sick Kids said. "Now perhaps you'd like to tell us how it happened." He closed his eyes and pretended to be asleep. The bastard deserved it but he was never a fink.

"You got too smarta mouth," his mother said that afternoon, when she surprised him with a visit. He knew then the hairy man was still there, and that he couldn't go back.

***

Rick was in Mr. Simpson's class in grade eleven. Mr. Simpson was very thin with longish fine blond hair. He didn't dress like the other teachers at Lord Dufferin, who wore sports jackets and trousers. He wore dark suits, always with a vest and tie. And he smiled like a male Miss Swinton before he asked him a question. Rick liked him. He reminded him of Steve McQueen, his favorite actor.

"He's a gearbox," said Diego, "I can always tell."

"Why, he do somethin' to you?" sneered Rick. "He give you a feel like Greenley?"

Greenley was the machine shop teacher and he was always groping the boys. But no one ever told.

On the second day, Mr. Simpson walked into his hospital room at Sick Kids. Apparently the doctor had phoned the school, spoken to him and said he suspected child abuse. But no report had been made to the Children's Aid or the police. Mr. Simpson was wearing his usual dark blue three-piece suit, but this time his shirt was unbuttoned and he had no tie. He looked at Rick without his usual smile. "They tell me, McCready, you've a serious concussion, but you're not giving information. I'm not asking for your cooperation, as I'm aware that in your part of the universe you'd be branded as a fink. But I'm here to make you an offer. I've an extra room in my condo with a bathroom and shower, and if you'd like to use it you'd be welcome. But there are rules: important ones."

Rick eyed him balefully, and thought of Diego's and his gang's comments. "Why?"

"Because you're a bright kid—the highest IQ in the class—and you're going in the wrong direction. I think I might be able to help you—if I'm not too late."

Rick kept looking at him: he knew people just didn't help each other. There was always an angle and Simpson must have an angle. The left side of his head was pounding and he needed a painkiller. "Why?" he repeated. "What's in it for you?"

"No ulterior motive. I'm not into young boys, if that's what's on your mind—not that I don't like you. I'm offering to help develop your potential, change your speech, perhaps even your name. Anyway, think about it."

He got up from the chair and gave Rick one of his tight smiles. Rick noticed for the first time how white and straight his teeth were.

"I don't need to think about it. I can't go home—but give me the rules."

Simpson told him he'd be taking speech lessons to cut "the gangster lingo," and that he'd be on a nightly study schedule, have an allowance, and be free on Saturday nights. But paying a lawyer was not part of the deal. And that he'd have to select a sport to increase his chance of future university entrance.

"I'm not into football or any of that crap."

"Just as well, you've already had one serious concussion. What do you do?"

"Run an' swim."

"Then we'll get you enrolled at the community center and get you on the school swim team."

Rick just looked at him—such a wholesome activity would conflict with his image—which would be damaged anyway, once word got out that he was living with Simpson. And it didn't take long.

"Everyone's sayin' you're livin' with a chicken hawk an' gettin' it up the ass." It was Chester, obviously upset.

"An' what did you say, ol' pal and buddy?" Rick sneered.

"I told them no way was you into that."

That night, in a penthouse full of grey leather and muted elegance, with pricey art and gleaming fixtures, all with a wrap-around balcony, Rick told Simpson.

"They're all sayin' I'm your ass-boy."

Simpson sat scowling and then said, "How'd you feel about going to Harbord Collegiate? It's far more academic and one way to cancel out your past. It'll make it easier for you to get into university later on. The principal's a friend of mine."

"Great," said Rick. Later, looking back, Rick saw the two years he spent with Alf Simpson as the best of his life; he sometimes thought if he'd continued with him everything would have been different.

After several months the diction lessons kicked in, and he found himself enunciating his words and even dropping the "fucks"—to a degree, not that he wouldn't fall back to his old lingo under times of stress, or if he spoke to someone from his old world. He learned a lot, and not just from his studies, which took place four hours each night under Alf's supervision—Simpson had become "Alf" after the first month.

On weekends, Alf played his "Golden Oldies" tapes, old numbers Rick had never heard before, but liked. Sometimes, if alone, he'd sing along with them—Armstrong, Como, Martin, the whole package— and then one Saturday afternoon he saw Alf standing by the door, smiling and listening. "Great voice you've got there," he said, "Not that you'd want to do anything with it—bad for the tough-guy image." Rick stopped singing from that point on, unless he was sure Alf was away from the penthouse.

He stopped poker on Saturday nights and Alf took him out. He took him to the symphony, which he liked; the ballet, which he loathed; and even to the theatre, which he thought was cool. He started appreciating the good food that Alf picked up, at times cooked, or when they ate out. At first the study pattern made him restless and it was agony, but he adjusted. "You're a bit ADD," Alf commented. "You don't focus well over time. I could get you some drugs for that, but you're doing quite well—considering." Rick could have said it was all about pleasing him. But he didn't.

The rumor had hit the eleventh grade at Harbord that he was a former gang leader—which was somewhat exaggerated—but it kept mouthy students in their place. "Heard you led a gang back in Regent Park," said a kid with skin and freckles like Marlene Drover, who'd obviously been put up to it by a grinning group standing nearby.

"So?" replied Rick.

"No offence," said the kid and scuttled away, with the four onlookers laughing—but not too loudly.

After that there were no more challengers. He was accepted—not as he'd been at Lord Dufferin—but as a member of the class. Girls liked him, and he took out the occasional classmate on a Saturday night when Alf was busy, using his twenty-five-dollar allowance. But after sex, or the lack of it, he'd lose interest. And girls who wanted more than one or two dates gave up on him.

He thought about the way he was and it concerned him. It was as if there was a hollow space inside him when it came to girls, a puddle of nothingness. He wondered if he was gay, but was convinced he wasn't. He enjoyed sex with girls while it lasted, and he didn't want to have sex with men, although his best relationships were with them: Pa, Chester and Alf Simpson.

Perhaps it was her, with her mean mouth and leather belt. And what she'd done to Pa. But if it was her, there was nothing to be done. He'd heard of talk of therapy from Alf and his friends—spilling your guts to some dude and paying for the privilege—but he didn't buy it. It would expose him as some sort of nut. And what would he say? I can get it on and bring the chick and me off, but there's no feeling inside. None.

CHAPTER 7

There were two more months left in grade eleven when it happened. Alf was out for the evening to meet some university buddies, rather than stay in his study writing away and coming in periodically to check Rick's work. It was near the end of April and outside there was a cool mist, and from the balcony the trees surrounding the ravine were barely visible, cloaked in this mist-like fog. Mists always reminded him of Pa. He wanted a butt, although he feared smoking would cut his breathing for the swim team.

Al's desk was cluttered, but there was a pack of open Players by a large folder. He picked up the folder and on its side was written "PhD Thesis." And inside, the heading: "The significance of cultural and behavioral patterns in establishing the future of students attending Lord Dufferin High School in the years 1986 upward, including the impact of race, social mobility, parental influences and environmental factors."

He sat down and started to read. Iggy, Diego and Chester were all there: IQs, family life, criminal behavior and parental involvement. There was a separate file on Ricardo McCready: I.Q, parental input, criminal behavior, gang involvement and the influence of a change of environment on learning patterns and future potential. He started reading: there was nothing Alf Simpson hadn't found out, like some snooping private eye gathering a piss-pot of information.

Now he knew why Alf had done it, and why at the beginning he'd been asking him why. And he'd never got an answer. Alf was using him as some sort of lab rat. He couldn't care less about him and his life, but only about how he could change it and then write about it, like he was some science experiment. He went out to the balcony, looked at the fog-wrapped trees, and had a butt. And then another. Fuck the breathing. At eleven he heard the key and the door open. Alf was there, flushed and a bit wiped.

Rick didn't even wait for him to sit down. "I been reading your files—especially mine. Why didn't you tell me I was some sort of experiment rat in your book—or whatever? I even thought you were interested in me." He despised himself for that last comment: it showed a neediness and a vulnerability he hated to display.

Alf reached out and took the file gently but firmly from his hand and beckoned him into the living room. He ran his hand through his long blond hair dampened by the outside mist, lit a cigarette and sighed. "I wanted to tell you, but I was afraid then you wouldn't cooperate. I'm not a teacher—you may have guessed that, although I managed to get a Type B certificate for my Lord Dufferin job. I'm getting a doctorate in sociology from the University of Toronto, and all this information is to be part of my thesis.

"You've probably read about your former friends—remember none of their names will be used, nor will yours. But as far as my not being interested in you, you're wrong. Perhaps at the beginning my interest was to use you as part of an experiment on environmental change, but now I'm very interested in you as a person. I'm gay and you're not. But you're the closest thing to a son I'll ever have. This may sound daft, as I'm only ten years older. But please don't think I don't care about you as a person. I care about you a great deal. And stop smoking, it'll ruin your breathing for swimming."

Rick stubbed out his cigarette and smiled. And Alf continued. "My family, by the way, owns Simpson's Foods, and the company owns this apartment, but I've a lifetime lease. I'm indulged as the family academic. I haven't come out, but my mother's stopped introducing me to nice eligible girls on my occasional trips to Montreal. So I suspect they know."

Rick felt a suspicious burning in his eyes. He knew Alf was giving him the straight goods and felt the urge to reciprocate. "I got problems too—with girls. I can fuck, really good, but I got no feeling for'em. Perhaps it was my ol' lady—a walking and breathing cunt—but girls never last for more than two dates. An' don't mention therapy."

For the first time, Alf smiled. "When you get upset, you forget those diction lessons. I won't be stupid enough to say the right one will come along. She may not. Life's not a Harlequin Romance and a therapist may suggest that living with a gay mentor may not be the best solution. So let's hope time may take care of it."

After this, things continued much as before. Al squeezed his shoulders with his long slim hands, brushed his thick black hair from his forehead, and checked his homework nightly.

At times, on weekends, he brought some dude home, but never the same guy more than once. Rick felt a pang of jealousy but never spoke of it. When it happened, he rejoined his Saturday night poker group. He had an occasional party pickup, a few who he brought home. But stopped when he saw Alf raise his eyebrows and pull a sour face. He stopped dating classmates as the ones he'd dated didn't speak to him. "Hit an' run Rick," one of his buddies on the swim team, where he was captain and strongest swimmer, called him.

Rick was in the top five percent of the class in June. "A real accomplishment," praised Alf, "seeing it's far ahead of Lord Dufferin in academics. I'm taking you to Europe this summer as a reward before grade twelve."

**

They went to London, Paris, all over Italy, and then Barcelona and Madrid, where he surprised Alf with his rough fluency in Spanish. "I'd forgotten your mother was Spanish," Alf said.

"Central America," Rick replied. "And she was a lot of other things."

He'd loved Europe, loved Italy's little towns with their narrow cobblestone streets, and cafés that served pasta with rich sauce like Mrs. Canarella used to make, and the many courses of dinners the French served with their assortment of wines. Alf took him to the Louvre and Prado, getting guidebooks and reading to him about the artists. He liked it, more Alf's attention than the paintings and lives of the painters. Sometimes they went to old churches where he marveled at the women praying and the statues of a bleeding Jesus and the saints.

"You believe in all this?" he asked Alf once. Alf merely smiled and replied, "Only when I'm in heavy trouble." Alf sometimes drank too much, and when Rick helped him back to the hotel he thought of Pa. One morning, over endless cups of cappuccino, Alf apologized.

"It's okay—Pa used to drink all the time and take Percodan for his back. I was always dragging him around."

They were sitting under an umbrella in front of a hotel in Italy. On the sidewalk the tourists walked by, and the Mediterranean sun baked everything in soft golden warmth, while in the distance a wedge of the sea winked blue.

"You miss him?"

"Yup. I try not to think of him too much, but every now and then he comes. He always stank of booze and butts, so when I smell those he's here—or even when I look at the sea. He hated Toronto and then wrecked his back, which made it worse—he got hooked on Percodan as well. But he always had a problem with booze."

"The Irish curse," murmured Alf. "I'm cursed with it and I'm not even Irish."

"It's okay, Alf," said Rick. He could have said he loved him so much it didn't matter, but he didn't want Alf to get the wrong idea about him.

"Not to change the subject," said Alf, "but we've got to get rid of that *Ricardo* label. There's nothing wrong with a Spanish first name, as long as you've got a surname to go with it. You don't. Your name's a weird combination of Spanish and Irish. I'll have my lawyer change it. You're eighteen now, it's your decision. How about Roderick? That's a class name and you'd still be Rick."

"Great idea," said Rick, basking in the warmth of the Mediterranean sun and Alf's interest.

At Monaco he won five hundred at roulette, and then another three at the tables. He insisted that Al take the money as his contribution towards the trip. He'd had a taste of the good life and from now on he didn't want to settle for less.

***

Rick found grade twelve harder than grade eleven. He didn't take bird courses, but those that would set him up for university like math and science. He was strong in math, and Alf had suggested engineering. They had started to apply to various universities including Waterloo, but Nova Scotia Tech had offered him a scholarship after Alf had given them his history and his final grade eleven marks.

"I really need to be where you are," he said to Alf. They were sitting at the kitchen table and Alf had been checking his work, although having some trouble with the math. It was a freezing January day, and outside a thick snowfall had muffled any sounds of returning cars and the harsh wind made the balcony squeal.

Alf sighed. "They accepted my thesis and my defense, even suggested publication. I was thinking of applying as a lecturer at Cambridge—I've friends there. Remember the group we went to the pub with in London?"

"Good to know you got payback for finking on me and my buddies and our scummy lives." It was mean-spirited and he knew it. Alf didn't deserve that from him after all he'd done. But he was afraid he couldn't make it without him. Even the thought of it panicked him.

Alf folded his arms and looked at him. When he spoke his voice had a harsh unfamiliar edge. "What do you want from me Rick—to be your permanent babysitter? I've got a life too."

After that they were both silent for several days except for Alf checking his homework, but slowly things slipped back to normal. But Rick was scared. He had been redeemed but now his redeemer was vanishing—perhaps forever. At Harbord he was friendly enough with members of the swim team, but there was no one like Chester—or even Iggy or Diego. There was no one he could relax with, and talk the tough street lingo he'd been brought up on that lurked beneath the surface of his new and improved diction. The Harbord kids were from middle class homes, most of them north of Bloor. They were ambitious—their parents even more so. They'd never robbed a house or a hotel suite. Or had mothers who paid for groceries by doing blow jobs. Or who beat the crap out of you because she hated your old man, who hanged himself rather than stay around.

The summer before Rick attended Nova Scotia Tech, Alf spent a lot of time with him. They'd go out to eat and see plays at the Royal Alex. Alf had been gentle, as if dealing with an invalid. Finally, a week before they were both leaving, Rick said, "Last January, what I said, I'm sorry. I just don't think I can do it without you." And for the second time in his life he'd covered his face with his hands and cried. And there was no Miss Swinton with a soft white blouse—just Alf, looking sick and guilty.

"You can use the condo when you come back—I'll keep it set up with automatic deductions from the company's account for taxes and common expenses. You can use it until the family wants it sold. I don't know when I'll be back. And you'll get five hundred a month for yourself as long as you're enrolled. You'll do fine. They're a friendly, hard drinking bunch of kids—it'll be like going back to Lord Dufferin."

He'd driven Alf to Pearson Airport, parked, and carried his bag to the check-in, nodding a mute thanks when Al told him to use the Audi until he came back. And he tried to control his sobbing when they hugged for the last time. "You'll be okay, little buddy," Alf said. And then suddenly he was Pa—better dressed and educated—but inside the expensive sports jacket and designer jeans there was Pa, saying goodbye.

He turned and rushed away, head down. And when he got into the Audi he sat behind the steering wheel, gripping it until his knuckles turned white, trying to stop the burning tears waiting to pour down his cheeks.

***

He'd been right. He needed Alf. He'd tried to join in and go to the endless Halifax bars, watch the guys drink till they puked, and study his books for hours. But Alf was not there to check his work. He tried listening in class but his mind wandered endlessly. He finally found a poker group and played most nights, usually winning. He picked up the usual types at the bars, and did his customary hit and run. But he was restless and unfulfilled. One girl, a Dalhousie student, lasted for a few weeks. She broke it off. He was "not serious enough," she said.

Following the first term's exams, after he'd returned to Toronto, the letter came: he'd lost his scholarship and his marks were such that he was advised it was pointless to continue—a Christmas graduate. The situation was, as the letter said, "highly regrettable." Alf was notified. He sent a telegram saying, "Sorry Buddy," which was followed by a phone call, where, in a voice echoing his disappointment, he told Rick he was throwing away all the work he'd put into improving him, and it was time Rick grew up and found some independence. But he could continue to live in the condo, and Simpson's Foods would continue to carry it, and he could drive the Audi. But there would be no more allowance. And he should get a job.

CHAPTER 8

For weeks Rick hung around, walking around the downtown streets, looking through store windows with temporary nodding Santa Clauses and reindeer. A feeling of heaviness weighed on him. Once he had even driven to the old duplex on Dundas in Regent Park. There was a new family where they'd lived, but Mrs. Canarella was still there, with three remaining children. "Ricky," she said, loudly kissing him on both cheeks, "you still like-a my pasta?" He sat in her warm kitchen waiting to be fed, while outside the window the street light, the one he'd been looking at after he found Pa, was surrounded by hive-like bees of snow.

"He beat your mama up, a while after he beat you—really bad, an' she left and never come back. I guess it stop her from doin' what she used to do." She turned her head and he saw her trying to hide a smile, and remembered how they'd hated each other. It occurred to him that it was Mrs. Canarella who'd phoned the Children's Aid when he was younger, and they'd taken him to Sick Kids. And he'd never finked.

He left the house entering a soft white world, and drove the Audi back to the penthouse. He was glad the bitch had gotten hers, and felt no desire to track her down. But he wanted to see Chester, perhaps even Diego and Iggy. Finally he tracked Chester down: he was running an all-night gas station. A sucker's job, thought Rick; guys get killed when non-paying customers take off and they try to stop them. Chester was off on Sundays and they would meet at the condo and have a few beers.

Chester's eyes widened when he looked at the penthouse. "Yours?"

"How the fuck you think I could afford this? Alf Simpson's family owns it. And Diego was right, he's gay. An' I'm not. He treated me good though an' I blew it." Then he told Chester everything, including the thesis and the write-ups on all of them. "I was sort of an experiment for him an' I proved I couldn't make it on my own."

"Motherfucker," said Chester in affectionate disbelief, and for a while they were both silent. Then Chester continued. "Yuh know who's makin' it, *really* makin' it? Diego. He met a daughter of Cosmo's at a party an' got her knocked up—tho' they still had a big wedding. Not that me or Iggy was asked. Now he's general manager of one of Cosmo's supermarkets. Don't even speak to any of us." He and Rick both laughed. "Always a jerk-off," said Rick. But it started him thinking.

After Chester left, he went out on the balcony and smoked, looking out at the blurred lights surrounding the condo building. The flakes kept falling on the sleeves of his pullover and then dissolving. His allowance was gone. He was not qualified for employment—the kind of employment he'd consider. And he refused to take risky, low-paying jobs. He'd be good working at a casino as a dealer, but he was reluctant to apply. Then he thought about what Chester had told him about Diego.

The next month, he started a series of what he considered low-end, dead-end, jobs: several months as a sous chef, painting walls as an assistant to an interior decorator, even a period waiting on tables, which ended up with his being a bartender at the same restaurant. His employers never complained of his competency, but of his "attitude." His employment both bored and irritated him, and he did not attempt to hide it. He had tasted a different life: the casinos of Monaco, the majesty of Rome and London, and the restaurants of Paris. Now he refused to sink back into the ordinary—or worse. But he needed money.

The cactus, for which Chester had innocently planted the seeds when he spoke of Diego, was stirring and scratching his brain. He started to evaluate the condo's contents, as he had at the suites at The Four Seasons—but with no jewelry available. There was the painting above the stone fireplace: the one Alf said was worth more than the condo. It was a gift from his mother. The artist was one of The Group of Seven: a painter of a different kind of Canadian landscape. He hoped it was insured, but knowing Alf it might not be. He looked at some gold-embossed Royal Doulton dinnerware, but decided against it. Marty, if he were still in business, would cheat him blind on it. As well, he dismissed some ivory carved decorative pieces, vases and small crystal statues, probably also supplied by Alf's mother, all traceable and ripe for Marty's huge discount.

When he'd left, Al had left his winter clothes: a thick fur-lined suede overcoat and some cashmere turtlenecks. They would all fit him, although he was much stockier than the emaciated Alf. Some of the three-piece suits were still there. He felt sad just looking at them, remembering Lord Dufferin and the way Alf had always smiled before asking him a question. But he'd never wear any of them, not that they'd fit him. He pictured Alf, sitting in some pub in Cambridge with his old and new buddies, and felt a pang of resentment—even anger. If he'd stayed none of this would have happened. He'd have gone to York, even U of T. And he'd have passed.

It was a high-end art gallery in Yorkville and Rick had dressed well, wearing Alf's suede coat, black cashmere turtleneck, and his own designer jeans and boots. He carried the painting wrapped in sheets of plastic. The owner of the gallery was an older woman with a perpetual frown and glasses. "Oh," she said softly, "this is just beautiful, so in demand. Of course I'll have to have it authenticated."

"Say it's the real deal, then how much?"

"About $600,000 less our commission—all dependent on authentication. We have buyers who collect the group's paintings: they go up every year. Would you like to leave it here while I have it authenticated?"

He left it but felt uneasy. If it could be sold for the right price, he wouldn't have to carry out the black cactus invasion that kept growing in his brain. He went back three days later.

"It's authentic. We can pay you $700,000 less our commission." For the first time she smiled. "And that's it?" asked Rick.

"We need a notarized declaration of ownership by the owner."

He couldn't do it. It would mean forgery and involving a notary or lawyer. It could mean future criminal charges.

"$100,000 tops," said Marty, looking old but still dealing. The kid was looking good, a far cry from the boy he remembered from five years ago.

"Then fuckin' forget it. I got a letter of authentication and an appraised value of $700,000."

"Don't have the cash Rick, don't have it. Remember what I used to handle for you—crap of a couple of hundred if I was lucky. Where you think I got anything like you're askin'?"

Look, I'll give you $150,000—that's top dollar. Where'd you get this kind of art—steal it?"

"It belonged to a friend of mine—he gave it to me." He tried but Marty wouldn't budge. Finally he made the deal. He had to have money for what he was planning. And it was going to take some time. In the meantime, hesitant to proceed, he drifted aimlessly, taking occasional what he considered low end jobs for diversion and walking around money, and trips to Vegas and Niagara. He spent months in the Bahamas, visiting Atlantis on Paradise Island and spending hours at the tables. He swam in the Mediterranean, and walked the beaches with an assortment of visiting female tourists, who he accommodated sexually later in the day. And he watched as, month after month, the money from the painting's sale to Marty kept shrinking.

CHAPTER 9

1997–2001

A decade later, dating sites were just getting started, and True Connections was one of the first. It interested Rick because it only dealt with "professionals," which to him meant money. The girl from the dating site was drop-dead homely, with an overbite that showed her folks weren't into braces and a height that showed they weren't into protein. And she actually thought he was into dating her. But after a great meal at Sotto Sotto, a restaurant that he thought was the best place for certain types—types who were into hunting down movie stars—he got down to business.

"I want to see background information on ten girls I'll pick from your site. I know you only show an edited version and I don't want to waste my time."

"They'll fire me," she sputtered. "They're really into privacy an' all."

"They don't have to know—just stay late one night and run off copies. It's worth $2500 to me." He could have added, "And for you to see an orthodontist," but didn't. He was lucky his teeth had turned out so well with all the crap he'd eaten as a kid.

She sighed and he could see she wasn't happy. "Nothin' to feel bad about—not like you're robbing a bank—just helping a friend so he won't waste his time." She shook her head and agreed. She would add the $2500 to her implant account.

Patsy Worrall was number three on the list. The first two were too smart and too old: university grads—a divorced stockbroker and a widowed dietitian—although in 1998 he seemed older than his twenty-eight years. Patsy was the only child of a successful insurance executive from London, Ontario, so there was a big dollar background. Her mother was a home-maker. She'd gone to a Catholic girl's private school which was good: he'd always scored with Catholic girls. And she had a little weight problem, had even joined Weight Watchers for a while—a fine prospect for insecurity. She called herself "pleasingly plump," which made him smile. Her picture just showed a head shot, a smiling girl with dimples and very blond hair.

He rehearsed his own criteria: graduate mechanical engineer—he'd find an iron engineering ring and create a story involving wealthy parents—both killed in a head-on collision in Ireland—an orphan in the process of establishing his own engineering company. He'd say he spent considerable time in Europe and spoke Spanish. He was looking for a fresh, unsophisticated, future companion, with a goal towards a permanent relationship.

"This is so beautiful," she'd gushed on her first visit to the condo, "so absolutely amazing, and with a balcony—you could drink champagne on that balcony in summer, so romantic." She wore a sleeveless dress and her arms were round and milk white. He'd bitten the under pad between her elbow and armpit very gently, and she'd giggled with delight. She shared an apartment in North Toronto with a fellow female teacher, and taught kindergarten at a nearby elementary school. There would be few problems with her, but he wondered about her father.

He met her parents when they'd come to Toronto where the father was meeting an important client and the mother was shopping. He appeared to pass scrutiny, although the father questioned him closely. The mother liked him. It was obvious that they were concerned about their only daughter's future. And briefly, just briefly, he started to reconsider.

In April, she told him she had missed her period. He wanted to puke—apparently she'd not been on the pill as she'd told him. "But Ricky," she'd pouted, "they were making me fat. And I've always had this teeny-weeny weight problem. And I could never do anything: I'd never forgive myself. It just means we have to speed things up." She'd loved their sex—which bored him after the first time—and she said he was the first. He found that hard to believe.

Alf was not coming back, and Simpson's Foods had decided to sell. Alf's friend, a real estate agent, had already contacted him, so there'd be showings. "Why are we selling our beautiful condo?" she'd pouted.

"Business is slow: we really shouldn't be having this big wedding," he replied.

"But Mommy and Daddy are paying," she'd wailed, "and Mommy's already ordered my wedding gown with the long train—just darling—and my bridesmaids have ordered as well, all summer colors. And you still haven't your best man or tuxedo."

Diego would come with his new wife, but you never knew what he'd let slip after a few drinks, and Chester and Iggy were too Regent Park. He'd rent a tux, tell her his friends were all in Nova Scotia or out of the country, and she had to supply a relative. The engagement and wedding ring had set him back $8,000. He hated everything about it.

The ceremony took place in a large Catholic Church with Father Burns officiating. Father Burns had discussed a possible conversion, a contingency Rick assured him he'd consider "later on." This brightened the father up, who remarked, "With a handle like McCready you should have a faith to go with it."

After considerable correspondence his birth certificate and certificate of baptism were received from Nova Scotia. He found to his surprise he'd been baptized a Catholic. He would, he thought, have told this to Diego and Iggy during the infamous collection plate robbery. His violation of church monies as a Catholic would have given him a much larger piece of the pie.

He'd stumbled through the ceremony, his tongue thick and face burning, while she'd caroled her vows in a voice that rang through the packed congregation. He hated himself for being there.

"Come meet my cousin—he went to Nova Scotia Tech." The speaker was her uncle, a fat, bald, pleasant man who was to deliver the toast to the bride. The cousin asked him about the staff. "Yes, Punch Mitchell had been there, and coaching boxing on the side." He breathed deeply, thankful that he'd spent at least three months there, although most of the time playing poker.

"But I don't want to go to Vegas," she'd protested. "That's an awful surprise, Rick McCready—not one bit romantic. An' all you'll want to do is gamble."

They were at a hotel at Pearson Airport following the wedding, and they were catching an early morning flight. He was sick with exhaustion. It had been a nightmare, surrounded by strangers, while she'd stood in the midst of her group of giggling bridesmaids. He saw her father look at him strangely a few times, and as they were leaving he'd said, "Not your kind of crowd here?" And then, "You better take care of her . . . y'hear?" Her mother had kissed him on the cheek and then wiped off the lipstick with chilled fingers. The toasts to the bride painted a spoiled, yet insecure, little princess, and he had to kiss her every time they banged the cutlery against their plates. If he'd known, he'd have escaped. It was the worst experience of his life—aside from losing Pa and Alf.

"I'm wiped," he said. "That was a circus. We gotta do away with any sex tonight."

"Ricky McCready, it's our wedding night. I even got a black satin nightgown—really darling—for the occasion." So he took a shower and had a three minute fuck, without any of the Marlene goodies she liked.

"Your heart wasn't in that, I can tell. I don't believe you love me at all."

"Sure I do," he mumbled, the lie tumbling from his dry-as-dust mouth. "The wedding took the crap outta me. Those people were all your friends, or your parent's people. I got nothin' to say to any of them." She looked at him long and hard.

"Guess what I got," she said, having put on her black nightgown again. She produced a box full of cheques. "These are our pressies. Let's count them. It'll make you feel better." There was sixty thousand in total. He did feel better.

"Shouldn't be traveling with these," he said. He'd been going through the remaining money from Marty with all the wedding garbage and other expenses. Now with this influx of money, he could carry on.

"You should kiss my tummy," she demanded. "That's what men do when their wife is preggums." She pulled up her nightgown and sat waiting, her pale distended abdomen cupped in her hands. He bent down and gave it a brief kiss. "You're not kissing it like you mean it." He thought of the sixty thousand and kissed it again.

They stayed at Caesar's Palace. The wedding suite bed had a mirror underneath the canopy. The thought of having mirrored sexual acrobatics with this plump woman carrying his child put him off, but it was making the decision he'd made earlier easier. "I don't think it's a good idea, twisting every which way when you're pregnant," he warned.

"I asked Dr. Gordon and he said sex was perfectly fine; it's stuff like jogging and horseback riding you have to watch out for." He groaned inwardly but complied. Funny how he could function like an energized robot, when just touching her made him want to recoil.

They went to the Fashion Mall by cab: it was about 110 degrees outside. He sat in a stuffed chair at Saks while she modeled maternity clothes. "I'll be teaching until my eighth month," she explained, "and it's important how I look—even if it's only little kids. Their moms and dads see me."

He glumly sat and watched, hour after hour, as she pranced in front of him, a five-foot two, plus-sized model, striking pose after pose like some tabloid glamour girl. And having no idea how stupid she looked. For a moment he felt a nudge of pity, but it was displaced by irritation, and then anger.

"Tonight," he said, "I'm playing blackjack. You can go to the Spa for a massage—they're open till ten."

"You just want to get rid of me . . . sometimes I think you don't love me at all, Ricky McCready—not one itty bitty bit."

She went with him, standing behind him in one of her new honeymoon gowns, watching the players, making remarks, and distracting everyone until half of the players left in disgust. Surprisingly, he won two thousand in spite—or probably because—of her.

They ate at the Bacchanal Room, where belly dancers gave neck rubs and poured wine two feet away from the gold-edged goblets. "You liked that, I know you did," she said, after he'd been given a neck rub.

"No, I hated it. They just go around to the tables torturing men to piss off their wives." He didn't care. He couldn't stand her. But perhaps it would make things easier later on. He only got in one other session of blackjack after persuading her to go to the spa. Despite being alone, he gave back the two thousand. He took her to a lot of the shows, except the strip shows, his favorites. The extravaganza with six-foot-tall showgirls was a mistake.

"You'd love me more if I looked like that," she accused him. "Nope," he replied, "I hate tall, sexy showgirls with big tits. I can't stand 'em. I just like little fat bleached blondes—with small boobs and short legs."

He shouldn't have said it. They had to leave. After his shower he'd come out and she was crying. He felt both ashamed and repulsed. He picked up a small padded foot with newly polished toenails from her last spa visit and massaged it gently, moving it back and forth.

"Look, you've got to stop with this insecurity. I married you, remember that. I see deeper than all this superficial crap." It was a total lie, but it seemed to make her feel better. The truth was he was overwhelmed by "this superficial crap." He would, if possible, drown in it.

They visited the large pool with the waterfall located at the back of the Palace. He rubbed the SPF-50 sunblock on her pale boneless body as requested. But she wouldn't go in. "I can't swim," she said, merely venturing down the concrete steps and getting her feet wet. He did an expert crawl around the pool.

Chapter 10

In September, Patsy went back to teaching. She was six months along and kept cradling the swelling with her hands, which annoyed him. She had stopped asking him to kiss it. In the second week of September, he made an appointment with an insurance company. "It's for the baby's education," he told her. "People die young in my family. I don't want to leave you with nothin'—as parents we gotta think of things like that. It's term, not whole life, a twenty-year policy. We can afford the premiums. A million clams'll send the little guy to Harvard."

"Perhaps I should ask Daddy: Daddy's in insurance."

"What kind of shit is that? What is it you want to ask your father about? To give us permission to insure ourselves so our little guy can go to college?" So she didn't.

His painting stash was long gone and the wedding gift money was down to ten thousand: a crib, a pram and a redo of their second bedroom. And he lost some at poker. Her fellow teachers gave her a baby shower: an assortment of small blankets, knitted caps and Dr. Denton's sleeping suits, from six to twelve months. "Really darling," she said. Her birthday was October 6. She would be twenty-two.

"I got a surprise," he said.

"Not Vegas again," she replied. She suspected he was gambling away their money on his poker games, but didn't want to fight with him with the baby coming. She wondered sometimes if he had a job, or if it were all a big lie—like his pretending to own that beautiful condo. She didn't like to think of it.

"We'll go to Algonquin Park: there's a class place near a lake. Beautiful up there, seeing the leaves change. There'll be great food and we'll almost have the place to ourselves. They even have canoes, so we can paddle on the lake. It'll be peaceful—'so romantic,' as you always say. They even have candles, stuff like that at dinner. We'll leave Friday night an' come back Sunday night."

The drive took several hours. Once they stopped for coffee and he had a cigarette, leaning against the car door. She said it made her sick when he smoked in the car. She lay back in the car seat during the drive, her plump hand constantly rubbing the growing bump. "Give the kid a break," he said, "maybe he's not into getting massaged all day long." She smiled and kept on.

They drove through the night, and darkness covered the car like a soft cool blanket, while other cars with yellow cat eyes heading for the city streamed past them. Against the dark grey sky the pines and spruce bulked black, and a bulb-like moon buried in mist pushed from the clouds.

"This is crazy," she said, her voice low. "We could have gone to dinner in Toronto. No need to drive way up here."

"It's your birthday present," he said.

"By this time next year we'll have a little baby, and that'll be my birthday present."

Hearing this, all of a sudden he felt sick. He drew up to the side of the road, got out and lit another cigarette. "You're smoking too much," he heard her say through the slightly open car window. They checked in with the smiling elderly proprietor of the inn, who commented, "You'll have the place almost to yourselves: we're only open 'til the end of October."

The room was slightly musty, but the bathroom had a bath and shower. "I'm going to give you a special tonight, seeing it's your birthday," he said, wondering if he could even perform. But he did a lot of oral sex—and she really liked it. "You don't do that often enough," she said.

After she was asleep, he opened the bedroom window. The mist had gone from the moon that reflected on the lake, leaving an amber path, and the surrounding trees stood rigid in the silence. He quietly left the room, walked down the stairs and left by the back door. He saw a line of canoes lined up against the back wall of the inn. He breathed a mixture of spruce and cedar and walked near the lake. It appeared deep and cloudy and he remembered it had been raining earlier on. He threw his butt into the water and slowly walked back to their bedroom. He lay down beside her but he could not sleep.

The breakfast room overlooked the lake, and there were only two other full tables. Both had older couples, neither of whom were speaking, perhaps talked out after all those years together. After studying the menu, she ordered Scottish, whole-grain, slow-cooking oatmeal, with ten percent cream and brown sugar, and a pot of tea that she poured into one of the china cups to sip from. He drank cup after cup of coffee, and only ate a portion of his Canadian bacon and farm fresh scrambled eggs.

"I'm so glad you thought of this," she said brightly. "It's the best present ever—just amazing." She stretched out a puffy, small, white hand and placed it on his. The diamond on her engagement ring sparkled. He felt the eggs and bacon flip over in his gut.

There was a faint drizzle and the sky was low and mottled grey when they headed for the line of canoes. "I'll carry it—it's portage, something they taught poor kids at the community camp." This was not the image he'd always given, but now it didn't matter.

"How about a life jacket?" she asked.

"No need. You'd be uncomfortable and I was captain of the school swimming team."

She sat smiling at him from the bow of the canoe as he paddled southward, away from the inn. From the distance there was a faint rumble of thunder. "It's gonna rain," she said. "Best we head back."

It was then he tossed the paddle away, stood up, and started rocking the canoe back and forth. She staggered to her feet and, leaning forward, grabbed the edge of the canoe. It tipped over. They were both in the water and she kept trying to stay afloat, flailing her arms and calling, "Ricky, help me!" He went underwater and swam towards where she was struggling. He grasped her from behind and pulled her under. He held her firmly in lethal intimacy. He felt her struggling to get away and then go heavy against him. Leaving her, he swam to the capsized canoe and banged his forehead against it until he tasted the metal of blood. He looked to where he'd left her. He saw a small white arm surrounded by mist rising up from the waters of the lake and then disappear.

The thunder was now directly above him and black and grey clouds were hovering low. He felt icy drops of rain lacerate his scalp. With his arm around her body, he swam to the shoreline. There were two fishermen in oilskins. "Phone an ambulance," he croaked. "We've had an accident and my wife's hurt." He saw them looking at his bleeding forehead and the limp bundle in his arms.

Cell phones did not work at the inn. The inn owner called a park ranger, who called an ambulance and the OPP. The medic in the ambulance said she was gone and now it was a job for the coroner. But they took the body. In a small room, located at the side of the reception desk, he spoke to two members of the Provincial Police. They looked at him with narrow-eyed suspicion. Apparently her father had been notified and was insisting he be charged with murder based on the very recent million-dollar insurance policy, with an extra half a million for accidental death.

"Any reason no life jackets, sir?" the tall one who'd given him a cigarette asked.

"She was seven months pregnant and she wanted to be comfortable. Looking back I should have insisted, but I'm a good swimmer—didn't ever think of getting my head banged so I couldn't think straight. Now I gotta live with thinking I coulda saved her." He placed his face in his hands and shook with remorse. The Mounties exchanged glances, then the smaller one said, after clearing his throat, "Your wife's father says you took out a million and a half policy a month ago—fortunate timing."

"Jesus," he exploded, "she was pregnant and it was for our kid's future education—in case something happened to one of us."

They didn't charge him. "Not a scratch on her—she drowned," one of the Mounties told the homicide detective from Toronto who the father had insisted be involved. "The policy and lack of life jacket's suspicious but he explained them, and his forehead was banged up pretty bad. The fact he lied about his background before the wedding's not enough to charge him—like the father seems to think."

He was banned from the London funeral, which was a relief, but he visited the funeral parlor the night before. She looked peaceful, with that buttery fold under her chin and a little cardboard smile. He felt really bad looking at her, and wished it hadn't happened: even whispering sorry when he bent over to kiss her goodbye. Her father kept railing about the stupidity of the OPP but eventually got a girlfriend and her mother got really sick. He felt bad about her mother as he'd always liked her. The insurers refused to pay him anything, saying it was a suspicious death. He hired a lawyer and they offered a million to settle—but no extra five hundred thousand for accidental death. He was broke, so he took it.

***

Driven by guilt and a need for distraction, Rick wasted much of the money. He took six trips to Vegas, dropped thousands at the blackjack tables and on an assortment of strippers and hookers. He'd even gone to Europe and hunted down Alf. He'd found him in a Cambridge pub surrounded by his buddies, drunk and fifty pounds heavier. He didn't even stay until he sobered up. He had been relieved that the insurers had covered the painting. He went to Barcelona and then back to Toronto. Nothing had been the same without Alf.

Sometimes he'd think back and see that little white arm rising out of the brown water surrounded by mist. Then he'd try to think of other things.

He only had $200,000 left when he met Steamy in 2001, but she bought his fake history and married him. She wanted "a father figure" for her sons—funny when those same sons would run him out of the house. It seems they'd found out a few things. He thought she would have put up with him, the sex was that good. He made a mistake one night when he was stoned, and told her about Patsy, although he denied it the next day. She was very quiet for a few days after that, but when he suggested putting fifty thousand into her townhouse to pay down the mortgage, and putting it in both names, she flat-out refused. She was making $6,000 a week as a top stripper, but they both knew it wouldn't last, although her cans were real and she didn't even need implants. He liked being with her as they spoke the same language.

After he was out on his keister, thanks to her young bastard sons, he contacted True Connections, thinking it may have folded after six years. To his surprise, Mindy was still there. He gave her $2500 again, and she gave him background information on his ten top picks. The one he liked most was the one with the dying mother and a future house in Lawrence Park. She even made decent dollars as a dental hygienist. Her name was Rosemary MacKenzie.

CHAPTER 11

2004

If she hadn't been twenty-nine, and had never had a boyfriend, she wouldn't have bothered with any of it. But she had decided, and joining True Connections was to be her first and last effort. The dating website had stated that it would cost $200 to join and then $100 a month for six months—with a guarantee of three introductions a month. And all members were to have professional careers.

"You'd think," her mother had murmured, lying there, her organs filling with carcinogenic ash, "you'd have lotsa chances of meetin' young fellas at the clinic." Her mother kept traces of her Belfast accent, and as her cancer progressed it seemed to thicken.

"I don't get past their tonsils," Rose muttered, "Nothing romantic about scraping plaque from under some patient's gums." She had known after the first year of training that she didn't want to be a dental hygienist. It had been a mistake. But by that time money had been spent. She tried to think how well she'd do once she started working. Not less than seventy-five thousand a year, she'd been told, depending on her patient stream. Perhaps it would be worth the endless scraping, cleaning and X-rays, all part of the job.

"Be sure you get someone good enough for yuh," her mother whispered. She closed her eyes and Rose thought back. She was in their Lawrence Park home and her father was dead. She felt her mother's warm hand on her back and smelled the meat loaf strong from the oven. "How's my wild Irish Rose?" her mother would say.

"Wish your Rose was a little wilder," her sister Del would reply, aware she wasn't her mother's favorite and disturbed by Rose's drab teen years. Del had a taffy-colored mop of hair and an easy laugh. She was out every night and every weekend. "Up to no good," her mother would sniff. Del looked and acted much more like her Scottish father, who had kept his pharmaceutical clients by his relentless joviality: so different from Rose, with her nose in an assortment of novels, and her dark hair, clear green eyes and luminous pale skin. "The face an' eyes of all of you, more beautiful than pretty," her mother would confide in her letters to her sisters who'd never left Belfast.

Del slipped through the hospital-room door but her mother's eyes remained closed. "Mom's accent's changed," she whispered to Rose, "Really weird. You'd think she was just off the boat."

"Regressing,"

"You asleep Mom?" Del asked, but there was no reply. "You're the important one, anyway," she said, remembering the years her mother had favored Rose—starting at age three, and ruining both their lives in the process. And she still loved Rose more, although Del had become a top legal clerk, had a happy marriage, and had produced her mother's only grandchild.

Rose sighed. She read Del's thoughts as clearly as if they had been typed across her forehead. It was unfair. Del was so much more attractive, so much more outgoing, so much more fun. Perhaps, she thought, her mother knew this and felt sorry for her. But she knew it was much more than that: her mother had needed her. But before that, she had needed her mother.

She reached out and took the cold, mauve, shriveled fingers in her hand, "Del's here Mom," she said softly. But her mother gave no sign of hearing.

"I'm supposed to meet one of my one-hundred-a-month wonders for coffee at eight, then I'll come back and sit with Mom till eleven; so why don't you go home, feed your crew and come back."

Del only picked up the first part of the sentence. "Hate those dating websites," she sniffed. "I keep waiting for the call: the one that says you've been found in a ditch with your throat cut, smeared all over with some loser's DNA."

"Oh shut up," Rose muttered. She didn't need that from Del—she was neurotic enough. She'd had two sexual relationships—one-night stands really—that she'd been too nervous, and drunk, to enjoy. She'd never heard from either of them again, not even a call the next day. They'd ghosted her. She was sure this meant she was bad in bed.

"Sorry," said Del, coming over and nuzzling her, smelling of Chanel and hairspray. "Don't get mad because I worry about my little sister."

She forgave her. She knew despite the harsh exterior that Del cared about her, and later when Mom passed, which could be any day now, she knew they'd be close. They'd always been close when Mom wasn't around—which was, unfortunately, not often.

***

They were to meet at Starbucks, although he'd first mentioned Tim Hortons—a bad sign. She'd straightened her dark curly hair, whisked some blush over her pale chiseled cheekbones, and traced some shiny rose gloss over her lips, after drawing a soft grey pencil around her green eyes. She wore jeans, a mock turtlenecked sweater, and a cropped leather jacket. And she was slim, except for her breasts that swelled unexpectedly on her slight body. Looking at herself in the bathroom mirror she appeared attractive enough—not hot or amazing, as Del would say, but not the hopeless sight she always feared. Then she felt guilty, sizing herself up for a date while Mom lay dying at the Trillium.

She knew right away he was wrong: a waste of time. He did not resemble his True Connections picture, where he wore dark framed glasses and showed dazzling square white teeth in a broad smile. He was slight and pale, a male replica of her. She was sitting at a table by the window as they had planned. He smiled when he saw her, and kept smiling as he sat down. He stretched out a thin cool hand and she took it, thinking it resembled the hand of her dying mother.

He was, as his profile said, a professional certified accountant for the Toronto branch of a well-known computer company. He liked spectator sports, a hobby that would bore her. He read books—"Nothing heavy, just some non-fiction or political and sport figures." And he didn't see a family in his future, "Not in the state this fucked-up world is in." He smiled at her, as if she agreed with him, and she saw some recession and plaque ripe for removal. She decided she would not waste time telling him her favorite pursuit was reading feminist fiction by and about women she wished she resembled or seeing foreign films, and that one of her objectives was having a family.

"I really should have canceled," she said, draining her latte. "My mother's dying in hospital and I can't think of much else. I'm sorry to have wasted your time—perhaps later on when things get better for me."

He lost his smile and frowned. He didn't believe her and his irritation was obvious. Bending towards her, he said in an accusatory voice, "I don't need to remind you that we pay one hundred a month to that crazy site for three introductions."

What did she expect from an accountant who loved spectator sports?

"I'm sorry, I really am. I didn't know this would happen to my mother. You'll have to forgive me—let me pay for our coffees."

He pushed his chair back and stood up. He wasn't more than five-foot-six and his jeans were too big.

"Perhaps you'd give me the name of the dentist you work for: you could do a job on my teeth and we could stay in touch."

"Dr. Blackler on King," she lied. He was Del's dentist.

"Do you want me to see you home?"

"No. But thanks. I'm going back to the hospital."

"I hope your mother makes it," he said. And he was gone, walking in an almost jaunty way, as if he believed what she'd told him.

True Connections owed her one more introduction but she was finished. It wasn't that their selections were losers, which she could almost tolerate, hardly considering herself a winner. But she had nothing in common with them, and could hardly imagine closer contact than forty-five minutes in her hygienist chair—for which at least she'd get paid.

***

Very few attended her mother's funeral, just a half dozen of Del's friends, a handful of neighbors and two hygienists from the dental clinic. Her mother had stopped socializing after what she always referred to as "the accident." She no longer played bridge or had lunch with old friends. She did not even write weekly letters to Belfast as she'd done before. She had just focused on her, who she sometimes referred to as "Poor little Rosie." And, she thought, as she looked over the almost empty chapel, had, to use Del's expression, "stopped you from getting on with your life." Her mother had insisted she remain with her in the family home, "Or I'd go cracked with loneliness." Not to forget that Rose paid the carrying costs.

When her parents had purchased their Lawrence Park home some thirty-five years earlier, they had paid a modest amount, an amount to be expected from a salesman of pharmaceuticals and a stay-at-home housewife. Prices however had soared, and Del told her they could expect "well over two mil," which Rose found surprising, although aware of the increase in real estate.

"Location is everything," Del had pronounced. Del was so smart, so much savvier than she was, and it would never do for her to know that her mother had wanted to leave Rose the whole house.

"No, Mom, don't even go there," she'd pleaded, not wanting to face a future laced with hostility from Del. So her mother gave in and split the house equally in her will. But Rose was the beneficiary of an insurance policy for $200,000, and the stock portfolio her father had left to her mother, both payable to her directly.

The organist played "Abide with Me," and the pastor of Lawrence Presbyterian, which her mother had attended on occasion for thirty-five years, had read the Twenty-third Psalm, and had the congregation recite the Lord's Prayer. He spoke of her mother's absolute devotion to her family, which provoked a deep sigh from Del. The sparse group had gathered in the room adjoining the chapel for coffee and egg salad sandwiches after the service. Her mother was to be cremated the next day and just Rose and Del would be attending.

"You'll miss your mother, Rose; Del says you two were real close." The speaker, who worked with Del at the law firm, had a small shriveled face puckered in sympathy and she patted Rose on the arm.

"Maybe now she'll be able to have a life," sniffed Del, standing nearby. "Mom was real selfish when it came to Rose, monopolized all her time." She slipped an arm around Rose's waist and gave her a gentle hug. Rose silently thanked God she had insisted on her mother's dividing the house. It was turning out as she had hoped: Del's jealousy was gone and it would be as it had always been when their mother was absent. She would not mention the insurance policy or stock portfolio, thankful they went to her directly.

"We'll have to think about listing the house when we get rid of all the clutter," Del said, as she drove Rose home after the cremation, her mother's ashes sitting in a golden urn in the backseat. "No point you being there by yourself—better you get a nice condo downtown and join the land of the living. Nobody under fifty left on the avenue."

Rose hummed her agreement, knowing Del would take over, including getting the house ready for sale and ruthlessly disposing of Mom's accumulated clutter, a chore that would cause Rose pain.

She kissed Del, and leaving the car, walked up the wooden steps and entered the silent house. She carried the urn carefully and placed it gently on the mantelpiece above a fireplace where she'd never seen a fire. Then a wave of loneliness and sadness choked her. She had yet to cry for her mother, perhaps out of a reluctance to let Del see it and associate it with a closeness she had never shared. But now she was alone. She trudged up the stairs to her mother's bedroom, lay down on her bed, breathed in the familiar smell of Pond's cold cream and Johnson's baby powder, and sobbed into her pillow. She had loved her mother and would miss her. It was impossible not to care for someone who so openly cared for you—unfortunately to the exclusion of all others.

Later, eyes burning and head throbbing, she went out the back door. She sat on the wooden steps, breathed in the darkening damp March air, and looked at the bare tangled branches of the lilac trees and the patches of stained snow still remaining on the lawn. Two fat brown doves and a jay hovered around the bird feeder that was always full, something her mother insisted on. She would remind the new owners to feed the birds, who were dependent on their diet of sunflower seeds and corn during the harsh Canadian winters. She thought of her mother again.

As the years passed she had sensed within herself a growing vulnerability, which had started with the accident when she was three. She had tried to curb it, attempting to fend off troubling thoughts, but failed. Newspaper and television reports of abused children and animals—and more recently, child refugees—haunted her and caused insomnia. She finally confided her problem to her mother, who referred her to their family doctor, who prescribed anti-anxiety pills. Dr. Dunstan, a kind elderly man who'd seen her since the accident and through all her childhood illnesses, had frowned his concern.

"Try not to read or listen to things that bother you," he cautioned, "and try to find some activities to distract you—sports, things like that. You're too young, Rose, to be taking on all the world's problems."

The anti-anxiety pills helped her sleep and she became addicted, slipping one under her tongue each night to rid herself of the disturbing thoughts that the pills blurred but did not stop. It was after this that she joined the True Connections dating site. For once her mother did not object, having received her own disturbing prognosis from the same doctor.

Strangely, her empathy and sensitivity had enhanced her popularity as a dental hygienist, and she was in demand at the clinic for her "gentle hands," many patients insisting on "Rosie" when they phoned for appointments. She still read the newspaper and watched the nightly news for stories that disturbed her. Her mother, knowing her problem, at times got rid of the nightly paper and distracted her from the news on television.

"You can't rescue the world, Rosie," her mother would warn. "The poor child's suffering is over. I wish you were more like Del." She agreed but knew she couldn't change. She sometimes felt she needed a protective salve between her and the rawness of life. But it—or he—wasn't available.

***

When she arrived home the next week, driving her mother's Chrysler, a welcome change from the Yonge Street subway, Del's Honda was there. There was also a van with "Mighty Maid Cleaners" painted on its side. Another unfamiliar car was in the driveway. Inside, Del appeared to be listing the furnishings and fixtures that could go with the house. Standing beside her was a squat, thick woman, who introduced herself as Frances Hutchings, and who told her she was LePage's top seller in Toronto for the past year.

"It just needs a few coats of paint and a general clean-up. It's the location. You and your sister will be over the moon when you see what you'll get for this little hovel. We might even have a bidding war. You'll both be able to take a world cruise on a tear-down like this."

"She can do that on her insurance money," muttered Del.

So she had gone through her desk. Rose felt a throb of annoyance and was again relieved that she had insisted on an equal division of the house.

"And the stock portfolio," she added, her voice showing a rare edge.

Del looked alarmed, not used to seeing her sister express irritation.

"And you deserve it," she replied, too quickly, "giving up your life to cater to Mom and paying for everything. Don't think I begrudge you a thing. You can have your pick of furniture for your new place—I don't even want a credit."

"Thanks," replied Rose, but added, "I'll buy new stuff. I might even take that cruise."

"Wonderful idea," gushed Del, who, Rose suddenly realized, was not as tough as she sometimes seemed.

Frances stood watching them, her full arms crossed and her short legs rooted to the floor. "Sisters," she said, with a curled lip and eye roll. But Frances was right about the house: the $2.2 million listing brought them an offer of $2.5 million within five days. And the purchasers did not want to close before June, which meant she'd have plenty of time to find an apartment near the clinic. In the meantime there was the cruise: a fourteen-day respite around the Mediterranean, that, Del reminded her, she could well afford. She had never had money and she found it exciting. Once she had started to work, she had paid for all household expenses, and had donated to The World Animal Fund, Doctors without Borders, and two Bangladesh foster children for whom she had purchased goats. She kept their pictures, showing their smiling faces, arms around their goats, tucked in the edge of her bedroom mirror.

"So quaint," Del had murmured, when she'd inspected Rose's room.

"It's tax deductible," Rose explained apologetically.

"Go to Holt's spring blow-out sale—time you slicked yourself up. You know what they say about first impressions: silly to meet some dude—a professional no less—looking like you cleaned houses. No wonder these dates don't want past first base. Show a little flesh for God's sake. No point having boobs that look as if they're $10,000 implants unless you show them."

"The first dates are usually at Starbucks and I don't want to look common. I'll pick up something in France or Italy."

"Oh wow, forgot about that. You'll come back, as Mom used to say, 'all gussied up' in Europe's haute couture. Wish I could go—more fun than running a law firm."

It crossed her mind that Del may be jealous but she dismissed it, lying and saying, "I'd love you to come, but then no one would look at me."

Del smiled and didn't deny it.

Chapter 12

The Mediterranean Princess, owned by the prestigious Empress Cruise Line, was advertised as being "The Single's Dream Ship." It had two Olympic pools, ten "meet-up bars," a casino, a dance hall with piped-in music, or even on occasion a small ship's band that also played as back-up for the nightly entertainment in the ship's theatre. The theatre featured plays and professional dance and musical groups, some well past their prime, and others just temporarily unemployed, needing a payday and the pleasure of cruising the Mediterranean.

Several of the ship's officers hovered around the ship's singles, fetching drinks and inviting them to dance. One incredibly handsome officer with a British accent chatted with Rose, who was charmed.

Three of them were sitting at a table in the dining room, while soft show tunes from the '60s played. There were starched white tablecloths with gleaming cutlery, and a fresh rose in a silver vase on each table that made the dining room resemble a five-star restaurant. Rose's companions, Dora and Georgie, were plump pleasant girls from Sudbury, who laughed a lot, had hair unstylishly curly, necklines too low and lipstick too dark. They worked for the same mining company and, judging by their conversation, Rose assumed they had been saving for the cruise for some time.

"Isn't Rodney hot?" she asked, using one of Del's old expressions. She had decided to eat with them after spending her first two evenings sitting with a group of older couples from Calgary, who ignored her after introducing themselves, and asking her where she came from.

"Don't go there, Rose," warned Dora. "He's gay. I saw him out on the deck the first night kissing his lover, another officer. The cruise line hired them to live up to their dream single ads. Straight men might end up having sex with us singles, and cause trouble for the cruise line when the single found out about his wife and kids."

After pronouncing these words of wisdom, Dora fished a compact from her sequined purse, and using the mirror carefully rubbed lipstick from her upper teeth with her finger.

"Not a straight officer," agreed Georgie, "and no single men. It's a big rip-off for anyone who's in the market to meet one. It'll be Club Med next time for us."

Rose nodded her agreement, and repacked most of her new cruise wear wardrobe, deciding to just enjoy the sights with her two friends. Her most expensive purchase, a backless black gown with a plunging neckline, which had taken hours to decide on, had only attracted two elderly men. One had confided to her over a drink at the bar that he had six great grandkids, and was recovering from a divorce from his third wife. "She cleaned me out," he told her, in what he'd sadly described as "a financial castration."

"Beautiful church," she'd murmured to Dora and Georgie in Venice. They merely took a fleeting look. No eligible singles hidden in the pews, just tourist couples and middle-aged women dressed in black, either kneeling or doing the Stations of the Cross, with black prayer beads wrapped around puffy pale hands.

"I lost my faith when Mom died," muttered Dora, to no one in particular, but giving a suffering Jesus on the cross a particularly nasty look. After that Rose decided she'd visit the palaces, galleries, and other churches alone, but did go with them to various bars, ending up at a small one in The Rialto. A few men drifted their way, but the one she liked had a problem with English, and ended up shrugging his regrets and kissing her hand. She would have, she thought, been better off alone. The three of them, with Dora and Georgie so obviously on the prowl, would scare anyone off. But she would not go to bars by herself.

Rose loved Rome, with its statues and fountains. She would, she decided, visit for weeks should she be lucky enough to find a permanent escort.

There were the three of them standing on the corner near the Trevi Fountain when the squeal of a Vespa cut through the air. "Can I show you around, *bella?*" he asked. He was so handsome, with his tanned face, wide white smile, and black hair curling from under his helmet. He was directing his words at her, waiting for her to agree to perch on the back of his motorbike. Rose smiled, but reluctantly shook her head, while all around her Rome erupted in the sunbaked noise of squealing scooters, yelling cab drivers, and the ever-present mob of tourists.

"I'll go," shrilled Georgie, bursting out of her jeans and T-shirt, made even tighter by her love of pasta and vino. He shrugged his consent but his eyes met Rose's, obviously his first choice.

"See you back at the ship," called Georgie, while she climbed on and rode away, curls flying, waving a short plump arm, which she then clasped around the waist of the handsome biker. They were leaving the next day.

"Isn't that a little risky?" Rose asked.

"Jeez, Rose," said Dora. "You're such a tight-ass. And he wanted you."

"I had a neurotic mother," Rose replied, by way of explanation, not adding she was even more so. And that it was a long story.

She and Dora returned to the ship and had a sandwich in the casual snack room for dinner, both full from their three-course Roman lunch of minestrone soup, pasta and rich tiramisu.

"I hope she's okay?" Rose asked.

"She'll be fine," answered Dora, somewhat impatiently. "She'll probably get lucky, but he'll be disappointed she's so poor: they all think we're rich Americans, not poor Canadians."

The last water taxi came at eleven, and in it a smudged Georgie, eyes blurred from vino, with a face for once without make-up, but flushed and swollen. Rose and Dora bumped into her as they were exiting that night's musical, *Guys and Dolls*.

"Oh Rosie," she slurred, "Did you miss it! But I'll save the details for breakfast."

But the next morning as they sat together, plates heaped with scrambled eggs, bacon and pancakes, a more subdued Georgie informed them, "I'm itching like crazy and stink like a polecat—that creep gave me an STD. I'm heading for sickbay as soon as I finish my coffee."

"Trick," said Dora, too loudly, after she left. "They'll give her some Flagyl and she'll be fine. She should have thought of picking something up. Those guys probably hit on a dozen of us a month."

"Awful," whispered Rose, "and not even using protection. She might even be pregnant."

"No way," scoffed Dora, "She's on the pill so she doesn't carry condoms. And the guys hate using them. I hope it was worth it—she'll tell us when she stops itching and stinking."

"Terrible," Rose whispered to Dora, after Georgie left for the loo with her drugs.

"It's like hiring a male stripper," agreed Dora, who then added, "but at least her cruise memories will be more exciting than ours."

"Whatever," shrugged Rose, remembering that Dora and Georgie were friends and worked together.

They flew together from Heathrow, or "Thief-row," as Georgie called it, as she'd had her wallet lifted there on a previous trip. Upon arriving at the Toronto Airport they all professed lifelong friendship, exchanged emails, and promised to go to Club Med together the following year. Rosie wished them both well, knowing she'd never see them again. They were not her type. She did receive an email from Georgie describing "the best lay I ever had," but adding, "I could swear he wanted me to pay him."

***

Rose was sitting in Del's warm living room, savoring the comfort of the overstuffed chintz sofa and looking into the flames of the gas fireplace, leaping orange, and adding to the cozy atmosphere—so different from the sterile living room on Dawlish with its grey fireplace and plastic-covered chairs. Del had opened a bottle of red, and from the next room Gwennie, Del's eight-year-old, played a painful "Fur Elise." Del's husband Fred, who repaired computers, was on a call.

"I'm considering upgrading," she confided to Rose, taking a sip of wine, after proposing a toast "to the sale," and giving Rose one of her gum-exposing smiles. "But what I have in mind may take a mortgage, or we'll move to Mississauga for something cheaper, but bigger, and with more class." Mississauga was a rapidly expanding city in Peel County: a thirty-minute drive west of Toronto.

"Gwennie?"

"She'll adjust—kids always adjust—and she's a friendly little creep."

"Stop talking 'bout me," yelled Gwennie, stopping her torture of Beethoven.

"Stop snooping and think about your playing," Del yelled back. She turned back to her sister. "Get lucky?"

"The ones I liked were gay. The ship was full of girls like me, looking for a man. The only one who got lucky was a friend from Sudbury, and it was with a Vespa biker in Rome. She got an STD along with the orgasm—or orgasms, according to her."

She was being too frank, unlike her usual self, but she appreciated Del's interest and she couldn't confide in her friends at the office, to whom even having a friend who picked up a STD would contaminate her immaculate image—the Blessed Rosie, gentle remover of stains and plaque: the most hygienic hygienist of them all.

Del gave her usual lecture about being too picky, and extolling the virtues of Fred, "a good solid guy who wouldn't even be accepted by True Connections."

"I've got one more left for my $100 for March that I put off because of the cruise. I was going to toss it, but now I'll give it one last try. It gets so tedious."

Del sighed. "Third time's lucky, but these dating-site intros scare me. Probably better than a bar . . . though I met Fred in a bar."

Rose sighed, got up, and sauntered to the next room and Gwennie. She gave her thick blonde braid a slight tug before she sat down beside her, placing her arm around her waist.

"You're getting better, you really are," she whispered.

"I suck and I really hate it," Gwennie burst out, but she started again with more enthusiasm. She loved Rose, threatening her mother she'd go live with her after every spat.

CHAPTER 13

2004

His profile said he was thirty-four, had a master's in Electrical Engineering from MIT, and his own successful electrical engineering company. He was divorced, but he and his ex-wife had remained friends. There had been no children. His picture showed a serious-looking man with regular features and thick dark hair and brown eyes—a Greek or Italian mother perhaps, although the surname McCready was Irish. When asked what quality he most cherished in a woman he'd answered "sweetness," which she thought unusual—but nice. His name was Roderick but his friends and employees called him "Rick."

"Starbucks for coffee?" she emailed.

"Can do better. The bar at Pangea, a restaurant at Bay and Bloor. Five Friday."

Rose was glad she'd gone shopping in Rome, breaking away from Dora and Georgie and their relentless bar searches. Her outfit was so unlike her—snug grey leather pants, a cropped stylish grey and green wool jacket with large silver buttons, and high-heeled boots which inspired comments from her co-workers. She even had a blow dry at 4.15, which meant she canceled her four o'clock. It was the end of May but the evenings were still cool, with just a touch of the sweetness of spring in the air.

She was nervous and she hated it. This was the last time she would subject herself to what she mentally categorized as "hideous scrutiny." She'd worn her date outfit to work, changing into her working coverall at the clinic.

She parked her car in the city parking around the corner and strolled to Pangea. Even at that early hour the bar was crowded, and the tables at the adjoining restaurant were filling up. The man with the dark hair, cut short like fur, was better looking than his profile picture had indicated. He had an empty bar stool beside him, with a cocktail on the counter in front of it. It was a mahogany-colored cocktail, straight up, with two coral cherries nestled at the bottom.

She walked slowly toward him, conscious of her bottom moving under the fitted leather pants and treading with care on the unfamiliar high heels. His eyes licked her briefly and then he smiled, and patted the leather top of the stool next to him.

"I ordered you a Manhattan—you seemed like a Manhattan girl, but I was wrong. You're a Martini girl: a vodka Martini girl with olives."

He gave her a tight smile. His teeth were white and even, and when he stood up she saw that he was about six feet, with a chest and arms underneath his black leather bomber jacket that showed he either worked out or didn't need to. He reeked of casual understated cool. She felt overdressed in her Roman outfit, when he wore jeans that clung to his long legs and Adidas that she was sure were top of the line.

"She's a martini girl," he told the bartender—too loudly, she thought. "You can donate the Manhattan to the blonde at the end, or drink it yourself, and bring her a Grey Goose martini, straight up with olives. I'd order her a dirty one but she wouldn't appreciate it."

She felt her face flush and the couple at the bar next to them giggled.

"The Manhattan is fine, but you could have waited and let me order my own drink." Her voice was cool; she meant it to be.

His smile never wavered: he was obviously amused by her annoyance. "Just aiming to please, Rosie."

He was presumptuous and overbearing—and intriguing and interesting. She liked his fixed smile and his nonchalant take-charge manner. He ordered another Crown Royal for himself, and watched her with narrowed brown eyes and the ever-present smile as she sipped her Manhattan.

"Something sweet for a sweet girl on a soft spring night," he murmured, and she remembered that had been his application criteria: "sweetness."

"I've a table for us in the dining room at six-thirty, that is, if you'll have dinner with me."

"We'll go Dutch," she replied—too quickly. It was what the site suggested for a first date, if anything other than coffee or wine were involved.

"I'm taking you for dinner if you want to come—forget the Dutch. Another Manhattan?"

She shook her head and felt gauche and embarrassed—her lack of sophistication obvious. She was sure he could see that underneath the elegant jacket, which had cost her so many euros at the store next to the Spanish steps, beat the heart of a naïve and overanxious teenager, aged twenty-nine. She was angry with her dead mother, an anger that produced a surge of guilt, but still remained.

She finished her Manhattan and they walked together to the adjoining dining room.

"Manhattan or wine?"

She chose another Manhattan, and ordered pasta primavera, the cheapest dish on the menu.

"Not a steak girl?" He smiled, and she was conscious of not pleasing him again. She felt she owed him an explanation, although she did not know why.

"I've spent my life taking care of my Mom," she said, after starting her second Manhattan. "I haven't been dating. She died in March and since then I've been trying to do . . . normal. You were to be my last connection."

"I'll be the last one, period," he assured her. He leaned over and took her slight cool hand.

His hand was large and warm, and a little rough. She saw his engineering ring on his pinky figure. He ordered a carafe of white to go with her pasta and started asking her a series of questions. Some seemed personal. He volunteered little about himself.

"I'll drive you home," he said, as they walked into the sidewalk of a busy Friday night on Bay Street.

"My car's around the corner in the City parking: you can walk me there if you don't mind. I shouldn't have had the white with the pasta, but I think I'm all right. I'm not a drinker—my sister Del always said I was the cheapest drunk in town." He didn't smile.

"Lawrence Park's a class neighborhood—but a bit of a schlep."

"We've sold the house," she said—too quickly. "I'll be moving."

She asked herself how he knew where she lived. It was a rule of the site that the addresses of its members were not to be released.

"We?"

"Me and my sister Del. Mom left it to both of us."

"You should have got it all, after all those years."

"I insisted on including my sister," she said, annoyed. He was so presumptuous.

"Such a sweet girl," he murmured. So she forgave him.

He lit a cigarette. It surprised her—so few were still smoking. And how did he know so much?

"Don't worry, I'm a considerate smoker," he said.

He walked her to the car, his hand firm under her elbow. He kissed her cheek, a brush of a kiss, opened her car door and settled her in the front seat. She backed out painfully and drove slowly from the parking garage.

She could have sworn a car followed her home, but when she turned at the driveway it sped past. She was relieved. She was being overanxious as usual.

Later she lay in bed after taking two of her anti-anxiety pills—ignoring the alcohol warning—and thought about the evening. He had spoken so briefly about himself: the electrical engineering degree from Waterloo followed by a master's from MIT, and his year-long marriage followed by "a civilized divorce." There were no children. And he had his own electrical engineering company with eight employees. None of this was new. It was all part of his True Connections profile. She did not know why it made her uneasy, perhaps his lack of spontaneity, as if he were reciting it from an online prompter.

"I can afford to buy you dinner, even steak," he'd smiled.

She had looked at his flawless white teeth with interest. "I'm sorry for being so personal but as a dental hygienist I'm always aware of teeth, and yours are amazing."

"Glad you approve. As I'm sure you tell your patients, the secret is flossing, and it helps that my mother fed me greens, one of her very few good qualities."

She didn't ask further as he was frowning at the memory.

Besides, he was busy asking her questions about herself, and what had started as interest became intrusive. She felt she was being interrogated but no charges had been laid. Finally she threw up her hands. "Enough please. I'm not that interesting, really I'm not."

"You are to me," he answered.

So she forgave him again. It crossed her mind at the time that this forgiveness would happen often, but then she dismissed the thought. "Oversensitive and overanxious," Del had said after one of their rare quarrels. She must fight it.

Chapter 14

He phoned at eleven the next day. She was still asleep. The stew of her double-dose of anxiety pills, plus two Manhattans and a glass of Chardonnay had knocked her out.

Her excitement—and anxiety—at hearing his voice made her catch her breath.

"No, it's fine—I should be up by now. It's the Manhattans and wine. I should have let you drive me home."

"Sorry," he said, his voice indicating he really wasn't. "I thought we'd walk through High Park, look at the cherry blossoms, and go to a little Thai restaurant where you'll only have one glass of white, but lots of cream of coconut soup and chicken on a stick with a peanut sauce dip."

She had promised Del she'd babysit Gwennie. Del's law office, Pascal and White, was opening a new branch in Mississauga, and there was to be a large cocktail party to celebrate. Even Fred had been talked into going, together with many Toronto lawyers.

"Good PR for me," Del had said, "just in case I decide to change offices someday—never hurts to have connections." Del was, Rose noticed, very ambitious, even having a crew of connections on the social media site LinkedIn.

"I'm so sorry," she said, her voice heavy with sincerity. "I'd really love to see you and you've planned a perfect day, just perfect, but I promised Del I'd babysit Gwennie and she asked me a week ago. Her law office's having a big celebration—even Fred's going. She'll never get anyone this late and Gwennie was looking forward to seeing me. I was ordering in pizza as a treat: Del doesn't approve of fast foods."

There was a pause, and then he said, "Well, I wouldn't want you to let Del and Gwennie down. I guess I'll have to see my other girlfriend."

The edge in his voice choked her, but instead of saying, "Why don't you?" she repeated lamely, "I'm sorry, I really am."

There was a moment of silence and then he said, "The cherry blossoms will still be there tomorrow and the Thai restaurant's open all weekend. I'll pick you up at two. Best to Gwennie."

He had not asked her if she wanted to go, just took her for granted. And how did he know her address? She thought of the car that followed her home. He was too domineering, too intrusive, too controlling. She should end it now—or at least on Sunday.

***

"I've met someone," she said, as she sat on the edge of Del's bed, brushing Gwennie's thick blonde hair in preparation of making a braided coil for the top of her head, knowing Del would brand it "way too sophisticated."

"Great," said Del, removing her hot rollers, and brushing her hair into a golden apricot helmet around her head.

"Those are great streaks," Rose said, not wanting to continue. She knew Del wouldn't like the controlling Rick.

Del ignored her comment. She knew her streak job was amazing; it had cost her four hours and a fortune. "So what's he like?"

"He's good looking with great teeth, an electrical engineer. He went to MIT and has his own business. That's the good part."

"And the bad?"

"He's pretty overbearing. He might fit into one of your chauvinist pig files."

"Good thing I'm not the one dating him."

"It would be nice if you liked him though."

"I'm sure he's great, when you gonna bring him around?"

"When I feel more confident about him: it's only been one date. He wanted to see me again today, but I wanted to see Gwennie and I'd promised you—"

"Why in hell do that? asked Del, struggling to pull down her new black dress over hips that showed her love of wine and desserts. "She could have stayed at Lilly's: her kid Bunny's her best friend. You make me feel like shit. Don't do that again. Time you enjoyed life, not spend it catering to family members."

Rose smiled, pleased that Del cared enough to be annoyed.

"I think you're more important than any date," she whispered to Gwennie, lifting up her blonde curtain of hair, as yet unbraided, and depositing her words into a pink ear, one of two that stuck out enough to have Gwennie wail to her mother that she wanted them "pinned back."

"No, she's not," shrilled Del, who missed nothing. "Nothing's more important than you getting on with your life." As she spoke, she slapped on golden beige foundation that made her look as if she'd spent her winters on a sandy beach, rather than the air-conditioned confines of Pascal and White, where she'd gone from receptionist to legal secretary, to legal clerk, and then head legal clerk, and had been told by Pascal, the senior partner, that her services were "indispensable."

They left within twenty minutes, Del perfumed and sprayed into cocktail party glamour. Fred had a face as red as the tie Del had purchased for him for the occasion, and looked as if he'd be much happier heading to the nearest bar for a beer with his buddies.

"Say you're in computers," Del hissed, as they walked out the door, "not that you fix them."

Rose got Gwennie ready for bed after supervising a bubble bath and painting Gwennie's toenails with the newly purchased bright pink polish.

"Sometimes," sighed Gwennie, as Rose finished a chapter from the second book of the Harry Potter series, although they both knew Gwennie could read it herself, "I wish you were my mother."

"You mustn't say that, Pussycat, you've a great mom," said Rose severely, although inwardly pleased.

"Yes, but she's not a *fun* mom. Sometimes I call her 'Bossy Boots' the way she orders Daddy and me around. She doesn't mean to be mean—it's just her."

Rose went silent. Gwennie was right; she'd nailed Del with her nagging ways. But it wasn't something she should agree with.

"She's got a big heart and loves you a whole bag full. If I were your mom nothing would get done—not even homework—we'd just giggle, put on make-up, and watch silly shows on TV."

"Yeah," agreed Gwennie, as Rose turned off the light and got up from the side of the bed, "It would be awesome."

Rose curled up on the sofa, still wiped by the Manhattans, wine and pills, turned the TV on, watched an old movie with Grace Kelly and Jimmy Stewart, and dozed. Del and Fred came trooping in after eleven, Del glowing with wine and forced sociability, while Fred's face was even more flushed than before they left. He sat down heavily on the sofa and swore, but not loudly enough for Del to hear him. It was obvious he'd taken advantage of the open bar.

"To hear your sister introduce me you'd think I was CEO of a publicly traded computer company, instead of being a computer repairman. Jeez, if she's that ashamed of me you'd think she'd let me stay home. No way did I want to mix with a bunch of tight-assed lawyers and hear them talk shop all night."

Del bent over and kissed a full burning cheek. "Darling, you were the most handsome man there, and lawyers, except for a few members of the criminal bar, are the most boring people alive. You shouldn't be cross because I build you up a little. After all, you could be CEO of your own computer company if you really wanted it."

Fred sighed, the burden of being a computer repairman heavy on his broad shoulders.

"I feel affectionate, Pie. It must be the vino and you looking so handsome in your dark suit and red tie."

Fred looked at Rose and pushed himself up, giving her a blurred eye roll.

"And if I don't feel affectionate?"

"Good things always happen eventually," Del replied, giving Rose a broad wink.

"Stop discussing our sex life in front of your sister."

But by that time Rose was at the door.

Chapter 15

The next morning Rick phoned at eleven. It was obviously the hour he expected all civilized people to be up and she was—all traces of alcohol gone, and with only enough Ativan to take the edge off. She had read an article about some refugee children detained at the American border, separated from their parents, and it bothered her. She would, she thought, adopt some of them if she could. She would comfort them, feed them tacos, give them bubble baths like she'd given Gwennie, and brush their shiny black hair before snuggling with them at night. Had her mother been alive she would have removed the section, knowing it would disturb her. She felt choked and missed her mother. And then he phoned.

"The cherry blossoms are still waiting for you at High Park, and Thai Delight is open from eleven to eleven on Sundays. We can see a movie at Cineplex, or you can have your usual six Manhattans at the Four Seasons." He laughed when he said it, knowing what two drinks and some wine had done to her on Friday night.

"I'll take the movie," she said, glad that she'd at least seen movies with Del and Fred and her mother throughout the years.

"I'll pick you up at two."

She started to give him her address, but he cut her off with, "I know where you live."

She felt uneasy and thought of the car that had followed her home, and then sped away.

"How do you know?" She thought of Del's warnings.

"I followed you home Friday night. I saw you weren't a drinker and I wanted to make sure you were all right."

His voice was rich, sincere and assured. She was being ridiculous. He was being considerate—she'd been listening to Del too much.

The sky was blue that morning, with puffs of clouds blown across it by the soft breeze; it was, after all, cherry blossom time. She wore a white dress with a full skirt, high round neck and a pattern of pink flowers, topped off by white sandals and a pink cardigan. It seemed so unsophisticated for twenty-nine, she thought, but she thought he would like that look of innocence. He still wore jeans, but his leather jacket was replaced by a tan blazer. He knocked lightly at the door at two minutes to two. He was always on time, he said. She joked in response that she never was. "Well, lateness is an insult to the person you keep waiting," he said. He was wrong; it was her shyness and insecurity that always made her late, but she did not say so.

"Don't *you* have any failings?" she asked, not rudely but out of curiosity.

He smiled at her. "Many—all much more serious than being late."

She wondered what they were, but she didn't ask—to do so would be worse than being late.

Later, as they sat in Thai Delight dipping skewers of chicken into peanut sauce and sipping their glasses of house white, he leaned back and looked at her without his usual smile.

"Are you a virgin?"

She should tell him that asking such a question on a second date was an intimacy violation, and much ruder than being chronically late. But after taking a sip of wine, she looked at him and said, "No."

"How many?"

"One. It only happened once."

There had been two, but she decided he did not deserve that information.

"You didn't like it? Was that why it was a one-night stand?"

She felt flushed with irritation. He was such a snoop and she had been stupid enough to go along with it.

She got up and headed for the bathroom, after saying, "Perhaps you think it's all right to discuss my sex life on a second date but I don't. And you should never lecture anyone on rudeness, though you seem to be an authority."

She stayed in the bathroom for five minutes, touching up her make-up and washing her hands. She was glad she'd shown her annoyance. He was insensitive and lacked class, and she wanted to leave. But she did not want him to drive her home. She would call a cab and leave thirty dollars with the waiter—her contribution towards the lunch.

But he had read her mind and was standing by the bathroom door when she came out.

"Look, I was way out of line. I'm not used to girls like you. You were sitting there in your little flowered dress looking so prim, pink and virginal that I couldn't resist asking. I shouldn't have. The women I'm used to dating would do a *When Harry Met Sally* orgasm scene in the middle of a restaurant—even better than Meg Ryan. You're a reserved girl and I should have appreciated that. Forgive me?"

She nodded and followed him back to the booth, not appreciating his admission that he associated with the Georgies of this world—the kind that hopped on the backs of Vespas in Rome and picked up STDs like spare change.

"A banana split with two spoons," he ordered. "It's the only restaurant in Toronto that still serves them. I used to love them when I was a kid: I used to buy them from money I robbed when delivering papers."

She smiled, not believing him.

They did not speak for a while, and then she said, "I guess my kind of girl would bore you eventually."

He took a cherry tucked into the whipped cream that covered the bananas and, leaning over, popped it into her mouth. "God no, it's refreshing. Think of all the things I can teach you."

She didn't answer and didn't smile, although he smiled at her and even winked before she turned away.

They walked to the Manulife Building hand in hand as if nothing had happened. She had offered to pay for half of the lunch, but he had merely looked at her, one eyebrow lifted. It was still light and Indigo on the first floor appeared busy.

"Are you a reader?" he asked. "I see you as a reader."

"Yes, I love books. I wanted to teach English, but the money was better being a hygienist. I don't really like what I do—it's messy and invasive. But I'm good at it. Everyone seems to like my soft hands."

"A good sign," he said smiling.

She did not reply, aware he was giving her soft hands a sexual connotation, so he became serious. "I'm not into *The Passion of the Christ*," he said, "but anything else you pick is fine. But I don't recommend *Dawn of the Dead*, you're not the type to be into zombies." They both laughed.

"As long as nothing happens to kids or animals—my mother used to throw out pages of the newspaper so I couldn't read about things like that. I saw our doctor way back and he gave me some anti-anxiety pills and I'm hooked. Sorry to be such a wuss. I really wish I wasn't like this—it complicates life."

"But life is often cruel and tough: you just can't hide from it."

"I can try."

"I'll try to protect you," he said, so earnestly that she started to like him again. "If there's some shooting and killing in a movie—will that bother you?"

"Not really," she said, and they both laughed at how silly that sounded. They settled on *Troy*, despite all the killing and violence, because she liked Brad Pitt and he liked Peter O'Toole.

The theatre was air-conditioned—not necessary for May in Ontario—and she gave an involuntary shiver after five minutes. Without asking he removed his jacket and wrapped it around her.

"You don't have to, but thanks," she said, and forgave him for everything. And decided she really liked him.

"I'm always hot," he said.

***

Later, he drove her home and walked her to the door. In two weeks the home would be sold, and she would be moving to her new apartment on Heath Street. He bent down and kissed her firmly on the lips. His breath smelled of peppermint that wiped out the residue of wine and cigarettes. She knew he had planned the kiss, but it didn't matter. She kissed him back.

"You nervous? Want me to check the house?"

"No crime in Lawrence Park, and it's just kids and animals that bother me. I'm braver than you think."

Later she went out and sat on the back steps. She breathed in the sad, sweet, smell of lilacs that were finally sprouting and looked at the stars. And for a fleeting moment was sorry she hadn't asked him in.

Chapter 16

They were sitting on her new sofa, and Del had opened a bottle of champagne to celebrate the move. "I've met someone," Rose said, "the one I told you about. It's been three weeks. We have dinners out and go to movies and on walks. I like him."

Del had helped her move, hiring the movers, supervising the placing of furniture, helping with her choices, even giving her a huge pile of sheets and towels as a moving gift. She had considered asking Rick to help but knew Del would be hurt.

"Sex?" asked Del.

"Not yet. I'm nervous: I haven't been around much. He's my last connection." She gave Del Rick's profile information, including his master's from MIT.

"Why haven't you brought him around—think he won't bear a once-over?"

Rose felt annoyed in spite of Del's help.

"That's not it. I wanted to feel more secure about how I felt."

"Have him over for dins Sunday night; we'll size him up and see if Gwennie approves."

"I don't need a nine-year-old's approval," she said, which was not quite true. She wanted Gwennie to like him.

***

It was Friday night and they were in a trattoria on Dundas because she said she wanted to walk and he said he wanted pasta. The June nights were becoming warmer, and they both wore jeans and running shoes. They ordered lasagna, because the menu said it was the house special, and it would go with the carafe of Chianti he'd ordered. She was drinking more and gaining weight, which was why she suggested the walk.

"What do you do when we don't meet up?

"I hook up with other women, big sexy women who don't want ties: I get them through the Big Sexy Women Dating Site."

The look on her face stopped him and he laughed, obviously pleased that the thought of it upset her.

"What do I do, really, when you're too exhausted from scraping off plaque to see me? I work at the office, and once in a while I get together with some guys and play poker. I even make the odd coin there. I'm very good and I cheat."

"You gamble?" her voice had a tinge of disapproval.

"A little. It's at a guy's apartment, not the Casino Royale. I thought you'd like that better than my meeting big, sexy women."

She didn't answer, merely took a sip of wine and pushed her fork into the thick slab of pasta, bursting with layers of meat and tomato sauce.

"My sister Del wants to meet you. She's asked us to dinner Sunday night—if you're not too busy chasing big sexy women or losing money at poker."

He ignored her comment, but smiled into his lasagna.

"Gwennie's mom? The legal clerk who helped you move instead of me, and who thinks her sister shouldn't polish a nine-year-old's toes? And whose husband Fred fixes computers?"

"The same."

"That would be great: a first step in being accepted by the family. By the way, what did you do with the house money?"

She drew in her breath sharply. He was so aware of things, more aware than she liked.

"It's in Pascal and White's trust account, in a thirty-day term deposit in both our names. Why? Do you need a loan?" She was showing an edge, which was so unlike her. He was, after all, a businessman and engineer, who would be interested in such things. But she felt as she had after the virgin question, somewhat violated and uneasy.

He was not offended but merely smiled at her.

"I'll let you know. Business has been slow lately and I may need a stash for my poker."

She sat, arms crossed, face expressionless, staring at him.

"Rosie, for God's sake, I'm kidding around. Don't you think you've got more to offer than money from a house sale? You disappoint me, sweetheart. I didn't realize you had such a low opinion of me—and of yourself."

She felt ashamed, and more so when he reached out, took her hand and gently squeezed it.

"I'm sorry. I'm a private person. That was nasty. Forgive me."

After they'd finished, she said, "I'm paying. You never let me pay."

He shrugged.

They walked down the sidewalk on Dundas towards the car, but instead of holding hands he placed his arm around her waist, and she felt his hot strong fingers rub against her T-shirt.

"I've been," he said, "very patient. It's not because I didn't want you, but because I knew it would mean more to you if we waited. But now I think we should make love. I'll stay overnight and make you Saturday morning breakfast. We've waited long enough."

She was aware of her heart thudding and an unpleasant dampness under her arms, in spite of her meticulous deodorant applications. She would have a drink before it happened. It would relax her.

"I hope I don't disappoint you."

"What kind of crap is that? You'll be as good as I am. This is not the Sex Olympics."

This made her feel better, and when they went into the apartment he made her a Manhattan out of the rye and vermouth Del had purchased for her "visitors" and poured a rye for himself.

"I'll take a shower," he said.

She was still sitting on the side of the bed when he came out, rubbing his hair, his arms well-muscled and his chest tanned and surprisingly hairless. He had a towel around his waist.

"Didn't want to scare you."

"You've been in the sun and you work out," she said, for lack of better words.

"Aruba—the week before I met you. And I swim: I'm one helluva swimmer."

As queen of the slow breaststroke, she smiled her appreciation.

"You need some help in removing your clothes?"

"I need to use the bathroom."

"I used your toothbrush. Hope you don't mind, bein' a hygienist and all."

She didn't know why she didn't take her clothes off. It was ridiculous and stupid, like a teen-aged virgin. But not even a teenager, certainly not a modern one, would be so clumsy and nervous. She brushed her teeth with a new toothbrush and waited.

"Are you okay?" He was standing just outside the bathroom door when she came out, still dressed. "Late as usual," he added in a teasing soft voice. "Looks like I'm going to have to help you." He undressed her as he would a child, saying "arms up," as he pulled off her T-shirt, asking her to lift up her legs as he removed her jeans, and undoing her bra with what seemed to be a practiced hand. It was, she thought, as if he'd spent his life undressing women, yet the women she suspected he'd been with surely didn't need his help.

When she stood before him, he smiled and said, "Why would you want to keep this hidden? You're beautiful, gorgeous, right from that black triangle to those fabulous breasts; I wouldn't insult them by calling them 'boobs.'" He started to kiss her all over, light butterfly kisses, and then licked her nipples. She felt an unfamiliar twinge through her vagina, and when he moved his fingers between her legs, rubbing them against her, she felt a choking sensation, so unlike the brief moments of nervous masturbation that she'd indulged in to help her relax before the Ativan kicked in.

They walked to the bed together and she was no longer afraid but alive to his every touch. She felt a relaxation of her essence, far beyond what she had read in her novels. He was no Darcy, but a magician with his hands, and she had never thought she could feel such longing and urgency.

Then he was lying beside her, rubbing her all over with those large warm hands and cupping her bum. "Nice you've got a good ass," he said, "I was into asses long before they became publicly loved. But tonight I won't even go down on you—it'll be straight sex, no kinky stuff. I don't want to scare you the first time."

She put her arms around his neck and pushed her nose in the hot hollow directly above his collarbone and whispered, "It's all right, you can do anything you want," then she added, "Do you have protection?" He laughed and said, "Don't worry, I'll protect you," and when he came she felt the jelly of his sperm on her belly and she had never felt so alive.

"You're a great lover," she said softly.

He was obviously pleased. He took one breast in his hand, massaged it gently, and whispered back, "I know." And then he said, as if it was a surprising afterthought, "And you're very responsive."

The next morning he squeezed her fresh orange juice, and made her pancakes and bacon and eggs for brunch. He cooked like an expert and she watched him from the kitchen table, sipping coffee, her eyes narrowed in thought.

"Like a professional chef," she marveled, "an expert in so many things—like cooking and making love. I should send True Connections a bonus."

He smiled. "I worked in a kitchen briefly: it paid for some of my university fees—a lousy job. The kitchens of most restaurants are hell-holes, but I picked up a few things."

She nodded. She knew his background lacked money, but he said little about it only to make an occasional nasty remark about his mother.

"Your mother didn't teach you?"

"My mother only taught me about women: she used to beat the hell out of me because she hated my dad."

Rose gave an involuntary shiver, "That's awful. Why didn't your father protect you?"

"He couldn't control her: he ended up hanging himself from the belt she used to whale me with. How's that for symbolism for your reading?"

"Why didn't you ever tell me this? That is so awful, so shocking. What's it done to you?"

"Made me a certain way about women—but she stopped when I was nine and started giving her money."

"Did you ever get therapy?"

"Why would I do that when I know what caused it all?"

She got up from the table, placed her arms around him and pressed against him. "I'll try to make it up to you," she whispered.

In the afternoon they shopped: two bottles of expensive imported French wine for Del, and a manicure set for Gwennie, although Del had objected to her last pedicure.

"Gwennie'll love it," he said with confidence. "The shade is Pink Princess, not Orgasm Red. Your sister won't like me—you know that, don't you? I'm nothing like Fred, the computer repairman."

She thought his prediction odd, knowing he could be charming when he wished, but she did not ask for a further explanation, saying only, "Sure she will."

He changed the topic. "Better get some pills. I hate those damn condoms: I want to feel you when I go inside." He had dismissed the importance of Del's acceptance.

"She's my only relative, except for a handful of Irish aunts in Belfast who I've never met, so it'd be nice if she liked you." He gave an inconsequential, "whatever," so she could see he was indifferent—or was pretending to be.

CHAPTER 17

They were underdressed for Del's Sunday dinner: much too casual, when the hostess was wearing a long, silk gown, and there were candles burning on a table that had a white linen tablecloth and Del's best china. Rose felt annoyed rather than grateful. Del was making too big a deal over a Sunday night meal. It was embarrassing, as if Rick was her last resort and she had just hobbled out of *The Glass Menagerie*.

Rick just handed Del the two bottles of wine, thanked her for having him, and shook hands firmly with Fred, who had refused to dress up for "some dude Rosie picked up on a dating site." He then focused on Gwennie, who fell in love with her manicure set and then Rick, in that order.

"Can I call you Uncle Rick?" she asked, smiling as Rick gave her braids a gentle tug and said, "Great hair."

"No, you can't," blustered Del.

"Rick would be fine," he answered, "as long as it's not Roderick. That would be like me calling you Gwyneth instead of Gwennie."

Gwennie smiled. She liked him regardless of labelling.

Del's roast chicken, vegetables and Caesar salad were good, as was the tiramisu, obviously picked up at Bruno's Bakery. At nine, Gwennie turned to Rick and said, "You can come up and read to me if you like."

"That won't be necessary, Gwennie," said Del. "Rick's a guest. It's rude to make demands on guests—besides you're getting too old to be read to at night."

"And too young to be escorted to your bedroom by a male guest," Rick said.

Del frowned and Fred lost the beginning of a smile quickly. It was obvious they thought the remark to be in bad taste.

The rest of the night consisted of a discussion of a new court case that did not permit the admissibility of evidence of previous related crimes and a proposed new act that was tougher on juvenile crime.

Del was against the court ruling, but was in favor of the new act, while Rick disagreed with her on both, even saying, "I wouldn't want you for my judge."

Knowing Rick was not that interested in legal proceedings, Rose could only think he was deliberately baiting Del.

They left shortly after, Del saying ominously to Rose, "I'll phone you."

"I went over like a lead balloon," Rick said as they walked down the path toward the Chrysler. "I don't think there'll be any more invites from sister Del—although we could have Gwennie over anytime—she's a really cute kid."

"What went wrong? She went to so much trouble making that dinner, and then her coldness was so strange.

Your crack about escorting Gwennie to her bedroom was a bit off, but not enough to bring about that kind of hostility. And why your sudden interest in the law?"

Rick sighed, and came up with what she knew was his most condemnatory size-up,

"Your sister reminds me of my mother."

Later they made love, and she was extra affectionate to make up for what she referred to as "Del's off-putting behavior," and his former child abuse. Much later, she said, "Don't think it matters to me what Del thinks of you. I care about you and that's all that matters."

His voice came from the darkness. "You always said Del was jealous of you and your mom. Perhaps she's still jealous of you, and was comparing me to Fred. I liked the guy but he fixes computers and Hollywood won't recruit him. Could be she didn't think baby-sister would come up with much while cruising dating sites."

She put her arms around him, loving the heat from his body that contrasted with the June breeze that came in from the half-open window of the bedroom.

"Are you hinting that she's jealous of my handsome successful boyfriend?"

He said a muffled, "Could be," and then his breathing became even.

But she couldn't sleep and she let a second Ativan dissolve under her tongue.

Del phoned her during her noon break. But before she could say anything, Rose began, "I know you don't like him, you made that obvious—but remember, I do. And there's no line outside the door waiting for me."

There was a moment's silence, then Del's voice, icy and firm. "Rosie, I know you've been very sheltered, but that guy's what our criminal lawyer Gerry White calls a 'rounder.' He's no professional engineer—or MIT graduate. He's slick and good-looking, but you'd better take care. He's not for you."

Rose hung up. Del's voice had rung with conviction and it worried her. She could not attribute her concern to jealousy as Rick had suggested. Del wanted her happy, she knew that. But her warning was too late in coming. She cared about Rick, loved the sex, and his protective ways made her feel secure. She could not face life without him. And she didn't care if he had attended MIT, but was concerned that he felt he had to lie about his background. It meant that there may be other lies . . .

He phoned at five, just after she'd finished her last patient.

"Swiss Chalet on Bloor at five-thirty?"

She parked behind the Chalet, thinking she'd turn in her car for one easier to park, and walked slowly towards the entrance on Bloor. She'd ask him about MIT, and if Del was wrong she could dismiss her other concerns. Then she recalled she'd never seen his office or knew the name of his business. He was sitting in the last booth and her heart surged at the sight of him. Then she remembered that she'd read in one of her very occasional thrillers that this was how gang members sat, facing the door, their backs to the wall. She hated herself for her thoughts.

He stood up and kissed her before she sat down.

"I'm up for a vodka martini," she said. "It's been a rough day: five patients, four who've never flossed in their lives."

"Vodka martini, two olives, and a straight shot of Canadian Club—make it a double." He sat looking at her, his dark eyes watchful, unsmiling.

"Did your sister Del phone?"

So much easier to lie and say no, and not confront it.

"Yes, and I hung up."

"Why?"

"She thinks you're some sort of con-man: you're like Gerry White's clients—he's the criminal lawyer. She says you never went to MIT."

He smiled. "She's right, I never did. I just thought it would add some class to my True Connections profile. I was going to tell you but you

8ontaosyの

really seemed to get off on it, so I didn't. Think about it; where's a kid from Regent Park going to get the bucks to go to MIT?"

"You should have told me. It wouldn't have mattered—really it wouldn't. What hurts is that you lied to me. These things aren't important to me."

"Sure they are—you're just the kind of girl they'd be important to—a little snob from Lawrence Park. I bet you even went to private school, even though Daddy just sold pills and Mommy stayed home and baked cookies. I wasn't the one who told Del about MIT—you did, to impress her, because the poor jerk she married only fixes computers."

She was shocked at the quick way he'd turned on her. "I'm no snob. I went to public school just like you did—although perhaps a better one. You're just being an ass because you were caught in a lie and now you're attacking me." She gulped one-half of her drink and stood up.

He started to speak and then stopped. She threw five dollars on the table and marched out.

The booths in the Swiss Chalet were filling up. When she went into the June night the air was soft but it was not yet twilight. She did not want to go back to her apartment, but the only other choice was Del's. And she was angry with Del for being right, and angrier with Rick for trying to impress the sweet girl he was trying to meet online by giving a phony degree.

She got in her car and turned on her Sinatra tape. Sinatra was singing "Summer Wind," which perversely increased her annoyance. He had lost her to the summer wind, just as she would lose him with all his lies and hang-ups.

The apartment did not have indoor parking, so she parked the car clumsily in the resident's section. Then she saw him. He was leaning against his Mustang, smoking. She felt torn between relief at seeing him, and annoyance that lingered from their fight.

"I brought us takeout. I took a chance and got you a white quarter-chicken: you're a white quarter-chicken kind of girl."

It reminded her of his opening first-date comment about her being a vodka martini kind of girl, and it increased her annoyance. He was so lacking in originality. She did not reply, only turned and walked slowly towards the entrance. She did not tell him to leave, and he obviously saw this as an invitation to stay. He threw down his cigarette before entering. He was, as he had often told her, a considerate smoker.

When they entered the apartment he walked to the kitchen as if he lived there, removed the chicken from the white paper bag, and took some cutlery from the kitchen drawer, throwing the plastic forks and knives into the garbage.

"I don't know if I can eat."

"Sure you can eat. You've spent the day looking at your patient's tonsils. I'll eat what you leave, but you gotta eat. It'll take the edge off. Your bitch sister caused all this."

He was the cause of it, with his phony credentials, but it was pointless to remind him. Besides she felt drained.

There was no make-up sex: the lovemaking had changed. He was rough and flipped her around like a fish. At one point she yelped, and he said, "Sorry, didn't mean to hurt you." But she knew he did.

Looking back, there were three things she remembered his saying: "I think you should stop seeing Del," "I'm out of condoms," and "Did you get your pills?"

Del kept phoning, but Rose didn't pick up. And she didn't reply to the email that said Del wanted to talk about "something important."

CHAPTER 18

Rick had started to move in. At first it was an extra jacket, and then some underwear and socks in her empty bureau drawers, and then more jackets, pants and one dark suit that altogether took up a third of the closet.

"Might as well," he said. "I'm here most nights anyway."

After a few weeks, he said, "I don't want to get between you and your sister, but don't you think it's time you got your half of the house money?"

She decided he was right. Perhaps Del was trying to protect her, which was insulting. She phoned Pascal and White's accounting department and asked for her half of the trust money from the house sale, together with the reporting letter. She would pick them up the next day.

"It's good you phoned," said Louise Martin, the firm's bookkeeper. "We were going to put it in a thirty-day term again, but we'll prepare your check. Your sister will need her half for her own house purchase anyway. It'll be at the desk tomorrow afternoon."

Rose changed her four o'clock and walked to Pascal and White's. When she arrived the receptionist used the phone and Del came out of the reception door. She walked over and hugged her. Rose felt her eyes burn. She had missed her, Gwennie and even Fred.

"We've missed you so much, Rosie. Gwennie's always asking when you're coming: the fickle little toad's already forgotten her crush on Rick."

When Rose spoke, her words seemed hollow and fabricated. "You've made it very hard for me. I'm living with Rick and I'd have to visit without him. It would seem so disloyal, after what you said."

"And you told him."

"The way you were I didn't have to—it was obvious."

"Sorry, sweetheart—I had such an aversion to the guy, but I should have controlled it. It's just that you're my little sister and you've been so isolated, so all my mother hen instincts came out. I saw him as such a sleaze, just not up to your standards."

"I have to go," Rose said and turned away abruptly, with Del's last words ringing in her ears: "Don't let him get his paws on that money: it's your lifetime security."

***

The July heat embraced her like a blanket and she wanted to pick up an iced latte at Starbucks, but instead she walked briskly to the Royal Bank on Front. While waiting at deposits, she opened the envelope. The cheque attached to the reporting letter was over a million. The reporting letter detailed the sale of the Dawlish property and showed no fee, only out of pockets. It was a kind gesture, a nod of appreciation to Del. Her personal bank account held only $983 and she thought of the cruise, the clothes purchased in Rome, the moving expenses, new furniture and monthly rent. Rick never contributed, although he was living there, having given up an apartment that she'd never visited. She would add some money to her personal account, open a special account for the sale money, and have what Rick always referred to as "walking around money." She was annoyed with Del, but she would not ignore her warning.

"I'll take nine hundred in fifties and twenties," she told the teller. She'd take Rick out to dinner. They no longer ate out, but he picked up Thai or Chinese take-out or made her dinner, usually frites and steak, which she bought from a nearby specialty butcher. Later they'd walk down Yonge and sometimes pick up an ice cream at Baskin Robbins.

"You always get vanilla," he'd tease. "Such a bland choice."

"That's because I'm so bland," she'd reply. He'd merely smile.

Sometimes they'd shower together, and she'd feel his strong hands soaping her breasts and crotch, and she became even more aware of the new feelings of arousal that she'd started to have. She knew she couldn't live without him.

CHAPTER 19

It was a warm September, the skies were still summer blue and the leaves of the maples had not yet turned yellow. She remembered them lying in the gutters of her Lawrence Park neighborhood where, as a child, she had romped through them on her way home from the near-by elementary school. Having so much money in her account gave her a sense of satisfaction, a pleasing sense of security she'd never before experienced. And it gave her choices about changing a career that was becoming increasingly burdensome.

A few times before Rick left for his poker games on Tuesday and Thursday nights, he would ask her for "a little advance," as the line of credit for his business was "out of control." She'd never refuse, merely asking "How much?" One night in August he'd thrown $2,000 in bills on the bed where she sat reading at two a.m. waiting for him. "Here's for the advances plus interest," he'd said. And she'd replied, "Sure you don't need it?"

He replied, his voice testy, "I said it was a line of credit problem with the business: it'll straighten up soon."

They were walking together in late September. She remembered it as she'd worn only a sweater and jeans and the nights were becoming cold. She began to shiver so he'd taken off his jacket and placed it around her shoulders, and she'd felt his heat against her arms. Later he'd said, "Why don't we have a joint account like a normal couple? We can put a thousand a month each in and both draw. I feel like a jerk asking you for money every time there's an overdraft."

"Sure," she said, and opened a joint account at the Toronto Dominion on Bloor. She placed $1500 in it and gave him his own checkbook when it arrived. He seemed pleased and was extra affectionate that night.

But he never contributed to the account, and she kept using her personal account at the Royal Bank, the bank that also held the money from the house sale. In October, when she checked the joint account, there was only $300 left. This concerned her, but she did not mention it, as he had complained that the business was "going through a rough patch." She did not want to embarrass him.

She had started on the pill in early August, a month after he had complained about condoms. Dr. Dunstan was on vacation and his associate had prescribed them. Now, in late September, her breasts were swollen and tender and she was nauseated in the mornings.

"My boobs are huge and I could puke before breakfast," she complained.

"Your body's just getting used to the pills," said Rick, who saw himself as an amateur doctor and who showed his appreciation for her new boobs on a nightly basis.

"Perhaps he can give me a weaker one," she said.

Dr. Dunstan seemed glad to see her and said he was sorry for missing her August appointment. But he frowned at her symptoms.

"Never heard of birth control pills giving morning nausea," he growled. Then he did a urinalysis and an internal—and frowned again.

"You're about three months pregnant. Stop those birth control pills; it's too late for that."

She went weak with shock. "But I've been on the pills since August. You were away and Dr. Murdoch prescribed them. My partner used condoms—or withdrew."

"The withdrawal's a Vatican Roulette type of thing: a smart girl like you should know that."

But she hadn't known and believed him when he said he'd protect her. And now asked herself, "From what?"

Dr. Dunstan kept looking through his file. "How'd those anti-anxiety pills work? I guess you found something to replace them."

She gave him a weak smile. She did not tell him she took one, or more, every night.

"You'll have to come in and get monthly check-ups. Get some vitamins; folic acid's important. And don't drink. It's too bad your mom's not still here—she'd be delighted with another grandchild."

"I'm not married," she muttered.

"Oh well," smiled Dr. Dunstan, "many aren't these days: it doesn't seem to make much difference."

It was four o'clock, the fall sun was still shining, and little white puffs of clouds scudded across a blue sky where a convoy of Canada Geese was flying south. He would not be home this early: it was Tuesday night, his poker night. She wondered if he'd borrow from her. Then she remembered there was $300 left in the joint account to which he'd never contributed. She would transfer $500 from her personal account—or better, a thousand. But she felt a flicker of annoyance at the thought. He was, after all, an engineer, and if his business was failing, then perhaps he should consider working for someone else.

She wanted a drink, and then remembered she shouldn't drink. She worried that the baby had been harmed by the cocktails and the useless birth control pills. Or even her anti-anxiety pills which she couldn't give up. Then she wondered what Rick would say.

She went into Starbucks and ordered a double latte, making ridiculous mental rationalizations, like calcium for the baby instead of the caffeine rush she needed. She kept thinking of Rick. It had been five months but she knew so little about him. She knew he hated his mother, that she may be in some long-term care home "somewhere," and he never visited. And there was a first wife with whom he remained "the best of friends." And he always seemed broke in spite of his business and education. And he gambled—and occasionally won. He also appeared to like kids, if Gwennie was any indication. And he was a great swimmer.

She should know more. The only thing she really knew was that she cared for him and wanted him in her life. She went to the TD Bank and deposited a thousand into the joint account.

***

She decided she would put off telling him until Wednesday night. It was important how she told him and how he reacted. It was, after all, his fault. She thought of that night in June, the night of their fight at the Swiss Chalet, when he'd been so rough she'd yelped. She didn't believe he'd withdrawn that night. She felt sorry that this unknown little being, like a small fish swimming in her lower abdomen, was the product of a painful lovemaking session that had made her yelp.

She drove to Bruno's in North Toronto, an unnecessary trip, as there were delis much nearer, but going back to North Toronto gave her a sense of comfort—even nostalgia. She purchased several cartons of potato and egg salads, meatballs, and selected some chicken liver pâté for herself—fattening, but chicken livers were full of iron, she'd read it somewhere. Then she purchased two beef fillets for the next night. On her way back, she'd driven across Dawlish, passing her old home. The new owners were doing renovations, putting in a room over the new garage. Seeing her old home and the staunch maples, leaves now turning brown, made her think of her mother who'd be horrified by her predicament—and certainly by Rick.

"Sorry Mommy," she said.

Chapter 20

Rick ate the deli portions, presented on one of her mother's china plates. He shoveled everything down. So not a gourmet, she thought, brought up on fast foods so that everything she fed him was a banquet.

"See the doctor?"

She just said, "Yes."

He didn't ask for details, so she gave him none.

She did say, "I put a thousand in the joint today: it was getting low."

"Good of you," he replied, and she thought she detected sarcasm in his voice.

She did not want him to ask for poker money, knowing it embarrassed him and, although she tried to hide it, irritated her.

"There's some guys there tonight from stateside, one is loaded, and he can't play worth a damn. I should be able to give you back something of what you've advanced."

He did not meet her eyes when he said it, but looked into space, as if seeing a bouquet of dozens of bills and playing cards.

He looked scruffy and hadn't shaved or showered. She sometimes wondered if the only time he took showers was before they had sex.

"Good luck," she said at seven-thirty as he ambled out the door.

He turned, came back, gently kissed her on the mouth and said solemnly, "You're the greatest Rosie."

It was, she thought sourly, a compliment due to the thousand-dollar deposit and the gobbled deli food. Her good luck wishes were sincere: she wanted him in a good mood when she told him about the baby.

She was bone-tired but she couldn't sleep. She took her usual pill but her thoughts kept jumping around. She finally dozed off, but woke up when he crawled in beside her at two, leaving, she knew, his clothes in a tangle by his side of the bed.

"How'd you do?" she mumbled.

"A bunch of jerk-offs. The dude they said couldn't play worth a damn had horseshoes up his ass, and he wouldn't shut up so no one could think. He's a nut job from Buffalo, an' he went on an' on about U.S. politics, but no one told him to shut the fuck up. He was the guy with the bread and they were waiting for him to start losing. But it didn't happen. I've had it with that bunch of asshole losers."

He smelled: the raw stench of failure, the smell of tension and sweat. He never smelled. It showed his anger at what, she concluded, was a wasted night of loss. She had five patients the next day and wished she didn't. Her pleasure in the popularity of "Rosie's soft hands" had worn thin.

Before she slept again, she wondered what she'd do if he left when he found out—just up and left. Some men did that and she'd be a "single mom," a phrase she detested and associated with welfare. But she wouldn't be poor.

She'd phone Del, and after an initial bluster Del would tell her exactly what to do—right up to getting a nanny and to finding a two-bedroom apartment. She missed her and wished she didn't detest Rick, although at times she saw some merit in her assessment of him. But it hadn't stopped her from caring for him, although more and more often concerns crossed her mind.

He was still asleep when she left, one muscled furred arm clutching a pillow, the duvet kicked off, and just the sheet wrapped around him, with a hairy calf hanging free, as if to be sure it received enough air. She wrote him a note and left it on the kitchen table: *Steaks in fridge, potatoes under sink. I'll pick up pie at bakery. Please shower. Didn't want to wake you, you had a late night. XXX*

That day her patients were all Dr. Henderson's referrals, and the four o'clock appointment hadn't been seen by a dentist for years.

"Your right back molar has a large cavity," she cautioned. "Dr. Henderson may have a problem filling it. If there's an extraction you can always get an implant, or perhaps he can save it with a root canal."

"That'll cost a fortune," the patient complained in a muffled voice, "just pull the damn thing out."

"Dr. Henderson doesn't do extractions; you'll have to see someone else on staff."

"Any more good news?"

"You've got a lot of recession and serious gingivitis. He may want you to see a periodontist to cut away some of the diseased gum before starting. I notice some of your teeth are a little loose."

She could have sworn she heard him mumble, "A fuckin' money pit," but when she said "Excuse me?" he merely gave a muffled, "Never mind."

"His toothbrush has been his enemy for years and now we are," she whispered to Dr. Henderson, "He's your challenge for the day—or should I say year?"

Dr. Henderson smiled.

She left the clinic at five, picked up a pecan pie at the bakery and a carton of chocolate-chip ice cream at Baskin's. She hoped that would sweeten him up before she broke the news. October was coming, with its mottled ashen skies, harsh winds, and bare branches, and in Lawrence Park there'd be gutters full of paper-like maple leaves. And inside the cushioned pocket of her abdomen a small being was coming to life, hopefully not damaged by the wine and cocktails she had been drinking since its conception.

She sniffed the smoke-filled air as she entered: so unusual, as he always boasted of being a considerate smoker. He was sitting glumly at the kitchen table in front of an ashtray full of butts, and was wearing his jeans and a stained T-shirt. He hadn't showered, but had lavished some aftershave over his stubble in her honor. The steaks rested in a bowl, covered in spices and red wine. He could actually marinate, she thought, and the potatoes were peeled but not cut in strips for the frites as yet.

When he spoke his voice was grating and harsh, "Ever ask yourself what you're doing with me? I guess if you had less cash I'd be long gone."

"Is this because you lost at poker last night?"

"I wrote cheques for every cent you put in the joint and the three that was left. The account now has twelve dollars. Just ask yourself what you're doing with a loser like me. It must be like having some little dog you picked up out of the rain, and now you've paid so much money in vet bills that he's become an investment. Or is it that on occasion I'm a good lay, and you never had one? Perhaps it's that you're pushing thirty and think I'm as good as you'll get."

This was not the time to tell him about the baby. This was the time to say, "Yes, you're right. You do nothing but mooch money off me and if we stay together I'll be broke. And you're right again, I was feeling hopeless about ever having anyone. And I'd never had good sex before you. And I don't believe anything you've told me about yourself: nothing.

I'll be a single mom but at least I'll have a baby. But you've got to leave. You're a sick gambler and a lying sleaze. And my sister Del was right."

But she didn't say any of it.

She just said, "I'm pregnant—about sixteen weeks. The doctor told me yesterday. If you're not up to being a daddy you should leave as soon as you can. I'm not worried about being a single mom: the world is full of single moms. At least I'm lucky enough to have a job and enough money to support myself and the baby. This is a result of your withdrawal method, which was supposed to protect me."

He sat looking straight ahead. He lit a cigarette and as quickly put it out. He put his face in his hands and muttered "Jesus." But when he took his hands away, he was smiling.

"You're not the type to be a single mom: I guess we'll have to get married—if you'll have me."

***

When she thought of it later, it was a sad little wedding. His witness was Al, one of his gambling buddies, who showed a grey dead front tooth when he smiled. And he wore what she understood was his best jacket, which resembled a horse blanket. Rick wore his only dark suit, and she wore dove grey, with a pink corsage. Her witness was Alice Morgan, a fellow hygienist, who pronounced it all, "real romantic." The brief ceremony was performed by a jaded-looking Justice of the Peace with severe halitosis. Later they went to Anthony's, opposite the Old Courthouse, and everyone, except Rose, finished a bottle of Merlot, and they all ate bruschetta and pesto pasta—an awful wedding meal—paid for from their joint Visa.

He had purchased a ring that she suspected came from a pawn shop, which he assured her was "a real antique." It was too big. In retrospect, the only romantic moment was when, after the ceremony, he had whispered, "Congratulations Rosie McCready. I hope I can make you happy—at least some of the time—and be a good dad."

After Alice and Al went home they drove silently along the Lakeshore, parked the car, and stood looking at the lake. The waves were dark and restless, and above them the sky was low, brooding, and swollen with rain. She shivered and he took off his jacket and wrapped it around her.

***

He felt bad about the wedding. Rose deserved better—a girl like her. It needed a little music and some flowers, perhaps even a white dress, after all, it was her first marriage. It was a hell of a lot better for him than that torture he'd undergone with Patsy. But not nearly as good as the one with Steamy in Vegas, with the Elvis impersonator doing the deed, and a lot of bubbly and laughs, followed by a great meal at the Bacchanal Room with all the gamblers from their winning blackjack table at Bally's. He remembered Steamy showing yards of tits so that every man at the table had his eyes glued to her chest.

He picked up the ring from Marty for $500, after listening to a spiel about how it was breaking his heart to part with a $5,000 ring for a tenth of its value. It was too big, and he knew she suspected he hadn't bought it at Tiffany's, as she didn't even ask him where it came from. The meal was no great hell, nor were the witnesses. He hardly knew Al except for an occasional poker game, and he'd seen Rose looking at his dead tooth—so conscious of teeth, always taking a professional interest. It would be worth introducing her to Chester just so she could see *his* teeth. He had whispered about his being a good husband and dad just to make up for things. And when he'd said it, he'd meant it. It was the least he could do.

CHAPTER 21

It was November and she was showing. She had decided to work only until the end of January, thinking that she'd be too clumsy to work after seven months. Rick had become increasingly irritable and critical—even hostile. She had suggested he might spend more time at the office, instead of lounging around watching "the boob tube." This had caused such an outburst that she did not mention it again. He picked up the bottle of anxiety pills by the bed and took them, accusing her of being an addict and endangering "her." After a sleepless night, the next day she visited her old pharmacist near Lawrence Park and begged him for a refill, saying she had lost the original bottle. He shook his head but succumbed, and she hid the new bottle under the mattress.

"Why do you keep calling it 'her,'" she complained, as she had deliberately not inquired as to the sex of the baby.

"Little girls have it much better than little boys," he answered.

It was early December and it had been snowing all day, large lazy flakes drifting from a frozen white sky. She'd bought home Thai take-out as she didn't want to go out, or cook, or have him cook. The night before she'd seen him watching porn, slouched in front of the television, drinking beer and chain-smoking. The porn made her sick. A small woman with huge augmented breasts was being tossed around by three men like a rag doll, all taking turns, or sometimes making it a threesome.

She closed the bedroom door with a sharp click and he came in. "That bother you? You're in no shape for it: you shouldn't begrudge me gettin'off watchin' it—not like I'm the one doin' it."

She did not reply, but felt an unsettling revulsion. He had changed, but perhaps this was the real Rick, and all the rest had been as synthetic as his master's degree from MIT.

He had fried steak that Friday night, some two weeks later, purchasing it as usual with their joint Visa. "It'll be good for Katy," he said, "protein and iron."

"Katy?"

"Katherine, but we'll call her Katy. She can use the Katherine when she's a CEO and Katy in her teens."

"This must be after some old girlfriend, though I doubt she's a CEO. Do I have any say in this?"

"Not when it comes to naming my daughter," he answered. But smiled.

She looked at him, expressionless.

He continued, his voice taking a tone that always came before some unsettling comment she did not expect—or appreciate.

"You do realize that you've given no thought to the baby's future. You don't want to bring her up in some one-bedroom apartment in the middle of the city, do you?"

She had thought of it, but more often had thought of separating from him once the baby was born.

"We could get a two-bedroom in North Toronto, although I'd have to take a subway to the clinic . . ."

"What about a yard and a neighborhood—a class neighborhood—with good schools, where she could have play dates with executives' kids. We should buy a house."

The steak caught in her throat and she started to cough. When she spoke her face was burning. "And who's going to fund all this? You know real estate prices in this town are through the roof. This house, with a yard and a nursery for Katy in this affluent executive area, is going to be funded like everything else—by the money from Mom's estate. What's it feel like being such a leech? I don't believe there's a business, a degree, or anything else. You were just looking for 'a sweet girl,' but you should have said, 'a stupid girl with funds, so she can support me.'"

He did not lose his smile. It was uncanny, weird, the way he could smile while she berated him. She thought of John Gotti: the Teflon Don. Rick was as untouchable as John Gotti.

"You're hardly a prize," he said softly, smile still intact, "but I think your pregnancy's getting to you. It's hormones. Sure I'll pay towards a home. I'll clean out the business account."

There was no business account: she knew that now. The engineering expertise she had expected went no further than changing a lightbulb.

"You're very selfish," he chided. "You disappoint me. I thought you'd want the very best for our daughter. You're also very cheap. You must know that—having me beg for every cent when you're sitting with a million in the bank. I was going to suggest we each get insurance, so that Katy can fund her university should one of us go before that happens. You know about these things: your mother put you on hers—*you* told me that, and that you didn't want your sister to know. She'll be buying a house for Gwennie and the computer guy—guaranteed."

She sat frozen. He saw nothing wrong with her supporting him, and now that she was pregnant, he could claim expenses on behalf of the baby. He saw her as cheap, as he had to ask for money, money that she'd never refused. He clearly thought she should be showering it all over him like leaves in a windstorm. She remembered a book she'd read on abnormal psychology, before she'd switched to college and dental hygiene, and the word *sociopath* flicked across her thoughts. No empathy: a moral idiot, while she on the other hand was just an ordinary one.

They looked for homes in North Toronto, nowhere as lofty as Lawrence Park, but on the west side of Yonge. They finally found an unimposing bungalow. It needed work, but had a small garden, three bedrooms, two bathrooms, and an old-fashioned kitchen. And the street was filled with better homes, which pleased him.

"It needs work," said the agent, one that Rick had chosen by studying the real estate section of the *Star*, "No open concept, granite kitchen counters, or even a good shower, but Lawrence Collegiate and North Toronto Collegiate are close, and there are good elementary schools nearby. It's really a good starter home and the vendors want a fast sale: it's a break-up. They're asking 1.2 million, I could get it for 1 on a fast-cash closing."

"Sounds good," said Rick, not looking at Rose.

"I work downtown," Rose said.

The agent shrugged and looked at Rick, who she obviously thought was paying.

She was, Rose thought, just his type. Everything enhanced: breast implants bulging from her low-necked sweater, bright red lips with a permanent synthetic pout and a teased, bleached mop of hair—so old-fashioned when everyone now was going straight. She probably reminded him of the old movie stars that inspired him to wank off from the back seats of darkened movie houses in his early teens. She wished he hadn't told her that—although he thought it was funny. It was a picture of him she always held when thinking of his youth. He loved to tell her things to upset and shock her, and always laughed when she bit her bottom lip and looked away.

During the ride back to the Heath Street apartment, she finally broke the silence. "Do you have anything to contribute?"

He did not answer, his eyes staring straight ahead, driving too fast, and she felt "it" move. She hoped "it" was a boy, a tough, naughty little boy, and then a teenager who worked out. She had never felt more female, more helpless—and more stupid.

"Hungry?"

He ordered a hamburger with "the works." She had been brought up never to eat "garbage foods," as her mother called them, and even her birthday parties served egg salad and peanut butter and jam sand- wiches on white bread with the crusts cut off, not like the other kid's parties with hot dogs or pizza—and coke. There was no Coke in her home—only milk, her mother's Bristol Cream sherry and her father's Johnnie Walker Red Label.

She wolfed the hamburger down, filling her mouth with raw onion, tomatoes, mustard and ketchup, and pebbly, harsh, ground beef. The hamburger sustained her, even though the flames of heartburn licked at her throat within minutes.

"Eating for two," he commented, still not looking at her.

She went to bed as soon as they arrived home. She did not want to talk to him, to listen to his lies. There was less than a million in her estate account not enough to cover closing costs if a one million offer were accepted. A mortgage was out of the question, he had no income flow and she had too many expenses.

She looked through the *Star:* an emaciated child from the Caribbean had been beaten to death by his stepmother after months of abuse. There was a tooth found in his stomach at the autopsy. A school picture of the child's face, twisted and unhappy, wrenched at her heart.

At ten, Rick opened the bedroom door.

"They'll take one million on a fast closing, and we can have all appliances, fixtures, and the dining room furniture. We have to close in two weeks."

She did not answer, only pressed her face into the pillow and thought of the child's suffering. Later, she placed her hand under the mattress, took out the small bottle and placed the tiny white pill under her tongue.

CHAPTER 22

She decided to take the agreement of purchase and sale to Pascal and White, not that she expected them to do another pro bono, but she could be sure they'd give her extra time if she was short on the closing costs. She longed to see Del. She missed her. Being loyal to Rick was no longer a priority in her life. Rick refused to go to Pascal and White with her—because of Del, she was sure.

"It" was due the end of March, but even at the beginning of March, she looked ready to deliver: on such a slim girl, her baby bump appeared enormous. She had parked in the clinic's parking lot and walked the three blocks to the law firm on Adelaide. It was wet and cold, and she felt the wind lash her face and embrace her with chill. The receptionist seemed glad to see her but raised her eyebrows at her obvious pregnancy. "When are you due?" she asked. "Soon," Rose replied.

"How nice," she murmured, "I've always pictured you as a mom."

Then there was Del, beaming at her, although her smile stiffened when she saw the bump.

"Rosie, Rosie, and you didn't even tell me."

She didn't answer but started to cry. Del put her arm around her as they walked slowly together into Del's small office. They sat looking at each other across Del's desk, Rose's face wet with tears.

"I didn't tell you because you were right, right about everything. He's a sleaze and a bully and he wants me to support him. I find it hard to confront him, though I've been doing it lately—but not enough."

"And this house purchase?"

"All my inheritance money: he says it's for the baby, who he's sure is a girl." Then she gave Del all of Rick's purchase criteria, ending with, "He sees me as a mark—that's his word—and a dumb pushover, which I am. And when the baby comes, I'll leave him. But it'll cost me."

"But you didn't marry him: it's not a matrimonial home, is it?"

She turned away and Del gasped, "Oh, Jesus."

She left the office after Del had placed her arms around her and rocked her like a child.

After she left and walked east towards the clinic's parking lot it began to rain, a soft drizzle that added to her already damp cheeks.

He was gone when she arrived back to the apartment, so she lay down on the bed, conscious of the bump that suddenly became more active—all the walking, perhaps. She felt a heaviness of both body and spirit: a mixture of pregnancy and depression. Seeing Del's horror when she heard of the marriage increased her feelings of frustration and self-loathing.

She had been cajoled and bullied into buying a home she did not want, on the pretext it was for her unborn child. But she had learned from Del that he would have a claim against it—for usually half of its value—as it would be, as Del said, "a matrimonial home." Upon a break-up—and there would be a break-up—he could be walking away with up to half of her inherited money, all as a result of her stupidity.

***

He came home around six.

"No dinner. And did we see sister?"

She did not answer.

"Did you tell her she was right about me?"

Again she did not answer: a silence he took as an assent.

When he spoke again, his voice was grating. "I think you need a little excitement. I want to introduce you to an old friend of mine. I was going to do this before, get both of you together, with me, of course, and she could teach you a few things. But it's not a good time now. Hungry?"

When she didn't reply, he said, "I'll heat up a can of pork and beans: good iron for Katy."

"I don't feel like going anywhere."

"Sure you do, get a little excitement in your life: Take your mind off all the things your sister said."

Was this some sort of payback for seeing Del?

When they went out it was still raining but the rain had become heavier, and she was grateful that he held an umbrella over her head. Sometimes when he was considerate, she felt a softening towards him. But then other thoughts took over.

The rain kept pelting against the windshield, and the wipers clocked away the silent minutes.

"Where are we going?"

"A gentlemen's club in Mississauga: The Priceless Pearl."

"What will they think of a very pregnant woman going to a gentlemen's club?"

"They don't care as long as we pay. They'll be glad to see anyone on a night like this."

He seemed to have money—perhaps he'd been lucky gambling.

The Priceless Pearl smelled musty, but with an undercurrent of Opium perfume she had once sniffed at The Bay, and fried fish, advertised as the Greek cook's special. Rick paid ten dollars admission each, and they walked down a dimly-lit corridor lined with pictures of women in various stages of undress, ranging from naked, to pasties and G-string. He stopped before one picture and tapped at it with his finger. The woman had a mass of black curly hair, huge breasts and black nylons, stretching to mid-thigh, held up by suspenders, and an abbreviated patch covering her crotch. Under the heavy make-up her face was beautiful, like an old-time movie star: his teen-aged target in the dark movie houses. On the side of the picture was written in a round childish hand, "Love, Steamy Arab."

"That's what she calls herself," he explained, "That's an old photo— she's over forty now."

"Is she Arabic?"

"Her mother's Lebanese, her father's Italian. Her real handle's Pina Gatto."

At the end of the corridor, there was a door opening into a large room that was covered by a stage, as in a theatre, with seats circling around it. Most of the seats were empty except for those occupied by a group of college boys in their late teens who were making a lot of noise, and who kept beckoning to the girls on stage. Across from them was another group, much quieter and older, who might be construction workers. They also beckoned the girls, and occasionally left with one to go to one of the three side rooms.

"Lap dances in the first, massages with happy endings in the second, and some tame S&M in the third: price varies with the extras," Rick said.

Two young slim girls with ponytails, bare breasts and g-strings were making love to two shiny striped poles. The more athletic one was straddling hers and leaning back, her long blond ponytail swaying.

Rick beckoned and a black-haired woman, who was in the process of completing a split, got up and sauntered over, ignoring the college boys who called out, "Steamy, don't forget us."

The other group just smiled knowingly and she tossed them a half smile and wave. They seemed to be regulars.

Her breasts were large, too large for pasties, so she wore an underwire bra that served as a display shelf. Her crotch was obviously shaved, as the small satin patch covered very little.

"Long time, Ricky," she murmured.

She squatted in front of them and Rose felt enveloped by the smell of ripe sex, a blend of dying tuber roses and frites, which seemed to ooze from every pore. Up close her age was starting to show: there were fine lines beneath the heavy make-up surrounding her eyes and mouth, and the huge breasts had stretch marks not completely disguised by the tan make-up that covered her body. There was a fine line going from her navel to the black patch—a c-section perhaps?—and her legs in the spike-heeled sandals, although molded and firm, showed some spider veins that the tan make-up was bravely attempting to cover.

Rick leaned over and pushed a one-hundred dollar bill into the patch, delaying taking his hand away, and Rose saw him rubbing her clit with his finger.

"Bad boy," Steamy murmured, arching her back like a cat, and then gently removing his hand, "and in front of your sweet, pregnant little girlfriend here."

She looked at Rose, gave her a conspiratorial wink and smile, and said in a low drawl, "Nothing a guy does ever surprises me."

She got up and moved away, hips swaying, down to where the college kids were waiting. Rick got up and headed for the bar, telling Rose, "I'll bring you back a ginger ale."

Suddenly Steamy left the college kids, and she was crouching in front of her like a black lioness on her hands and knees. "Sweetheart," she said, in a low urgent voice, "be very careful of him, y'hear. Can't be careful enough."

All of a sudden Rick was next to her with his drink and hers. "Woman talk?" he asked, obviously annoyed—and curious.

"She was wishing me good luck," Rose said, "Woman do that when you're about to deliver."

With another wink and a flash of white capped teeth, Steamy was gone. Rose watched her and she was squatting in front of the college kids and they were all copping a feel, and filling the patch, most likely with dollar bills. When she left the patch was bursting, as was the under-wiring supporting her breasts.

"Great jugs," said Rick, "and they're real, no implants, nothing. And one touch on that joy button's enough to bring her off. It may be worn out by now. The body's hanging in, but it's showin' wear and tear. I wouldn't give her more than another year to keep making the bread she makes."

He finished his double-whiskey, Rose finished her ginger ale and they got up to leave.

"Take care of your little friend," Steamy called out, coming over.

Rick scowled. "I know how to take care of my women, or don't you remember?

"Sure I remember, Ricky," she said, and gave Rose another wink, and ambled towards the construction group, the star tattoo on her left bum-cheek moving with the tanned muscle. She left with one of the construction workers for the lap dance room.

Rose liked her. She felt Steamy was trying to protect her: she'd been warning her about Rick.

"An old girlfriend?" she asked, as they settled in the car.

"My first wife: she was in a lot better shape then, a great lay, and she still makes a bundle of tax-free dollars."

"What happened?" The rain was still coming down, just not as hard as before and silver tears were sliding down the windshield.

"She had teenagers, twin boys, and they hated my guts. They told her it was them or me, and she made the choice."

"I liked her," said Rose.

"Christ, you're full of surprises. I would have thought you'd think she was the worst trash known to man—a tight-ass like you."

"She's just making a living. Her sons probably adore her."

He didn't answer.

CHAPTER 23

The weeks crawled by and the bump became more and more active. Rose got up during the night to go to the bathroom but Rick never woke up. The co-seller's wife permitted them to go to the house before closing to fix up a room for the nursery. The husband had gone.

"You're alone?" Rose asked.

"Thank god," said the wife. "Worse things than being alone: it's a good thing we didn't have kids."

Rose felt the usual choking concern when she thought of her marriage and the baby.

Rick was painting the room they had decided on as a nursery—pale pink from the original lime green. He painted carefully and expertly. She wondered whether house painting was yet another of his undisclosed talents, much more likely than a degree in electrical engineering.

"Del is giving us Gwennie's old crib for the baby; we're the alternative to Goodwill."

"Why couldn't she have her own nice new crib?"

"Because we're broke. This purchase has cleaned us out, unless you can come up with some of the overdraft money you're always talking about. Without it I can't meet closing costs, that's why I'm using Pascal and White—they might cut me some slack. Del will know—it's so embarrassing."

She had changed and she knew he hated her for it. She no longer sat silently, her mind making its own soliloquy. The purchase of the home that she felt she had been pushed into, and the visit to Steamy, had triggered an ongoing sense of futility and disgust—the latter with herself as well as Rick. She should have been firm and refused, rather than allowing him to set her up for a purchase that would wipe out her inheritance—and from which he would profit. Steamy's warning—"Can't be careful enough"—ran through her thoughts. She had not been careful; she had allowed herself to be manipulated and used.

Even an exotic dancer in a strip club had shown more common sense. And two teenagers had gotten his number.

The small nursery was pretty, with its pink walls and Gwennie's old crib and change table, retrieved from Del's basement, and fluffy pink-and-white curtains, another of Del's donations. And a custom-made white blind Rose had ordered.

"Looks great," Rick commented, "A perfect room for a little girl."

And a ridiculous room for a little boy, she thought, angry that she had made a point of not inquiring as to the sex of the child.

The house closing was March 15 and she produced a certified cheque from her account that covered most of the purchase price—after asking Rick for his contribution.

"Blame the bank, they won't advance it."

She ignored the surge of anger she felt, went to the brokerage holding the stock account, and sold everything, thankful that many of the stocks had gone up due to a surging market. The moneys received would cover the shortfall and legals. Her insurance money was long gone.

"Hasn't paid a cent, has he?" snapped Del. "That's why he hasn't shown his face here."

Rose wordlessly signed the deed.

The reporting letter came a week before the birth, complete with a copy of the registered deed. She was lying on the bed, too heavy to move. Rick had supervised the movers, showing unusual energy, but she had done most of the packing. She wanted this baby to come. Dr. Dunstan had told her "it" had dropped.

She heard his voice, then the curses, and he was there, standing beside the bed.

"Playing tricks, cunt?"

He sat down heavily on the side of the bed, and she felt his large hot hands tight around her neck. Then he stopped.

"I'm not even on the deed, and your bitch sister had it say that it wasn't a matrimonial home. I'm going to report those bastards to The Law Society."

"I don't know what you're talking about: I just signed where they told me to sign," she rasped.

He stamped from the room and she heard the toilet flush.

When he came back to the room he was still angry, but he was smiling.

"I'll get my old divorce lawyer to do a new deed tomorrow. I just flushed your ol' lady's ashes down the crapper after I pissed on them. You won't be able to scatter them in the Irish Sea like she wanted."

A voice whispered in her ear, it said, "Be careful."

She would leave him as soon as the baby was born—"Worse things than being alone," as the seller of the house had said. The next day she went with him to his lawyer and signed the amended deed. "If one of you dies, the other will get the house," she explained with a smile. "It's called the power of survivorship that goes with the joint tenancy. It's the way most married couples take title."

She did not protest. Now she was afraid. She took her mother's empty urn from the bathroom, wrapped it in a silk scarf and placed it in the bottom drawer of the nursery bureau. She felt sad. And then angry. The violation of her mother's ashes was a personal affront and it shattered her. Her mother had deserved better.

***

Rick had always believed in sharing: with Pa, Chester, Diego, the other gang members—even with his mother, much as he hated her. But Rose wasn't into it, sitting there with a million in the bank, and making him grovel for every lousy dollar; opening a joint account and putting in fifteen hundred. It was a joke—a dirty one. He'd liked her at the beginning, not loved—that was out of the question—but he found her unique. He'd never known a girl like her, but now it gnawed at him, her anxiety, fragility, and most serious, her frugality. Then she'd started to turn on him, lashing out, showing her true self: a total lack of the sweetness he'd listed as a connection requirement. She had, he decided, no juice. And he wasn't thinking of the sex. It was her personality: it was dry, no give to it. And, after the first few times when he had instructed her, the sex bored him. Not that he couldn't perform—he could always perform. And she had responded, much more than he'd thought she would.

After all, he'd married her when she'd become pregnant, knowing she couldn't make it as a single mom, and considering the legal advantages that his old divorce lawyer had told him about. But she'd even tried to do him out of his share of the house, lying that it was her bitch sister and she didn't know what she was signing. But when he'd called her on it, she'd made the transfer into joint names, proving her guilt. She wasn't the first woman to lie to him, but he didn't have to take it anymore. And although he felt some guilt about the ashes, he had only to think of how destructive mothers were. But he wouldn't let her destroy his daughter, like his mother did to him. Now, it was just a matter of time.

CHAPTER 24

The cramping started at midnight, and became stronger as the hours went by. At two o'clock she went to the bathroom and warm water streamed down her legs, and the cramping increased. She wanted to call Del, but he would be furious.

She stood by the bed. "I'm having the baby." He let out a muffled "fuck" and sprang out.

They were driving up Bayview in her mother's car, and snow was falling straight down although it was the end of March.

"Sheila's Brush," she murmured, "that's what my mother used to call it: the last snowfall after St. Patrick's Day."

She thought of her mother, whose ashes had been transported through pipes filled with the sewage of those who lived in North Toronto, and mixed with her fear was a sense of repugnance.

"I'll stay with you while she's being born."

She didn't want him there. Didn't want him watching as "it" came out and the bump was gone. It was invasive, as if he were an onlooker, watching the intimate process of birth as he would one of his porn movies.

"No need," she whispered. "I'm fine. It turns some men off. What if you don't get your girl or she's born with two heads."

It was a silly thing to say, but better than, "Don't come. I can't stand you and don't want you watching. It's an invasion of privacy and I can't forgive you for urinating on my mother's ashes and choking me."

But he came along with her anyway.

It was an easy birth, although the baby was over eight pounds with a round head covered with Rick's hair and wearing Rick's face—but a sweet female version. It was the girl he had ordered.

The nurse said, "Would you like to hold her?"

He took her gently from the nurse's arms and rocked her.

"Hello Katy, I'm your daddy," he crooned.

"A daddy's girl," one of the nurses murmured, "I can always tell."

Rose watched him with half-closed eyes, his face awash with tenderness. It crossed her mind that he had met the only being in the world he could wholeheartedly care for. Yet she knew she must protect her from him, even though she appeared to be the sole unit of light that leaked through what she thought of as his grey flannel blanket of sociopathy.

Del arrived that afternoon, complete with diapers, shirts and sleeping suits, all for a six-month-old.

"She's gorgeous: a female version of him. It was never his looks I couldn't stand—it was everything else. He's out there now, watching her through the nursery window, so mesmerized he didn't notice me. Weird, absolutely bizarre. Maybe he's a pedophile. Gwennie thought he was the second coming. Still leaving? You'll have to leave him the baby."

"I would never do that," Rose muttered.

They were discharged the next day. He carried "Katy" or whose birth certificate said, "Katherine Patricia McCready," in her car seat, and Rose carried the bag of baby clothes from Del.

"Who's Patricia?" she asked. "I thought Steamy's real name was Pina, or is Patricia some other girlfriend?"

"It's a nice name for a girl," he growled, "just in case she doesn't like the Katy later on. We have to get a pram and some bottles and formula. It's good that we have that rocking chair."

"I'm nursing."

"You may not have enough; besides I may have to feed her sometimes."

"Really?"

Then he said nonchalantly—too nonchalantly, she thought—"I made an appointment with an insurer. I told him to prepare joint policies—for Katy's education, private school, university and all that: a million each. It's great security for her future. It should see her through Harvard if one of us doesn't make it."

What was he up to? Or was she being paranoid? Then she remembered Steamy's warning voice. But she attended with him, together with Katy, the next day. She could think of no excuse not to.

Katy screamed all night and wouldn't nurse.

"She won't latch on," she complained, "and when she does, I don't have enough. And she's got colic."

She was startled to see him get out of bed, appear with the baby in his arms and as she drifted off to sleep she heard him pacing the floor, humming some old song popular long before both their times. She did not notice when he got back into bed.

The next day it happened again. The only time the baby stopped crying was when she attempted to give her a clumsy bath.

He stood watching, shaking his head.

"Let me do it: you're hopeless. A lousy nurser and you can't even give her a bath."

She handed the wet child over and watched. She was amazed at his dexterity: the gentle lathering of the plump pink limbs, even the head, where he massaged her scalp with a firm but tender circular motion, her dark hair so much like his.

"What are you—some sort of baby nurse?"

He gave her one of his weird smiles. "Just good at certain things."

She thought of the sex. It seemed so long ago, back when she used to like him.

He kept hanging around the house, watching her failed attempts at nursing that his presence made worse.

"Haven't you anything better to do?" she burst out in exasperation. "Other than standing around smirking while I try to nurse your impossible daughter?"

She wanted to phone Del. Del would tell her how she'd managed Gwennie, and what she was doing wrong. But she couldn't, not as long as he was lurking around. Finally, after a week of Katy's screaming and engorged breasts that she obviously found unworthy, he went out.

"She screams all night—I think the word is colic—and refuses to nurse, although I'm loaded with milk."

"You must be exhausted." It was so good to hear Del's voice

Rose paused before saying, "He walks her all night. He sings to her, old numbers like 'Melancholy Baby.' He's like a male nanny."

"Lordy," said Del, "I'm shocked. If this keeps up you're going to have to put her on the bottle. They do survive without breast milk, you know. I only nursed Gwennie for six weeks."

He returned in a few hours with cans of formula to put in the bottles he'd purchased while she was in hospital. "I got a lot of information from the salesgirl at Shopper's."

"You're encouraging me not to nurse this baby," she yelled, "because you don't think I'm fit and you want to take over!"

He sighed. "You're stressed out. I'm going to fill up the tub and you can try to relax. I'll even get you a glass of warm milk and honey—good for the milk supply, but that doesn't seem to be the problem."

CHAPTER 25

He'd checked out postpartum psychosis online. That was, he was convinced, her problem. Lashing out and accusing him of taking over when she couldn't nurse, couldn't even give Katy a bath: so stupid, so clumsy, so deranged. They would be better off without her—just the two of them. It wouldn't be a suspicious death: she was depressed, unable to function and she'd been dependent on her anxiety pills for years. And she'd chosen a way out: a lavender-soaked coffin of foam—much better than the muddy rough cold waters of a lake in Algonquin Park. And he wouldn't even be there.

He'd prepared the bath, pouring her lavender shampoo into the warm water under the running tap. Then he knocked softly at the door of the bedroom. "You've got to relax," he said, his voice soft, almost tender, "Your hormones have gone haywire. I've prepared a warm bath so you can flake out. I'll take Katy out in the car—the movement may help her go off."

She hadn't even protested, even giving him a small grateful smile as she headed for the bathroom, wearing her toweled bathrobe and another towel wrapped like a turban around her head. He would remove it later—it looked as if she intended to get out. You would not worry about your hair if you'd decided to drown yourself.

He went into the bedroom closet and removed the bottle of Ativan from the inside pocket of his leather jacket and went into the kitchen. He took out a carton of milk and warmed it in a saucepan on the stove. He shook all the pills from the bottle into a glass tumbler and added the milk, stirring the whole time. And then he added a squirt of honey. He touched the mixture with his tongue. There was an aftertaste. He added more honey.

She was lying back, her turbaned head resting against the rim of the tub, her eyes half closed, the pink of her nipples shining through the foam. "I want you to drink all of this. It'll relax you. I'm going to stand here 'til you finish," he said.

She gave him a grateful smile. "Sorry for being so difficult: you're so good with the baby."

"Drink," he said.

Small demanding hiccups could be heard from the nursery. "Keep drinking," he said, but he knew he had to leave. "Yessir," she whispered, her voice almost loving, a reminder of things long past. For a moment he felt like leaning over, taking the glass and helping her out. But he just said "Drink" once more and left for Katy.

*****

She heard the bathwater running, his soft invitation, and when she went into the bathroom the tub was full of lavender bubbles and froth. Taking off her robe, she slid into the water, and felt herself relax. Then he was standing by the tub, a tumbler of warm milk in his hand.

"Drink it all," he said, "It'll relax you. I'll drive Katy around—some babies sleep in cars, even one like ours."

The milk was sweet but with a chalky aftertaste: she kept sipping it and a drowsiness and numbness crept over her. The glass with the remaining milk slipped from her hand and into the water. She felt herself slowly sliding into the foam and she breathed a throat full of water. Then a light bulb turned on in her head and she heard Steamy's voice.

She threw a leg over the side of the tub and forced herself up, only to fall back. Using her remaining strength, she turned on the cold water tap with her foot, and a snake of cold water wrapped around her, jolting her back from her stupor. With a painful effort she pulled herself over the rim of the tub and landed with a thud on the bathroom floor. She lay there unable to move, then, gathering the little strength she had left, she crawled over to the toilet and pushed her fingers down her throat. Some of the milk came up. It had a white powdery residue that clung to the side of the toilet bowl.

Still wet, she crawled into the bedroom, pulling herself up on the bed, fighting the numbness and dizziness. She slept until noon the next day, and when she woke up she heard him singing to the baby. She tried to focus through a drugged fog. He had put something in the milk, hoping she would drown in the luxury of the warm foamy bath. She thought of the pills he had taken from her night-table: there must have been eighty left from the hundred prescribed. He must have put all of them in the milk. She was thankful for the dropped glass, the years of addiction that had built up a resistance, and her forced regurgitation. She ran her hand under her mattress. The substitute bottle was still there.

"Jesus," he said, when he came into the room with the baby in his arms, "You must have been exhausted. You even dropped the glass in the tub."

"You can give her the formula," she said, not meeting his eyes. "I'll use the pump."

He must know she suspected. Naiveté rather than stupidity had been her problem.

"Already have," he said, giving her one of his weird smiles, which were, she thought, really just baring his teeth like a dog. The baby lay against him, her round head with the dark moist hair heavy against his white T-shirt.

"I'm going back to work next month: I'll get a nanny for Katy. We need the money. I can't expect you to be responsible for her care."

"Why not?"

After another week of failed attempts at nursing, she surrendered Katy to him, although as soon as he left the house she would pick her up and nuzzle with her, attempting to bond without his monopolizing presence. She was such a pretty baby, with her slits of black eyes, full cheeks and cap of black hair that curled in fine tendrils towards her pink creamy face, with its rosy petulant little mouth. She would run her finger down the warm quilted cheek, and sometimes she thought she detected the faintest flicker of a smile, but decided it was merely gas or a muscle reflex.

Sometimes he would come in and say, "Trying to be a mommy?"

"She's got your coloring, like a little Italian baby. What nationality was your mother?"

"The bitch? Some place in Central America. She spoke Spanish, I know that. Another woman who should never have been a mother."

"I can be a mother," she protested. "You just don't give me a chance."

"You have no appreciation for all I do," he replied. "You're the only mother in Canada who never gave a two o'clock bottle."

CHAPTER 26

The baby was crying—not lusty yells, but soft hiccup-like sobs, like the doves he'd heard over at the island with Pa when they'd stayed all night. He felt the diaper; it didn't feel damp but he changed it anyway, gently stroking the soft small thighs. Then he picked her up, and with her heavy on his shoulder, took the formula from the fridge and placed it in heated water in a saucepan. He held her cheek against his and hummed to her, one of the old songs Stormy used to sing at The Pearl when she stripped. He took the bottle from the pan, shook some of the formula on his wrist and sat with her in the rocking chair, the one they had purchased from the baby store on Bloor.

She gulped down the formula and started to choke. He removed the nipple from her mouth, placed the bottle on the table, and rubbed her small back, moist against her cotton top. Then she started to drink again, and after a few minutes her eyes, black and almond-shaped like his, began to close. He waited until the bottle was almost empty and then gently removed it, and nestled her to his shoulder, rubbing her small warm back again.

He never thought it would happen, the way he felt when he held her for the first time: the flood of love that washed over him. It was stronger than anything he'd ever felt, stronger than his love for Pa and Alf. It was a love that fulfilled and energized him. And that's why he took over, not just because Rose was a hopeless mother—which she was—but because this small female replica of himself gave him what he'd been seeking, perhaps forever. And he could never lose her.

Rocking in the chair, a peace came over him. It was as if this small morsel had traveled to that unfilled pool within him and had taken up residence. His love for her pressed against his throat, choking yet fulfilling. Alf had a passion for old jazz, and he had played it on weekends and downtimes, old hokey numbers like "Million-dollar Baby" and "Walkin' My Baby Back Home." He used to sing along with them when

Alf was away. Now he sang them to Katy, and just the sound of his voice stopped her from crying. She didn't need anyone else.

***

At the beginning of May, Rose hired a nanny: a pleasant smiling woman who sent money to the Philippines, and who was in the process of sponsoring her three children into Canada. She had recommendations, and was well worth the fifteen hundred a month.

Rick was furious, but hung around for a week, watching her closely. Then, one week after she'd started work, Rose came home and Elena was gone.

"Why? Aren't you ever going to work? There's no business, I know that. But you're very good with your hands. I know you're not an engineer, but you could be an electrician, you could paint houses, you could be a male stripper—anything. You could even sing. You can't leech off me forever."

She listened to her own voice, marveling at how she'd changed and at her own bravery. This was, after all, a man who'd tried to drown her while he'd chauffeured a colicky baby around town.

"I can take care of Katy: better than you, better than any nanny. You can pay *me* the fifteen hundred a month."

There was no longer a marriage. Sex was out of the question—neither of them wanted to touch the other. They were separate and apart in the same bed, or he slept on the sofa. They ate in silence, some take-out she brought home, or something he threw together, which she hoped wasn't poisoned. There were no more marinated or fried steaks. Sometimes he went out at night, to gamble or perhaps get laid. She placed her cheques in the joint account and paid the bills. He took out fifteen hundred a month, calling it "nanny pay."

Katy knew him: flaying her arms and legs in excitement when he came near her.

They had bonded, through hours of colic and the singing of a dozen versions of "Melancholy Baby." It would take time for Rose to win her back but she would do it—once he was out of the picture.

"She knows you," she said.

"Why wouldn't she?" he replied.

She wondered when he would try again. He would be so rich—almost two million, counting the house and insurance proceeds. He'd tried the doping and drowning; next time it might be anti-freeze in her orange juice, or arsenic or cyanide sprinkled over her macaroni and cheese. No, that would be too obvious. He was too clever for that. But she knew she must leave and take Katy. Katy would miss him but she would make it up to her. And she would hire Elena back.

Spring was slow in coming in 2005. May was full of rain and Rick had complained that the weather was not fit to take Katy out in her new pram, a luxurious British import paid for by her mother, and, according to her, needlessly extravagant.

"Must be nice, a stay-at-home daddy, pushing his baby in her pram, and chatting with all the mommies, while the baby's real mommy spends her days scraping plaque off teeth and looking at tonsils for eighty bucks an hour." Not only had she changed, but she realized she had developed a sarcastic edge that could cut concrete.

He smiled. His teeth were remarkable for a smoker who drank an abundance of red wine and coffee and who shunned dentists. "If you were a better mother I might be persuaded to start working."

It was all so exasperating and depressing and, as she drove back and forth from the clinic, sitting in the gridlock up and down Avenue Road, her mind worked feverishly on plans for escape. She hated confrontation, although now growing nastier and bolder by the day. The lilacs were finally in bloom in the front garden and she plucked one from the tree and sniffed it on the way to work. The scent filled her with nostalgia and she thought of how all her hopes had been crushed, turned into farce by her own bad judgement. She had even lost her baby, although she savored the times with her when he was absent.

One night at the end of July choked by her empty life, she confronted him.

"I don't want to keep on living like this. I'm all for equality, but there's no equality here. I'm supporting you, always have, and we can't stand each other. I want to end this sham of a marriage, and I want you to tell me what you want."

He appeared speechless. He rubbed Katy's small back for a final burp and walked with her slowly to the nursery as she nestled against him. When he came back he lit a cigarette, something he seldom did indoors, especially with Katy nearby. He frowned into the thin blue smoke.

"I want Katy. I'm her main caregiver, remember that. And I want this house. You can pay child support according to the guidelines plus the carrying costs of the house." Then, after a pause, he added, "You can see her every second weekend."

He had obviously seen a lawyer. Where else would he have picked up phrases like "main caregiver," and know about "guidelines?" She attempted to control the anger pushing at her throat and went to the kitchen. She poured herself a shot of vodka before answering him.

"You're mental, out of your mind crazy. Do you really think a court would give a four-month-old infant to a father and let him walk away with a house funded by the wife's inheritance? And have her pay child support, and carry the costs of a house she no longer owns because her husband refuses to work? Get a life, Rick. I haven't added that you doped me so I'd drown in the bathtub, flushed Mom's ashes down the toilet and fingered your first wife in front of me when I was nine months pregnant. And I haven't mentioned your porn addiction. You're *amazing* daddy material: the courts would just love you."

He dropped his cigarette into the whiskey he'd poured, looked at her and smiled. But his eyes were blurred with anger.

"You asked what I wanted and I told you. I didn't get into your sleeping pill addiction and pathetic attempts at mothering—not even taking your maternity leave. I answered a question. Jesus, you've changed—not a shred of sweetness left—but perhaps it was never there. And this attempted bathtub murder—you've gotta stop reading *The National Enquirer*. You've become a fucking head case."

They did not speak again.

She put her hand under the mattress, took an Ativan from the bottle, and slipped it under her tongue. But she couldn't sleep. She got up, and through the crack in the bedroom door she watched as he chain-smoked and sipped his whiskey. The porn he was watching was raw and violent and the victim did not survive. She went back to bed and took another pill. She knew he was thinking of her and she couldn't wait much longer.

Chapter 27

It was nearing the end of August—and hot. She was booked solid from nine to five. Then at lunch hour she received an email from Del.

Can you cm to office between 4 and 5? Imp I see you. Please confirm.

She phoned her four o'clock patient and offered an hour with Rita, another hygienist.

"No way. Give me one with you next week."

Instead of being flattered, she was annoyed. She apologized to Rita and left the clinic at four for Pascal and White.

The late afternoon sun blasted her bare arms and she felt sweat dribble from her armpits, and beads of perspiration cluster on her upper lip and the back of her neck. She wondered if he was taking Katy out for her afternoon walk, and if she was overdressed. She did not want to phone him as they had barely spoken since last month's confrontation. She saw herself reflected in the window of a restaurant on Adelaide: a tall slender girl, her dark hair with its side bang reaching her shoulders in damp waves, her slim arms as pale as her face. Her face had changed. The round cheeks and arresting green eyes were gone. Her face was more sculpted, with slight hollows under her cheekbones, and her eyes a little sunken. She looked older than thirty, but more arresting than she had at twenty-nine.

"She's waiting for you," said the receptionist.

Del was sitting scowling behind her desk in her small office jammed with filing cabinets.

Rose chewed on her lower lip and noticed a quickening of her heart, her old symptom of anxiety that had become chronic. Del began speaking slowly, as if presiding over a graveside eulogy.

"I'm sure you remember we've access to a P.I. here, Arnie Finch, who sometimes works for White and on Pascal's personal injury files: a great investigator, 'slick as a whistle,' as Mom used to say. I had him do a life history report on Ricardo or Roderick or Rick McCready. It took over a month but worth the cash. And Arnie's not cheap. You can pay me later—if you think it's worth it. Mad?"

"No, I'm not mad." The heat she'd felt when she entered the air-conditioned building was gone and her sweat had turned cold. Inside her rib cage her heart fluttered, as if it knew what was coming. She took the report Del had handed to her, and started reading. Del sat silent. It all made sense, things he'd told her about his childhood and mother and father. But then she read about the pregnant kindergarten teacher.

"Rosie, are you okay?"

Rose wanted to vomit. The room was spinning. Then she knew she hadn't really believed it: that he had been trying to have her drown. She had thought she was over-reacting, and that he could explain it. But now she knew it, knew it in her bones, as surely as she'd ever known anything. And she remembered his hands around her neck.

"Pina Gatto—or Steamy Arab—who thought she'd be able to stop the stripping business with a rich husband, who was to be a father figure to her sons, was the only smart one of the three of you. She refused to let him take out insurance, or transfer her townhouse into both names. Arnie thinks he told her about the first wife one night when he was drinking, although he made a joke of it the next day. But she believed him. He had some of the insurance money left. He blew it, gambling, and on weeks in Vegas—often with her. Once he spent his money, he started going into hers. And that's when she got rid of him. Her kids smelled a rat and wanted him out. He was into some kinky stuff as well: and the kids found that out and called him 'a sicko.' Suspect they objected to it more than Steamy, but she listened to them.

"Then, thanks to True Connections, you came along, the perfect mark: lonely, pushing thirty, insecure, with an anxiety disorder and a bundle of inherited money. And gullible as hell. But after a while even you figured him out."

Rose got up, felt weak and sat down. She put her hands over her face and started to cry. Then she told Del everything.

Del came over and held her wet face in her warm hands. "Rosie, Rosie, so sorry baby, so sorry. Mom kept you so protected, and you had no life experience—none. You were just hanging there, a sweet little peach, waiting to be plucked."

"I'll leave. I have to. It's just a matter of time and he'll make another try. I'll never trust again, never. But there'll be trouble, terrible trouble, over Katy."

"Katy?"

"He loves her. Perhaps the only person he's ever loved, except his dad or this Alf person he's talked about. And they've bonded. She loves him much more than me, as much as a five-month-old can love. He took over right from the beginning. He wouldn't let me be a mother."

"No court," said Del firmly, "would ever award a five-month-old to a father."

Chapter 28

At the casino, Rick felt the comfort of the familiar: the heavy smoke-packed air and the background clanging of the slots. He moved around the tables, seeking out his lucky end seat at a twenty-five dollar blackjack table. He'd only taken six hundred, not wanting to blow his fifteen-hundred nanny allowance. Miserable bitch—although she paid the carrying costs of the house he still couldn't forget how she'd been about divvying up her million, making him grovel for dollars. And she'd accused him, quite correctly, of trying to drown her. But the mental case had no evidence. He worried about leaving Katy with her, feeling her absence like a lump in his throat.

He won his first five hands, tipping the dealer, a heavy-set, dark-haired, smiling woman with the name tag of Renee, five a hand. He was up to nine hundred when there was a dealer change. Renee wished them all luck and gave him a special smile for the tips. The new dealer was an unsmiling Brit or Aussie, who dealt too fast and couldn't break. So he gave his winnings back. And then he doubled up, as he figured his run of bad luck couldn't last—but it did, and when he was down to two-fifty, he quit in disgust.

He made a quick tour of the tables, looking for Chester who said he'd try to make it. But there was no Chester. It was Chester's damn wife, who resembled Chester's mother, and who resented their friendship. She'd stopped him. She had objected to his sleeping on their chesterfield before he moved in with Rose, even though he was so good with their kids. He was grateful for Steamy and her absent sons. She let him stay with her, and she still had sex with him, all that time he was seeing Rose and not having it.

He left the casino around midnight, longing to see Katy. He hoped Rose had given her the formula that he'd prepared and put in the fridge. He knew Katy would cry if he wasn't there. Suddenly he was angry with himself for leaving her. It had been stupid and he wouldn't do it again. He pressed the pedal of the Mustang and headed back, hunched forward, flying into the night, the jazz station playing. He reached the dark street in North Toronto at one-forty-five.

He entered the house carefully. Everything was quiet. He turned on the hall light and walked to the nursery. The crib was empty. He checked the bedroom. She was gone with Katy. The lump in his throat that had pulsed with missing Katy now erupted, and he took one of the dining room chairs and bashed it against the floor time and again. Then he took one of the plates in the dryer by the sink and threw it against the kitchen wall. He thought of the joy of throttling Rose, placing his hands around that thin white neck and pressing long and hard until she fell lifeless to the floor. An abysmal mother, now she was robbing him of a child he had nurtured since birth, and who he loved without reservation. He would kill her. He did not know how, but it would happen.

Bitch Del's address was behind the wall phone in the kitchen. He left the house and headed for Mississauga.

**

Before she'd left that morning, Rick had said to her, "Try to get home early: I'm going to Niagara tonight. Can I trust you with Katy?"

She just stared at him.

It was an opportunity, as he would be gone for at least eight hours. She could pack and go to Del's, and she and Katy could share Del's spare bed. She'd phone Elena and line her up for next week, provided she wasn't working at another job. At six, he was gone and she was on the phone with Del; at eight, she was in her car, a car filled with suitcases. In the backseat, Katy was strapped in her car seat. Her heart was beating in her ears, her hands trembling against the wheel, and her throat tight. Del's new home was in Mississauga, where real estate was less expensive than Toronto's. She predicted she'd have trouble finding it. It would be her first visit.

The air had the drenched sweetness of late summer, and the grey sky was scattered with stars. As she drove west along the Lakeshore, she began to feel lighter and with a sense of freedom. She had been depressed—even afraid—but had not realized how much until now. She had started to realize that she was responsible for her own happiness. Her dating site searches and her longing for a man to bring her fulfillment were senseless: it was the stuff of her novels. Should she ever find another mate—and at the moment she wasn't interested—he would not be a necessity. She would not need him to complete her but only as an enhancer of her happiness.

She stopped the car near a streetlight and looked back at Katy in her car seat. Her cheeks were round, her finely sketched brows drawn together, as if she were pondering her life's future problems at five months. She swelled with love. Rick had not only taken her money, he had taken Katy, as surely as if he had boarded a plane with her and left Rose stranded at the airport. But she would win her back, and that would make it all worthwhile.

It was after nine before she found Del's house. It was a two-story, built back from the road on a quiet street, and much larger than her Toronto home had been. Gwennie had gone to bed, but Del told her she was wild with excitement that she was moving in. She and Del sat and sipped tea. She felt warm and safe. It reminded her of fifteen years before when they were still living in Lawrence Park. Mom and Dad had gone out, so Del had nothing to be jealous about. Now she could share her dates and crushes with Rose, and Rose would giggle as Del made fun of them—and herself.

While they were talking Fred came in, patted her on the shoulder, and said, "Sorry Rosie." Then he kissed Del on the forehead. She suddenly appreciated Fred, as well as liking him. He was so proud of Del, so proud she worked at a law firm. He had even encouraged her to try for law school as a mature student after their mother had died, rather than buying a new place. He would never try to steal her money, or take over Gwennie. Instead, he'd tell Gwennie how lucky she was to have such a great mom. He loved Del and wanted her happy. Who cared that he fixed computers and would not be accepted by True Connections.

It was three o'clock when loud bangs sounded at the front door, as if someone were kicking it. Rose knew who it was. She stood at the top of the stairs in her pajamas and watched Del and Fred stand by the half-open door.

"You've got my daughter and I want her."

"Leave or I'll call the police: your daughter's staying here." Del's voice was high and strained.

She saw him push Fred and then he looked up the stairs.

"Get her cowardly cunt—you waited till I was gone to abduct her."

Then Del was on the downstairs landline, "I'm calling the police if you don't leave."

He ignored Del and focused on Rose. "Call your bitch sister off—I'm leaving, but you'll hear from my lawyer tomorrow. No way am I losing my daughter to a half-assed mother like you."

Rose crumbled and sat down abruptly on the top stair. The front door slammed shut.

"Cancel work tomorrow, Rosie. I think he means it."

PART TWO

Part Two

Chapter 29

The years had not been kind to Martin Springer in the twenty-one years since he had represented Rick McCready, then known as Ricardo McCready, in juvenile court. The former natty, clean-shaven lawyer, trim in a dark suit, had been replaced by an overweight individual with a three-day growth of beard, stained poached eyes, and a belly that hung over a rumpled pair of trousers. But Rick, who'd been following the lawyer's career through newspaper articles for many years, hoped there was still lurking inside this new Martin the skills that had given him a conditional discharge at the age of fifteen.

Martin eyed his prospective client: a good-looking man, casually dressed in jeans and a leather jacket. He felt instinctively it was a criminal matter, just from his thirty-five years of practicing criminal work. He knew the man, knew his capabilities, and knew he was like one of a group of criminal clients he had defended throughout the years. And if he did not think of them with warmth, he at least thought of them with understanding. This was much better, as understanding did not always extend to his current family practice.

"I don't do criminal work anymore, Mr. McCready," he said, "they won't let me."

The would-be client smiled, a tight, somewhat mirthless smile. "I know about the tapes, Mr. Springer. Can I say how much I admired your loyalty towards your client? Even serial killers need good representation."

"Thank you," replied Martin. "Unfortunately the Law Society didn't agree with you."

They both sat silent. Martin took a cigarette from a pack on his desk and, after placing it between his lips, threw another across the desk at Rick, who caught it in mid-air. Then Rick spoke, reminding him that Martin had been his lawyer years before.

Martin rubbed his grizzled chin and smiled. "Didn't I call your teacher? She was the best witness I ever had."

"And the only woman I ever loved," Rick replied. They both laughed and he continued. "This is not a criminal matter, it's more serious—it's about the custody of my daughter." Martin thought he heard an unexpected tremor in Rick's voice.

"This will be a court matter?"

"For sure. I've been her only caregiver—there's nothing I haven't done for her except breastfeed. My wife's a hopeless mother." He continued with a list of Rose's maternal failures, and her abduction of his daughter the previous night, ending with "I want my little girl back." At the end his voice was thick with emotion, and Martin sighed to himself. He was just like his other family law clients.

"Age?"

"Five months." Martin sighed again, this time out loud.

"I'll need a twenty-thousand retainer."

Rick felt a surge of desperation and considered his very few sources, but he didn't even flinch. "I can't even think of money when it's this important—but you'll have to give me a little time. Can I come back this afternoon or tomorrow?"

"You can," said Martin, thinking back to the joys of representing those charged with attempted murder.

Rick made a hasty exit, and thought of heading for Steamy's townhouse in Brampton, but decided he'd see Rose first.

***

Gerda Heller, Senior Partner of Heller and Cole, had been practicing family law in Toronto for twenty years. She was well known and respected, having won a precedent-setting appeal during her first ten years of practice, and it usually took weeks to get an appointment. Then, there was the problem of affording her. But for once in a very long time, Rose was lucky.

Del's employer, Pascal and White, did not do family law unless it consisted of the most straightforward domestic contracts, so those who attempted to retain them were always referred to Gerda Heller. Since many were Pascal's personal injury clients, for whom he had acquired substantial settlements, these referrals were welcome and appreciated. Ernst did not ask for or expect a referral fee, only that Gerda send him any of her personal injury clients. There were none, as Greta specialized only in family matters. A box of fine wine at holiday time did not compensate for her debt to Pascal and White. So when Del McKee, senior law clerk at Pascal and White, asked for a favor, which was to see her sister Rose McCready on an emergency matter, she could hardly refuse. As well, she would accept an authorization and direction that any legal fees owing would be paid to her from the sale of the former matrimonial home, provided her out-of-pockets would be paid when incurred.

"You've lucked in, Rosie," said Del, as she watched Rose attempt to give a squirming Katy her morning bath. "Can I help you?"

"No, it's fine," said Rose, although it obviously wasn't. She tried not to sound ungrateful. After all, Del had taken the day off, as had Rose, after phoning Dr. Gruber, the clinic's owner, who sighed his irritation when she told him she had to cancel all her Friday appointments for "an urgent personal matter."

She was determined to become competent at handling Katy, to rid herself of the label "miserable half-assed mother." But it was clear that Katy missed her father, fussing and crying during a bath that Rose feared was not warm enough and only drinking half the bottle of formula Rose had carefully prepared.

"Too bad you couldn't nurse," said Del, in her clumsy but sympathetic way, "It would go over so well with a motion's court judge." Rose ignored her, refusing to revisit her history of painful nursing attempts.

Gerda was seeing them at five—her usual hour to exit the office, especially on Fridays. It meant Fred was coming home early with pizza to be there for Gwennie, and gridlock Friday night traffic. Katy howled until they reached Bay Street, then passed out as if dead.

"Do you suppose she's all right?" Rose asked Del, her voice high with anxiety.

"She's fine," Del assured her. "You two have got to get used to each other. You guys haven't bonded—I'm not sure she even likes you."

"Thanks, you're really supportive."

"Sorry, don't mean to make things worse. But you were always the one who loved kids."

After that they didn't speak, although she did say thanks to Del, whom she left holding a sleeping Katy as she walked into Gerda Heller's office.

Gerda had instructed her, through Del, to write a short history of the marriage and to email it to her before her appointment. She'd written it in twelve brief paragraphs starting with True Connections. On re-reading her paragraphs she was humiliated: she came off as a dental hygienist with, it seemed, a borderline IQ, completely unable to see an obvious con for what it was and handing over everything to a guy who'd lied to her the moment she'd met him. What if Gerda refused to take her on the grounds that she was too demented to instruct her?

When she went into the office, Gerda told her she'd been "off the wall" and had been unable to read the history, but she'd read it while she was there. Rose nodded mutely and at the same time pushed Arnie's report across the shiny mahogany desk.

"What's this?"

"Arnie Finch, Pascal and White's investigator did it. My sister was worried about me."

Gerda laughed. "Arnie Finch: I used to use him when clients were still using cruelty and adultery as divorce grounds. That's gone now—everyone does one year separate and apart. But this is custody and money, right? So it might be useful."

Gerda started to hum and searched out her email on her computer.

Rose watched her. She was about six feet tall and model-thin. She wore a navy knit suit with white piping in spite of the August heat, as a bow to the building's frigid air conditioning. She wore spike-heeled navy sandals in spite of her height, and her salon blond-streaked hair was pulled back in a tucked in a ponytail. Her make-up was immaculate, her perfectly arched brows tweezed to perfection, and her lined coral lips were smudge-free. Her nose was a little short for her rather full face and Rose suspected early surgery, but she was still a very striking woman.

Greta's humming increased in volume as she read, then she stopped midway, looked at her, and asked, "Were you on something?"

"One gram of an anxiety pill at night, prescribed by my family doctor years ago. Rick took the bottle; he said the pills might hurt the baby. I think he put them in some milk so I'd drown in the bathtub. I got a refill from my old pharmacist."

"It's a prescribed drug but be prepared to have him say you're a drug addict," Gerda said and continued to read, stopping only to ask, "Did you show anyone the marks on your neck?"

She did not wait for a reply, obviously concluding that Rose was incapable of anything so sensible. When she finished she sat and sighed.

"Is there any reason why you went along with all this?" Gerda gave a summary of her mistakes, which she'd already heard from Del, ending with "How will I explain that to a judge?"

Rose felt herself sliding into a second bath, one filled with depression and suicidal thoughts. "Arnie thinks he killed his first wife, and I know he tried to kill me. And there was the choking. He's never worked a day since he's married me—his second wife warned me to be careful." At this point her voice broke and her eyes filled with unshed tears.

"I know, I know," said Greta sympathetically. "But he was father of the year—that's a big deal, no? He was a stay-at-home dad who seems to be the sole caregiver. You'd have been fine years back when mommies were in, but now it's all equality and it works both ways. He's a stay-at-home dad, fully supported by his wife, and some so-called enlightened judge might ignore his pathology and just focus on that. And you're stuck with the status quo until trial."

"Status quo?"

"They like to keep things as they were so as not to disrupt the child."

"But she's only five months old." Rose let out a dismal howl and no longer held back the tears, mopping them up with a soaked Kleenex.

Greta got up from behind her desk, and coming over placed a perfectly manicured hand on Rose's shoulder. She smelled of spice and money. "Remember this, Rose: I'm a very good lawyer, and you're not there to help him pay his legals. Let's try to keep positive."

"You must think I'm the worst moron ever. I'm so overanxious and always have been. I had trauma from a childhood car accident and guilt about my parent's marriage. I hated confrontation. He exploited that. At the beginning his controlling ways made me feel secure, but just before I left I was standing up to him—or trying to. He's very manipulative and clever. But that's no excuse for my being so dumb and gutless." Greta nodded in unhappy agreement.

Rose signed her authorization and direction from the proceeds of the sale of the home for Greta's legal fees, which were six hundred an hour, and that she was to compensate Greta for out-of-pockets when incurred. Greta would prepare the divorce petition, the application for a sale of the home, and the motion for interim custody of Katy. Rose would be notified when she was to come in and sign. She was also to complete a financial statement. "Your sister will help," Greta assured her.

When she came out of the office, a tight-lipped Del was walking a screaming Katy.

"Maybe," she muttered, "You should just let him have her."

CHAPTER 30

By Sunday night, Katy had improved. Del concluded that she was hungry and had introduced some strained applesauce and baby cereal. Katy was responding to Gwennie's constant stimulation and to Rose's rocking her in Del's old rocking chair that had years before soothed Gwennie. Katy was even looking at Rose, her black almond eyes showing curiosity rather than dislike.

"Such a sweet baby," Rose cooed, running a finger down the plump cheek and receiving a very small smile. "She's smiling at me," she called to Del.

"It's gas. She's getting colicky again," she replied.

"You're so negative," complained Rose. "You're as bad as Gerda. She's afraid they'll keep the status quo."

"Our fault," said Del. "We kept howling for equality and now it's biting us in the ass. What you need is an old-fashioned judge who thinks mommies should be number one and that men who live off their wives are low-lives and parasites. But they've all retired and the new wave, male and female, may overlook the fact that he's a Grade-A user and psycho, and may focus on his superior daddy parenting that you permitted."

"I found it hard to stand up to him," mumbled Rose. She sat there thinking sadly of expensive prams, her possible loss of Katy, and her money problems, which meant she had to continue working. "Just imagine his parading up and down the street with the other mommies and nannies, with Katy beaming away from her exclusive pram."

Del shook her head. "Makes me want to puke."

***

On Saturday night she phoned Elena, who had been cleaning offices at night, and she agreed to start on Monday morning.

On Monday morning a letter was delivered to the Gruber Dental Clinic for Ms. Rose McCready. It came from the office of Martin Springer,

QC, who, it seems, was in the process of being retained by Rick McCready. He wished an immediate return of the child, Katherine McCready, who had been "abducted" by her mother on Thursday night last.

The second paragraph was especially chilling: "The status quo in this case has been well established. Your husband has been the principal caregiver of this child since birth, when you refused to breastfeed and wished to return to your profession as a dental hygienist less than a month after the child's birth. This was in spite of the fact that you were entitled to six months of maternity leave."

The remainder of the letter reminded her that she had never given a two o'clock feeding, had a "concerning drug dependency," could not afford "expensive litigation," and demanded "the child's immediate return." The first paragraph of an offer of settlement made settlement impossible.

1. The father will have interim and permanent sole custody of the child, Katherine Patricia McCready, born March 31, 2005. The mother will have access every second weekend, from Friday to Sunday night, at a time to be agreed on. The mother will be responsible for picking up and delivering the child to the father's residence. Christmas, Easter, and school holidays will be shared by the parties.

The second and third paragraphs were also disturbing, asking for guideline child support, and for all other future expenses which were to include French tutorials, private school and music lessons, all to be chosen by the father, who was to stay in the matrimonial home for five years, and she was to pay all carrying costs, followed by a sale and an equal division of sale proceeds. She was to receive no credit for any inherited money brought into the marriage.

Rose faxed the letter to Del, who emailed back that Martin Springer was a "legal psychopath, who practices family law like a criminal matter" and recommended Rose's suicide. But she did tell her to immediately fax the letter to Gerda, whose receptionist then phoned and told her to be at the office at five and to be on time as Gerda was cancelling an important meeting. Rose's one bright spot of the day was her phone call to Elena, who told her Katy was "jus' fine," had eaten two bowls of cereal, had drained her bottle of formula, and had not once cried.

Rose longed to go back to Del's, to take Katy's small warm body in her arms, hold her round cheek against hers, and rock with her in Del's old rocker. She thought of how Rick had made her feel inept and hopeless. Looking back, she saw it as a deliberate ploy so that he could make himself indispensable when the inevitable break-up happened. It would lengthen his mooching time if she had to pay child support. He did love Katy, though—that part she knew was genuine—which made everything that much worse.

Gerda was sitting behind her desk looking rumpled, unlike the model-like persona she had projected Friday night. Her voice was low, but contrived, and Rose felt that it was only her professionalism that prevented her from speaking in a non-lawyerly yelp.

"I wonder how that grasping gold-digger you married was able to retain Martin Springer? This matter will never settle now. There will be a sale of your bungalow, but years of bankrupting court appearances. His wish to stay in the home is a joke. He'll need every cent to fund future years of litigation. He shouldn't get a cent from the house—your marriage lasted less than a year and the home was funded solely from your inherited money, but you were daft enough to transfer it into joint tenancy. You'll have to claim duress: a knife, gun, or that brief period of choking. Fortunately, you used his lawyer, so you didn't have independent legal advice."

"She told me what it meant."

"No she didn't . . . think about it."

Rose thought about it. And Greta continued. "The support he wants for Katy and the carrying costs of the home mean you'll never be able to live anywhere but your sister's. And child support's not even tax-deductible. Seeing your daughter only four days a month would ensure against future bonding. It's a garbage offer and Martin knows you'll never take it.

"We can't stand each other. I've caught him putting forth false evidence on behalf of his rich fraudulent clients—which are pretty much all of them. I wonder what he's doing with Rick McCready, a gambler with no money, who kills or leeches off woman. Perhaps he misses his old criminal clients, or Rick fed him the same crock that he fed you. I'd have thought Martin was too smart for that."

"I'm glad I'm not the only one taken in," murmured Rose.

The upside is as soon as the money goes he's out of Martin's office. Martin won't carry him."

Gerda had so far spoken in a thoughtful flat voice, but she became animated when she said, "I'll turn down what I'll refer to as 'their totally unconscionable offer'; prepare your pleadings, throwing in Arnie's and your material; and draw up a motion asking for interim custody, a sale of the home, a declaration that he'll be holding any equity as a joint tenant in trust for you, and that he'll pay you guideline support. We'll have the court attribute a salary to him using his True Connections material. He can have access every second weekend, exactly what he offered you." Rose sat watching her, her mouth slightly open, eyes unblinking.

"All we need now," said Gerda, "is the right judge."

***

Rose left Gerda's office exhilarated, but terrified. Rick would be furious. She had seen flashes of his temper and knew that behind the fixed smile and the dead eyes lurked the ability to kill. Then what would happen to Katy when she went through the usual teenage rebellion? He saw his mother in every woman. Would he see her in a rebellious daughter? Somehow, she doubted it.

She drove back to Mississauga along the Lakeshore, watching the silver skin of the lake turn topaz. She thought of driving her car along the ribbon of the silver sheen and into the depths of the lake, her former sense of freedom replaced by the heaviness of fear. But then she thought of Katy.

When she finally reached Del and Fred's quiet street in Mississauga, Rick was sitting in his Mustang, waiting. She parked, got out, and started walking up the driveway, but then he was behind her. He grabbed her arm. He looked unshaven and tired and when he spoke his voice was harsh and broken.

"Look, I know you hate my guts but forget all that. Just give me Katy and I'll walk out of your life. You can have the house. And I don't want a cent. I just want my little girl, that's all. You can't do this to me: just let me take her and leave."

She kept walking, hating the wrench of pity she felt for him even after everything he'd done to her: "I want you to go. My lawyer will be starting an action next week."

"You're a stupid cunt, always were. Those shite-hawks don't care about us, they just want our bread. You're being dumb and naïve like always, listening to your sister Del and your bitch lawyer: Springer says she's a blood-sucking ghoul. If you had a clue—or half a clue—you'd get Katy and come home with me now. Just give me my daughter."

Del opened the door and called out, "Problems?"

Rick yelled, "Happy now, bitch?"

"I'm calling the police," said Del.

"All I want is to see Katy."

"I'm calling the police," Del repeated.

Rose watched him as he walked away, head down, and as he got into the car she felt another nudge of pity. And then she remembered.

Rose went into the house and entered the bedroom. Elena had fed and bottled Katy, who lay on her back waving her arms and legs, dressed in a thin cotton jumper patterned with pink teddy bears. Gwennie was leaning over making strange kissing noises that excited the baby, spurring her arms and legs into even more activity.

Rose leaned over the side of the side of the crib. "Hello, sweetheart, Mommy's home," she whispered. She was rewarded by Katy not only waving her arms and legs, but fixing her with her black eyes and giving her a pink-gummed smile. She knew her mother. Rose's throat swelled with joy—so much for Rick and his taunting of her lack of bonding.

"Come up, come up to Mommy," she crooned, picking up the small warm body and walking over to the rocking chair. The baby lay in her arms looking at her while she slowly rocked and made circles around her plump cheek with her forefinger. There was another smile.

"Katy's smiling at me," she called out to Del, "She knows me."

"You are her mother," Del replied.

CHAPTER 31

Rose sat in Heller and Cole's reception room at five-fifteen on a Tuesday afternoon, reading her pleadings in support of the motion for interim custody of Katy and the sale of the matrimonial home that Gerda had scheduled for the following week. Gerda left nothing unsaid, putting emphasis on Rick's damaging history plus his efforts to alienate her from her baby, and his abnormal relationship with the child that focused on cutting her off from any relationship with her mother, which would doubtless result in "future severe psychological damage."

"Well?" asked Gerda.

"It's . . ." said Rose, "a little harsh at times and not quite accurate, though most of it is. I'm not sure he killed his first wife, you know."

"Believe me," snapped Gerda, "It'll be a birthday card compared to Martin's work of art. You'll never read anything like it: you'll be sprouting claws and horns. Your financial statement looks a little too good: you hygienists make as much as some lawyers."

"I think you do a little better than our hourly rate."

"I wonder what he did with the million from the first drowning?" mused Gerda, ignoring Rose's comment. "Hard to believe he blew it all in Vegas."

Rose shrugged, signed all the papers, and wished it were over.

"I'll need the disbursement money," said Gerda. "This all has to be issued and served."

Rose wrote a postdated check for five hundred, grateful for Gerda's association with Pascal and White.

Rose walked back to the clinic's parking lot through a haze of late August heat. The sidewalk was filled with office workers going towards the subway, or just walking to meet friends at the bars and cafés on Queen Street. There were students from the university, and even lawyers from the courts, or late meetings, carrying briefcases. Strange, so many people, so late in the day. She dreaded entering the Gardiner and joining the sweating gridlock, but longed to see Katy, who now greeted her with a wide smile, waving her arms. All the suppressed feelings she'd had when she'd been with Rick came flooding back, and she was filled with intense love. Had she suffered from a post-postpartum psychosis? She didn't think so—just a husband who exploited her new mother nervousness.

As she walked to her car, she saw Rick leaning against the door. He was slouching, his arms folded, and he was wearing jeans and a T-shirt, which showed his muscled upper arms. His dark hair tumbled over his forehead, and his tan and dark glasses made him look like an actor filming in Toronto. For a moment she forgave herself for being swept away by his looks and lies.

"Wanna go have a drink?"

"I'm driving and I want to get back."

"Ooh, look who's starting to be a mommy—took you long enough. Can I have her for the weekend?"

"Everything has to be between the lawyers."

"Helluva expensive way to communicate. That bastard I'm hiring wants twenty-thou before he goes to court. Where in hell am I gonna get twenty thousand?"

"In the old days you'd get it from me, but I can't cover your legal fees."

"Look, can't we settle this?"

"We can't. Your lawyer sent a ridiculous offer of settlement. Move, please."

"Why so bitter? Because I tried to score a few bucks off you and took care of our kid because you were useless?"

"Move."

As he walked away, a tall muscular figure surrounded by the late afternoon light, he said over his shoulder, "You're going to be sorry for this, Rose."

She endured the hour of gridlock, listening to her Sinatra tapes, which even Rick liked. They filled the silence, which had often happened when they'd driven together. Rick could sing, but always stopped when he noticed her listening. To her surprise, she even found "My Way" inexplicably annoying, a smooth hymn to male chauvinism. She thought of her divorce petition and affidavits, and asked herself what parts were blatantly false: perhaps he hadn't killed his first wife, perhaps it had been a genuine accident, and perhaps the honeyed milk was meant only to make her relax. But she didn't think so. And the hands around her neck had really happened. Perhaps he was thinking of Katy when purchasing the house and getting the insurance. But she didn't believe that either. The only thing she really knew was that he loved Katy and that he'd never give her up. And neither would she. She thought of that when she looked at the glistening silver of the lake, and once again dismissed an impulse to drive in.

***

She was giving Katy her bottle in the rocking chair when Del came in.

She told Del what had happened at Gerda's and about Rick's threat.

"Disgusting," sniffed Del. "You should phone Gerda and ask for a restraining order next week."

"He didn't touch me, just snarled it over his shoulder. He can't afford Martin. I think he was actually trying to get me to pay for his legals."

"You've been such a patsy, I'm surprised you didn't do it. Seriously, if he wants to settle why not think about it—as long as it's reasonable. Once Gerda and Martin get into it you can forget settlement. They'll be worse than you and Rick."

"He wants Katy, that's the offer."

Del did not reply, just shook her head. And Rose kept rocking, watching Katy's lids begin to close over her black Spanish eyes, eyes that sometimes seemed so aware for a little baby.

***

The next Monday, the day before the scheduled motion, Gerda phoned the clinic.

"I've just received the answer and counter-petition, and the reply to your affidavit. According to this you're an evil, child-hating, drug addict, and I don't know how the child's survived the week with you. He wants an adjournment to cross-examine, provided McCready gets access next weekend—that's the condition of the adjournment. I have to reply to his garbage, so I'm all for the adjournment, but do you want me to agree to let him have her for the weekend? It gives a bad precedent, but we've never really said anything about his actual parenting—just that he's never let you have a relationship with her."

So he had gotten the twenty-thousand. Rose didn't know why, but she thought of Steamy Arab.

"How can you stand to have me as a sister?" Rose wailed to Del, throwing the legal papers she had picked up from Gerda's office across the kitchen table. "He's a baby-loving electrician whose business was failing, and I'm his millionaire skinflint wife who made him grovel on his knees before I tossed him a cent, all while being the worst mother on earth. I have never, ever, read anything like this. And he wants Katy every week, and three weekends, while I have her one weekend—provided I'm supervised. Did you ever?"

"Welcome to litigation," said Del. "I could have told you. Remember Gerry White used to do family law before he switched to criminal. He said defending a murderer was a piece of cake compared to family law. He was having a breakdown when he handed his files over to Gerda. You have to think a certain way if you do that stuff—the hatred between people who once loved each other is incredible. Now, write answers to his pleadings and email them to Gerda. But it's too late for her to file more material. And prepare yourself for the worst tomorrow."

Rose emailed her answers to Gerda and then lay down beside the sleeping Katy. She was exhausted but sleep was out of the question. She drew Katy close and felt fear. And then anger.

CHAPTER 32

The house was silent without Katy. The lack of her made him ache: her smile, her smell, her softness, her joy when he sang. No other woman could ever inspire this emptiness. He couldn't eat, just smoked and drank stale cold coffee from a cardboard container he'd picked up earlier. Then, as he sat there, there was an assertive knock at the door. He got up with an effort, depression making him heavy. Through the front door window he saw a young guy standing there with a bundle of papers in his hand.

"You're Roderick McCready?" he asked. And when he'd agreed, and shown identification, the kid continued. "Serving you, sir," he said, and gave him a smile. Rick noticed a front tooth was chipped, and he wondered if it had been the work of someone who hadn't wanted to be served.

He sat in the quiet house, reading and smoking, and becoming more incensed as he read. She had turned his love for Katy into a ploy to steal her money and had given him no credit for all he'd done. And she'd accused him of murder and attempted murder with no proof. Most of it was a pack of lies. He thought again of wanting his hands around her thin white throat. He threw the papers across the floor and sat shaking with agitation and anger. Then he went over, picked them up, went back to the table next to where the pieces of the broken chair still lay as a reminder of the night she'd taken her, lit another cigarette, and started writing his answers.

***

Martin sat behind his desk, dressed in what Rick presumed to be his court shirt, which was unbuttoned at the neck and revealed a tangle of grey chest hair. He fixed Rick with those pale blurred eyes of his and sipped at his cigarette like a glass of rare wine. "No need," he said, "to get yourself worked up like this—it's all typical. This is the garbage they throw at you. They'd never get away with it in criminal court. We'll answer it—it's a good thing you've done your homework."

"They've turned the way I feel about my daughter into some dirty joke. They say I've damaged her 'psychologically'— it's all complete shit. How do they get away with this crap, and when am I going to get my daughter back?"

"You'll get her the weekend after next week's motion, I guarantee that," murmured Martin, not unkindly. "And you've got to think about additional funds: this case will call for more court appearances, cross-examinations, and discoveries. I'll write up your answers to this nonsense, but you'll have to come up with more money before next week's court appearance."

"You've gone through the twenty thousand?"

"Will have, by the time we get to court."

Rick stood up. He felt hollow and desperate. Martin would drain him, and he had nothing more to give him. He'd had to beg Steamy for the twenty thousand and assure her she'd get it back from the sale of the house. He thought of Mrs. Laughlin: she'd always talked to him when he'd had Katy out for her pram walk. She was a friendly and sympathetic woman whose husband had left her a bundle. And she didn't have kids, which was why she'd been so interested in Katy. Women had always liked him, until they really knew him. And sometimes that took time.

CHAPTER 33

Judge Albert Denning—who bore little resemblance to Britain's great late Lord Denning—was due to retire in two months. He was tired. The motions court's list was too long; the lawyers too verbose, brazenly ignoring the twenty-minute time limit; and there was an unrepresented couple at the end—always a nightmare. Now he was facing the weasel Martin Springer, who had been exposed as hiding evidence on behalf of the accused in his last criminal trial. He had barely escaped disbarment. And his opponent was the strident Gerda Heller, who never shut up—even if ordered to do so by a judge.

Their clients were sitting with them: a handsome man with dark features who was wearing an open black shirt inside a sports jacket, and a rather pretty pale woman who looked abnormally stressed, a condition no doubt brought about by having her husband represented by the weasel Springer. He addressed both solicitors, although his narrowed tired eyes flicked over the clients.

"I had the unfortunate experience of reading the pleadings in this matter over the lunch break. If I can accept them, Mr. McCready should be serving a life sentence for murder and attempted murder, and Mrs. McCready should be taking time off from her profession to attend a rehabilitation center for drug addiction. In other words, they are both unfit parents, and should I be presiding at the trial I would be tempted to give custody of the child to some willing and good-living relative—if one exists. Fortunately, I won't be hearing the trial.

"For the present time, as a condition of the adjournment that both parties are requesting, the father may have the child for the weekend. I understand he was the main caregiver during her brief lifetime and he has not seen her since his wife's departure. You experienced solicitors can work out the details of her delivery and return. I shall deal with nothing else at this time, and will put this motion over to the next long motions day as I predict dealing with such allegations will take considerable time.

Such considerations as the sale of the matrimonial home, spousal and child support, and a shared parenting arrangement should be worked out by two such experienced lawyers. Collaborative law's the fashion now, even for the litigious.

"I will interject and make a suggestion for Mr. McCready, who is here today, and who appears able-bodied and employable. Perhaps, Mr. McCready, you should consider finding a job, not to undermine your considerable efforts in parenting this child since her birth. Your wife has hired and is paying for a nanny. There seems to be little reason why this cannot continue and you could obtain employment—just a suggestion, Mr. McCready.

"This motion is adjourned to the next long motions court's date. All matters will then be heard by the presiding judge, including costs."

"Happy now, bitch?" Rick asked, as they left the courtroom. "That's all I asked you for the other afternoon and you could have saved us both a bundle, but no, you had to have your day in court. And for what? What time do I pick up Katy?"

"Stop speaking to my client," snarled Gerda. "I'll convey her wishes to your lawyer."

"How much will that set me back?"

"He can pick her up at eight Friday night, and bring her back at five on Sunday," said Rose, in an audible whisper.

"Tell your client that's not a full weekend, and I'll bring her back the same time I pick her up."

Martin Springer suddenly came to life. He came to Gerda's shoulder and his long nose and chin, with his small pale eyes, close together, made him look like a particularly ill-disposed rodent—so unlike Gerda, whose black gown and crisp white court shirt, with starched tabs, seemed tailored by Dior. Martin's gown was long and rumpled, and his shirt looked as if it hadn't been laundered since his last trial.

"He's right," he wheezed, "What's your client doing—rationing the kid? He's the guy who used to take care of her every day, or has dementia set in with her drug use? We shouldn't even be here, the result's so obvious. And no way is my client facing cottage traffic at five on a Sunday night. I would suggest nine but we'll stick to eight."

"She's on solids now. I'll give you those plus her formula, and I'll give you her new schedule when you come to pick her up."

She wanted to cry. Just when she was bonding and Katy was adjusting, here he was disrupting it all, interfering and taking her away from her again.

"At least we're rid of Denning," Martin wheezed. "The old bastard's retiring, although he'll probably be back supernumerary. He won't be able to resist coming back to torture us all."

"At least he tried to persuade your client to get a job."

"None of his damn business, Gerdie. It's equality now and you'd be the first to clamor for it. We've got a genuine house husband, and if we get a modern judge, he or she'll be the first to see it."

***

"He's getting her next weekend," Rose sobbed to Del that night, rocking the sleeping Katy, "just when she's getting so used to her routine and bonding with me. It's really cruel: a little five-month-old."

"Get used to it. He'll end up with a couple of weekends anyway. Be happy they don't go back to the old status quo and he has her all week, and you have her only on weekends. I know judges who'd do that, but not Denning—he's old school. Sinclair might. She'd buy right into Rick's continuing to be a home daddy, and you'd end up paying a fortune in child and spousal support."

Del was so smart. Fred was right, she should have gone to law school. And her choice of Fred was such a good one. She didn't want a man telling her how to run her life—and Fred didn't: it was the other way around. But nobody seemed to mind.

On Friday night she packed a small suitcase for Katy—diapers, jumper changes, dry baby cereal, jars of puréed fruit and vegetables—all with a list of instructions. He arrived early. She answered the door and handed over Katy with her suitcase.

"Remember me kid?" he asked, his voice husky, his face grazing the pink bundle.

Katy looked at him, brows drawn together, obviously not sure.

He went down the front steps, Katy in his arms, carrying the suitcase that he suddenly pitched across the lawn. He then walked to the car, put Katy in the car seat in the back, and drove away much too fast, the tires squealing in a cloud of dust.

Rose collapsed in tears. "That's what scares me—he's so damn impulsive. Did I tell you he threw Mom's ashes down the toilet because he was mad with me about the house title? He might do something. You just don't know."

Del stood looking at her, her face pale and shocked. "You never told me about Mom's ashes," she whispered, "that is so awful." Rose didn't answer. Del's reaction made her reason for not telling her obvious.

***

At ten the next morning, Rick phoned and asked for Fred. Katy was fussing and he wanted the suitcase. Would Fred meet him halfway?

"I'm so sorry Fred," moaned Rose, "You don't know how sorry."

Fred smiled. "He's a head case Rosie; best you get rid of him. I don't mind him ruining my Saturday morning. What's a golf game when you can drive and meet the world's biggest shithead?"

After the door closed, Del spoke. "Fred's a saint," she said solemnly. "There's absolutely no one like him. And I did my share of shopping at some seedy dumps before I got lucky with Fred."

Rose nodded. "We should clone him."

"Clone?" asked Gwennie. "What's that? Would that hurt Daddy?"

Del and Rose laughed. It was good to laugh when nobody felt like it.

CHAPTER 34

When Rick brought Katy back on Sunday night, the fighting started.

"She just started remembering me, and then I had to bring her back so some nanny could take care of her. An' what do you care, you're working all day. Why not let me have her? You're wasting money on a nanny when the biological father is willing and able."

It was so strange to hear him refer to himself as the biological father, a phrase no doubt picked up from Martin Springer. "This should be settled anyway. We split time with Katy and the cash from the house sale."

"I won't have Katy bounced back and forth like a rubber ball, and it's criminal for you to want half the house money when you contributed nothing. I'll split the increase in value with you and that's it. The market's going through the roof, but you're not walking away with half the money Mom left me."

He gave her his usual tight smile, with eyes full of hate. "You forget, Rosie, the next day you made a gift to me of half —my old divorce lawyer will be my witness. There's a 'presumption of sharing,' when you transfer into joint, that's what Martin said, and he's one helluva lot smarter than your tight-assed ice goddess. They both charge an arm an' a leg, which means we may be walking away with zilch, with Katy a nervous wreck like her mother. She'll be taking a kid's version of your anti-anxiety pills at age five."

"I can't talk to you. You can have Katy every second weekend and that's it. And I want the house sold."

"Martin says they're keeping the kids in the matrimonial home now, and we take turns going there, a week on and a week off, 'cept I don't know where I'd spend my off week. Perhaps Steamy has a spare room now that the kids are off to college."

"No more garbage," Rose yelled. "Elena won't want to work every second week and it's disruptive for Katy. She's a little baby and thrives on routine. Look how she fussed when you took her after a week."

"She got over it. She was smiling away at me when I brought her back. She's my kid, every cell of her, and until you broke up this marriage I was the guy in charge. You don't remember that, do you?"

Del came out and took Katy, who was starting to fuss, from Rose's arms.

"Don't fight on my doorstep: you're upsetting your daughter. What have you done with my sweet, shy, little sister? This is not the sister I knew."

But he was gone into the darkening early fall night, tires squealing, running over Del and Fred's newly sodded lawn and leaving ugly gashes.

"Sorry," said Rose, "I know I've changed. Sometimes I don't know who I'm angrier with, me, for being so stupid, or him, for being such a bastard."

"Better tell Gerda to get a wiggle on," said Del. It was Mom's expression, usually aimed at Rose who was always late. They both smiled, remembering.

***

The next day Rose phoned Gerda's office about the cross-examination. "We're on it," said the receptionist. "The boss scheduled a whole day on September twentieth for your husband, and Mr. Springer will do you on the twenty-first. It's a combination cross and discovery—to save you guys time and money."

"Tell Gerda that I want the house listed: he'll squat there forever. I'm going to stop paying the carrying costs."

"Will do, but I believe it's part of the relief claimed in the motion. I'm sure Martin won't object. He's hot to trot for bucks, an' he told Ms. Heller she may not have him to kick around much longer. She said, 'He must be running short.' Martin Springer won't carry anyone, not like Ms. Heller."

"Can I sit in?"

"Better not. We don't want any hostility ruining the manuscript. Don't worry, you'll get your copy—it'll be expedited to be available for the motion."

Chapter 35

Katy was five months, and so cute, and bright, and pretty, with her dark curly hair, black eyes, round cheeks, and petulant rosebud of a mouth. She had adjusted to Rick's picking her up and smiled as she sat upright in his arms, after only a moment's hesitation.

"A Gerber's baby food baby," Del called her. "He probably gives her cake and cookies all weekend," she whispered to Rose, who scowled as she packed up her daughter's things for another weekend away.

"He has all her food, formula, changes, and pull-ups in her little suitcase. Mrs. Garafolo, who lives down the street, ran into me at the clinic. She said he parades her up and down the street in her million-dollar pram and she sits smiling at everyone like a little diva. The women on the street think he's just wonderful and can't understand my leaving. He's told them he's a published author and works from home, and that I found someone with more money. Mrs. Laughlin, the widow, really has her eyes on him, bringing him pies and casseroles. She's over fifty, but her ex left her loaded. God, how I wish he'd be out of my hair and into her bank account."

"Do you really wish that on some simple good-hearted widow? Let him get another Steamy."

"Whom I suspect gave him twenty-thousand for Martin's retainer."

"These women all have hearts of gold."

"She's not a hooker—just a little raunchy: she was kind enough to warn me even if she's helping him out now. You're too smart to believe in clichés."

"Oh Rosie, how you've changed! Where has my quiet, sweet, innocent little sister gone? My mother's favorite—not 'a piece of work' like she used to call me."

"You adapt," Rose replied.

On September 20, the evening following Rick's examination, Rose met with Gerda at five o'clock.

"How'd he do?"

Gerda chewed her lower lip, which was missing her usual well-applied lipstick.

"He was quite amazing: he should be an actor. He may be a genius, although an evil one. He had a perfect excuse for his application lies: he said it was to meet True Connections' criteria so he could meet 'a better class of girl.' He described his first wife's canoe 'accident' with wet eyes and a broken voice. No wonder he wasn't charged. He wants a week-on, week-off arrangement for Katy, and half the house money. He says you insisted on sharing it. He had a perfect excuse for the doped milk—he said he was trying to 'soothe' you, as he feared you were in the throes of post-postpartum psychosis. And he didn't dump your mother's ashes in the loo, he said—he found your accusation 'vicious' and feared you were becoming 'delusional' from drug use. I didn't know they taught Psych 101 in first-year engineering. By the way, Martin is still with us."

"He borrowed money from Mrs. Laughlin, the rich widow on our street."

"You know that?"

"No, I guess that."

"I'll run over a few questions Martin may ask."

"I'm not worried: the truth is horrendous enough."

"Martin will empty your Ativan bottle and count how many you've taken this month."

"I won't take it with me."

"How will you describe him as a dad?"

"I'll be fair, but I've got to say he's impulsive in many aspects of his life and may harm her later on."

"But not as yet?"

"Not as yet, except for throwing her suitcase across the lawn and driving too fast with her in the car."

***

Martin Springer took pride in his cross-examining. He would still be using this skill as a top criminal lawyer but for the John Rossi tapes scandal. He feared he'd never live it down. John's disclosure of these tapes to an undercover police officer in an adjoining cell, and his lawyer's knowledge of them, had doomed both Martin and Rossi, who was currently doing three life sentences for the torture and murder of three international students. Martin was doing well as a family law specialist, although his lack of credibility among certain judges aware of the Rossi fiasco was not helpful.

Martin began the cross-examination by asking, "Isn't it true that you were a totally incapable mother, so incapable that your husband had to take over the complete care of this infant?"

After five minutes, and several under-the-table kicks to Rose's shins from Gerda's high-heeled boots, Gerda said, "I have to visit the john. How about you, Rose?"

"No discussing the case, ladies," Martin ordered. "You're in a cross examination, Ms. McCready."

Upon entering the bathroom, Gerda grabbed Rose by the arm.

"What in the hell's wrong with you? Every time he starts with, 'Is it not true that . . .' you agree with him like a lobotomized robot. He's making chopped liver of you and you're helping him. If you don't stop, you're losing this case. Start defending yourself. Say you were a new mother and nervous. Say anything, but don't just sit there like a dummy and agree with everything he says."

"I'm sorry," Rose whimpered.

"You should be," stormed Gerda. "You're helping him win this case."

"Quite a long bathroom break, ladies," wheezed Martin. "May I ask the topic of conversation?"

"Actually we were talking about you, Martin, about your past as a criminal lawyer."

"Let's not waste more time," muttered Martin. "I charge my hourly rate, even if it's gossiping lies about me in the washroom. I'm surprised at your lack of professionalism Gerdy: I thought more of you." Gerda merely smiled.

The cross-examination continued, with Rose starting to assert herself, but the damage had been done. Gerda and Martin had lunch together "to discuss settlement."

***

It was the day after Rose's examination and Rick had an afternoon appointment with Martin Springer. He and Martin had established a camaraderie, which would have gone even further had Martin not stamped him as a viable money pit to be badgered for additional funds at every opportunity, even making the generous Mrs. Laughlin frown, perplexed by his constant requests.

When he entered, Martin was tilted in his high-back recliner, his feet on his desk, smoking his usual butt from an open package, from which he removed another and flipped it over to Rick as soon as he sat down. As usual his pants and open shirt looked slept in, and his eyes looked as if he'd spent the night before in a local bar. His secretary, who was dressed as casually as Martin, but with an even more exposed chest, served Rick a coffee with a hand displaying nails that were a different color on each finger. The coffee had slopped into the saucer but she ignored it, advising him, between chews on a massive wad of gum, to "give me a shout if you want a refill." Rick found it all very relaxing.

"So how'd she do?" he asked Martin. Martin smiled before answering and sipped another inhale from the butt moldering between his stained fingers. "Terrible," he said, "just terrible. It seems our ice goddess Gerda didn't prepare her, or if she did, she didn't listen. She agreed with every damning thing I put to her, fitting right into your hopeless mother criteria. It got so bad Greta hauled her off to the washroom to caution her, and when she came back she improved, but she couldn't erase those damaging admissions, which I'll read verbatim to our motion's court judge. By the way Greta paid for lunch and we talked settlement."

Rick's smile matched Martin's. He'd suspected this might happen.

"Of course," droned Martin, his familiar wheeze surfacing, "few in this field have had my experience in cross—I never knew an opposing witness I couldn't destroy."

"It all sounds great," said Rick, his spirits rising for the first time in weeks. "It looks like we've got a shot—Katy's fine by the way."

Martin lit up again, Katy appearing to be the least of his worries. Rick waited for the inevitable. "You received my last statement?"

"You'll be paid, right after the hearing."

"Better before," said Martin. There was a silence, then as an afterthought, Martin added, "Of course a lot depends on the sitting judge."

Chapter 36

After one adjournment, due to the lack of ready transcripts, the long motion was to be heard the last week of November. Katy was a knowing, precocious eight months, who never fretted, but beamed when going with her father every second weekend.

"She's doing so well," said Rose. "Why don't we keep things as they are, but we'll put the house up for sale and see what we get. But no doubt you'll miss all your free food donations and cash handouts from the rich widows on the street."

"Nope," Rick replied. "I want her half-time, and the court can decide about the house. You can't list a house in November, anyway."

"You're not thinking of Katy, you're thinking of you, as always, and if you keep this up Gerda and Martin will own the house."

"Then settle."

"Not on this crazy fifty-percent deal you can't seem to shake."

Then he was gone, wheels squealing, as usual going much too fast.

"Perhaps he'll crash it, some day when Katy's not with him," she said to Del.

"Don't count on it. You'll find out some day he used to be a race-car driver, just like all the other goodies you've found out about him."

***

It was a cold Thursday in November, and there were only two long motions to be heard. *McCready vs. McCready* was scheduled for two p.m.

"Damn," muttered Gerda to Rose, "It's Hollwell. She's a total idiot: a roaring feminist who prides herself on being politically correct. No kids, so you won't get a smidge of practicality. She's been appealed from time and again, but the judges never want to hear them. The last thing the Court of Appeal wants to hear is a family law appeal, so she's safe until she orders a spousal beheading. Robbie phoned yesterday and they told her it was Getty, who'd have taken instructions from his wife, mother of six. This is a nightmare."

"Get an adjournment."

"Your Honor, I notice we're only scheduled for three hours. The examinations and issues in this matter are extensive. Would you consider an adjournment so that all issues may be dealt with properly during a day's sitting?"

"Mr. Springer?"

"I strongly object, Your Honor. A counsel with the experience of my colleague should have no problem dealing with these matters in the allocated time. My client has shown commendable patience in waiting since early August to have this matter dealt with. He has been forced to accept access every second weekend with his daughter, a child to whom he was the main caregiver since birth, until she was abducted by the wife who has her parented by a nanny. He's currently in the matrimonial home, which is fully equipped with a crib, bath, and even a pram, ordered from London by my client. My client is the new man: a full-time caregiver of a child with a working mother."

Justice Hollwell's eyes shone with appreciation. She had been waiting for the new man and now here he was, sitting with Martin Springer, a notorious sleazebag, but his client looked handsome—even paternal.

Gerda tried. She gave a litany of Rick McCready's sins: his refusal to work, his impulsive conduct, his sponging off his wife, the suspicious death of his first wife, the dubious occupation of his second, even the deadly glass of milk to the applicant-wife. Then there was the disruption, inconvenience, and the uselessness of having a nanny for two weeks a month.

"None of this is relevant, counsel, none of it. What matters is his availability and his former excellent parenting of the child. Your client agreed at discovery that before she left he was an exemplary father. Surely it is better to have the child with her natural father rather than a hired nanny, competent though she may be.

"I feel tempted to have Mr. McCready parent the child every week, but I notice that he is only asking for the child half the time and that is what I am awarding him. This is the equality that we, as women, have been seeking for so long. Mr. McCready may stay in the matrimonial home until a trial and Mrs. McCready will pay the carrying costs, and fifteen hundred a month, which is what she paid her nanny plus one-half guideline support for the child."

Gerda kept arguing but Madam Justice Hollwell was firm. She had made what she'd considered a fine decision; moreover, a modern and enlightened one. The whole scenario pulsed with sexual equality.

Martin wanted costs. Her Honor hesitated, even when he read his offer. The offer concerned the splitting of house proceeds, something that had not even been touched on.

Martin handed her his Bill of Costs which caused Her Honor to lose her smile.

Forty-five-thousand dollars—even though the wife had been carrying the home, and they had been agreeing on weekend access without the court's help.

"I'll fix the costs at fifteen-thousand on a without-prejudice basis, and either party may choose to revisit them after a trial."

Rick was smiling as he got up to leave the courtroom, and when he passed Rose, crumpled and devastated, and still sitting on a court bench, he said in a husky yet confident voice, "Sorry Rosie."

"I can't afford it," she later complained to Gerda in her office. "I'll have to pay Elena the same $1500 as if she were full time, pay him for Katy, and carry the house. And I'll end up buying her food and clothes, work like a dog to meet expenses, and come home exhausted. And it's awful for Katy, all the driving and lack of consistency. Can't you appeal?"

"It's an interim order and I'd have to get the Court's permission. They won't allow it. It's a stupid order, but not so outrageous that they'll let you appeal. She'll cover her ass in her written reasons—she knows the score: been there, done that. What a fucking nightmare. It's times like this that I hate practicing. But in fairness you really flaked out in the early part of your cross. Every time Martin said, 'I suggest that. . .' you agreed."

"I know. I know. I'm not blaming you."

But she was. Gerda should have told her exactly what to say, even if it were a pack of lies, like the ones she suspected Martin had fed Rick. It was Thursday, and on Friday Rick would come for Katy and keep her for an entire week. During this time she'd have to put in long hours to meet her court-ordered expenses. It was all so depressing and unfair, especially when she'd grown so close to Katy. She asked herself why Rick was doing this. Was it in some perverse way to punish her for leaving him, or for not drowning in the bathtub as he'd hoped? Or was it for money, which always seemed uppermost in his mind? Or did he really love Katy? Was he even capable of love?

Chapter 37

"Where's my daughter?" Rick said, the Friday following Hollwell's order, smiling at the door at seven-thirty. "You better say a long goodbye: you won't be seeing her again till next Friday night. Martin turned out to be worth the cash." He'd come early and had waited outside in the car, but when he'd knocked at the door she'd kept him waiting, although she knew it was cold and time for his access.

Through the glass of the door he watched as she zipped up the pink snowsuit, and saw the round, solemn, small face, framed by a hood fringed with white bunny fur. He took her eagerly as Rose reluctantly handed her over.

"Glad to see your ol' man, Katy-Bird?" he said, holding her high. A smile crossed Katy's face and he saw Rose's face tighten. She handed over the packed satchel, the same one that he'd thrown across the lawn that first weekend.

"It's all organic, I puréed it myself and the feeding instructions are enclosed." Her voice was tremulous and what she said insulting, as if he couldn't feed his daughter, when all those four months before she'd stolen her he'd been the one feeding her and doing everything else.

"I'll be sure to give her hamburgers for breakfast," he replied. "Losing your memory as well as everything else?" But she'd closed the door, and he pictured her crying inside and he was glad of it.

Katy was quiet, but when he'd placed her in the car seat in the back of the heated car and had gotten behind the wheel, he heard a soft hiccup of bewilderment. He started to sing softly, "You Must Have Been a Beautiful Baby," a number from Alf's golden oldies collection. He had a great Irish tenor—"perfect pitch," Miss Swinton had declared, before urging him to join a youth choir for training. It was out of the question. Alf had said the same about his voice when he'd heard him singing along with his tapes: "a young Bing Crosby," he'd called him. "Jack of all trades, master of none," another line from a song he couldn't remember.

But it was dead-on. He was a failure at everything, too fucked up to focus—except as a daddy to Katy.

He kept on singing and Katy had gone quiet, but when he looked at her through the rear-view mirror he saw she had a little smile. Perhaps, he thought, deep down in her baby consciousness she remembered all those "Melancholy Baby" numbers that had helped her survive hours of colic. Or perhaps she just liked the sound of his voice.

When they reached the North Toronto bungalow she was asleep, lulled by the warmth of the car's heater and his singing. She woke up when the car stopped and he kept singing and talking away to her. She kept fixing him with those black eyes and soon she was smiling away again. He unzipped the snow suit, pulled off her corduroy overalls, and removed her soaked diaper. "Oh, oh," he said weighing them in his hand, "so much pee-pee." She smiled as if aware of the value of her production.

He noticed her thighs seemed long for a baby, in spite of the fold of baby fat. He pictured her as a tall beautiful girl with curly rich chestnut hair, travelling around Europe and speaking perfect French from her years of attending the French Immersion classes that he'd insist on. And he'd be by her side, grey and distinguished, protecting her from unsavory influences. He bent and kissed the softness of her stomach.

Later, he started a ritual that would continue throughout his access periods. He'd have her lie on his bed and he'd rub her back and sing to her, and then when she was asleep he'd carry her gently to her crib, kiss her warm cheek, and tuck her in with snug cotton blankets. That first night she'd taken a while to go off, probably because of her car nap and new surroundings, and he'd marveled at the peace that descended on him as he rubbed the small back and sang his love songs.

At breakfast, after she'd turned her head when he'd tried to feed her Rose's strained oatmeal, he'd spread blueberries and Cheerios on the apron of her high chair, and had made a game of her picking them up with her little clumsy fingers and putting them in her mouth. He then provided entertainment, singing and gyrating to his version of "Walkin' My Baby Back Home," all while he'd caught tossed blueberries with his mouth between musical pauses. Katy had actually laughed out loud, and he decided she was a genius, not just an audience of one, and that he'd get her a sippy cup rather than a bottle, and would encourage her standing and walking. After breakfast he'd danced with her in his arms around the kitchen, making little dance dips, and making her laugh again. His heart swelled with love.

At noon he'd dressed her in her pink snowsuit, and had taken her to visit Mrs. Laughlin, whose generosity had made her visit possible. She'd raved she'd never seen such a beautiful and obviously advanced child—and such an attentive daddy—and had offered a cookie, warm from the oven, which Rick accepted. He placed a small bite between Katy's four front teeth, thinking of Rose's disapproval with satisfaction.

On the Thursday night before her return, he'd spent extra time with her, singing and rubbing her back long after she'd gone to sleep. Then on Friday he'd delivered her to Rose, who clutched her as if saving her from an infant firing squad, even though Katy had fussed when he'd left. He'd driven home too fast, chain-smoking with the car windows open and music blaring.

Upon his return, rather than watch TV, he lay down on his bed. He felt Katy's absence with a hollow intensity. He thought of distractions—a casino visit, even contacting the Bergman twins, who although expensive, were known for their innovative threesomes. But he cancelled such thoughts. No distraction could fill this void. And he knew that he could not, and would not, live without her.

CHAPTER 38

Rose had spent Rick's access week doing extra hours to increase her pay. Then, on the Thursday of the Friday before Rick was to return Katy, Gerda phoned.

"We have to talk."

"Nothing worse, I hope."

"How could it be worse? It's about me—but you may not be happy."

Rose walked along Queen, looking at the Christmas window displays. Simpson's had a Christmas Winter Wonderland, with Rudolph flashing his red nose and Santa waving his arm. She thought of how Katy would love that by the time she was two. Such a smart little baby, those black eyes of hers following her around the room, and her little crow of delight when she came over after a day of absence. And Elena said she was crawling and trying to stand. She would never share her with Rick, with his dirty mouth and squalid background. He would contaminate this beautiful child as he had contaminated her. But she would save her.

Gerda was smoking when she entered the waiting room: Rose saw her through her half-opened office door. Strange, she didn't think she smoked. Gerda called her in and butted out her cigarette in her coffee cup. Not like Gerda at all.

She told her she'd been appointed to the bench, based on her successful appeal and committee work, perhaps even her political involvements, and that she was happy about it, although stressed. "But the downside is you'll have to get another lawyer."

Rose sat silent. Then she said in a low voice, "I'm finished."

"Stop it. I'm waiting for the house to sell before I'm paid, and I've got you a replacement. I've told him about you, and he says he'll wait as well. He'd appreciate a retainer for disbursements, but he won't die if he doesn't get it. His rate is far less than mine and everyone likes him, including the judges. He's not a shark like me. Even better, his office is in Mississauga. I've got your file ready and you can see him next week. He's very accommodating."

"I've got Katy tomorrow night until Friday the next week. I don't want to miss time with her. This one week on and one off is hell."

"It'll have to last a while: you're not even on the Court list yet, so you're stuck with Hollwell's order unless he does something completely outrageous—and he's too smart for that.

"Here's your new lawyer's card: Daniel Levine. He practices on his own: it's good he has a great legal clerk. Make an appointment. Here's the file—everything's there, including Hollwell's reasons for judgement and Arnie's report."

She stood up, a tall, slim, figure in the darkening office, but Rose remained sitting. "I do appreciate what you've done. I'll miss you a lot."

"Not as much as you think . . . just a hunch."

A strange comment, Rose thought.

***

Rose phoned Daniel Levine on her cell on the way home. She assumed there was no way he'd be at his office after six on a Thursday night and that she'd leave a message.

He answered. "Levine's office, Danny speaking. Can I help you?"

"Rose McCready. Gerda Heller gave me your card. I want to make an appointment. I'm getting my daughter tomorrow night for a week. I don't want to miss any time with her, so my appointment will have to be the week after. I have my file. You may want to look at it before you see me."

"Gerda's brought me up to speed: she's upset about that last ruling. I'm happy about her appointment—she'll make a great judge—but you may not be."

She couldn't say, "You're right," so she kept quiet.

"Where are you now?"

"On the Lakeshore, heading west. I'm staying with my sister and her family in Mississauga. I can't afford anywhere else."

He gave a sympathetic sigh. "If you want to drop the file off at my office, I'll make it my weekend reading."

She looked at his address on the card. He practiced from a cluster of townhouses where dentists, accountants, and other professionals had offices, off Highway 10, northeast of Square One Mall. "I'm on my way," she said.

***

The brick townhouse contrasted with Gerda's high-rise office, and the white sign, D.M. Levine and Associates, Family Law, hanging from a wrought-iron stand, seemed a little hokey, especially as there were no associates, just a law clerk. She parked her car in the back parking, and carrying her file, walked to the front of the house and slowly up the wet stone steps.

She knocked softly, using the huge old-fashioned knocker, and then when no one answered, turned the door handle and stepped inside. The reception area off the hall was small, with just a desk with a phone and computer, and a small leather couch and chair. To the left, through an open office door, a man in his mid-thirties was sitting behind a desk talking quickly and earnestly on the phone. He was going bald, but the hair remaining was dark and curly and he was not disguising his baldness with a comb-over. He wore dark-rimmed glasses, slightly tinted, and a tweed jacket over a dark T-shirt. She knew without waiting to see that he was wearing jeans and that he didn't work out. And that he was dressed much too casually for the office—but that he didn't care. He contrasted with the immaculate Gerda, although much cleaner than Martin. But she suspected in twenty years their court gowns would be identical.

He told his client, obviously a woman, to come to his office on Sunday afternoon, "to go over things."

"Examination, Monday morning," he explained with an apologetic smile, beckoning her into his office. The smile revealed a row of perfectly straight, white teeth. No hidden plaque problems there. He'd obviously had a mother who'd taken him to the dentist—and possibly a periodontist.

She handed over her file. "I hope you specialize in dumb women because I rank right up there in the top ten. And I'm paying for it in every way. I'm told I've lost my sweetness. It's gone. I now have an edge developed over two years. And I trust no one."

He stood up behind his desk. She saw he was about her height and had a slight paunch, and when he pushed back his horn-rimmed glasses his eyes were bright blue. When he smiled, considering his teeth and eyes, he was attractive, not handsome, but attractive—if you were into short men who didn't work out.

"Are you hungry? There's a restaurant called Antonelli's in a plaza at 10 and Steeles. It has lasagna made by the owner's mother, the real deal made from scratch, plus bruschetta and tiramisu, all responsible for my gut. We can drive there in my car: we might be the only diners—the place is too good for the area."

She smiled her encouragement, but wondered about his approach. So he continued.

"It's been two months since my live-in dumped me so now I can date. Not that this is a date. It's break-up etiquette: you have to wait that two months, even if you're the dumpee. It lasted three years: maybe a little too long. She was a stockbroker who did very well, and her mother told her she should marry a rich Jewish lawyer. The problem was she made more than I did. We used to joke about it, but after the first few months it stopped being funny."

She found his personal approach disconcerting. He was so not what she'd been expecting. But he continued.

"I knew we were wrong from the first month and waited for her to come to the same conclusion—no point in hurting her feelings—but it took her longer than I thought. The guy's richer and taller and we're still friends, although I'd cross the street if I saw her on the same side."

She laughed, but gave him a puzzled look, as if wondering why he was making her a confidante of his love life.

"I'm telling you all this boring crap because you're going to be telling me about life with Badass Rick, and I don't want you to feel shy about it. You seem to be beating yourself up and I don't like it. We all make mistakes. They say only hairdressers know about their customer's private lives, but I think it's lawyers—if they're any good. And remember, in a custody fight, everything counts."

She agreed to have dinner.

He guided her, his arm under her elbow, towards a dilapidated Chevrolet parked with hers behind the townhouse. It was unlocked. "No way would I be lucky enough to have this piece of shit stolen. It's seen me through undergrad, two years with my dad, law school, and five years here in Mississauga, suffering with the suffering. I feel about her like I hope I'd feel about my wife after thirty years, knowing all about her quirks, but loving her—and them, even if she's rusty underneath, is hard to get started and coughs in the mornings. My mother says it's an embarrassment and she's threatening to buy me a new one."

She couldn't believe he'd just compared a fifteen-year-old car to a future wife. But she found him entertaining. And even better, funny.

"What do you do, Rosie? Something in the dental field, I believe Gerda said. I can see you more as an English teacher."

"So funny you'd say that. I was heading for Honors English, but became sidetracked because of family finances, and began a dental hygienist course After a few months I knew it was a mistake, but I stuck it out. But I always felt confined, you know?"

"You wished you were a pair of claws scuttling across the floors of silent seas."

She smiled. "I didn't think lawyers read poetry."

"I hear the mermaids singing, but they do not sing to me."

"You like him?"

"I love him, even after I found out he wrote some anti-Semitic stuff. I memorized one-third of 'The Waste Land' and then stopped. "April is the cruelest month," is a good bar pick-up line—especially if it's April, and you want to know if your target went to college."

She didn't comment, thinking dour thoughts of her fatal meeting with Rick McCready.

"I met Rick through True Connections. Mom had died and I was afraid of being alone. I didn't want to go to a bar by myself and True Connections is supposed to canvass its member's background. I was looking for a professional and ended up with a con man. And then it was all lies—everything."

Danny was quiet for a moment and then said, "These dating sites scare me. My dad's a builder and in real estate. Most of your Jewish purchasers want to see the finished product before they firm up a deal. It used to drive Pop nuts, but I think it's smart. If you meet someone through the ordinary channels—an intro by mutual friends, or even at a wedding—the guy's been checked out. They'd hardly invite a scammer. These sites are fed a bill of goods. Some bad stuff has happened."

"He tried to have me drown."

Danny turned the car into the mall a little too quickly.

"That must have slipped Gerda's mind."

Then she told him everything.

"You didn't go to the police?"

"No, I didn't want to believe it: it was too awful. And I thought he'd convince the police I was some sort of psychotic. He's a misogynist, among other things, but he loves Katy. I hate to admit it, but he really does. She looks like him, but she's got a sweet little soul. And when she gives me those smiles of hers, my heart just cracks in two. But I don't want her with him—he's too dangerous."

Danny sat in front of Antonelli's with the engine still running, looking straight ahead. "I've changed my mind about discussing your file through dinner. I want you to enjoy your lasagna and stop thinking about it. I want to see you laugh. You said you'd lost your sweetness. That's not true. You've mixed up sweetness and naiveté, and the fact that you're more experienced and edgy now doesn't mean you can't still be sweet, in fact it may save you from the next creep."

They had a carafe of house red to go with the bruschetta and lasagna, and talked about books and poetry. He favored Auden and she liked Dylan Thomas.

"I loved the way he used words—'boys wild as strawberries.'"

"Both of us should have been English teachers."

"I couldn't do it to my Dad. That's a direct quote from my mother. *You can't do that to your father.* My dad has a construction company and he wanted me to get an engineering degree and take it over. But after a month at Waterloo doing engineering, I was bored. I got a B.A. in humanities: English, philosophy, the whole bit. After I finished I went with Levine Construction for two years. I hated it. I told the Queen of Israel—sorry, that's my mom—that I wanted to go to the University of Toronto and get a master's in English. Then she gave me her favorite quote about my not doing that to my father—but she added, 'At least be a lawyer.' I was a B-average law student—but I was still called to the bar. Perhaps not loudly enough."

She laughed—it felt so good to laugh—"Is your mom religious? You call her the Queen of Israel."

"Esther Levine is the most observant Jewish wife in all Toronto . . . or maybe Canada. When she met Dad, she was one of Canada's best-known models, but nothing cheesy like walking down a catwalk—she made the covers of all the better magazines, even *Vogue,* she tells us.

There was even talk of her making it in Hollywood. She came from a family of ten in Timmins, and her father was a goldminer from Dublin who drank. She had a head of golden red hair, bright blue eyes, and was five-foot ten. Too bad I didn't get her height instead of her eyes. My sisters are as tall as storks."

Rose smiled. "I noticed your eyes right away."

"And then I stood up."

"You're the same height as I am."

"Give or take an inch." They both laughed.

"Anyway my dad, who'd lost his own family in the Holocaust, fell crazy in love. But one thing worried him: she had a mean mouth and called her own family members a bunch of Irish lushes—or Mick maggots, or whatever. He didn't want to take a chance on what she'd call Jewish people during one of her tantrums, so when he slipped on that five-carat diamond, he told her, 'You'll have to convert, you know.'"

"Poor Pop. He thought she'd just be a normal Jewish wife. That would have suited him fine. He's a very casual Jew, paying a little visit to shul on high holidays so he can chat with his buds, and atoning for his few sins on Yom Kippur. And that was it. But he underestimated my mother. Once my mother was dunked in that mikveh she became the most religious woman in the Temple, which she attends every Friday night after she lights the candles and prays. And she prepares a Shabbos dinner right out of *The Joy of Cooking*. She's collected so much for Israel that they give her a parade when she makes her yearly visit."

"You're kidding."

"Yeah, I'm kidding. But she does go every year and had me and my two sisters in a kibbutz until we all rebelled in our teens: we didn't want to join the Israeli army."

"Your sisters?"

"Rachel—well, we call her Ray—has a degree in commerce and basically runs the business. Dad wanted me there and it's all a big disappointment. He and Mom want her to marry but she won't. She may be a lesbian but she's never come out. It would upset Ma, who keeps talking about 'grandbabies.' And there's my other sister, Mimi, who's in medicine at McMaster, interning to be an oncologist. She's dating a Muslim, which bothers my mother, who worries about her converting. He's a great guy, does pediatric surgery at Sick Kid's, and I suspect has better things to do than discuss conversion—but it bothers Ma. I think she suspects about Rachel, but the day that she brings some girl home and introduces her as her future wife will be the day Ma leaves for Israel permanently.

"So I'm the prime suspect. She was very annoyed when Pamela dumped me: she couldn't understand anyone doing that to her wonderful son. And when I told her how relieved I was, she freaked out. I'm her favorite. She whispered it to me starting at age two—which was probably very poor parenting on her part. It pissed off my sisters, who took turns beating me up. I look more like Pop and she loves Pop—in her crazy Irish way. He's a great guy, not the second coming she holds him out to be, but a good guy. And compared to her drunken brothers and father, he's a prince."

All of this was recited in a flat monologue, which made it all much funnier. He reminded her of a comedian she'd once seen on a comedy channel.

Rose giggled. "You have such an interesting family. Mine was so drab compared to yours." Then she filled him in, about her accident, her parent's troubled marriage, and her mother's attachment.

"If I'd been braver I'd have rebelled, left, and had a life. But I was just a mousy little girl who read a lot and who worried about the sad-eyed children in Africa whose parents had died of AIDS, and abused animals and kids everywhere. That's when I started my Ativan addiction: one gram under my tongue before bedtime. Del says it causes early dementia, and it must have been in progress when I married Rick McCready."

"A sad tale, Rosie," Danny said, in an exaggerated Irish accent. "You were hanging on the branch like a little ripe cherry, when the likes of Rick McCready with his evil ways came strollin' by, and just plucked you off and chewed you up, pit and all."

She laughed. He could make her laugh and no one else had, not really. He was her Ativan, the salve she always knew she needed between herself and the harsh reality of life.

"Del said something like that—but she said peach and missed the accent."

They stayed until Gino, the waiter, brought the bill, and told them how tired he was, and then they walked out into the freezing deserted plaza. Rose looked at the dark grey starless sky and saw their breath like whiffs of smoke.

The car hesitated.

"It's like your wife after thirty years," Rose said, "Takes a while to get her started."

He laughed. "I'm so full of shit."

"No, I really owe you for what you did for me tonight. I don't remember laughing the way I did, never. Sometimes Del would make me laugh when I was in my teens, telling me about some of her dates. But I've never met anyone like you."

He was quiet for a moment, and then said, "You know Rosie you underestimate yourself. Your humor could cut steak: it's very sharp and funny as hell, but I suspect you've kept it hidden. Why, I don't know. And you're very pretty."

It was then she was pretty sure she fell in love with him.

When they got back to the office he parked his car next to hers, took her keys, and turned on the car's engine and then got back into the Chevrolet.

"Wait till it warms up—it's a nice car."

"My mother's."

"Too bad I'm your lawyer."

"Gerda says everyone likes you."

"When you're a B-average law student you develop your personality . . . as your lawyer it would be very tacky if I kissed you."

"Well," she said, "We don't want to be tacky, do we?"

But when she closed the door of the car, she blew him a kiss through its icy window.

Del was still up when she arrived home at eleven, "Where have you been? I thought the evil one may have driven you off the road." Rose filled her in on Gerda's appointment and Danny Levine, who, she said, made her laugh.

Later on she used some of Del's night cream and checked her eyebrows for strays. But she found it hard to sleep, even with the Ativan. She thought of Danny, who heated up her car before she got in, and who drove a dilapidated Chevy even though Del said his family was so wealthy. He thought she had a sense of humor. She smiled into the darkness.

Chapter 39

Months had passed since the Hollwell order, but the pick-ups and drop-offs had gotten no easier. Rick was standing at the door with Katy in one arm and the suitcase in the other, and the cold was surrounding them, but she wouldn't ask him in. "She's cutting her teeth," he said. "I had to walk her one night and drive her around another. I fed her the food in the jars you gave me, but she didn't eat like usual, so I doubled up on the whole milk."

She was sitting up in his arms smiling, and when Rose reached for her she seemed to hold back.

"She's used to me," he explained, "even calls me Da."

"It's hard on her being bounced around like this."

Her voice was sharp, and as she spoke she looked at the yellow headlights with snow, like flour, pouring over them. "Why not let me have her during the week, and settle for weekends like other dads?"

He looked at her, his mouth open in shock. Flakes of snow kept coming down and settling on the shoulders of his jacket and his thick dark hair, and the boughs of the spruce lining the pathway looked so heavy and the silence was so silver and solemn.

"Why would I do that?" he asked, his voice hoarse.

"Because it might be best for your daughter," she answered and banged the door shut.

She watched him through the glass of the door, standing on the steps, and then he turned and stamped towards the car, banging the car door after he entered and revving the engine as he tore down the pathway in a cloud of snow.

"Did you miss Mommy?" she whispered into the cool round cheek, running her finger down as she always did. Katy smiled.

Rose cancelled her four o'clock appointments the next week, and made up for it by taking patients at five the week after: she wanted to spend as much time with Katy as possible. By the next Friday night they were as close as before, with Katy out of her crib and sleeping tightly pressed against her every night.

"It's so annoying that I have to purée the food because that bastard won't do it, and he'll buy processed baby food filled with water they use to purée that costs a fortune. It's all such a farce: he's loading her up with formula when she should be eating solids, and he doesn't have the sense to give her whole milk. I'll stress that in my memo."

Del nodded sympathetically.

Danny phoned her on Sunday and suggested that they get a psychological assessment. "It's our only hope to change this week-on, week-off thing. It'll take two more years for this to get to trial and Katy will survive—but you won't. And if we wait that long the whole pattern will be so ingrained that a judge won't want to change it." She knew it would cost her, but she reluctantly agreed. He asked her to dinner the following Saturday, joking that she was his best-looking write-off.

"All right," she sighed.

"Don't wanna twist your arm." He sounded hurt.

"Sorry, I don't mean to be an ingrate: dinner would be lovely."

"Two on Saturday. Write out all your concerns and why we need an assessment. Bring them with you."

On Friday at lunchtime she went to Del's hairdresser for a styling: her hair looked good afterwards, feathery and flattering, and she picked up a low-necked sweater, left over from the Christmas sales at Holt's. She had good skin: the result of a lifetime avoiding the sun. She even purchased some dark, rich, red lipstick by Dior.

"Your black leather jacket with the fur trim?" she asked Del.

"Wow, Rosie, what are you doing on a Saturday afternoon going around dripping with glamour? Is there something I don't know?"

"I'm meeting Danny Levine. We're preparing to apply for an assessment and he's taking me for dins after."

"Would you ever get married again, Aunt Rosie?" asked Gwennie. "You said you never would. You said you didn't trust men, I heard you say it to Mom."

"Still don't, Snoop. But you can never be sure of what you hear when you know you shouldn't."

"I really liked Rick," sighed Gwennie, "but he turned out to be a total asshole. That's what I heard Mom tell Daddy."

"You're eleven and your language is disgusting," snapped Del. "Stop slithering around like a little snake and listening to conversations you're too young to hear."

Rose looked at Gwennie and winked.

Rick came at seven-thirty on Friday night. She had spent the night before puréeing and sterilizing jars of fruits and vegetables, even enclosing a carton of whole milk. She had strained oatmeal that was to be heated up, a whole carton that he needed to refrigerate. She felt her throat fill with anger at Judge Hollwell as she completed her last batch.

"All her fruits and veggies are there," she said. "It should be enough for the week, but if not you can buy some jars, but they're not as healthy as what I've made: mine are organic. And no more formula, just the whole milk—I even got that for you. And you have to watch her. She's standing up and trying to walk. Dr. Snowden says she's very advanced, of course she's almost a year."

He looked at her, eyes narrowed, with that bitter smile of his. "Quite the mommy we've become—better late than never, Rosie. Got yourself all glamoured-up, I see. Trying a single mothers dating site? Martin says your shark is now a judge, so you gotta get yourself a new lawyer. Not hard to find someone better than that bitch: a no-nothing ice princess. Why don't we quit all this? I'm into Martin for fifty-thousand borrowed bills, and it'll be ten times more before a trial's over. And what makes you think a trial will change anything? The kid's smart as paint, saying words, and knows me better than you, because when I have her I'm with her non-stop—no nanny for this daddy."

He held out his arms and Katy almost jumped into them, with a gurgled 'DaDee.' Rose's heart gave a dull lurch.

"Someone has to work," she snapped. "I've no time to stalk the neighborhood for rich widowers I can leech money from. You're such a useless, lying, piece of crap."

"Jealous, Babe?" he asked, and took off for his Mustang with Katy cooing in his arms.

"If," she said to Del, "I was connected, I'd have him whacked."

Del's jaw dropped: so unlike Rose, talking like that.

"Have you been watching *The Sopranos?*"

But Rose merely went into the television room, poured herself a shot of rye, and lit one of Fred's cigarettes, which astounded Del even more.

CHAPTER 40

"Lookin' good," said Danny. "It's been three months, I should take you home and introduce you to the Queen. I'd take you somewhere high-end tonight, but I'm not dressed for it. Of course, I'm never dressed for it."

"Good of you to take me anywhere."

"A collateral benefit of having me as your lawyer."

"You feed all your clients?"

He smiled. "Only an occasional lunch. You're exclusive."

She sat across his desk after handing him her pages, watching as he carefully and silently read through them. Then he sighed.

"It's too bad you dropped your future English courses for tonsil-gazing: a budding literary talent lost to CanLit."

"Are you making fun of me?"

"Never. It's great stuff, and you've painted a brilliant picture of a raging psychopath. But there's not a shred of evidence that he's anything but a doting daddy, except he hasn't got your talent for puréeing fruits and veggies. And Katy loves him as much as a one-year-old can. The outbursts, the erratic driving, we can fashion all that in—and his homicide attempts, but it's still a bit uphill. The assessor mightn't believe you about the drugged milkshake, and he can't give much weight to the canoe incident as he was never charged. And as for Steamy Arab, that seems a bit rich."

"But she told me to be very careful"

"I believe you, sweetheart, every word, but the assessor may not. It's too much: it reads like a B-movie plot."

"What if I saw Steamy and asked her about that canoe death?"

"She'd never tell you. She's probably scared of him, as we all should be. But that doesn't seem to stop him from loving his daughter, although we don't know how he'd handle a mouthy teenager. And she's a very useful tool to get Mommy to pay."

Rose shivered. Danny may have been a B student, but he had something better than a fine legal mind—he had an intuitive one. Gerda, clever as she was, was far behind him.

"You're so clever, so knowing. Please don't go on about your B-student status ever again. You just get it. You're cool, as the kids say, and I'm so glad Gerda got appointed and I have you."

He smiled, obviously pleased. "I'll rework this and make it into an affidavit. Judges don't want to make decisions on issues like custody. They just want you to give them the law, nicely served, and how it applies to your case. Nothing makes them happier than to have an assessment they can follow, especially one that follows their own inclinations. We just have to get the right guy. There's an assessor who makes a point of saying he'd never give a kid to a father—seems his was a bit of a brute. Martin would love him. 'Is it not true, Dr. Silk, that you have said time and again you would never recommend giving a child to a father?'"

His imitation of Martin's wheezing voice was perfect and she laughed. "Poor Martin."

"Don't underestimate him. He was a great criminal lawyer. He'll cross-examine you like a hostile witness if this goes to trial and the judge would end up feeling very sorry for you, which would not be Martin's intention—at all."

"Rick asked me if I wanted to settle yesterday. He's borrowed fifty-thousand from one of the street's widows to pay Martin."

"Terms?"

"The same. One week on, one off. 'Split equally,' that's his mantra. He wants half the house money. I'd give him half if he'd just walk out of her life—but he'd never do that."

They both sat looking at each other and then they laughed, bitter laughs, with irritation scratching at their core.

"We'll go to Jacques Omelettes on Cumberland: you're still young enough to make the stairs. It's a real French restaurant, but not so fancy that I can't go dressed like a slob. The waiters are French—from France—and they have French Onion Soup that's really like French Onion Soup."

"You've been to France?" It was a silly question, as he obviously had. He described a two-month trip to Europe with Ma and his sisters, and she told him about her cruise and the Vespa biker, saying that if she'd taken him up on his offer she'd have been scared off True Connections, and would never have met Rick.

"Or Danny Levine."

"Are you my compensation for Rick?"

"Probably. It's a nice thought—a well-deserved mitzvah. And you wouldn't have Katy."

"I know. But I can't give her the uncomplicated life I want. There's always these shadows and worries in the back of my mind, these reservations that he'll do something and that I have to turn her over again the next week. It takes all the juice away. Her birthday was last week and I had a cupcake with one candle on it. She let Gwennie blow it out. She thought it was so exciting and I wanted to cry."

They left for the restaurant.

"Before Mom died I used to worry about not having children because I'd never had a date. I'd even think of freezing my eggs, and then having the doctor buy the sperm of some nice, clever, med-student. It was so silly—but I'd had such a sheltered life. Looking back, I read my life away—when I wasn't chauffeuring Mom around."

"I'm sure you'll find someone up to the task for number two, Rosie."

They parked at the nearest parking lot. The fierce April wind and icy rain lashed against their faces, and he said, "If you say 'April is the cruelest month,' I'll never forgive you."

She laughed.

"We should try to avoid what's foremost in your mind and keep things a little light. We could see a fun movie after dinner, a *Sleepless in Seattle* sort of thing, or the one with Meg Ryan faking an orgasm in a crowded restaurant, but I checked, and there's nothing on but vampire garbage and superhero crap for the kids. So maybe we'll go back to my place for a drink."

"Wouldn't that be tacky?"

"I hope so."

She had steak and frites, which reminded her of Rick McCready—when she'd thought he really liked her, and Danny spoke French to the waiter.

"Trying to impress me?" she asked.

"Absolutely."

His condo was in the Manulife Building. "I rented an apartment in Mississauga when I was living with Pam—my year is up Sept.1st."

"You miss her?"

"No. She never knew about April being the cruelest month. But she's so smart, organized and successful—makes you want to puke."

"I'm not a bit like that, but I'm good with plaque."

They both laughed.

***

The apartment was surprisingly neat and clean. When she gave him an inquiring look, he read her mind.

"The Queen: she sends her cleaning woman every week. The apartment in Mississauga is more like me."

"Does she know you call her The Queen?"

"Probably. I think my sibs tell her. I just call her 'Ma' to her face but as I said, she's not one bit like a Ma."

He turned on the gas-lit fireplace and asked her what drink she wanted.

"This is so nice," she said. It was. She felt so good with him, so safe, so relaxed.

"I'm gonna take a shower," he said. "I really didn't plan this."

When he came out she saw that his chest was covered with black hair and he had a towel around his waist, "Didn't want to invite any comparisons with McCready."

The bathroom was so clean. She took a new facecloth from the cabinet and washed. She noticed that her hands were shaking: she did not want to disappoint him. There was a toweled robe hanging on a hook at the back of the door. She put it on and opened the top drawer next to the sink. To her relief there was a new unopened toothbrush and a tube of toothpaste. The dental hygienist brushed.

When she came out he was lying under the bedsheet, and she went over and sat on the edge of the bed. "I want you to know that I only had sex with Rick, and that stopped as soon as I got pregnant, so it's been a long time." She was lying—there had been the two disastrous one night stands, but they didn't count.

"You cold? Take off my bathrobe and I'll warm you up. I'm a hot guy: I've had complaints." She slipped off the robe and got under the sheet with him. She felt his hot hands run over her.

"You're so slim," he said, "like a teenager: you'd never know you'd had a baby." Then he took her hand and placed it on his penis. It was large and erect and she gave a slight gasp: it was so much bigger than she'd thought it would be.

"God did it," he laughed, "to make up for the height: and the chest hair for the hair loss. It was one of his better moves." And then they were lying together in the soft bed that smelled of him and shaving lotion. She was covered by his warmth and longed to be closer. He held up a condom and asked, "Will we dispense with this and see if I can live up to the task of being your dream sperm donor?"

She knew she should say no: it was too soon. The divorce was not yet finalized and this was the second time she might be having a shotgun marriage—if indeed he even wanted to marry her. But she whispered, "It's up to you." And let herself flow into him.

"For such an inexperienced woman, you're very responsive," he said later.

She threw a long slim leg over him to emphasize her sincerity. "And I'm sorry I was so noisy."

"Why?" he said, bewildered. "I love that I can make you cry out like that."

***

Later she listened to his breathing, basked in the warmth emanating from him, and felt a ripple of tenderness sweep over her. Rick had known all the right moves, all the exciting and controlling gestures, but they weren't comparable. It all related to feelings, she thought, perhaps stemming from the early whispered words of love from Ma, as compared to the sharpness of the physical attacks by Rick's mother. Rick had not built up a reservoir of feelings, only a pool of bitterness, while Danny had an ever-expanding core of love. And she was the lucky recipient. It was strange that Rick still seemed to have a spill-over for Katy. Perhaps it was impossible to entirely extinguish love's capacity. She felt herself drifting off and she hadn't taken her Ativan.

CHAPTER 41

"This," said Del, "is so gross. And not even a phone call. And do you really think it's wise to be sleeping with your lawyer?"

"You're getting this all wrong. It's not a sex thing."

"So you two spent the whole night correcting your affidavit. Do you really think I was born yesterday? His father's super-successful, his companies have built nearly every home in Peel County. He's part owner of that construction company, he and his two sisters. Big disappointment for Daddy that he's not working there instead of Rachel, who they say is gay, and who Mommy and Daddy are waiting to marry and produce grandkids."

"Who's your informant? Arnie Finch again?"

"Who else? I told you I'd be watching out for you. Rosie, you hardly know this guy—it's way too soon. And I don't know if The Law Society would approve. According to Arnie he'd been common-law for a few years. She's very smart and pretty, from a well-to-do Jewish family, and she's a portfolio manager for Nesbitt Burns. Word is she got sick of waiting for a proposal."

"What's he doing with me?" murmured Rosie.

"Exactly," said Del. Just then, Rosie's phone rang.

"Are you up for fish or steak—or Chinese?" Danny asked. "Or do you want to visit my messy Mississauga apartment that Ma doesn't have her cleaning woman visit? It has a balcony we can fling ourselves off if we lose our assessment motion."

"It's Sunday night, we don't have to go anywhere. I'm working tomorrow so we can order in—pizza with the works or I can make you an omelette. And I'll clean up your kitchen and bathroom."

"Rosie, where did I get you? You cook, you clean, and have multiple orgasms. And if April wasn't being so cruel we could make love against the balcony rail."

She laughed. This was what she loved about him: no one had ever made her laugh like this. To think she had almost gone through life without this funny warm man, who lifted her depression and filled everything with sunshine, even at six o'clock on a cold Sunday in April.

"Danny wants me to go over," she said to Del as she hung up. "He has a condo a few minutes from here."

"So much for my Sunday night roast beef dinner."

"Sorry."

"Just go. And you'll be going to work from there tomorrow morning, I guess."

"Is he nice, Aunt Rosie?"

"Yes. And he makes me laugh all the time—that's very important."

***

She stopped at Whole Foods on the way over and picked up some fresh-squeezed orange juice, a dozen free-range brown eggs, kimmel bread for toast, organic butter, a jar of unpasteurized honey, some organic cleaning fluid, with sponges and rubber gloves.

She arrived at the condo, travelled to the fifteenth floor, gave a timid knock, only to have the door opened at once by Danny who said, "She shops, she cleans, she scores," before kissing her, and who watched in admiration as she deposited her purchases in the fridge, which needed and got a wipe-down, and cleaned the kitchen and bathroom, using new washcloths and mop and a pail under the kitchen sink, all unused.

"Whatever got into you to buy these? Expecting a visit from Ma?"

"Dunno. Perhaps someday I thought I'd meet a beautiful hygienic girl, appropriately known as a dental hygienist, who'd want to sub for a cleaning woman. One who doesn't mind not eating out and who can even tackle my loo, which may be a step up from scraping off plaque and avoiding her patient's halitosis? I never thought I'd be that lucky at thirty-six, after all the discerning broads I'd dated, who'd never think of buying brown, free-range eggs for breakfast."

"A rooster for every hen," she said solemnly. "Every hen sexually fulfilled. You can tell by the yolk. And I can scramble them and finish while they still glisten. They must glisten. It was the only thing Marlene Dietrich could cook."

"You're too young to know about Marlene. Thirty-one, right? I checked it in the file. You don't need to worry about freezing your eggs until thirty-five. I'm five years older than you, and sometimes I feel twenty years younger, and at times much older, when you start throwing out some of your poetry quotes."

"You make me sound awful—a tedious, poetry spouting bore."

He looked offended. "But I love that about you. Two years with Levine Construction, three years of tax, torts, and corporate law, followed by human misery—in spades. But now I have someone who hears the mermaids singing."

"You mean that?

"Damn right. And I never knew anyone who needed my tender guidance so much. Nothing wrong with sweetness, sweetheart."

She felt her eyes burning. She turned away and he said "I'm going to fill up the tub with some foamy shampoo. And I promise I won't pull a Rick McCready and bring you a knock-out milk cocktail, because I want you to be awake when we make love. This will happen after we have our Pizza special and watch Sixty Minutes. I hope you like anchovies. I'm the only Canadian alive who likes Anchovies on his Pizza—some places don't even carry them anymore."

"I like them."

"You're too much, Rosie."

And later, much later, as she lay warm against him, she said, "The week after next I want you to meet Katy and Del. Del thinks it's very poor taste for a client and her lawyer to be sleeping together. She's legal clerk and office manager with Pascal and White, and she had enough savvy to take an instant dislike to Rick McCready. I should have listened. She's everything I'm not: shrewd and practical and I do love her—most of the time. I love my niece Gwennie more, but she lacks her mother's smarts. She actually liked Rick."

"She had an excuse. What was she? Ten?"

"Nasty," she mumbled and pinched his gut, which showed he hadn't worked out for years.

***

Out of the four nights left until Katy was delivered on Friday, Rose spent three with Danny. They took a pass on Tuesday, as he had a motion on Wednesday in Toronto and wanted to prepare. She got her hair done and a mani and pedi, and when she walked in Del rolled her eyes and said, "Here she is, right out of *Vogue*, the glamorous Rosie McCready, for whom I've kept a chicken breast and half a baked potato. Thanks for telling me you'd be using your bedroom tonight and wouldn't be eating out."

Later, just after he'd phoned to say goodnight and told her he missed her, Del walked in. "Don't want to be a snoopy bitch, but I wasn't pro-active enough with Killer Rick, and I'm concerned about this Danny thing. Number one, you're not Jewish, and Jewish guys prefer marrying Jewish girls—and not shiksas. And all of Danny's girlfriends have been Jewish. And his mother, who's quite aggressive, is very, very, active in the community. She may not be happy about you. That is if it goes that far, which it may not."

"Is this straight from Arnie's mouth, with a little general knowledge from Pascal?"

"Of course. But I don't want you hurt again."

"His mother converted: very seriously converted. I know it's been a bit intense but I really care for him, and I think he cares for me. I love his mind: he's so funny and we laugh a lot and the sex is good too, but it's because I loved his mind before I loved the sex—if that makes sense."

"And his family is wealthy."

"That doesn't matter either, except it means he's not after mine, although there'll be nothing left by the time it's over. He drives an old Chevy and dresses like a first-year college student."

"He can afford to do that," said Del, with disapproval, "but I don't like it. Clients are a superficial lot and they go for two-thousand-dollar suits from Harry Rosen's. You should see Pascal when he attends a mediation—right out of *GQ*. He's trying to prove something with all this casualness, but clients like to see a guy who looks like he makes big dollars. You should tell Danny that."

"No, you tell him. I'm working on the Chevy. It will break down some night at Jane and Finch and someone who's in hiding will think he's undercover."

"Well," said Del, "that would certainly take care of future concerns."

***

There was, Rick suspected, something going on. When he'd come to pick up Katy, Rose looked as if she were going on a date—hair, make-up, the whole bit. He'd thought she'd be deflated losing the ice-goddess,

210

and perhaps back off and they could settle. But no, she was as bitchy as ever—even more so. That Friday night after he'd picked up Katy, he gave his daughter a lolly and parked in the driveway of a nearby house that appeared empty.

Rose came out after only about five minutes, tripping along in high-heeled boots, wearing a jacket with a fur trim he hadn't seen before, and took off without waiting for the engine to heat up. She was such a rotten driver, so crazy and erratic. He followed her, knowing she'd never notice, too focused on her destination. He trailed the car through a maze of streets, and finally into the entrance of a large apartment building on Highway 10. She parked in the visitor's parking, poorly as usual, and trotted, rather than walked, to the building. There was something confident, something new, about her walk. He found it irritating, and the word cocky crossed his mind.

He parked a distance from her car, and taking Katy from her car seat, where she was still sucking on her lolly, walked with her in his arms to the apartment. There was no concierge, only a line of names with entrance buzzers. He scanned the names. Then he recognized one: D. Levine. It rang a bell. It was the name of her new lawyer, the one Martin had brushed off as "no big deal." He felt his throat swell with anger. She was shagging her lawyer to cover her legals. This meant the case would never settle. Katy was pulling at his hand, obviously bored, so he attempted to swallow his rage, but as they walked past her car he made an ugly scratch across the car doors with his keys.

They drove towards Toronto, and he played the music station rather than singing. But then she started to fuss, so he started to sing. He knew she loved to hear the sound of his voice. He saw her in the rear-view mirror and she was smiling. His heart started to swell with love. "Does Daddy's little sweetheart want an ice cream?"

He saw them reflected in the Baskin Robbins window, a tall man wearing a black leather jacket and tight jeans, and a small figure wearing a pink snowsuit with a hood. "We want an ice cream for a very good little girl," he said, and then picking her up instructed, "Point to the flavor you want, sweetheart." She merely smiled, so he chose chocolate. Nothing bland about Katy, he thought, thinking of her mother, who, it seemed, was no longer vanilla.

"Tired *querida?*" he asked. He never spoke Spanish—too many bad memories. But he spoke Spanish to Katy. It made them even more special. She shook her head and he smiled, knowing she fought sleep, and that he'd have to back-rub and sing even longer that night. After he'd wiped the chocolate from her mouth and dressed her for bed, he lay down beside her and sang "Moon River," a song he'd always found sad. It reflected his mood. He carried her to her crib, as she'd fallen asleep faster than usual.

He went to the TV room, lay on the sofa, and considered his options. With Rose no longer having to pay her lawyer, the case could drag on for years. He'd been lucky with Hollwell; in fact had Martin asked for full-time custody, she said she'd have given it—a terrible error on Martin's part. But a new judge could make a different decision and he could lose Katy. His borrowed funds had been eaten up by Martin, who badgered him for more at every opportunity. He thought of Rose strutting into her lawyer-boyfriend's apartment that night, and felt choked with hatred. But he had not created this monster, she'd always been there, hidden under dresses covered with pink flowers and a cloak of fake sweetness.

While he lay there thinking, the black cactus that had been list-less and spent after Patsy's drowning started to bristle and stretch its arms, clawing at his mind. It had not been present during the bath-room episode: she had taken the milk willingly—he had merely been the bartender. But this new venture would need active planning. He thought of a series of car accidents caused by everything from cutting the brake fluid line—much too detectable—to loosening the lug nuts on her tires. The results would be made worse by her hopeless driving. He thought of the car spinning around on the 401, the target of a long line of speeding cars, a derelict tire bouncing across the highway. And his meddling would be impossible to prove. He doubted whether the spaced-out airhead had ever had her tires checked.

***

"I thought I'd drop in," he'd told Chester, who was now general manager of a large garage off Bayview that had a vehicle repair service. It was Saturday morning, the day after he'd returned Katy, always a hollow and depressing time. "What's shakin' man?" asked the familiar voice, and for a moment he relaxed and let the memories come, and he was back at Lord Dufferin with Alf as his teacher and his small gang of followers, which always included Chester.

"Just wanted to touch base and have my tires checked," he said.

"No problemo, Ricardo," Chester replied. They exchanged smiles of understanding. He felt good that Chester was doing well and appeared happy in spite of that god-awful wife of his.

He watched carefully as the mechanic checked his tire lugs—"nothing loose," he assured him, "it must be something else." He refused to leave it for a general check-up, but said he'd be back if the problem resurfaced. He had witnessed what he'd needed to see.

"On the house, ol' buddy," Chester assured him. And then asked, "Still battlin' it out for your kid?"

"Still," he replied. Chester placed a sympathetic hand on his arm and said, "Sorry." And he remembered the "Sorry" from Chester in Miss Swinton's classroom, the day after Pa had hung himself. He was the only one who'd said it. "Good to see you dude," he said.

***

On the Tuesday of the following week he'd gotten Katy off to sleep, and had recruited Mrs. Laughlin to babysit, telling her he had an emergency appointment with his lawyer. But by the time he'd reached Del's place, Rose's car was gone. He drove over to the apartment building but she had not parked in visitor's parking. Then, while he sat there chain-smoking and seething with frustration, her car appeared, but with a man driving. They headed into the underground parking where there'd be cameras all over. It would be safer to do it some other time, and he was sure there'd be other opportunities. Strange, her lawyer-boyfriend driving her car instead of his own, but perhaps the scratch had alerted them to possible vandalism: another impulsive act on his part that had backfired. He headed back to Toronto, deciding to pick up a little gift for Mrs. Laughlin at the Yorkdale Mall. She was, after all, funding his case.

CHAPTER 42

It was the second week of April, and on Friday night he delivered Katy back to Del's at seven-thirty as usual. She was beaming, with a mouth smeared with chocolate.

"She's only a year—she's too young for garbage food," Rose protested.

"It's her late birthday chocolate."

"She's already had a cupcake with a candle."

"I'm surprised you have time for such things." His grin was fixed, but his eyes were narrowed and dull with hatred.

"I always have time for my daughter." She hated herself for the defensiveness in her voice and the way her throat closed.

"I know you and the new lawyer are a thing now. I guess that's one way to pay for your legals: he's taking it out in trade. He can afford that. You can use some of the kinky little tricks I taught you—he should flip me a few extra bucks for that."

"Go to hell."

She grabbed Katy, who'd started to fuss about being deprived of her chocolate supplier, and banged the door closed, watching him through the glass panel as he swaggered towards his Mustang, so cocky and delighted that he had upset and enraged her.

Carrying Katy, she went into the family room where Gwennie was reading to Del and Fred was watching a hockey game.

"He knows about Danny."

"He's stalking you," spat Del. "Who has Katy while he plays Junior G-Man? You may have to get a restraining order. Not that it surprises me. *Nothing* about him would surprise me."

She walked with Katy to the bedroom, zipped her out of her pink bunny suit and pulled off her soaked diapers, kissing the soft folds of her tummy and noisily blowing on them, making Katy laugh. Del came and stood by the door.

"You should tell Danny he's stalking you."

She didn't answer, just kept making Katy laugh so that she wouldn't cry herself.

CHAPTER 43

There were no trials during the summer of 2006 on the Family Law floor of the tall building on University, but the motion for the custody assessment was to be heard on a long motions day in late July. Even then Martin Springer wanted the parties examined, and would not agree with Danny's choice of assessor, so it was put off until October for the cross-examinations and transcripts, and to canvass the availability and schedule of an assessor, who was to be decided upon by the motions court judge.

During the summer, Rose was spending every other week with Danny, and had introduced him to Del, Fred, and Gwennie, but most importantly Katy, whom he handled like fine china, carrying her from room to room and pointing out things she actually tried to pronounce.

"She's such a smart little kid," he raved, as she sat bolt upright in his arms, smiling, "and walking around like a big girl. She should be going to playschool next year, so she'll have friends. Ma sent us all to playschool 'for social interaction,' she'd say. The truth was she wanted rid of us."

"A great idea," Rose said. It would get Katy away from Rick during the day on his weeks with her, and she'd chose a place where they guaranteed healthy lunches and snacks—although she'd have to pay for it. She wondered where he was getting the money for Martin's appearances: he seemed to be running up fees like a crazy man. She imagined the street's widows were tapped out.

Del and her family had met Daniel and all of Del's concerns had vanished in an instant. "Daniel is an amazing guy," said Del, "reminds me a little of Fred. And he's so good with Katy. Even Gwennie said he was 'awesome' . . . though I thought that Judy Blume book he bought for her might be a little frank."

Danny did not resemble Fred in the slightest, but Rose did not say so. Del seemed to regard it as a great compliment.

Rose went with Danny one night to meet Ma, his father, and sister Ray, as Mimi was on call at the hospital.

The Queen reigned at a large stone mansion in Forest Hill. She was tall and thin, with her hair colored the same shade it had been when she'd been the first Canadian model on the cover of *Vogue*. She chatted incessantly, whether out of forced sociability or slight nervousness.

"Danny speaks so well of you, Rose, so much better than he did of those lovely dynamic girls who were all so crazy to marry him. I don't think they were his type. We all have our types, don't we?"

Rose gave Danny a quick glance and read his mind. Before him, her type had run along the lines of the psychopathic Rick McCready.

"And he's doing your divorce. So romantic. I've been so lucky with men. I grew up surrounded by Irish drunks and then I ended up with the most wonderful man in the world."

This last declaration was punctuated by her sweeping across the floor and planting a crimson lip tattoo on the forehead of Danny's father, who rolled his eyes in synthetic misery, but who, Rose suspected, loved every minute of it.

"Jesus, Ma," muttered Ray, "cool it. Do you want Rose to think we're a bunch of lunatics?"

"It's okay," said Danny, "Rosie is very tolerant: she appreciates emotional displays."

"She's come to the right place," said Ray. "We're *loaded* with emotional displays."

Between the chicken soup with matzo balls and the blintzes, Ma put Rose through a grueling examination—second only to Martin's—about her having children, even to the point of having Rose describe Katy's delivery, and then her thoughts on conversion.

"You're not Jewish, Rose, I know that. My mother was a Presbyterian, a rather bloodless religion—'tight-assed,' as the kids say—but good solid people. She turned Catholic for my drunken father. I attended the Kirk once out of curiosity, and my father whacked me black and blue for putting my nose inside anything but the Catholic Church. Not that he ever attended, though God knows he had plenty to confess. Cirrhosis of the liver got him before God did. It was a great relief for us all."

Rose smiled her understanding and support. "My parents were Presbyterian, but I've read a lot about Judaism. It's a wonderful faith—such an emphasis on charity—and Rabbi Hillel's writings are so similar to much of the teachings of Jesus. I would love to attend Yom Kippur. It would be like going to confession, but I'd be there all day. And then to have the shofar blow at the end—so sad and mystical. Nothing fascinates me more than the history of the Jewish people."

Danny sat with his mouth open, while Ray started to choke on her blintzes and Sol Levine cleared his throat loudly. But Ma beamed.

"So glad Danny brought you home, Rose," she said. "Danny always makes the right choice at the end, though sometimes it may take him longer than it takes others."

"You're something else," Danny said on the way home. "Where'd you get all that information about Judaism? Ma is out of her mind with joy. You're very calculating: I've seen an entirely new side to you."

"I read up on it. I was sincere: it's a great religion. I'm sorry—I wanted her to like me, and I believe she does. And I like your sister Ray, but I believe Ma will take the pressure off if there are other grandchildren."

"Are you trying to tell me something?"

"I may be."

He reached over, took her hand, and kept holding it. She looked at the rear-view mirror and saw a car that seemed to be following them. But she didn't mention it.

Chapter 44

It was autumn and the leaves from the maples lining Del's driveway had turned to yellow and were dropping to the dark earth. The air was heavy with the smells of sweet, rich decay and the mists of October. That morning Rose had recited the first few lines of Keat's "Ode to Autumn" to Danny, but he was too rushed to appreciate them. And she was almost three months pregnant.

It was seven-thirty on a Friday night and Rick McCready stood on the steps of Del's Mississauga residence, Katy in his arms, his face flushed with anger.

"You're living with your runt lawyer—now he's even taken you home to meet his rich folks. Why the hell don't you settle this? Christ, you're a fuckin' caution—screwing your lawyer to cover your legals. His family's rich and he's wasting time slumming, doing divorce work. Martin says it's worse than dealing with criminals."

At this point Katy, who was squirming in his arms, said, "Bye-bye, Dad-dee," and trotted inside to see Gwennie.

"Can't you limit your outbursts to when Katy's not here? Don't think I don't see you crawling around after us—and spying on me. Where's Katy when you do your snoop work? Or is your poor little daughter asleep in the back seat while you spy on her mother? And our divorce is final next week. I can't wait. I should sue True Connections for false advertising."

"What a mouthy bitch: it's your new Jewish family and your big-mouth sister. You pretended to be all sweet and innocent when I met you but you were phony from the word go. And no thanks to me for agreeing to split the divorce from all other grounds. Number one, I ran out of food so she had a hamburger and regular food like an ordinary kid. Number two, if I ever hear her call your creep lawyer-boyfriend Daddy, I'll run his wrecked car off the road."

"Do you know I just recorded your whole speech for the assessor?" Rose lied.

"Fuck. You."

He went stamping through the leaves and she heard the banging of the car door. She wished she *had* recorded him. She hadn't even thought of it.

CHAPTER 45

The cross-examination for the appointment of the assessor was to take place the following week. It was to be very brief. Rick had wanted to sit in but Danny had objected.

"Let him read the damn transcript, Martin. I won't have him in here upsetting my client. If she didn't think he was a threatening asshole she wouldn't have needed the assessment. Now I want it on record that I'm amending my pleadings, and asking for a restraining order against your client for following and threatening mine."

"Hope you're not getting personally involved," wheezed Martin with a snide smile. "A mistake for you to get emotional like this. Now if it were me, it'd be a different matter. But I'm not smiling Danny Levine, scion of Levine Construction."

"Enough, Martin, we both know this is a waste of time, so don't waste anymore."

Rose sat in the examiner's room, Danny beside her, facing Martin, who asked her to justify seeking an assessment, considering the time and expense involved. She agreed that Rick had never been cruel to Katy in any way, but insisted that his impulsivity and lack of transparency would make joint-parenting impossible. Challenged by Martin to concede that any fears regarding Rick related solely to herself, she stated Katy was only eighteen months old, and that "things might change." Martin then accused her of dealing with "hypotheticals." She went through it all with a sinking feeling, thinking how Martin would diminish and twist her every word as he had done before.

It went on, and on.

Then Martin suddenly stopped.

"You care to have her clarify any of her answers, counsel?"

"None. But I do want my client to clarify why she wants a restraining order against Mr. McCready."

"Rick McCready has followed me on several occasions since our separation. As recently as two weeks ago he suggested he would drive my lawyer's car off the road if Katy ever called him Daddy—that was at an access exchange."

"So this restraining order is not just for your safety, but for the safety of your lawyer?"

"Yes."

"Ah, Danny," wheezed Martin, as he ambled out of the examination room, "The plot thickens. Can't we agree on an assessor and I'll consent to a restraining order?"

"Abrams has been doing this for forty years. He's consented to start by November 1 and thinks he can finish by February. I don't know why you're fighting me on this."

"Doctor Ludlow's younger and smarter, and she'll have a more modern approach about joint parenting. She can start right after the Christmas break and she says she can finish in eight weeks. And she's cheaper."

"See you in court, Martin," Danny replied.

"Why are you so adamant about Dr. Abrams? And how bad was I?" Rose asked.

"Ludlow and Hollwell are good friends: I've seen them lunching together. And they tell me when Hollwell was practicing, Ludlow was always her choice of assessor. There's no way Ludlow won't pander to Hollwell's ruling. And stop beating yourself up, you were fine. I shouldn't have asked about the restraining order."

The motion to appoint an assessor was heard by a new appointee, Judge Edwards, who had made his reputation in criminal law. He had, however, heard of Dr. Abrams and his book on alienation, and appointed him as an assessor in the McCready custody matter. The restraining order motion was adjourned on Mr. McCready's undertaking that he would not come near Mrs. McCready or her solicitor without their express consent or during the process of picking up or returning Katy.

"Waste of time and money," muttered Rick loudly as they were leaving the courtroom, "driven by your spite, and wanting to hurt me through my daughter. But you're hurting her too, bitch."

"Control your client," said Danny. "He's just broken his undertaking by attacking mine."

"Do you screw all your clients, Levine? And I'm not just talking dollars."

"Enough," bellowed Martin, so that everyone on the benches outside the court turned to look. "Shut the fuck up, Rick, and I apologize on behalf of my client, Dan, but from what I hear you've placed yourself in an interesting position."

"None of your damn business, Martin," muttered Danny as he and Rose swept by them, "You've enough to worry about controlling your own nutter."

Later, Rose saw Rick standing in the parking lot, hands on his hips, as she and Danny got into the Chrysler, Danny getting behind the wheel.

"Where's your beat-up Chevy? Gotta use my wife's car?" he called out.

Danny swung past him, barely avoiding knocking him down.

"I'm pressing charges against you for that, Levine," Rick yelled.

Rose covered her face with her hands.

"If I didn't know he'd tried to kill you, I'd think the putz was jealous."

"It's going to get worse. In two more months I'll be showing, and then he'll go off even more, saying I don't need Katy as I'll already have a baby, or better, that I'm not capable of caring for two children. The house has to be sold. I can't keep supporting him."

"We've gotta think about getting married," Danny said softly.

"I thought you'd never ask," she sighed.

Then they both laughed.

Chapter 46

Ma arranged for the mikvah with her favorite rabbi, Rabbi Goldman, officiating. Mrs. Klein removed her toenail and fingernail polish and supervised the ritual before the mikvah submersion. "I was supposed to be naked but I had a sheet around me," she whispered to Danny, "and there were some elderly men with beards davening for me in the shul, which I thought was such a comforting touch. I think I need all their prayers."

Danny merely nodded solemnly. She suspected he found it all somewhat overwhelming and would have opted for a quick trip to City Hall.

Rabbi Goldman performed the marriage ceremony and the entire family plus Del and Fred were present. They all went to the Four Seasons for dinner later on. The sisters, whom Rose really liked, presented her with a set of Royal Doulton dinnerware, Sol gave Danny a cheque for $100,000, and Ma gave her a necklace with a huge golden Star of David sprinkled with diamonds, special-ordered, and a velvet bag filled with religious books, mostly written in Hebrew.

"Are you really going to wear Ma's necklace?" Danny whispered. "You could knock out your enemies with your Mogen David and they'd never survive."

"Sure I'm going to wear it. Why wouldn't I wear it? It's perfectly gorgeous."

Danny gave her a little smile and did not reply. She noticed he had taken off his yarmulke right after the ceremony. She would leave the children's religious education to Ma.

"My Hebrew name is Rebecca," she said.

"Just as long as I can keep calling you Rosie," he replied. "And just in case you were going to mention it, no, you're not taking a yearly trip to Israel with Ma. But you can go once —with me."

"I promised your mother I'd go to shul with her every Friday."

"That's fine—as long as you don't want me to go. Ma's excessive. Remember I didn't ask you for any of this. This was your decision and

I'm glad you're taking it seriously. But I'm not making any of these decisions for you."

She nodded. He was right: it had been her decision. But she was happy about it. And it made her feel even closer to him.

Chapter 47

Dr. Abrams was to start interviewing for the assessment on November 1 but then said he couldn't start until he read the pleadings. He then said he feared reading them would taint the interviewing process—possibly invoking prejudice—so he didn't read them. Then he was called as an expert witness on another file, so nothing happened until the middle of February.

Danny and Katy were bonding: Rose watched them together, amused by Katy's reaction to his gentle teasing. She was almost two and talking, and Danny spent hours pointing out objects and having her repeat his words. They were living at the Mississauga apartment but the child exchange still took place at Del's.

There was a Montessori School around the corner from the old residence, and Rose decided that the advanced Katy would benefit from playing with children in her age group or older. She and Danny could take turns picking her up and dropping her off during their week. But she needed Rick's cooperation.

"I'm enrolling Katy in Montessori," she told Rick at the next exchange. "She should be playing with other kids: she's so bright. She'll get a hot lunch and we'll do pick-up and drop-off depending on our weeks. It's expensive, but I'll pay as usual."

But he was looking at her five-month bump.

"Fuck. Knocked up again. Martin said something about you getting married, and I shoulda guessed you'd be up to your old tricks. What do his folks think of him marrying someone like you? Jeez, rich Jewish people and him the only son. They must be pissed. Didn't think their son would end up with one of his clients—a drug-addicted dental hygienist with a bun in the oven."

His last expression reminded Rose of her mother. It seemed so quaint and incongruous, considering the rest of his speech. Such a strange man: not a man who would ever even listen to, let alone use, such an expression. She looked past him and saw snowflakes falling softly, and looked at his dead dark eyes that did not go with his mirthless grin.

"I'm glad you picked Abrams," Rick said. "The rate he's going he won't be finished by next summer. Martin says the longer he takes the better. The trial judge won't want to disturb something that's working."

Rose tried to swallow the anger that was blocking her throat.

"But it's not working: it's disruptive. That's why I'm suggesting Montessori—it will be a constant in her life. And you have to list the house—you're tying up all my money. If she goes to daycare, you can get a job—not that you'll want to consider it. I'm quitting in my seventh month—I'll be too clumsy to manage it."

"I hope you do better with the new one than with Katy. Why don't you stop all this crap? We'll divide the house money and you'll let me have her, or we'll go on like we are."

"Why divide it? It's gone up in value and you can have half the increase, or $250,000, whatever is more. That's a good return for someone who hasn't put a cent into anything and was married less than a year. And you know you'll never pay back that poor widow you've been scamming to pay Martin."

"Two-fifty's chump change. Think how rich I'd be if you'd drowned in that tub with Katy's insurance plus the house. It would have kept Katy and me in style for a lotta years."

She stood in the doorway frozen: under the porch light he loomed, an ominous figure, his lips tight over his white smile, his eyes as dead and hollow as a corpse. She watched the dropping snowflakes and a chill swept over her. Everything she'd feared was confirmed. She knew if she'd stayed he would have killed her, as surely as he'd drowned the young pregnant schoolteacher.

She held Katy's hand, soft and trusting in hers. Rick bent over and picked her up, kissing her warm cheek. "Coming with Daddy?"

Katy nodded and smiled, waving at Rose as he carried her through the drifts that swept flour-like clouds from the waves of snow surrounding Del and Fred's driveway. She stood there watching them, stiff with fear, knowing he was capable of anything.

"Daddy missed you," Rick said, as he settled her in the backseat of the car. "Do you know how much Daddy misses you when you're not with him? Daddy has no one to eat with and no one to cuddle and sing to at bedtime."

Katy sighed. Then the small voice from the backseat spoke, "I here. We eat and have cuddle to-night."

"But then you have to leave."

"No. I tell Mommy and I stay. You be happy then, Daddy?"

***

That night Rose sobbed her concerns to Danny. It was after they had gone to bed and he became angry. She had noticed this before, whether it was a feeling of helplessness or frustration, it was predictable. She suspected the truth was that he could not remove the source of her upset—in this case the presence and behavior of Rick McCready—and he found it infuriating.

But she could not resist telling him everything. It was so cathartic and his anger soothed her. It was like a comforting blanket. She deplored her own selfishness but could not stop.

"It's bad for the baby, you getting upset like this. Perhaps Del could do the delivery and pick-ups at the door. If I was Italian, I'd have him whacked." Danny: another fan of *The Sopranos.*

"Don't Jewish people have people whacked?"

"Sometimes, I'm sure, but they're not as organized about it. But I'm contacting Abrams tomorrow and telling him to stop fucking around. He starts the assessment as of now—or I'll get another idiot appointed."

"But you want Abrams, you don't want anyone else."

"He doesn't have to know that. I'll tell him the delay is having a terrible effect on you psychologically and you're on the verge of having a miscarriage."

"Please don't do that. I don't want him to classify me as some sort of neurotic—which I am. Use Katy. Say the week-on, week-off is disruptive, and that you're going to need him to make some recommendations about Montessori."

"Anything else?"

"I always know you'll do the right thing," she whispered.

"I appreciate your confidence. Now that you've got me all keyed up, I'll probably need one of your stress pills."

"They're addictive." There was nothing better than transferring her anxiety: she felt so relieved.

Chapter 48

Dr. Abrams's office was on the fifth floor of the Medical Arts Building. It was small and airless, with one wall filled with serious-looking books and a shelf in front of a small window filled with pictures of the Abrams's extended family, all holding diplomas and dressed in graduation gowns. Attached to the office was another small room packed with toys and books, with a one-way window through which the doctor could observe the interaction between his patients and their offspring. There was even a microphone where he could overhear all conversations. The reception area was approximately the same size as the office, and had a pleasant grey-haired receptionist who distributed lollipops to child patients upon request.

Dr. Abrams started the interviewing process on February 15th and saw Rose first.

"Wear your Mogen David," Danny had advised.

"Why?"

"He's old-school: he'll appreciate it."

"How old is he?"

"About one-hundred and fifty: think Moses and the tablets."

"Be serious."

"About seventy-five."

Dr. Abrams had thick white hair, a grey brush-like moustache, and a saggy furrowed face that was surprisingly tanned, as if he had returned from a Florida beach or had developed some liver problems. The pronounced furrows in his face made him look like a benign bull-mastiff. She noticed when he smiled at her that he still had his original teeth, which were large and somewhat stained. He would have benefitted from a visit to her, she thought, but she had stopped working. She had never realized how much she disliked her work until she stopped doing it.

"So you're a dental hygienist," he said, smiling again. "Enjoy your work?"

"Not really, but it pays well."

"Your father-in-law's Sol Levine?"

Dr. Abrams was thinking she didn't need the money.

"I'm Danny's wife, but I like to be independent."

He shrugged, clearly not an adherent of feminism.

"And you're due . . . ?"

"The end of April."

"I'm sorry for the delay. Now what I'll do is interview you and your former husband separately and then with the child. Then I'll see you together. At the present time I understand that you see the child on alternate weeks, and your position is that it's disruptive for the child. You'd prefer the more orthodox every-other-weekend access for the father and you wish to have actual care and control the rest of the time. Am I correct? You don't believe the present situation is working for you or the child, although the child's father is willing to accept it?"

"Right."

The interview took two hours. She told him about her accident at three, her years with her mother, her anxiety, and her dependency on anti-anxiety drugs.

The last revelation appeared to interest Dr. Abrams. "You're obviously over-empathetic and sensitive. Have you ever thought of getting some therapy rather than drugging yourself?"

She knew she shouldn't have told him—but she knew Rick would, making it much worse than it was.

"I've improved now that I'm with Danny. He gets upset on my behalf and it makes me feel much better."

"Rather hard on Danny."

"Yes, it's very nasty of me."

They both laughed. After that everything got much better, and by the time two hours were up they had reached True Connections, which interested Dr. Abrams.

"Why a dating site? And why one in which only professional men are possible partners?"

"I just thought they'd be superior and better able to support me and the future kids. I'd always wanted a family. My sister Del warned me that I'd be found dead in a ditch somewhere using dating sites. I never thought that someone would make up a phony CV to impress a possible partner. And he was so smooth—he always had an excuse for being broke. Del nailed him right away. Then she had her firm's investigator check him out. But by the time she told me about him, I was married and pregnant. But not in that order." She felt embarrassed just listening to herself.

Dr. Abrams sat, bent over, his right hand cupped over his eyes, occasionally giving her a hum of encouragement.

"He knew all about my being left a share of Mom's house and later on we had joint insurance policies for Katy's future education. I went along with everything. Perhaps it was because I wanted to believe him so much, or that he scared me with his temper. I was not sexually experienced, and he did things—some were exciting. Please don't mention this in your report: I'm so embarrassed about it. His second wife was a stripper and he took me to meet her at her club. She warned me to be careful. Please don't mention this either—I don't want to get her in trouble. I really liked her."

Dr. Abrams was shaking his head when she was getting ready to leave and said he was looking forward to their next meeting. It must be, she thought, like reading the worst trash ever, just listening to her.

***

"How'd it go?"

Danny was picking her up after the assessment. She somehow feared Rick would be there, lurking among the snow-covered cars—a silly fear as it was his week with Katy. As well, Danny did not want her driving which was still hazardous, the road filled with patches of ice. He thought it would be a threat to her swollen belly—not that she had ever been a good driver. Danny made her feel valued and she felt a warm glow when she saw him after an absence.

"How do I love thee, let me count the ways."

"Never mind Lizzie Browning, how'd it go with Abrams?"

"I felt I was giving him exciting material for his memoir, *Weird Patients I Have Known*. I don't believe he knew much about dating sites, so perhaps he should be paying me for all the new information. I don't think he approves of my anti-anxiety pills: he thinks I should have had therapy. But I told him you were my therapist and absorbed all my anxiety, which we agreed might be hard on you."

"Hold it, Rosie, you're not there to talk about me, but heavy topics like Katy's upbringing and your concerns about McCready's future parenting."

"You know he's not a bad dad and he cares about her, it's just that he's such a dangerous human being in every other way."

"You mean you're not worried about him insuring her and pushing her down the basement stairs someday when he's down to his last poker chip?"

She felt chilled, even with the car's heater blazing hot air. "He'd never do that," she said quietly.

This wasn't like Danny, especially given that he knew how anxious she was. She knew he was sorry as he reached out, took her hand, squeezed it, and said, "Sorry, darling, that was a very stupid thing for me to say."

It was hard on them both, she had to remember that. He was not the Mister Cool he liked to project, but worried about things in his own way. And it was all because of her. She'd make it up to him and produce a big, fat, smiling baby, anxiety-free as a result of his mommy's anti-anxiety pills that she felt guilty about taking while pregnant.

Snow was coming down and building up beneath the wipers. They kept driving and got caught in the pile-up at the Gardiner exit. Danny broke the silence. "The car was acting up, so I took it in for a check-up after I dropped you off: one of the tire-lugs was loose. It's good you weren't driving." She didn't reply, but thought of Rick, although she didn't mention it. Why worsen an ever-worsening situation? Danny kept on. "It was a rough morning. I had Driscoll's motion and Greenley sitting. She accepted all of Bitch Booker's lies and made an order the poor bastard can never comply with. Who said it was professional negligence to go before Greenley if you were representing a guy—Gerda, I believe. I repeated that to Driscoll and he said, 'I guess you're professionally negligent.' I told him, 'I didn't get up there and lie like Booker—if that's what you mean.' And he said, 'maybe you should have.' You know a lot about this legal profession is overrated.

"Fuck, I just remembered, Ma wants a family meeting tonight. She says it's very important. I said, can I bring Rosie? And she said, 'She's family, isn't she?' I thought you'd like that."

Rose smiled. "I love your mother."

"The most difficult woman in the world: she needs all the love you can give her."

"Your dad loves her."

"Absolutely."

"Why the hell are we heading for Mississauga? Let's turn around and go to Ruth's Chris and have a steak—you're due for a shot of iron—and I need sustenance if we're having 'a very important family meeting.' The doctor's too important to be there, so I guess there'll just be unimportant people like you, me, and Ray."

She took his finger and bit it gently. "You're very important: No one more important than you."

He smiled, "We sound like the Queen and Pop."

Danny had a drink at Ruth's to fortify himself for the meeting, and she had ginger ale. It was bad enough to be addicted to anti-anxiety pills while pregnant, let alone drink.

They drove to Forest Hill and parked in front of the imposing residence. Lights shone through the glass entrance doors, and she could see the orange flames of the fireplace through the large front window. They entered and saw Ray and Ma sitting on the sofa in front of the fireplace. Pop was absent. They both got up and hugged them. Rose sat in a chair next to the fireplace and found the warmth comforting. But she felt uneasy. Perhaps it was Ray's expression and the unfamiliar scowl on Ma's face.

"Where's Pop?" Danny asked.

"He's in bed."

Then everyone went quiet.

Ma continued. "He was dizzy yesterday morning and I was worried. I got him down to Mount Sinai and they did a battery of tests. His blood pressure was through the roof and he may have had a slight stroke. He's on medication and dismissing the whole thing, but the doctors are concerned. And I'm concerned."

"Why the hell wasn't I told about this? This happened yesterday and you wait till tonight to tell me. Jesus Ma, what is your problem?"

Danny's anger was a sign of caring. Now Rose understood and was glad she was there.

"Sweetheart," she said, putting her hand on his arm, "you're being told now. I'm sure your mother didn't want to worry you until she had all the information."

Everyone breathed a sigh of relief except Danny, who kept scowling.

"So?"

"Well," continued Ma, "this morning I get more news. Your sister Rachel informs me she's in love—with a doctor, a *lady* doctor, whom she met six months ago in San Francisco. This is not just an ordinary doctor, I'm told. This is a plastic surgeon with a big name and practice—a practice she could not possibly leave while your sister stays in little Ontario and runs Levine Construction. And yes, they intend to get married. Your sister will be artificially inseminated with the help of California's top fertility specialist using the sperm of her new wife's brother—another doctor I understand. They miss nothing in California. This, she tells me, is her one chance at happiness. And now she wants to be a wife and mother—at thirty-eight."

The room became very quiet again. Ray sat smiling, as if her mother had just conveyed the most exciting and pleasing news in the world, ignoring her voice which could have cut the steaks Danny and Rose had just eaten at the Ruth Chris Steakhouse.

Danny said, "Jeez."

Rose said, "I'm so happy for you, Ray! And you'll have such brilliant children."

Ray gave her a grateful smile—but no one else did. And Ma kept on.

"I think the point you're all missing is that there's now no one to run Levine Construction. Your dad's really not up to it, Danny—the best he can do is drop in for an hour a day and everyone will pretend he's still the boss, or we attempt to sell the business, or—"

"Don't try to guilt me, Ma," said Ray, her smile collapsing. "I've given that business my best years."

"Of course you have," cooed Ma, "but it's somewhat unfair coming out of the closet at thirty-eight with a bagful of plans. I'm not a narrow-minded person. In the modelling industry I was surrounded by gays and I just adored them. But to have my daughter hide her sexual identity until she's thirty-eight and spring this on me, after all the men I've tried to hook her up with, leaves me breathless."

"Perhaps Ray thought you'd be upset, Ma," said Rose.

"You're right," said Ray.

"I'm not upset," said Ma, who was more upset than Rose had ever seen her, "I'm insulted and hurt that you thought you couldn't be honest with me. But upset? No. Certainly not."

Danny stood up suddenly. "I have to discuss this with Rose. I know where you're coming from, Ma, but it's a big decision. Does Pop know any of this?"

"Of course not," said Ma, "Do you want him to have another stroke?"

"There are builders who might be interested but we'd be taking a bath," said Ray, never losing her smile. "And they'd want us to stick around and run things."

"Look at Rachel," Ma hissed, as she showed them out the door. "She hasn't stopped smiling for two days."

"She's happy, Ma," said Rose. "You want her to be happy."

"At our expense," sniffed Ma.

"We won't talk about it till we get home," said Danny, as they got into the car. "It's a big decision."

Rose nodded. It was all very exciting, and she had not thought of Rick McCready and her custody case for at least an hour.

The drive back to Mississauga seemed endless. The snow had started again, and solid white V's had started building up and the wipers kept clicking a dull refrain. She knew it was annoying Danny, as was everything and everyone. And she did not want to join the club. But she knew she must.

"Imagine Ray pulling this," he said between clenched teeth, "like a freaking teenager—and taking for granted we'd all fall into line. She's been running the business for ten years and has been smart enough to let Pop think he has. Poor Pop, it will depress him all to hell to let it go—and we won't get anything like it's worth. Any buyer will know he's paying for goodwill, a few garbage contracts, and Brampton properties."

Rose hummed. In the old days before Danny, and certainly before Rick McCready, she'd have listened silently, busy with her interior dialogue, not venturing to comment. But she had changed.

"You and Ma are being really selfish when it comes to Ray. You disappoint me. She's thirty-eight and I'm happy for her—and you should be too. Ma knew she was a lesbian, she even asked me once what two women do together sexually. She just didn't want to acknowledge it, that's all. Now she's acting as if Ray cleaned out the family silver and bank accounts—it's so unfair. Perhaps it's because she's so worried about Pop that it's taken over everything else, including common sense."

Danny did not answer but stared glumly ahead, while the wipers clicked their dull refrain. "Anything else?"

"Yes, you. I think you should ask yourself if you want to spend your life doing family law. You get emotionally involved, which I'm sure your clients appreciate—I know I did—but it's draining you and your clients take advantage. And you beat yourself up if you don't win. And there are things you can't win, as some of the judges are as unpredictable and crazy as your clients. To Gerda and Martin it's a job: they do it and get paid and then they walk away. But that's not you. You worry. Even Gerda was getting sick of it when she was appointed and she didn't have half your dedication."

"So you're saying I'm a lousy lawyer."

"No, I'm not saying that at all. It's a personality thing. You're a *great* lawyer. But do you really want to spend the rest of your life worrying because Mister Jones didn't bring the kids back at seven sharp and he let them meet his girlfriend, and that Mrs. Jones's standard of living has taken a dump? Do you know how often you're fed up because of some stupidity your client is hounding you about, and half the time they've run out of money, especially the women, and you're carrying them? Gerda and Martin would dump them, but not nice guy Danny Levine."

"So in other words I'd be happier running a million-dollar company, though I hated it before."

"Everything's changed. You've got a law degree now. Ray's gone. Pop's not well enough to be in your face and you'll have a family. You'd be building up a legacy for Solly Jr."

"Nathan."

"Okay, Nathan."

"You've really changed: my sweet, quiet, little wife who allowed husband number one to take such advantage of her. It must have been the mikvah."

She ignored him. "It's your decision. I wouldn't presume to tell you what to do. I'm only reminding you of things I believe you're forgetting."

They parked the car in the underground parking and took the elevator to the condo. Neither spoke, but she knew he was thinking.

They went to bed without speaking and she did not take her anti-anxiety pill. Then after half an hour she got up and cut one in half.

"Anxious?"

"I just took half. I shouldn't be taking any."

"Normally I'd suggest we'd have sex, but I'm not up to it."

"Me neither."

They both laughed, there in the dark room, when outside the snow kept falling and the wind pressed against the balcony doors. She thought of Katy and wondered how she was, and tried not to think of her. And of the other half of the severed pill that she longed for.

"I'm glad you opened up," he murmured. "You said things that were on my mind but that I didn't want to say. You did and it made them real. I did take corporate and commercial law at York—even real estate. And I did all right. It would be a big relief not to be expected to solve the personal and legal problems of clients. I really wanted to help people. But if so I should have been a social worker—which would have driven me even crazier. I haven't made that much in six years—not enough to buy us a house in Toronto without a mortgage. I'd be broke if I didn't get the checks from Levine Construction."

"I'll contribute my house money to our new place."

He laughed into the darkness. "That's pathetic. I'm in the same league as McCready."

She put her arms around him and felt the comfort of his warm gut. "No, you're in a league of your own and that's why I love you."

"I'll phone Ray and Ma in the morning."

"Who'll get your files?"

"Booker: my clients deserve her. I'll keep my favorite client unless it looks as if I'll be called as a witness. You can phone my clients and tell them I'm packing it in because of family illness. I'd really appreciate that—no way I want to do it."

"Sure," she whispered. And thought about the other half of the pill.

Chapter 49

"Can you get Katy when he comes? I don't want to talk to him. He upsets me."

Del shrugged. "Sure. No problem. But he may want to talk to you."

"Please."

"Katy's getting so smart she'll soon be able to convey all messages."

"What a burden to put on the poor little girl," said Rose. But she smiled. Katy was very advanced. Whether it was Danny's reading to her from the dozens of books he brought home to her during their custody week or Rick's absorption when he had her, she reflected the attention.

"Now what book tonight?" Danny would ask.

"*Cat in Hat,*" she'd reply, and he'd roll his eyes and say, "Whatever did we do without Dr. Seuss?" She'd smile at him, open the book, and say, "Read."

Once she'd said, "You're not my daddy." He replied, "No, I'm your big buddy and I buy you books."

She was, thought Rose, so lucky to have him. And then she'd worry about her with Rick.

"Prezzies," she'd demand as Danny entered.

"Only for good little girls," he'd tease.

"I a good little girl," she'd insist, and out would come a new book and on occasion a pink brush and comb set with a small mirror, or a necklace with a little pink heart.

"You spoil her," said Rose in her eighth month, sitting soggy and motionless in her chair.

"Nah," said Danny, looking more at home in his work clothes than he ever had in his court gown, "She'll just be a girl who expects guys to give her things—not like her mommy."

Sometimes Katy would kiss him spontaneously on the cheek, her dark curls bobbing, plump arms resting on his shoulders. Then she'd draw back as if betraying "the other," the one who came every second Friday and gave her chocolate cake for breakfast.

Seeing her concern he'd wipe away the kiss and say, "Uh oh." She'd smile and say, "It okay, Danny."

Rose watched. Katy loved him: it was as obvious as the guilt the love brought.

***

It was April 15 when Rose saw Dr. Abrams again. She was huge and sat uncomfortably in the chair across the desk. Seeing her discomfort he told her to lie on his sofa, telling her, "This sofa is usually reserved for Ziggy Freud's patients, but we're not doing a psychoanalysis on you, although some shrinks would say that most assessments contain an element of this—if they're good assessments."

She lay on the couch, her hands holding the squirming bundle she longed to push out.

"Uncomfortable?" asked Dr. Abrams.

"No, I'm fine," lied Rose. "I just wish it were over."

Rose and Dr. Abrams discussed the discrepancies between her and Rick's version of their first dates, and Rick's professed line of credit problems. And then Dr. Abrams went quiet. He sighed, tapped his fingers against his pad, and asked, "Did Rick McCready ever share his childhood with you?"

"To a degree: I knew he hated his mother and I believe she used to beat him. Every time he didn't like a woman, he'd make a comparison. He never sees her. I believe she's in a nursing home in Nova Scotia. I remember he once said, 'I hope she dies alone in her piss.'"

Dr. Abrams frowned. "Too bad you didn't talk more: it might have alerted you. His mother was a raving psychopath and he suffered early horrendous abuse—so bad that I didn't believe him—until he authorized the release of his records from Sick Kids. The abuse stopped when he started to give her money. His father drank and was addicted to Percodan. He found him hanging in the basement at age nine and blamed his mother. It seems he cared for his father, but his father didn't do much to protect him. I'm surprised he's never told you more of this."

"He did tell me his mother abused him and about his father's suicide. It upset me. I may not have believed him later on; remember he lied to me about everything and built up his own mystique: a successful professional engineer with a flourishing business."

They continued talking: of Patsy's drowning, her new-mother problems with Katy, and of Rick's wish to settle on an equal division of everything, including Katy.

Dr. Abrams got up and stood looking out the narrow window facing the parking lot. She heard him sigh. She saw the grey sky framing his white hair and slight shoulders.

"This equal sharing, you wouldn't consider that? I suspect she's the only person in the world he's ever really loved—or even formed an attachment with—except perhaps his father, who let him down badly, and an Alf Simpson, who took him in for two years."

Then it hit her, like an unpleasant smack to the side of her head; Dr. Abrams felt sorry for Rick. It was there, a certain note of compassion in his voice for this man who'd drowned the trusting schoolteacher, and who'd tried to murder her. And whose entire life was a fabrication because the truth was unspeakably tawdry . . . and sad. Did Dr. Abrams think his love for Katy had redeemed him? That this bright, smiling, plump little girl had been a poultice to his ravaged psyche? A little female Christ figure? She had always envisioned Danny as a more well-nourished Jesus, but would never tell him. Danny would not appreciate it. Jesus had, after all, caused the tribe a great deal of trouble.

"I can't agree with what he wants. Katy deserves better. He's agreed to Montessori, and she loves it, because she's very, very social—for a two-year-old. We can give her so much more stability. We're buying a house and she'll have a baby brother. Danny's such a great dad."

Dr. Abrams kept looking out the window—but answered her.

"Unfortunately he's not her biological father, and I can predict future hostility from McCready if they become too close. It's a troublesome case."

Dr. Abrams had moved from the window and was back behind his desk, his drooping face resembling more than ever a depressed, aging— but aware—bull-mastiff. He sighed heavily. "I'm seeing McCready within the next two weeks with Katy, and then I'll be seeing you with her after the birth. I also thought I'd see her with your husband—as a household member. I sent the schedule to Springer and got a ridiculous letter back. No doubt he shared the schedule with McCready who objected strenuously.

"You do realize, Rose, that I can't comment on the alleged murder or the attempted murder allegations. It would impinge on my credibility as a psychiatrist if I appeared to be swayed by unproven allegations. This doesn't stop you from telling the court what you believe.

"Unfortunately, I can't interview his second wife, Pina—I suspect she wouldn't cooperate in any event—or your sister, whose bias would be obvious. My only focus is to consider Katy's best interests; that's what the court order and the law says."

Rose pushed her swollen body from the sofa, thanked Dr. Abrams for his efforts, and assured him the next time they met she'd be in much better shape. She waddled to the door, after again thanking him, this time for his wishes for an uncomplicated birth.

"Name?" he called out.

"Nathan."

"Good Jewish name," he replied.

***

Danny was sitting behind the wheel of the Chrysler looking into space. He was, she thought, as preoccupied with running Levine Construction as he had been with his divorce practice. That was what he was like, obsessive about things. He told her he had dozens of ideas about expansion and wanted to go more heavily into condominium construction. To everyone's surprise, Sol was so pleased with his interest and involvement he didn't interfere.

She opened the car door, pushing herself in and getting his attention.

"Sorry about that: just playing with the idea of buying some land in Mississauga for future condo development. How'd it go?"

"Terrible. He feels sorry for Rick because of his childhood abuse, which bothers him more than the possible murder of his first wife, my attempted murder, and that he's such a pathological liar you can't believe a word he says."

"Jeez," muttered Danny, "he's getting senile. Where's the best interests of the child?"

"Martin didn't even think he needed to see you with Katy—that's Rick. Martin couldn't care less."

"Want to drive north, past our new place? They've finished Nathan's nursery, and made Katy's bedroom more sophisticated. They've finished the built-in bookcase for the books her buddy Danny brings her."

"Lovely," she said, and then convulsed slightly.

"You okay?"

"Nathan's asserting himself: he's getting tired of the delay. But not as much as I am."

Danny reached over and rubbed the restless Nathan.

"I may start taking English courses through the university's extension program. I can't even think of going back to being a dental hygienist."

Danny hummed. "Looks like everyone in this family's having a second career."

***

Nathan Saul Levine was late—seven days in fact, a pattern he was to continue throughout his life. A rollicking nine and a half pounds, he arrived after an induction that had been scheduled the same day as the birth. His father was present, but left at the crucial time of the crowning. "Just as well," whispered the nurse. "We thought he was going to faint."

Nattie screamed for two minutes, then started to nurse and never cried again.

"He's bigger than I am," whispered Danny.

"But much more relaxed," replied Rose.

And he was.

Nathan was surrounded by adoring fans, especially Katy, who was fascinated by this chubby, bald, smiling creature she referred to as "my brudder." Ma arrived at the hospital laden with gifts, held the child against her emaciated chest and looked at her crimson talons with disgust.

"When are you going back to work?" she asked Rose. "I'll have to cut my nails."

"I'm nursing, Ma," she replied.

"So?" sniffed Ma. "Haven't you ever heard of breast pumps and leaving bottles with an alternative caregiver? No need for you to disrupt your career."

Rose smiled. Danny had been dead right about Ma: she would take over if permitted, fawning over this plump, affable child, so different from the colicky screaming Katy. And he actually liked his mother. Except, Rose thought, for the ongoing litigation, things would be perfect.

Danny had managed to eliminate her child support payments, telling the court as the former wife was no longer working, the child support payments were effectively against him; and then attempted to get a sale of the house. The Judge agreed on the child support argument, but refused to order a sale, ruling that Rose was to continue to carry the home—but would receive credit for the payments made upon the eventual sale.

"It makes no sense," growled Danny. "Letting him squat there and making you responsible for his upkeep. It reminds me of why I quit this stupid game in the first place. I can't even get a positive result for my one remaining client."

Rose insisted on paying the carrying costs of the home from her exhausted stock portfolio: as a matter of principle she would not have Danny pay. The dislike between Danny and Rick, especially since the parking lot incident, had gotten worse, and Rick was taking the new home purchase and Nathan's birth personally.

"Now you've got your boy, perhaps you'll let me have my girl," he'd snarled the week after she'd arrived home with the baby and he'd come for his Friday night pick-up.

"She's my daughter, not just yours, and she loves her brother. If you really loved her you'd let her live a normal life."

***

It was the middle of May, and the trees lining Del's pathway were sprouting and the air was becoming sweet. Rose watched as Katy walked beside Rick, holding his hand, her chocolate curls bouncing on the shoulders of her new spring coat, while he carried the small suitcase with her daily clothing changes, and the small, zipped plastic bag with chicken cut in cubes and carrot and celery sticks.

"Put the food in the fridge," she called out.

"I can feed her," he yelled back. "She gets lunch at daycare, toast and orange juice for breakfast, and normal stuff for dinner. She's not starving—she's overweight. I grew in spite of my old lady's crap food, bigger than the runt you married."

She followed him up the pathway, breathless with annoyance. "Just go. Leave. I have to get someone else to do this exchange. You don't know how to be civil—in fact you don't know how to do anything, including work."

"Say goodbye to mean Mommy," he instructed Katy, who called out, "Bye-bye Mommy," as she got into the back of the Mustang. Rose stood watching them, wondering how long it would be before Rick succeeded in damaging her relationship with Katy.

***

"Daddy missed you all week," he said, as they drove towards the highway, "Daddy couldn't eat or sleep because he was so lonely."

"I here now, Daddy," said the high voice from the back seat. "You not be lonely this week."

***

They were moving the next week, near another Montessori school, and unfortunately nearer Rick. But she could not let Danny be part of any exchange. Katy loved them both and Rose did not want her witnessing the inevitable confrontation. Katy had, sadly, grown used to Rose's confrontations with Rick, which were worsening over time. Her appointment to see Dr. Abrams with Katy was during the second week of June. He had already seen her with Rick and with Danny.

"I'm going to ask Dr. Abrams about the exchange," Rose told Danny. "Perhaps it could happen at some supervised place. It's ugly for Katy to witness what goes on, although I'm ashamed to say she's used to it—her parents hurling hatred at each other. God knows what damage it's doing, though it doesn't seem to bother her—and that says it all. But she's so smart she takes it all in."

"This is all the result of Hollwell's stupid order, thinking about gender equality and not the kid's interests. Once this is over I'm going to write her and tell her what hell her stupid order has caused."

And what would be the point of that? she wondered—but she didn't say it, although she no longer went through life communicating through an interior monologue. She knew Danny suffered as much as she did with the whole Rick-Katy situation, feeling as her lawyer he was responsible for not fixing it and that he had failed them both, even thought it had happened with Gerda. It was all made worse by his growing affection for Katy, whom he was as proud of as any biological father.

CHAPTER 50

It was exactly eleven when the phone next to Pina Gatto's bed started to ring. She knew who it was, although she was expecting a call from Omar, her most academic twin, about the results of his law school admission rewrite. But only someone like Rick McCready would phone at exactly eleven, because he took the position that everyone should be up at that hour, even those who worked all-nighters. And this was from a guy who never worked a day—or night—in his life.

He probably wanted more cash, but there was no more. She'd cleaned out her retirement account for that twenty thousand, and if Omar or Abdul found out it would be game over—they'd never forgive her, not when she'd increased the mortgage on the Brampton townhouse her folks had left them to put Abe through Ryerson, and Omie through his first degree at the University of Toronto. As well they'd both had summer jobs and worked part time to meet expenses, and she'd done extra shifts at the Pearl.

The phone kept crowing, so she picked it up. "Yes." Her thick voice needed coffee.

"Figured you'd be up."

He knew the club didn't close until two, but not about her talk with Vince, the club manager. "Vince fired me last night, not that he said it right out, just gave me the same line he gave Rita: said I was lookin' tired and should take a few months off. I knew it was coming, but hoped I could hang on until the boys were finished. So if you're looking for more cash for your court case, forget it. If the boys knew about that twenty they'd bury us both in the same box."

"I'm not hittin' on you for bread," he rasped, sounding indignant and really hurt, as if he hadn't done it a year and a half earlier, and for the year they'd been together. "My name's on the house, an' you'll get it all back, plus interest. I just wanted to thank you, an' tell you I got my little girl half the time an' I'll bring her around. You never seen a kid like this, guaranteed."

She didn't reply, just kept lying there, breathing into the phone, so he went on. "Still got your little French Bully? Katy'd just love that little bully." So she said, "You can come around three." He didn't reply, which she took as an agreement, and then he said, "Sorry about Vince: that son of a bitch, after all you've done for that club." She just sighed and said, "I guess forty-four's not the new twenty-four." He didn't answer, but said, "I'll bring takeout."

"No need, gotta get in better shape, and talk Vince into a few more years so I can see the boys finish. I'll waive the basic and increase their cut. I'll never make what I make anywhere else." He didn't disagree, just said, "Three o'clock."

She pulled on her Lululemon stretch top and pants, and carried Mignon, who was at the foot of her bed, out to the backyard for a piddle. Mrs. Nuttall, who used to look in on the boys when she was working, was planting spring daffodil bulbs and she gave her a wave. She carried Mignon back through the kitchen, and noticed she had already left a small puddle in front of the sink. She sighed and mopped it up with a paper towel. She and Mignon: both losing it.

She made coffee and then started her routine on the living room carpet, a modified Pilates—stretches, pelvic tilts, and leg lifts—putting off the smoke she was longing for. Then the phone rang from the kitchen. "One-sixty-five," said the familiar voice. "This'll clinch it."

It was only three points more on the LSAT, but he seemed happy. "Good?" she asked.

"Damn right—really good, now I've got a chance with U of T."

"That's wonderful," she breathed, "Really proud of you honey."

"Talk later," he said, and he was gone. Now she knew she had to talk to Vince, although Omar had mentioned law students getting a bank loan. If everything went badly, she'd try to increase the mortgage again. They should let her. She'd never missed a payment, and the property was up in value.

She went in and started her leg lifts again with more enthusiasm. She thought about her boys and her mind went back. She'd been twenty-four, living at home, and waitressing at the King Eddy when she'd met their father. He was to die for: a guy from Egypt who looked like

Omar Sharif. She moved into the Palace Pier with him a month later, much to her mother's disgust. They didn't even tell Papa. He seemed to have money, so she quit her job. Then she got pregnant. She wanted to get married. Then he told her he already had a wife in Egypt, but he'd go back and get a divorce. Three weeks later he was gone, and she found out he'd owed rent on the condo—which he didn't own—so she'd moved back home. She never heard from him again.

She would, she promised her mother, have the baby adopted, and they told Papa the daddy was coming back—but he didn't believe them. And then the baby was two babies, and Ma and Papa fell in love, so there was no more talk of adoption. She gave the boys Egyptian names, just in case he did come back, although she knew he wouldn't. Her mother babysat, and she got her first job as "an exotic dancer" at the Brass Rail. She never called herself a stripper. Ma made a lot of her costumes, as this was before they started taking so much off.

When the boys were ten, Papa died, and everyone was glad she made the extra money. Then, when the boys were fourteen, Ma passed away from cancer, and they were all upset, especially the boys. They had a family meeting, and she and the boys decided they would continue at Cardinal Ambrozic, where they were top students, and she'd continue her dancing, but she'd change to The Pearl in Mississauga, as it was closer. And that they'd keep studying hard and not let her—or themselves—down.

There was no social life or dating. When the boys came home after school, they'd bring her up to date on their day, and she'd give them a hot meal at five. Then before she left, they'd be settled in with their books at the kitchen table, and she'd phone them every hour between performances. She didn't finish grade ten, but she ran a tight ship. "They're a real credit to you and the school," Brother Davis had said after the grade twelve graduations, where the twins had shared valedictory speeches.

The boys were both in residence in Toronto for their first year when she met Rick at a bar around the corner from the Pearl. She couldn't believe her good luck, then she figured the Blessed Virgin had sent him to make up for all the bad times and hard work. At last, someone the boys could look up to, a successful businessman who was a really big spender, and who was great on looks and sex. There was the Vegas marriage, and all the trips back and forth, and San Francisco, Palm Springs, and even

Monaco once for a week. And Vince let her do it, perhaps because of her work record and house following. It was the best year of her life. But then he started "running short," and she started "shelling out."

Then there was Omar and Abe at the kitchen table, Abe with a pile of papers because he was such a computer nerd. And they gave her the down and dirty: she'd given fifty thousand to a con artist who'd been living off the insurance proceeds of his wife's suspicious death, a dirt sandwich who liked threesomes—a fact she was already aware of, but pretended disgust—and if it kept up he'd be walking away with the Brampton townhouse and any savings she had left. And she might even be another "suspicious death."

They gave an ultimatum. Then she remembered some drunken raving about a woman who'd drowned in Algonquin Park, and how he'd wanted to invest in the townhouse, even talked about mortgage insurance, and how his stories about his business kept changing. And she knew the boys were right. And yet, after all that, she'd still loaned him another twenty-thousand two years back: perhaps in memory of that one great year.

After the exercise she had a butt, and examined her face in the hall mirror, looking at the small lines around her mouth and eyes. She whipped a raw egg white with a fork, and rubbed it over her face, and ate a half a grapefruit and the remaining egg yolk for breakfast. Surgery was out—too expensive—but perhaps she'd get some filler and Botox.

Rick was standing on the top step at three sharp, with this really pretty little girl by the hand. She was dressed in cords, a denim jacket, and those trendy running shoes she'd seen kids wear at the Bramalea Mall, and she had a long curly ponytail anchored by a fancy bow and two butterfly clip-ons. Pina bent over and gave the ponytail a gentle tug—no one loved kids more than she did. "Who does your hair darlin'? If you give me the name of your hairdresser I'll go see her right now." The child smiled, and she saw Rick's smile, and knew right away why he wanted her. She was so much more like him than the little pale girl she'd seen pregnant at the Pearl.

"Daddy did it."

"Oh wow, really! Your daddy's so great with his hands!" A few memories crossed her mind, but she kept smiling at Katy as if they didn't.

He'd brought some hamburgers and fries, and a milk shake for Katy, who also ate some fries, gingerly dipping them in ketchup and taking small bites. "Such a little lady," Pina said, eating a hamburger and breaking her diet. She told herself it would be her last meal of the day. "Mignon's waiting in the bedroom when you're finished with your fries."

"The puppy?" Katy asked.

"The puppy, but she's an old puppy—more like a little ol' dog."

Katy and Mignon started a love affair, and Mignon let her carry her around, even letting Katy put her in Pina's unmade bed. Rick stood watching them, smiling, and said, "When you come and live with Daddy you'll have your own puppy, a fluffy little white puppy."

Rick never took his eyes off Katy, even when Pina produced some of her old bracelets and necklaces, letting Katy try them on, together with some feathered boas she'd worn, before they'd started asking for complete nudity. Katy never stopped smiling.

"She's adorable," she whispered. He just nodded his agreement and said, "Sorry about that Vince thing: when they order a sale of our house I'll give you fifty thousand." She nodded, but didn't look at him, knowing you couldn't believe a word he said.

They left at four, Katy clinging to Mignon whom she didn't want to leave. Pina watched as they walked down the sidewalk to the car, hand in hand. She no longer regretted giving him the twenty-thousand, although she knew she'd never get it back. Katy's ponytail waved a goodbye, and she put her arms around Rick's neck as he eased her into the back car seat. They seemed very attached. Perhaps, she thought, even con artists like Rick were capable of love.

Chapter 51

Mid-June was warm in 2007, and Rose and Katy were dressed for early summer on the morning they were to see Dr. Abrams. Rose had bunched Katy's curls into her usual rich ponytail and she wore her new yellow cashmere cardigan and the running shoes that lit up as she walked.

Rose watched Katy check herself out in the hall mirror and heard her whisper "bootiful." Vain little creature. Danny was right in his prophesies: she would be the kind of girl who expected guys to buy her things. Prince Nathan was with the adoring Queen, who almost pushed them out the door telling them not to hurry back. Two bottles of pumped breast milk were waiting for warming in the fridge.

"We'll go for ice cream later," Rose told Katy.

"Daddy buys me ice cream all the time."

"That's nice," said Rose, her voice flat.

"You can buy ice cream too."

"We'll go after we see the doctor, and you'll have a special two-flavored cone, chocolate and vanilla, with chocolate sprinkles on top. When Nattie is old enough, you can share your ice cream with him."

"He have his own ice cream." Rose laughed.

They parked in the parking lot behind the Medical Arts Building. Later, when Rose thought about it, it was as if she were watching an old noir movie, in black and white slow time.

They went to the fifth floor by elevator, walked down the hall, and into the empty reception room.

"There a playroom with books and toys. I go there with Daddy and Danny."

Dr. Abrams came out. His receptionist Judy, the lollipop distributor, had gone to the dentist, fortunately in the same building.

"How's my best girl?" he asked, a smile lifting his furrowed face—apparently the two previous visits had created a bond.

Katy smiled. "Mommy's taking me for ice cream."

"Aren't you the lucky girl."

They sat in front of the desk—Katy in a small chair the doctor had probably purchased for visiting children.

"We go to playroom?"

"In a few minutes, Katy."

Then Katy, her voice ringing like a small bell, said, "Danny put fingers in my pee-pee."

The room became thick with silence, and Rose fought an impulse to throw herself out the fifth-floor window.

But except for a momentary widening of his eyes, Dr. Abrams did not react.

"Who told you to tell me that, Katy?"

"Daddy did. He said he buy me a puppy."

"Did Danny put his fingers in your pee-pee?"

"No," said Katy, shaking her head vigorously, "but Daddy say he did."

"You know," said Dr. Abrams to Rose, "I'm under a legal obligation to report this kind of allegation to the CAS. I may have to phone a friend of mine there, and tell her what was said. She may or may not want to speak to the child, who's made the source of the allegation clear—and that she was bribed to make it."

Rose sat frozen and bizarrely felt her breasts fill up. Then she felt her face burn with anger.

"Have you read my book on alienation?"

"No."

"I know this is a false allegation, but we need to take it seriously, because any allegation of sexual abuse could have ruinous, far-reaching effects, and the party promoting them could ensure a complete severing of the relationship between the so-called abuser and the child. Criminal proceedings could be brought."

"This would destroy my husband."

Dr. Abrams shook his head. "Katy has made clear the reason for her accusation."

He paused, sighed, and asked, "Katy, do you like Danny?"

"I love Danny. I love when he reads to me."

"And he's never touched your pee-pee?"

"No."

"Then why did you say it?"

"Daddy said to."

"I won't go into this again, but I'm forced to make the call. I know nothing happened. McCready's a classic caution against dating sites: I underestimated his capabilities. Do you and Katy want to go to the playroom?"

When Rose spoke her voice was hoarse and she felt unpleasantly warm.

"I'm sorry, Doctor Abrams, I'm very upset. I don't think I can be myself. I'd like to postpone this—though I'm more than happy to pay for your time."

"My receptionist should be back from her appointment any minute. I'll let her take Katy to the playroom and we'll have a brief chat."

"Katy, do you want to play with Judy for a few minutes?" asked Dr. Abrams.

"Will she give me a lollipop?"

"She usually does."

When they were alone, Rose, sitting across the desk from Dr. Abrams, started to cry.

"You have to understand Danny has a really special relationship with Katy. He says he's her big buddy, but he's so much more. He'll be devastated and then so angry that Rick bribed Katy to say this. It's diabolic and vicious. If Katy were believed, he'd not only get custody, but I'd no longer have a lawyer. As it is I'll have to get someone else as Martin will call Danny as a witness."

Dr. Abrams sat back in his chair frowning. Outside the window behind him, the sky was a bright solid blue and the June sun streamed through the glass. Rose felt the air-conditioning, but now instead of the heat that had enveloped her, she felt chilled, as if she were looking down from a frozen height.

Dr. Abrams leaned forward, his furrowed face quivering, his voice threaded with conviction. "I won't discuss with you how this will be factored into my report, but it impacts on your ex-husband's credibility in a profound way—this will have a far more dangerous effect on Rick than on Danny. Now go into the playroom and have fun with your daughter. I know you're upset and I do understand. But this matter must move along. There's been too much delay."

"Danny will be afraid to go near her when he hears about this. This will hurt her—she really loves him. I don't want to tell him."

"You have to."

"Do you suppose Martin . . ."

"Never. He's a criminal lawyer. He'd be as upset as Danny. It's not his style, not like hiding evidence tapes in a murder trial. He hates divorce work: this will bother him."

Rose went into the reception room where Judy was showing Katy pictures of her daughters, and Katy was sucking on a lollipop.

"I have a brudder," Katy told Judy, "and I play with him, but next time Mommy get me a sissor."

"Your daughter's ordering another baby," said Judy, "a sister."

"She may not be as smart as you, darling."

"I teach her," sighed Katy, "or we send her back to baby shop."

They played, but there was more cuddling than actual playing. Rose needed physical contact—to be close. She was fighting feelings of fear: fear of losing Katy. She saw herself on this high icy mountain, standing alone, and searching downward among the frozen folds for a small body.

**

"How'd it go?" asked Danny after they arrived home, "You're very quiet."

"We'll talk about it later." Her breasts were hard with milk and she needed to nurse, but Ma kept holding on to Nathan. She looked at Danny for help, pointing to her breasts.

"Give him up, Ma," he ordered. "You've done a great job but you don't have the equipment for the next stage."

"He drained those two bottles," Ma sniffed. "He's so big perhaps he's ready for solids."

"It's a little early, Ma," said Rose, lifting Nathan from Ma's reluctant arms. "Once he gets some nice sweet applesauce and pablum he'll lose interest in my boobs."

Ma nodded. She'd ordered Chinese takeout and Rose was appreciative. The episode at Dr. Abrams had drained her—as did the prospect of telling Danny.

"I'm afraid Katy's becoming a sugar junkie: her father feeds her ice cream nonstop and she lives for carbs."

"Shocking," said the former model. "I lived on protein and greens for years. She's a beautiful child but we don't want a little tub."

"I love ice cream," protested Katy, an eavesdropper on every conversation.

"Yes, we know," said Ma. "We used to say a minute on the lips, a lifetime on the hips when I was a model, sweetheart."

Katy looked perplexed, and Rose felt a flash of annoyance, not wishing Ma to start body-shaming Katy about her weight at the age of two.

"You've put in a long day Ma," said Danny.

"Trying to get rid of me, Sonny-Boy?"

"Never," lied Danny.

***

Propped up by pillows, Rose lay on the bed, looking down at the reddish down-covered bald head and round cheeks. He nursed with such vigor, so different from Katy. She felt his eager mouth and the hardness of her left breast started to dissolve. After he was finished she burped him, rubbing the small damp back and sniffing his sweet soft neck, grateful that she had him. Then the fear came back, and she was looking down from a mountain and all around her the wind was howling.

"Ma's gone, but not forgotten," cracked Danny, when she came out of Nathan's room. "I guess Nat's worn out from all the entertainment— she told me she didn't put him down for five hours. I put Katy to bed without her bath, just washed her face and hands, and had her brush her teeth in honor of her mother."

"She's exhausted, full of crap ice cream, lollipops, and sweet and sour chicken, the only Chinese food she likes. Ma's right—we need a change of diet."

They sat silent. Danny spoke first.

"So?"

"So?"

"How'd it go with Abrams?"

Rose wanted to avoid it: a shameful and cruel accusation towards this loving tender man who had shown her daughter nothing but kindness, and who deserved credit for her love of books and advanced state of curiosity towards the world in general. Instead, she had been bribed into branding her self-named "buddy" as a loathsome pedophile. He would regret ever having married her. Not that he would say so—but he would regret it.

"Katy told Abrams you molested her: put your fingers in her pee-pee, to be exact."

She said it without looking at him, but when she did she saw the color had drained from his face. Then she spoke quickly. "Abrams questioned her more closely. It seems that Rick had promised Katy a puppy if she told Abrams what you'd done. But no, she told Abrams, you'd never do that, it was what daddy had told her to say. And she loved you because you read her books. Abrams questioned her twice and she was steady in her denials. He's legally bound to tell the CAS and they may want to talk to her, but he knows it didn't happen. He's disgusted. He says it fractures Rick's credibility. It scares me. I knew he was bad but not bad enough to involve Katy. I thought she'd be the exception. But there are no exceptions."

Danny got up and walked slowly from the rec room. She followed him to the kitchen. He was leaning over the kitchen sink, his hands gripping the counter, his head bowed. Rose went over and rubbed his back, feeling the padded warmth, and a feeling of tenderness swept over her, the same feeling she'd had when she'd rubbed Nathan's back after nursing.

"You don't deserve this. I know you wish you'd never married me, and you have to forgive me for bringing this sick person into your life. And if it wasn't for Nattie, I'd just walk away. But Nathan does need a dad like you—and so does Katy."

He turned and held her. And they stood swaying, just holding each other, and he whispered, "Shut up, just shut up." And when she felt his cheek it was wet against hers.

Later they lay silent in bed, and she knew he couldn't sleep, but was lying there looking into the darkness. "Do you want to do it?" she whispered. "It might relax you and I'll help."

"I'll never have another erection."

"Sure you will. Katy told Abrams's receptionist that she wanted a 'sissor.' He did not even laugh but sighed, so she got up and returned with two pills. "Put these under your tongue,"

"Trying to hook me?"

"No. Trying to ease your hurt and pain."

She kept rubbing his back, but before he went off, he said, "You'll have to get a new lawyer, Martin will call me as a witness."

"Booker?"

"Good choice," he mumbled. "No more Mister Nice Guy."

Chapter 52

"I'll give you a special rate because of Danny," said Barbara Booker. "He's sent me a piss pot of files—whatta mensch. Too fuckin' nice to be a lawyer—let alone do family law. You're so lucky getting him: horseshoes up your ass, Rosie."

As Danny had warned, Barbara Booker had a potty mouth. Rather than be appalled, Rose found it strangely comforting: she knew that few could compete with Barb along these lines. And she remembered Danny's anger when she represented the other side.

"Dr. Abrams hasn't finished his report," she ventured.

"Jee-sus," spat Barb. "I'll tell the old bastard to pull his head out of his ass."

Rose smothered a smile. "He did say he was ordering a psychological report to support his psychiatric assessment, which means we'll have to do a battery of tests. He was upset when it came out that Rick had bribed Katy to say Danny had sexually molested her. Apparently, it's right out of his alienation book. He was willing to give him a pass on many other things, but that really bothered him. Not as much as Danny, who had to be sedated when he heard about it. I'm sure he's sorry he married me, no one deserves that kind of garbage."

"A lot of girls were after Danny Levine, but he chose you, so cut the crap. Cunt Hollwell fucked you up giving that order when you had Gerda, so you're one of Hollwell's parade of victims. Someday someone will take her out: I'm counting the hours."

Barbara Booker was an extremely pretty woman, with a face like a Madonna, enhanced blond hair, styled in an inappropriate halo, and a navy Armani pantsuit just pulled off the runway. As such her language, which was much closer to a trucker or a biker than a lawyer, seemed even more shocking and made double the impact.

"You've read the file?"

"Rick McCready leads the male asshole parade—a sick fuck if there ever was one, for which we can partly blame his sadistic nut of a mother. It's a mix of nurture and genes: remember Psych 101? But it is as it is and we have to deal with the finished product. I'm glad Abrams's getting a psychologist for testing: he probably wants someone to confirm what he already suspects—that there's a serious pathology. There goes another six weeks. And then he's got to cough up the report—which isn't easy when you're older than God. After that I'll have to make a motion getting you interim custody. Bloody fucking hell: it'll be December. How's the kid? Really?"

Rose filled her in.

Barbara groaned but made no further comment, so she went on.

"If I wasn't so afraid her father was a narcissistic psychopath I'd probably keep things as they are—though I'm paying for everything. He doesn't work and he's squatting in the matrimonial home—that I paid for and have been carrying for over two years."

Rose paused and looked at Barbara Booker, who was looking into space with narrowed eyes. So she continued.

"He only has three months of university, but he's got lots of talent. He can do anything with his hands, which I'm sure the women appreciate. He could hire himself out as a hit man—he's gotten away with one murder and another attempted one."

She stopped and Barbara spoke: "All that and asshole Martin—I can't tell you how happy I am to have your file."

They sat, eyes meeting, and then they both started to laugh: hollow, bitter laughter, laced with venom.

***

The psychological testing took place at Dr. Marie Kennedy's downtown office in August and took all day. There were questions and checklists about moods, anxieties, empathy, and even a Thematic Apperception Test, which showed a picture with a shadowy individual in a doorway, presumably waiting for a returning figure. Rose said the woman was waiting for her daughter. She noticed many of the questions were repetitive, with small spins and twists and there were many multiple choices. Her testing and interview with Dr. Kennedy seemed calculated to catch a dishonest test taker—as did many of the questions. She wondered how

Rick would manage to slide through them, although she did not underestimate his capacity to deceive and ingratiate. She liked Dr. Kennedy and was straightforward and careful not to contradict her written answers.

"How'd it go?" asked Danny, who picked her up after both the Booker and Kennedy interviews.

Rose filled him in.

"I hope to God you modified some of that: you sound like me. Booker's terrible. She just likes me because I gave her some files. She's a nightmare to deal with—a female Rick McCready. Two divorces—and she's not that old. Her nice conservative parents, who she refers to as "two old crocks," don't know where she came from—but wish she hadn't."

Rose laughed and didn't say that she liked Barb, and found her male assessments and potty mouth hilarious.

"Let's get some take-out—Ma'll be exhausted. It's so soft and warm. If it weren't for Nattie we'd walk through Yorkville hand in hand, sit at some café with a patio, drink dirty martinis and watch the world walk by."

"My boobs are bursting and I don't want to give your son a second-hand dirty martini. Can't you imagine Kennedy's summary, "A limited but sincere woman, gullible enough to be the victim of considerable manipulation."

"You're too hard on yourself, sweetums—you're better than that."

She reached over and rubbed his cheek and then picked up his hand and kissed it.

"Barb's right. I've got horse-shoes up my ass marrying you."

"She said that? Just imagine being in bed with her and having her snarl, 'Get your goddamn pecker out of my snatch.' You'd never rise again. And I'm only wonderful in comparison with McCready."

She laughed, opened the window, and felt the warm breeze against her arm. And wondered how Katy was.

CHAPTER 53

The Abrams Report, which came out on the second week of December, contained the essence of interviews with Dr. Abrams, his professional opinions, and the results of Dr. Kennedy's psychological testing. Barbara Booker sent an email with the report as an attachment.

"Rosie, herewith report. Read it and share with Danny. If we put our case on trial list we're waiting another year, and in view of conclusions and recommendations I don't think waiting is an option. Martin will want an alternative assessment, to cross-examine Abrams and Kennedy, and crap all over it—as it's highly damaging. Phone me after you've read it and shown it to Danny."

The first few pages gave her background and a history of her relationship with Rick. She was categorized as oversensitive, bookish, and somewhat naïve about relationships. Her lifestyle had been curbed and impeded by her devotion to her mother. She had a natural shyness and literary leanings, so her choice of being a dental hygienist was somewhat surprising. With Katy, she was described as loving and maternal and appropriately concerned with hygiene and diet. Any shortcomings described by Rick McCready after the birth could be seen as the result of new mother nervousness and not a lack of devotion. "The present arrangement of alternate weeks by the parties has resulted in concern and frustration on the mother's part and she believes it to be disruptive for the child.

"As Mrs. Levine's IQ appears to be in the solid upper range, her acquiescence in permitting Rick McCready to take such financial advantage of her is surprising and can only be explained by a deep reluctance to confront the unpleasant, and Mr. McCready's quite ingenious aptitude in twisting the truth. Suffice it to say, Mr. McCready has succeeded in financially exploiting his former wife for the past two years—with the aid of the court, a situation he quite happily acknowledges."

On reading this Rose sighed: Nothing harmful to her as yet, just her general financial idiocy when it came to Rick.

Then there was a paragraph on Danny and Katy. She wished Dr. Abrams had left that out; although it would please Danny, it would incense Rick.

"Katy has bonded with her mother's second husband Daniel Levine, who may be credited for some of her surprising sophistication for a two-year-old, even displaying a sly sense of humor at times. Her behavior resembles a much older child attending elementary school. She told the assessor that Danny brings her books, "all the time," and she not only knew the titles—but recited a few lines from Dr. Seuss and laughed while reciting them. She says she likes him and they have fun. At Montessori she said, "We mostly play," although sometimes, "Mrs. Brown reads us stories."

"With her father she watches TV, eats ice cream, and goes to McDonald's. She said Daddy liked movies "with guns and scary stuff" but sometimes lets her watch cartoons. Her father does not read to her, nor does he make her brush her teeth, but he gives her an apple at night which he tells her is as good as brushing. He sings to her at bedtime. He does see that she has baths and he brushes and combs out her hair. She says, "If I live with Daddy, he'll buy me a puppy." She says they drive around in "Daddy's car," and sometimes ladies come to visit. She says they are all "nice." They talk to her, and on occasion bring "treats."

"Both men are appropriately affectionate with the child, although a slight withdrawal on the part of Mr. Levine was detected, which the assessor suspects may be related to certain allegations which will be discussed later. Katy is spontaneously affectionate with her father and twice during the play period and once in the assessor's office, she placed her arms around his neck and kissed him on the cheek. These affectionate gestures were not initiated by the father, and he appeared delighted by them. If the child were older, one might suspect that she sensed his need for affection. There is little doubt that these two love each other. This makes any decisions brought about by some of the father's upsetting characteristics very difficult.

"The assessor interviewed Mrs. Brown, Katy's main teacher at the Montessori School. She said Katy was an easy child, happy and eager to please. She played well with both her age group and with older students. Her one fault was a tendency towards bossiness. She smiled when she said she had heard one of the boys complain, 'You're not the boss of me,' after Katy ordered him to pick up his toys. She was often late for class 'on her father's week,' and a few times had complained she'd had no breakfast and was given a muffin and juice. She was, however, always clean and well dressed, with her curls in an elaborate ponytail which she says, "Daddy does."

"She always seemed happy to be at school, and Mrs. Brown noticed Katy and her father hugging goodbye. The father always picked her up on time and they hugged again, and she appeared happy to see him. During one of the play sessions everyone was asked about their favorite meal. Katy said "Hamburger and fries," and told them that her Daddy took her to McDonald's.

"Mr. McCready's childhood was described to the assessor with such chilling detachment that he found it difficult to believe him, and suspected he was embellishing his history in an effort to gain sympathy. Indeed, the facts were found to be so disturbing that his authorization was obtained to obtain his file from the Sick Kid's depository. On perusing the file it was discovered that not only had Mr. McCready not exaggerated his disturbing childhood, but had, if anything, underplayed it.

"There were instances of physical abuse that started with a broken arm at age four and that continued with other injuries on a yearly basis. The explanations for these injuries appeared to be blatantly fabricated by the mother. There was even a photo of a brutally scarred back at age seven. The last entry documented a stage-three concussion thought to be inflicted by the mother's boyfriend, which was reported to both the police and the CAS, with an annotation that "this sixteen-year-old is temporarily living with his teacher." There were no further injuries documented after this. The assessor could only think that at this point in time he had left the home and was still residing with his teacher.

"The assessor found it confounding that no intervention had taken place to help this child in his removal from this abusive environment. His mother, judging from her constant cruelty, appears to have had a pathological disorder. His misogyny, obvious in his personal history as relayed to the assessor and shown in his testing, stemmed from years of relentless abuse and a father who deserted him by hanging himself when he was nine. This appeared to be severely traumatizing, especially when the child found the body. Psychopathy, as manifested by the mother, may have a genetic core. In this case it was exacerbated by environmental factors, and this individual may be unable to form meaningful attachments or show even normal empathy towards others. He did form an attachment with his father and had a relationship with Mr. Simpson, who took him in after his concussion. And he led a gang in high school. But he could not sustain a relationship with a woman.

"There is one marked exception to his misogyny: Mr. McCready loves his daughter unconditionally. I marvel that he is capable, considering his history, of forming such an attachment. Any concern would be that any threat or severance of this relationship may end in an impulsive act of desperation. It may not, but given the background such would not be unreasonable to predict.

"Mr. McCready's first marriage ended when his wife, a pregnant elementary school teacher, drowned in a canoeing accident. There was a joint million-dollar policy that he said was to be used for the unborn child's education. The insurers waited several months before paying, as it was considered 'a suspicious death.' Mr. McCready spoke about the accident with little emotion but expressed regrets he could not save her. He had banged his head against the canoe which had disrupted his efforts and she had disappeared in the muddy water. She was dead when he finally retrieved her body. She was, he said, "a good kid."

"She was the only child of reasonably well-off parents from London, Ontario, who had accused him of murder, especially when they heard about the policy, but nothing had come of it. He had not revealed the details of either his first or second marriage to Rose Levine personally, or in his dating site disclosure, only that he'd had one "friendly divorce." He did take her after the marriage to meet his second wife, Pina Gatto (a.k.a. "Steamy Arab") at the strip club where she worked. Rose had surprised him with her acceptance of Ms. Gatto, whom he thought she'd see as "a low-life."

"Ms. Gatto was, he said, "a great lay" and made "good money" before she started "going downhill." Her sons made her kick him out, but they'd remained on good terms, and she'd occasionally slip him a few bucks "for emergencies."

"He admitted he falsified his background on the True Connections dating site. He'd wanted to attract a woman "with money and class," so he'd falsely claimed he was a graduate engineer with a flourishing business. Rose was made to order: "without a clue sexually and an airhead when it came to real life." He knew she was practically a virgin, but she wanted kids, so he "made a play for her." He estimated she made about $100,000 a year as a dental hygienist, and at the time of their meeting she was the beneficiary of her childhood home, along with her sister.

"Mr. McCready is an attractive man who dresses well, and although he had almost gone through his insurance moneys from his first marriage at the time of meeting Ms. Gatto, he had been lucky at the tables in Aruba the month before he met Rose, so he had been able to fund their first few dates, although he said she had insisted on paying.

"Although Rose had been "sweet and undemanding" at the beginning of their courtship, as things progressed she started to resent his lack of financial contribution to the union. She did not appear to believe that the bank had cut off the line of credit of his business. She told him there was no business—a perfectly true comment that he nevertheless found insulting. She married him because she was pregnant, but he felt she was glad that her sister's law firm had placed their new home in her name alone. She did agree to reverse this when he became upset, and she had also signed a million-dollar policy for Katy's education in which the surviving partner would hold all moneys in trust.

"Her accusation of his giving her drugged milk after Katy's birth so she'd drown in the bathtub was "pure and utter crap," he said. He put only a couple of stress pills that he had confiscated during her pregnancy in the milk "to chill her out" and to make her feel better, as she was "the most clueless mother on record." He did admit she had improved with age and was "not a bad mother now," although her parenting qualities could not be compared with his. He had, he said, saved Katy's life after her birth from "her hopeless mother's bad parenting."

"Katy, he told this assessor, was "a brilliant child who loved him best." Rose had "pulled a fast one" by marrying her lawyer and was "a real bitch" for fighting him for half the house money when she had "a loaded husband." Her vicious nature was obvious with her pursuit of a court action that was "bleeding him dry," especially when she knew how he and Katy felt about each other. Mr. McCready's sense of entitlement and narcissism is such that he sees nothing unusual about Rose Levine supporting him and carrying the home for over two years since the separation.

"This lack of empathy and sense of entitlement indicate a narcissistic pathology, as does his cheerfully admitting that he'd "scammed an old broad for bucks" to pay his lawyer.

"Mr. McCready showed a superior score of 140 in his intelligence testing and under normal circumstances could have easily acquired a degree in electrical engineering. He cheerfully acknowledged that he completed high school often without owning textbooks for the courses in the early years, and by just listening in class. In his two final years of high school, when he was living with his teacher, he came within the top five percent of his class. I commented to him that he was underachieving, and did not have to live by exploiting his wives and women friends. He smiled and agreed, but said, "life's easier this way." He agreed that the former matrimonial home should be sold but insisted he deserved his equal share, "If there's anything left."

"Mr. McCready's other test results show a brooding paranoid individual who feels isolated and alone. In his Thematic Apperception Test he saw himself in a doorway, totally deserted, and waiting for his daughter's return, as did Rose Levine. The answers on a pathology index showed a marked lack of empathy for others, and acceptance and indifference to his own misconduct. His interests were hedged around his own financial survival and the sole individual with whom he professed to feel intimacy was his daughter Katy.

"Mr. McCready clearly cannot see himself functioning without this child, but it is troublesome that he sees her as vital to his own happiness, and not as a developing other, with her own needs and wishes. This could cause complications when the child reaches her teenage years and may wish to achieve her own independence. He does not see the incongruity of his not making practical contributions to her upbringing and yet being a viable presence in her life. When queried as to his future plans he expressed the wish that he would receive half the proceeds of the house he has been residing in for "seed money," and that he would be carrying out "more of the same." The assessor inquired whether this would be scouting dating sites to initiate viable relationships. He merely shrugged and smiled. When asked about future employment he mentioned his gambling, or any position where he could keep flexible hours. He is apparently an excellent electrician but refuses to apprentice so has no "papers."

"Should the assessor focus only on Mr. McCready's best interests there is no doubt that it would be recommended that he have custody of his daughter Katy, the sole person to whom he can and will relate. But the assessor's appointment is based on determining Katy's best interests, which not only includes her emotional wellbeing, but her right to live in a stable environment with consistent parental figures. These parents will meet her physical and intellectual needs, but will not use this bright, advanced, and affectionate two-year-old to support their shortcomings.

"Katy's life with her father could consist of adjusting to a revolving door of women, all selected to meet Mr. McCready's material needs. Quite possibly by the time Katy formed an attachment they would be gone, because Mr. McCready's pathology is such that it is impossible for him to form solid permanent relationships with women. These comings and goings could be devastating to a sensitive and perceptive child such as Katy. From a practical point of view, even if Mrs. Levine were ordered to pay child support, it would be strange if any court would order that she support Mr. McCready indefinitely, as she has been doing by carrying the former matrimonial home since separation. Mr. McCready is definitely employable and the marriage lasted less than a year.

"Mr. McCready wishes to support himself by gambling or as a predator to financially viable women. My impression is that all he wishes from women are money and sex. I am not basing my conclusions on Mrs. Levine's belief that Rick McCready drowned his first wife and drugged her milk after she gave birth. She points to insurance policies, and his insistence on changing the title of the home, which would ensure him the home upon her death. I am not a police officer but a child psychiatrist. All I can say is that Mr. McCready has psychopathic traits, stemming from possible genetic propensities and childhood abuse. This is not Mr. McCready's fault, but we are left with a clever, manipulative, potentially dangerous individual, so damaged that he cannot sustain relationships except with a two-year-old child.

"The week-on, week-off arrangement was not to go on indefinitely, and can only be disruptive to the child and the mother's family. Mr. McCready would prefer sole custody, but is content that the week-on, week off, continue. I am not. I also find the joint custody concept farcical if the parties vigorously dislike each other as in the present case.

"Mrs. Levine has matured significantly since her marriage to Mr. McCready. She is happily married to Daniel Levine, and is quite open in expressing her affection for him, and her appreciation for his involvement with Katy and their son Nathan. She finds his humor a foil for her more somber personality and relishes their closeness. They have purchased a home around the corner from the Montessori school, and when Katy has finished elementary school she will be attending one of the private schools in the area.

"Rose Levine takes her conversion to Judaism seriously and attends Friday services with her mother-in-law, also a convert. She is, she laughs, much more observant than her husband. She has stopped her work as a dental hygienist since Nathan's birth, and is taking online English courses, which will hopefully result in an undergraduate degree and a future teaching career. This will give her more time with the children. She hopes to have one more child and says Katy has "ordered" a sister. She finds the current week-on, week-off distressing, and believes it is difficult for Katy to adjust to such different styles of parenting. Although she does not deny that Katy and her father love each other, she believes the absence of routine, constant trips to McDonald's, and a diet of takeout and processed sugary foods are unhealthy and Katy is already overweight. She also professed future concern with Katy's watching of adult movies and keeping her father's hours. Mr. McCready watches violent pornography and she would not wish Katy to be inadvertently exposed to it.

"In addition, there are several female visitors whom Katy says she likes, and they frequently stay overnight. Mrs. Levine does not believe such an atmosphere qualifies as an acceptable home life, and simply does not believe that Mr. McCready can provide Katy with a home life as would she and Daniel Levine. I must agree with her. It is not a matter of affluence compared to possible impoverishment; it is a matter of emotional stability and family values, neither of which will prevail should Katy live with her father full time or continue the present routine with him.

"There is another aspect to custody that I feel compelled to bring up because it disturbed me at the time and exemplifies the lengths to which Mr. McCready will go to gain custody of his daughter. It also shows his disregard as to the feelings of others, which would in turn impact on his daughter. This came to light when Katy told me that Mr. Levine had sexually molested her. When questioned closely, however, this two-year-old denied that this had occurred, but said she was merely carrying out her father's instructions to tell me this and that she was to receive a puppy as a reward.

"Mr. McCready's indifference to severing an important relationship in Katy's life that would, if accepted, bring about a serious family rupture in Katy's other family, is very worrisome. False allegations of sexual abuse reflect a pathological lack of empathy for both the supposed abuser and victim. It was at that time that I started to question the nature of Mr. McCready's love for his daughter.

The above is followed by recommendations that follow the wife's request for custody and access relief.

D. Abrams, MD, FRCP, Registered Child Psychiatrist

M. Kennedy: PhD, Clinical Psychologist

CHAPTER 54

"Well the Old Cocker finally delivered," said Barbara Booker. "Think it had anything to do with my telling him to piss or get off the pot?"

Rose's heart began to pound in her ears, as it had when she had received the copy of Abrams's report attached to Barbara's email, with the comment, "That says it all."

The report frightened and confounded her. She was perplexed by Rick's candor with Dr. Abrams. Perhaps he thought that if he told some damaging truths, Dr. Abrams would accept some of his more damaging lies. Or did he see Dr. Abrams as a father figure he could trust? He had not even attempted to hide that he was a financial predator of women and that he intended this to continue: an unbelievably crass and troublesome admission. Why, she asked herself, had he done it? Dr. Abrams was an elderly and respected child psychiatrist. Why would he think Dr. Abrams would accept such a lifestyle? Was his pathology such that he deluded himself into thinking it would be acceptable to any source? He had not revealed himself when cross-examined. It baffled her. Even if Dr. Abrams were sympathetic after considering his tormented youth, Rick should have known he'd not condone his psychopathic behavior. And how could a two-year-old be expected to be a source of redemption and support, regardless of their strong bonds of affection?

The recommendation of sole custody to her, and every second weekend access to him—provided he could show available and suitable accommodation—would enrage Rick.

"We'll apply after the holiday break. If not, we'll be looking at a two-year wait before trial. She'll be almost five and Martin will be looking for another report. He'll want to examine Abrams on the report anyway. No fucking way, we've got to move. Make me a list of all the advantages of her living with you: Abram's solid on this. He even told me, in confidence, that he was considering supervised access. But he'd never hurt Katy—right?"

***

She handed the report to Danny that night and went inside to nurse Nathan. From the windows she saw the cedar hedge of their driveway packed with snow, and across the street the Kelly's doorway was surrounded by spruce boughs, packed with red and white lights. When she was finished she went in to read to Katy. It was her week with her daughter and she was glad. She knew the report would incense Rick and Katy would see it.

"I want Danny to read: he's more funny."

"He can't. He's reading important papers. You'll have to put up with me and I'll try to be funny."

She looked at her: the round cheeks and pouting little mouth, large brown eyes and dark curls spilling over her shoulders, covering the pink pajamas with the dancing unicorns. She was, she thought with relief, looking a little less like her father.

She read *The Grinch who Stole Christmas* with as much drama as she could muster. Katy patted her hand and said, "Thank you, Mommy, that's good." Then in a small sleepy whisper she said, "It's good when I'm here." A small hand squeezed Rose's heart.

"Then perhaps that's where Dr. Abrams will say you should be."

She shook her head. "Daddy would be by himself."

"But he'd have his lady visitors."

The voice was barely audible, "He only wants me."

Rose wanted to cry, but that would make everything worse, so she kissed the soft round cheek, sniffing Johnson's baby shampoo and the sweet essence of Katy.

Rose walked back to the living room where Danny was finishing Abrams's report. He was scowling and rubbing his scalp through his fast-diminishing hair.

"Well?"

"It's bloody awful. He's characterized him as a psychopath whose only link to humanity is a two-and-a-half-year-old, but he doesn't give weight to the drowning that gave him a million, and the knock-out milkshake that if you hadn't managed to crawl out of the tub, would have given him another million-plus ownership of the house. This would have paid for about five years of strippers and gambling, depending on how lucky—or extravagant—he was. Abrams seems to give all that a pass. But his recommendation gives us exactly what we wanted."

"We can't knock his recommendation, but he sees me as an overanxious—but literary—neurotic, and sees Rick's pathological narcissism, which is a pretty mild label for what he does, or tries to do, from the pages of the latest *New York Times* best seller. He took Katy's puppy bribe seriously, though, and the result if Katy hadn't straightened it out. That really bothered him—Rick attempting to sever her bond with you and shatter our marriage. And he didn't like his porn watching and visiting ladies, although Katy liked the ladies. It's nice he thinks I've matured. I guess the fact that I got duped by Rick McCready speaks for itself, but then I had the good taste to get together with you."

Inside the room the gas fireplace flickered, casting shadows against the white walls, and Danny sat by the table lamp, still rubbing his scalp as if seeking inspiration. Outside the December snow blew like flour against the large window that overlooked the tree-packed front yard.

"Barb wants to bring an application to vary Hollwell's order during the first week of January. She says everyone's away and there's only a few supernumeraries from out of town available—but they'll be old school which is good."

"Martin will insist on examining Abrams and he'll probably push for another assessment as he'll say Abrams is biased, or some other crap they won't buy. I think you've got to go ahead. The longer you wait, the less impact that report will have—and it's pretty damaging."

"Katy wanted you to read *Grinch*. She says you're 'more funny' than me."

Danny smiled. "Should've been a comedian: my third career change."

"Katy said she was good when she was here, but then Daddy would be alone."

Danny started on his scalp again, and Rose looked into the red flames of the fireplace. And then out the window at the drifting snow, which she could barely see through the darkness.

***

Christmas came and went, with Ma bringing baskets of "prezzies," for Nathan and Katy. "Christmas presents?" asked Rose archly. "Late Hanukkah gifts," Ma replied. There was a huge leg of roasted lamb with about ten vegetable dishes, and six bottles of Chardonnay, imported from France.

"No stuffed turkey and gravy?" smiled Danny.

"No stuffed turkey and gravy," snapped Ma.

Ray appeared glowing, with a smiling Dr. Sherman by her side. She would, she told Ma, after her third glass of Chardonnay, be artificially inseminated with the sperm of Dr. Sherman's brilliant surgeon brother the summer following the wedding that was to take place in San Francisco in May. "A quiet affair," she told the table, "Only about two hundred, mostly family."

Dr. Sherman smiled her approval and took a sip of wine. She was, Rose thought, so striking, with her streaked, bobbed hair and fine features. She looked at her pale hands with their long fingers and short unpolished nails, and decided she'd head for her when her face collapsed and hopefully receive a family discount.

Chapter 55

January 5, 2008, blew harsh and white: large flakes of snow whirling from the brooding grey skies. Barbara Booker had taken her notes and Dr. Abrams's report and had welded them into an affidavit that, even to Rose, seemed shocking.

"Inflammatory," said Danny, "but that's Barb Booker."

"She spins things," said Rose. "They're even worse when she's done. You know it's true: but not that true. He'll be furious."

"Martin's was rough as well. Jeez they're an evil pair: not fit to take care of the family cat."

"He's not as vicious as Barb," said Rose.

"No one's as vicious as Barb," agreed Danny.

They dropped Katy off at daycare where the exchanges had been working well, and although the snow and gridlock had slowed the traffic, they made court by nine-forty-five for the ten o'clock hearing.

Rick was lounging outside the locked courtroom door where *McCready vs. McCready* was the sole case on the posted list. His eyes narrowed as they approached.

"Your cousin Abrams did a job on me, runt, guess it doesn't hurt you bein' from the same tribe. Terrible—crappin' on me like that—after I did such a great job teachin' your wife how to fuck. You owe me big-time for that."

Danny sprang at him, but as he was shorter his fist merely grazed Rick's shoulder, so he grabbed him by the throat, while Rick started punching him in the ribs. Rose attempted to jump between them while the court clerk, who'd just arrived, said he was calling security.

"You're such a pig," yelled Rose at Rick, but suddenly Martin was there and pulled Rick away. "And what tribe do you think your lawyer comes from, asshole?" yelled Danny.

Rose was shocked, but she knew it wasn't Rick's snide anti-Semitism that bothered Danny. It was the remark about his teaching her how to fuck.

"Cool it, for God's sake: I hated having sex with him," she lied in a whisper. "I couldn't even climax, ever" — another lie. "And he's always said Jews were the smartest people in the world, and he'd never have a lawyer who wasn't Jewish," which was finally true.

But Danny kept scowling.

Then Barbara appeared from the cloak room, looking immaculate in her black gown, fresh white tabs, newly pressed black trousers, and high-heeled boots. She collided with Rick, who Martin had unleashed so he could go to the robe room.

"Careful, cunt," he rasped.

"Don't you dare disparage me, cocksucker."

"It must," commented Danny, back to himself after hearing Rose's lies about her unfulfilling sex life with Rick, "be deeply troubling for a refined woman like Barb to hear such disgusting language—I'm sure she'll carry the trauma of it for weeks."

At that moment, Martin ambled out of the robe room in a robe that looked as if it had been slept in by his decrepit German shepherd, who had also chewed his tabs to cure his insomnia. Barbara immediately accosted him, "Your Jew-hating asshole murderer just called me the c-word."

"Sorry about that, Barbara, but your pleadings are highly inflammatory and packed with lies. He's very upset."

At this point, a police officer stepped from the elevator and asked for the McCready courtroom. The court clerk had obviously called him. Everyone appeared relieved.

Mr. Justice Stewart Ennis, who at seventy had been supernumerary for five years, had been asked to come from Sudbury to hear the McCready interim motion to vary. Brought from Edinburgh at the age of five by his industrious and frugal parents, he had been taught to save every penny he received as payment for keeping his room "spotless." At age six, he had opened his own Royal Bank saving account, an account which slowly increased when added to by his paper-boy money. So by the time he was to enter his first year at York University, his account had become so substantial that it would cover the costs of his BA in Honors Economics. It, together with a scholarship for academic excellence, would see him through law school, where he had received awards in corporate law and insurance.

"I worked like a dog," he always told his three boys and two girls, and indeed his sole diversion was as leader of the Young Conservatives, which some had suggested was behind his appointment to the bench. He was also an elder of the local Presbyterian kirk. His life had been dictated to by prudence and industry, and his five children were all achieving university graduates. "The apples," he was prone to saying to his quiet smiling wife, "don't fall far from the tree."

At the time of his appointment to the bench, he had been senior partner of Ennis, MacGregor and Ennis, a firm that represented some of the most prestigious insurance companies of Canada. He was a bad choice to judge a man with a work ethic and a marital history like Rick McCready.

Martin Springer knew it. He also feared that Justice Ennis, a well-known and well-regarded reader of the law and a former bencher, would have heard of the infamous case of *The Law Society vs. Martin Springer*—the case of the hidden tapes—so that his bias towards Rick McCready might also extend to his lawyer.

Martin's first thought was one of flight: an urge that became even greater when he saw Judge Ennis look at his client as if he were a piece of walking excrement. He got to his feet and cleared his throat with a mucous-packed gargle.

"The assessment, which is of great importance in this matter, only arrived some two weeks ago. I would be doing my client a grave disservice should I not examine Dr. Abrams. The report is—no disrespect intended—completely biased against my client, who has overcome horrendous early difficulties to become a loving and exceptional father, a father closely bonded with his daughter. His labelling of my client as a psychopath is false and unforgivable, and it should, I submit, be given very little weight when considering all the circumstances."

"He just said he had psychopathic traits," Rose wrote on the pad that Danny had given her to make notes. As her former lawyer, Danny was sitting beside her at the plaintiff counsel table, as well as Barbara Booker.

"Dr. Abrams," said Judge Ennis. "Was he the author of that book on child alienation?"

"He was," shrilled Barbara, jumping to her feet. "It has biblical status for those of us who practice in family law and for judges who preside on these cases."

The comparison of the bible with Dr. Abrams's book on alienation did not sit well with Justice Ennis. He ignored Barbara, a pretty, but he feared over-dramatic, young woman.

"Were you finished, Mr. Springer? Your time will come, Ms. Booker."

"I can't emphasize enough the importance of examining Dr. Abrams on this more than biased and damning assessment that shocks me in its libeling of my client, and in its ignoring of the best interests of this child who is so closely bonded with him."

"Ms. Booker?"

"Your Honor, this matter started when Katy, the child in question, was only five months old, and she's now two months shy of three—a very advanced three, I understand. Dr. Abrams was appointed by Mr. Justice Edwards, who, conscious of time, obviously thought the report would be completed in just a few months. As a result of Madam Justice Hollwell's preliminary interim order, the couple have been sharing this child on a week-off, week-on basis, which is very disruptive to the child and has become progressively so. It was certainly not Her Honor's intention to have this matter drag on indefinitely. We would be doing Mrs. McCready, now Mrs. Levine, a grave disservice should it be permitted. If we are to accept even half the findings of Dr. Abrams and his colleague, Dr. Kennedy, we would be perpetrating a grave injustice against this vulnerable child to have this matter further delayed."

Mister Justice Ennis had received the pleadings and the attached assessment report that had been sent to Sudbury by special delivery two days before. He had read it, pursing his mouth in disapproval at Rick McCready's work ethic—or lack of it—regardless of his abominable childhood. He looked at the attractive, pale, Mrs. Levine, a former dental hygienist, who'd since had another baby. She appeared restless and nervous, biting her lips, while sitting beside her husband, a former lawyer, who was now running the family construction company. The Jewish people, he had always thought, resembled the Scottish with their work ethic and industry. No doubt the days of exploitation that had prevailed during her time with Mr. McCready were over.

Surely this child would flourish more with this industrious couple, rather than spending half her time with a father whose idea of making an income was the nearest poker table, and who refused conventional employment, although blessed with high intelligence, preferring to make a living by sponging off susceptible women. Mrs. Levine had been paying for him while he remained in their former home, a home that had been totally funded by her inheritance.

All of these thoughts ran through his mind as he looked down at the disgraced Martin Springer, the evidence hider, and the useless Rick McCready—a bad pair and well suited to each other.

"I notice that the Court of Appeal, and now the Supreme Court, have voiced their displeasure at the intolerable delay that is taking place in current trials; and that in a recent case the accused, a wife killer, walked free after a three-year wait. This is an unacceptable state of affairs, and I suggest the court's displeasure may be applied to civil actions as well as criminal. As such I am going to hear this motion today. No one should have to tolerate this type of delay, especially when it concerns a young child, in this case a three-year-old girl, who one would assume would be best suited living with her mother. So we will continue. I am giving Ms. Booker an hour for her submissions and equal time for Mr. Springer. Then Ms. Booker may have an extra fifteen minutes for her reply."

"I wish my objection noted on record," huffed Martin Springer, "and that Your Honor has already shown a bias in favor of mothers: an anti-quated concept that went out with the Family Law Act and Children's Law Reform Act that both stress parental equality."

"Be sure to note Mr. Springer's objection and his comment concerning my so-called bias, Madam Court Clerk. Things have indeed changed, including common sense. This is an application to vary an interim order made by Madam Justice Hollwell over two years ago. Should you wish to examine Dr. Abrams you may do so pending trial, which by the way things are going may take another two years, or you may wait until trial. This will give Mr. McCready even more time to squat in the marital home at Mrs. Levine's—or her husband's—expense, while she pays for the Montessori school and all other expenses relating to the child."

In a clear bell-like voice, untainted by her usual profanity, Barbara Booker told the story of Rose McCready Levine: the sacrificial waif who had cared for her widowed mother and then, because she felt life passing her by—and wanted a child, connected with Mr. McCready, who smothered her in a web of lies and deceit, misrepresenting his education, financial position, and ignominious past, which might possibly include the murder of his first wife.

At this point His Honor stopped her: "Such has not been proven and it is highly improper for you, Ms. Booker, to mention it. I'm surprised that Mr. Springer has not moved to strike that part of your pleadings, together with the milkshake episode. They can only have been included to inflame the court."

Barbara Booker apologized profusely, such was certainly neither her nor her client's intention, and had Mr. Springer shared His Honor's position then he had been given ample time to move to strike.

Rick gave Martin a withering look, and Martin scowled at his file, obviously wondering if it were too late to apply to return to a text he knew all too well: the Criminal Code. But it was when Barbara Booker started on Rick's usurping Rose's mothering abilities and preventing her from bonding with her daughter that the outbursts started.

"All lies," thundered Rick, from his seat next to Martin at the counsel table, "I had to take over or my daughter would have starved to death."

"Control your client, Mr. Springer," warned Justice Ennis. "Your lawyer will have his opportunity, Mr. McCready."

"This type of allegation, Ms. Booker, although relevant, is not helpful to the court. The child has obviously survived, and indeed from what I've read is somewhat plump."

"She's such a liar, exaggerating everything," wrote Rose on her pad to Danny.

"Forget it," he wrote back, "You can't stand up and say your lawyer is lying to the court."

Barbara finally finished, after placing Rick McCready in a house of sin, bubbling over with pornographic movies and visitors who, she submitted, resembled his second wife, the stripper "Steamy Arab." It was in this house where the child would reside, as opposed to living with a baby brother she loved, a mother who had stopped her employment to be available, and a surrogate father who read children's books by the hour.

"The court will recess for fifteen minutes," rumbled His Honor, who had developed a headache listening to Barbara, whose voice had, towards the end of her submissions, developed an unbecoming squawk that he found grating.

"Well?" asked Barbara, turning to them outside the court, obviously expecting an accolade.

"Great," said Danny, nudging Rose into silence.

Rick sauntered up to Rose, his face mottled an unbecoming red. "Jesus, how can you live with yourself—such a lying bitch? Don't think this won't come back and bite you in the ass."

"He's threatening my client," screamed Barbara to Martin Springer.

"You should be disbarred, spewing lies to judges," snarled Martin.

"Almost as bad as hiding evidence for your client in a serial killer case."

The police officer strolled over. "I thought it was clients and not their lawyers I was called for."

At this point Rick disappeared into the elevator, probably heading downstairs for a smoke, Barb went into the lawyer's lounge for coffee, Martin disappeared, and Rose and Danny sat miserable, mute, and motionless on a bench outside the courtroom.

Martin Springer, unlike Barbara, spoke in the most dulcet of tones, as if he were addressing a large hall full of funeral attendees. He spoke of his client's abusive childhood and all he had to overcome. He compared him to a soldier with PTSD, just returning from two tours in Afghanistan, an analogy that caused Justice Ennis to lift his eyebrows. He then spoke of even more trauma: the death of a beloved and pregnant first wife, and then harsh and untrue allegations, accusing him of attempted murder, when he was merely trying to soothe the petitioner from what had obviously been a post-postpartum psychosis following the birth of their first child. His client was a maligned and damaged figure, who was now being further penalized by efforts to deprive him of being with a much-loved daughter. It was extreme cruelty, and both he and the child would suffer as a result.

"A job," interrupted Justice Ennis. "Why hasn't your client a job? Why has he chosen to live off women? He's in his late thirties; time for him to overcome his PTSD."

"He's gotten one this week, apprenticing with an electrician," lied Martin.

"My friend's giving evidence," hissed Barbara. "This is the first we've heard of it."

Justice Ennis pulled his glasses down and looked balefully at Martin, and Martin knew he was thinking of the hidden tapes.

"He just told me this morning," Martin lied again.

"Indeed," said Justice Ennis.

"In any case, it's irrelevant," said Martin.

"You think so?" asked His Honor.

Martin Springer, spurred on by Barbara's lies and his own, ended on a bombastic note, saying how well the child was doing under Madam Justice Hollwell's order, and how harmful it would be to impair in any way "the vital bond that exists between this child and her father."

"King Lear," whispered Danny, "Cordelia: she'll come no more."

Rose sat numb, long past any Shakespearian quotes.

"Frankly, I thought he sucked," said Barbara Booker. "I'll spend my fifteen minutes on the money stuff—that seems to be Ennis's main focus." And she did, calling both Mr. McCready and "my colleague, Mr. Springer," deceitful in fabricating employment for Mr. McCready, when, to the best of everyone's knowledge, he'd never had a job in his life. And it was a strange coincidence that one had materialized out of thin air just before court that morning.

"The Court will adjourn for lunch," sighed Justice Ennis, appearing exhausted, as Ms. Booker had that effect on him. "I will give my judgement at two-fifteen. I have heard of unseemly conduct not only between the parties, but between counsel, and I note a police presence. I hope there will be no reoccurrence of this. It discredits counsel, and worsens an already strained situation between the parties."

"Ciao," caroled Barbara, "or do you guys want to join me for lunch at the lawyer's dining room at Osgoode Hall?"

"I'd rather die . . . slowly," whispered Rose.

"Great idea, Barb," said Danny, "but Rosie's upset—some other time."

"Not to worry, guys, Ennis' so disturbed by McCready's work ethic— or lack of it—that nothing else matters; though I'd like to think I did a good job. Christ, Marty sounded like he should be saying Kaddish: I think that tape thing really got to him. His reputation is zilch with the bench."

"Let's get some Chinese food and a drink, you don't look good."

"Can't."

"I'll get you some coffee from downstairs then."

***

At two-fifteen Judge Ennis walked into the courtroom, sat down, and started to read his order. "This matter was commenced over two years ago. At that time, Madam Justice Hollwell made an interim-interim order, which I doubt she expected future justices to be bound by, as she did not consider herself seized with the case. Her order ruled that the parties were to share the custody of the child, Katy, now almost three, equally, on a week-by-week basis. The Respondent was to be given exclusive possession of the parties' matrimonial home, to which the wife had been the sole contributor, and the wife, who was the sole working party, was to carry all expenses and pay child support for the period that custody had been allocated to the husband.

"To have this unfair and disruptive order continue is contrary to both law and common sense. I am convinced that had Madam Justice Hollwell predicted the future delay she would never have made it. At present, the former Mrs. McCready lives with her second husband and infant son near the former matrimonial home and within blocks of the Montessori school that Katy attends. Mrs. McCready pays for the child's school fees. She believes the current situation to be disruptive and that the child would have a more stable family life living with her new family and baby brother."

Rose sat numb and choked at the counsel table, but there was little doubt that Judge Ennis was presenting her side of why Katy should be living with her and Danny, and that he was going against Judge Hollwell's order. She looked over at Rick, sitting to the right of Martin at the counsel table. He was sitting back, eyes narrowed.

"Roderick McCready had a wretched childhood, which no doubt damaged him. Although of superior intellect he has chosen not to work, although when his gambling is going poorly he benefits from the largesse of women, who either work, or have acquired money some other way. He was the recipient of a million-dollar policy from the death of his first wife and received handouts from his second wife: an exotic dancer. His third wife, now Mrs. Levine, paid for the matrimonial home from her inheritance and carried all expenses from her salary as a dental hygienist."

Rick, his arms folded, sat looking at Judge Ennis. He knew the judge was winding up for the pitch, classifying Rick as a gigolo to justify what he was going to do to him and Katy. A flood of anger washed over him.

"Mrs. Levine speaks of a lifestyle of pornographic films, gambling, and violent movies, the latter which he watches with the child. This not-quite-three-year-old, when not with her mother, lives on fast foods, is often late for daycare, and her friends are ladies who visit her father.

Dr. Abrams speaks of Mr. McCready's pathological difficulties. Dr. Abrams is a well-respected child psychiatrist. He has not been examined, but I cannot ignore his report. It is disturbing."

It was all lies. He did not watch violent movies with Katy, or even watch porn when she was in the house. The visiting ladies were not hookers; they were women he'd met through Steamy, who needed a temporary place to stay. "All lies," he said loudly, before Martin shushed him up. And the bastard Abrams had betrayed him, after he had believed he was on his side, after he had shown such sympathy about the beatings, his love for Pa and Alf, and his great love for Katy. And it was all because of Katy's accusing the runt Danny of molestation, an accusation caused by his own stupidity.

"I attribute Mrs. Levine's early maternal difficulties to typical new mother nervousness and I agree that Mr. McCready's taking over the baby's care at that time was commendable. Katy and her father love each other, I don't question that. I do however question the environment supplied by Mr. McCready and the effect of his lifestyle on a susceptible bright child. It seems relevant that Katy's favorite foods when with her father are hamburgers. I understand both his food and legal fees are subsidized by a sympathetic neighborhood widow."

More lies: one hamburger a week at most. He was losing his daughter because of one hamburger a week. "More lies," he said loudly and hoarsely. Judge Ennis stopped, looked at him, and said to Martin, "Control your client, Mr. Springer." But Rick's mind would not stop: Rose and her lies; Abrams, the betrayer, who had turned on him like a viper; the lying bitch Booker, they had all trapped him in a leaden web from which there was no escape. Except perhaps one.

Rose looked over. Rick's face was grey, his mouth twisted in bitterness and despair. Booker had gone too far. The truth had been sufficient.

"I am ordering this matter be expedited: at the present time there is a two year wait on the contested Family Law list. Another judge may well see this matter differently, but at the present time I order: interim custody of the child, Katherine Patricia McCready, to her mother, Rose McCready Levine."

Rose felt a gush of relief. Then she looked over at the counsel table. Rick was gone, as if he had dissolved, and Martin was sitting alone, bent over and rubbing his stubby fingers against his temples. And Barbara Booker was punching her arm in triumph.

"Access to her father, Roderick McCready, every second weekend from seven-thirty p.m. on Friday night to seven-thirty p.m. on Sunday night, delivery and pickup to be carried out by the father, preferably at the home of a conveniently located friend of the family. Holidays to be shared on an equal basis. Costs will be dealt with after a trial of this matter.

"As no relief was requested as to the sale of the matrimonial home, I will give no further order, but I would prevail on Mr. McCready to have it listed forthwith in order that a statement of net family property may be agreed upon. I am willing to make myself available in any future pre-trial relating to any of these matters."

Barbara Booker was hissing "awesome," through her perfectly veneered teeth. But Rose felt a sense of panic and knew that she and Danny had to go and get Katy.

"There, Rosie, that's a relief. We should go somewhere and celebrate," Barbara said.

"We'll go get Katy at Montessori: it's our week." Her throat was closing and her heart was beginning to flutter, like a caged sparrow imprisoned beneath her ribs.

"I'll take out the order and have it signed. And I'll get you a copy of the endorsement," said Barbara. "You okay, Rosie?"

Chapter 56

The wind was becoming more piercing and the snow heavier as they walked towards the underground parking in front of City Hall. She felt it sharp against her face, blinding her. She took Danny's arm. "We have to get Katy," she gasped.

"Katy's fine. You're just having a delayed panic reaction."

By the time they had located the car and were driving from the underground parking and across Queen to University, the snow was piling on the windshield, and she thought of the rainy night they had left the strip club after seeing Steamy. She was full of Katy and Steamy's words were now ringing in her ears: "You can't be careful enough."

"Phone Montessori."

Danny was leaning forward, eyes narrowed, hunched over the wheel, and the cars going north on University were crawling: strange, sedated, humped insects, their backs packed with snow. He took his cell from his pocket and handed it to her without comment.

"Mrs. Brown, we're coming for Katy: don't let her go with her father. There's a court order."

Then she asked, her voice barely audible, "How long ago?"

Danny looked at Rose as she snapped the phone closed, her eyes wild.

"He took her ten minutes ago. He told them the court had given him the go-ahead."

Danny kept leaning forward, his head almost touching the wheel, and muttered "fuck." Then he said, "I hope we're overreacting, but do what you want to do."

Rose phoned 911 and put in an Amber Alert, describing the Mustang, its license number, the individuals in the car, and the area last seen. There had been a court order against the male driver. He was impulsive, unpredictable, and he had made threats. The child was in danger.

Then she knew it was all true and she started to cry, tears silently running down her chilled cheeks. She looked at Danny. His face was ashen and mouth tight and that made her feel worse.

They drove to the former matrimonial home: it was dark and deserted, the tire marks on the pathway covered with snow. Two neighbors came to the car, the grizzled brothers from Syria, whom she'd helped with their papers and English.

"He not here," said one. "He leave and take kid."

Then a woman in her late fifties crossed the street, her short hair as white as the snow blowing in the wind. "Did the Court give him Katy?" she asked. "I've been giving him money for it. He'd die without that little girl."

Nobody answered.

Then the cell rang, and a voice said an empty Mustang had been spotted outside Chesapeake Park and a delivery man had seen a man carrying a child going through the gate. He thought it strange, a man carrying a child into such a treacherous park, full of ravines and ice-covered crags in a storm like this. And then he heard the Amber Alert.

"We follow you," said one of the Syrians.

Danny was biting his lips and seemed to be holding back tears and that frightened her more than anything.

It was getting dark, and the wind blew grey arrows of hail against the windshield. They drove in silence, not daring to speak. The car was filled with fear, the only sound an occasional muffled sob from Rose. It was taking too long. It was cold, freezing, and there was so little time.

At the mouth of the encrusted gate leading to the park were three police officers, with regulation duffels and hoods covered with snow, together with several other men, men with woolen caps pulled over their ears and stout jackets. The Syrian brothers joined them.

"I'm going with them," Rose said.

"You'll freeze," Danny said. "I'll go, you stay in the car."

She was deaf with fear. She got out, and the cold cut her legs and slashed her face. They trooped in together, these rugged men with two of the police officers, following faint footsteps filled with snow. It was getting darker and the two policemen, and men from the search party, pulled out flashlights that gleamed with bright crystal eyes. And Rose could see the fine snow blowing against the light. They kept on, heads down, and she kept saying to the inside Rose, the Rose who sometimes believed that He would not let bad things happen, and who kept saying, please God, please God, aware of the beating sparrow still trapped beneath her ribs. They walked to the edge where the crag ended and the ravine dipped deep.

***

Rick lifted Katy from the car and stamped through the drifts, surrounded by the smell of spruce, and feeling the lash of the wind-driven snow. The hurricane of his thoughts were like the blizzard: he heard his mother's yells and felt the sharp of her belt, and saw the silver of the lake as he pressed against Pa on the deck of the ferry, then he saw Pa hanging there, in the mist of the basement. He heard Chester's soft "sorry," and felt the silk of Miss Swinton's blouse against his face. And then Alf was hugging him, that last time, and he heard him calling him 'little buddy,' like Pa used to do. And he heard Patsy, wanting him to kiss her pregnant belly, and how she'd been heavy against him in the water after it had happened. And he and Pina living it up in Vegas, before she found out what he was. And he and Rose, walking and eating ice cream, before she'd started hating him. And Katy, and how she used to smell when she was just a baby, a Melancholy Baby. And all the songs, when she'd smile, just hearing the sound of his voice.

He kept on carrying Katy in his arms and all the time the needles punctured their faces and chill whirled around them. "I want to go home, Daddy," Katy said, "I'm cold."

"You'll fly away with Daddy, we'll fly away together, like two birds."

"I want us to go home," she said again, "We'll fly away tomorrow."

He stood with her in his arms and all around them the sleet arrows came and peppered their faces, and she grasped him tight around his neck, and in the distance he saw a small pale arm stretching upward through the sharp white curtains. And then he jumped.

CHAPTER 57

"He jumped with her in his arms," rasped one of the flashlight bearers. "Jesus, why the hell take her? Why not leave her out of it?"

"Because then it wouldn't hurt me," the voice said, the voice right behind her eyes. "It was useless if it didn't hurt me." At the bottom of the ravine two figures lay side by side. Danny sobbed, "go back," but she would not go back.

They formed a human chain and slid down the steep, snow-encrusted hill, and when they reached the bottom she looked at him. She saw his neck was twisted and that he was gone, his arms held out against a cross of ice.

She knelt beside the child and touched the icy still marble of her cheek, pulled off the frozen mitten and took the small hand stiff with frost in hers. And then Katy moved.

"She's alive." Her voice cut through the frozen air and drifts of snow. "Oh my god, get an ambulance, she's alive!"

"Got one," said the officer.

The ambulance was parked outside the gate with its engine running, and a hulking man wearing a dull green coverall, and who had thick freckled arms and a mop of tousled red hair, approached her.

"You're the mother?"

She nodded, "Please God," spinning in her head like a top.

"I'll help," he said. "I'm a Glasgow nurse, a Toronto paramedic, and I know about hydrothermal therapy after two years in Yellowknife. Let me see the poor wee lass."

Rose sat in the warm ambulance as it screamed through the night, watching him cut away the pink snowsuit and then the stiff overalls and shirt, and wrap Katy gently in the heated blankets he had prepared, until all she could see was the still, small face. He pressed gently on her rib cage and blew into the small mouth. He was so gentle, she had never seen anyone so gentle.

"Her poor wee arm may be broke and her little leg, all on the left side. She was clinging to his neck, that's what saved her. They may take some blood out, warm it, and put it back, and once she comes to they'll cat-scan her extremities—she may have a concussion—an' they'll put a cast on her arm and leg, depending on the breakage. I'd like her to sip something warm but she's not up for it." He pressed gently against her ribs and blew into the still mouth again. She thought she detected movement. But she wasn't sure.

"I'm praying," she said softly, "and you're one of the answers." He was a big, freckled, gentle angel, so he didn't reply.

She phoned Danny, his voice unrecognizable.

"We're almost at Sick Kids. Pray."

He didn't answer—too choked to speak, perhaps.

She waited outside intensive care, and then the cold and fear kicked in and she started to shake. A nurse came towards her. She looked Filipino, with a soft, smiling face.

"Her temp's up to ninety-five, and she breathes okay. They take X-rays and brain scan. That the worry, the brain. The damage on left side: she holds on to him and that save her."

Then later, it seemed like hours, the nurse came back. "No brain bleed—or damage, but bad break in arm and many in leg. She needs casts but spine's okay, that's a big deal."

"Get yourself tea or coffee, machine down the hall." She came over and rubbed her shoulder gently. Rose resisted the urge to kiss her hand.

Danny arrived about eleven with coffee and a doughnut. "The desk just said her brain's slightly concussed but her spine's all right. They'll have to cast her arm and leg, and tape some cracked ribs. They'll be moving her to her own room tomorrow. I'd like her to wake up, that'd be good. You should go to a hotel, you look like hell. Ma's taken over with Nathan, you'll never get him back. I'll wait here with Katy. Where in hell's the doctor?"

"You look like hell too," she murmured. They looked at each other and exchanged wan smiles. She had never loved him more.

It was around noon the next day when Katy woke up. Rose must have slept in the chair in her room, as when she woke both Katy's left arm and leg were in casts with the left leg elevated. Her face seemed so small, surrounded by the tangled mop of hair she had always loved.

"Mommy," she whispered.

In one moment Rose was awake, and then it all came flooding back, and for a fleeting moment she was standing at the top of the ravine, with the wind and snow howling and whirling around her, looking down at the two figures, the larger one with his arms stretched out.

"Daddy's gone?"

Rose breathed deeply, "Yes."

From one large brown eye a pearl leaked and rolled slowly down the pale cheek.

"Daddy want me to fly away with him, but I keep holding on to Daddy's neck, so he have to fly away with no me."

Rose sighed and said, "yes," again. What could she say? What could anyone say?

"Where's Danny?"

"He was here. He'll be back."

"He my daddy now."

CHAPTER 58

In time, the casts were removed, Katy had completed her physio, and the limp was gone. But more than the casts were gone, more than the baby fat.

"Katy lost her joy," Rose said to Danny one night two years later, after he had read a chapter of *Emily of New Moon* to Katy, which the saleswoman had warned was "much too advanced" for a five-year-old. "She never giggles or has fun the way she used to. There's no frivolity. She's like a little mother to Nattie, not like a fun big sister. And Nattie does everything she tells him: he's much more obedient with her than he is with me. She waits for you by the front door and won't eat until you come. She wants to eat with you. She says she doesn't want you to eat alone."

"Ridiculous," said Danny, "just ridiculous," reveling in every aspect of being the object of such adoration. But Rose knew, although Katy loved him, he was a surrogate, a stand-in, for the one that had flown away that stormy day and stole her joy. And she was doing what she'd do for him—if he'd not gone without her. But Rose could never tell him that. There are so many kinds of love. And Katy did love him—but behind those dark brown eyes lay a well of sadness, so deep, so bottomless, that there was no end to it. And the joy that had been Katy's had flown away with him and now lurked like some small frozen bird hidden behind the snow-drenched branches of a thick black spruce, its song forever stalled.

"She's so much more serious," Miss Brown had whispered the year after, "and when our day is over I see her waiting for him, although she knows he'll never come."

"She won't eat ice cream—and I suspect hamburgers," Rose replied, "painful memories, perhaps."

Danny had gone to a builder's meeting, and Rose was putting Katy to bed, a rare occurrence. Prayers had been said and Katy asked—in her new voice without its old lilt, "Daddy used to sing to me at night. . . and in the car. He wanted me to fly away with him. I said no. I just clung to his neck. Do you think he's lonely by himself? He always said he was lonely without me."

"No. Daddy was not well; he didn't really want you to do that."

"Then why did he ask me?" said Katy. Rose didn't answer, but kissed the round warm cheek.

CHAPTER 59

Seeing Dr. Abrams brought back painful memories—apparently to them both. He sat behind his desk looking oddly shrunken, although it had only been two years. Rose was pregnant with the "sissor."

"I'm glad you finally came," he said, "All of this has caused me a lot of grief. I've been second-guessing myself—and of course the report. Perhaps I'd been too harsh, but I'd predicted his reaction, remember? I should have been more diligent in warning you."

Rose felt moved—and relieved. Dr. Abram's humanity and guilt was shining through, making him so approachable. "Pregnant again?" he asked with a smile, followed by "How's Katy?"

"She survived the plunge, after some very hard months. And she'd wanted a sister. But she's why I'm here. She's changed: her joy has gone. She's so serious, at times I fear depressed. The love she felt for Rick has been transferred to Danny, but not without mixed feelings, I suspect. She feels guilty she didn't fly away with Daddy as he'd asked—it's horrible: a little five-year-old."

Dr. Abrams's furrowed face fell into full mastiff folds. He got up abruptly from his chair and stood facing his square window. He spoke without turning around. "It's the result of childhood trauma. You and Rick McCready both suffered from it. You tried to conquer yours by becoming over-attached to your mother and by taking anti-anxiety pills and making disastrous life choices. Rick turned to criminality and suffered from an inability to relate to the opposite sex emotionally—unless it was a two-year-old child. I did not mention in my report that his mother was a street prostitute. He begged me not to: he was so ashamed of it."

They were both silent. Dr. Abrams kept looking out the window and then continued.

"The mother's sole motivation was relentlessly economic and she actually stopped beating him when he started to contribute to the family finances at age nine—using monies acquired from being a very successful thief. His tattered self-esteem mixed with a disconcerting narcissism prevented him from pursuing conventional employment and his career as a financial predator of women was just starting. His mother hated his father and Rick had been her scapegoat. He hated her—yet had a more than passing interest in hookers and strippers. And yes, I believe he drowned his first wife and tried to kill you. His much-hated mother had taught him money was the answer to everything. Nobody needed therapy more: but at fourteen, not thirty-eight.

She kept silent. It was obvious that Dr. Abrams had been torturing himself about the case, and she wished she'd come sooner. His anguish showed a lack of professionalism. And she loved him for it.

"And Katy?"

"She's got to get therapy: there are specialists in childhood trauma. We can't have a five-year-old torturing herself because she didn't join her daddy in a suicide pact. I can't do it. I'm too close to it. And I'm carrying my own share of guilt in all this. But I'll get you someone."

Rose thought of Martin's speech in court concerning Rick's PTSD, and remembered Danny's saying, "Don't underestimate him."

Dr. Abrams had moved from the window and was standing beside her chair. He obviously wanted her to leave, as discussion of the case had obviously drained and worried him. She got up, put her arms around him, and hugged him for what seemed like a long time. He smelled old and tired, but lovable, like an old slipper that had been worn for years and you just slipped into it.

"You mustn't worry. It was a great report, and none of this was your fault," she whispered. "And thanks for not being professional—perhaps you'll see me occasionally—I've always missed not having a dad."

Dr. Abrams patted her clumsily on the shoulder and the last she saw of him was he was looking out the window again, his slight frame surrounded by the blue of the sky.

Epilogue

It was January, the same time of the year that it happened, but five years after the fact. Katy was almost eight, no longer guilty after two years of therapy, but her joy had not returned. Rose went alone; she didn't want to tell Danny, who would not approve. "Stirring up things best left alone," he'd say. But she was on a search, the object intangible—even frozen.

She parked the car outside the park and entered. This time there were no needles, only snowflakes floating down, frozen moths drifting from a low-hanging grey sky on a sunless day. She walked to the ravine, this time knowing her way as if guided. She stood at the top looking down. She saw him, arms outstretched, and the small, still figure beside him. She wondered where joy went to die and where tortured souls find peace. She looked at the surrounding black spruce and for a moment thought she saw a bird half-frozen on a bough.

She thought it was Katy's joy, gone fluttering away on the day of the piercing needles, gone to nestle in the boughs of black spruce . . . perhaps forever. And all the while the frozen moths kept falling.

ACKNOWLEDGMENTS

I would acknowledge my wonderful editor Jen Hale, and Mark Anderson for his expertise and patience. And my fellow lawyers who read the book, attested to its typicality, and encouraged me to continue.

Author's Note

Every year 30 children in Canada, and 900 children in the United States are killed by their parents, many during contested custody cases. During my 32 years of practicing law, I represented many parents in these custody actions. At times either they, or the opposing spouse, was fraught with vindication and anger, damaging to themselves and more especially to the children. These children carry their wounds into adulthood, and also suffer from the sometimes permanent loss of the alienated parent. If the child survives, however, they sometimes, like Katy, suffer from a permanent loss of joy. An unfair psychic burden to be placed on an innocent child. But it happens.

MORE STORIES

If you enjoyed *Last Connection*, you may also enjoy Hillier's other novels. Here are some comments from fellow writers and critics giving their opinions of *Sonja & Carl*, and *My Best Friend was Angela Bennett*.

"With searing clarity and poignant insight, Suzanne Hillier takes readers into one woman's personal hell. *My Best Friend was Angela Bennett* is a transformational exploration of abuse, sadism, shame, entrapment, and injustice. A truly harrowing journey."

—Angie Abdou
author of The Bone Cage

"*My Best Friend was Angela Bennett* is a fierce provocative novel about love, loyalty and survival. It's harrowing, funny, tender, unforgettable. It will stay with you."

—Libby Creelman
author of Walking in Paradise

"*My Best Friend was Angela Bennett* is a gripping and compelling tale."

—The Historical Royal Novel Society, UK

"If you're always looking for another book to read, as I am, *Sonja & Carl* is a brilliant choice. What engaging storytelling. Suzanne Hillier is overdue to burst on the literary scene."

—Adair Lara
former columnist for the San Francisco Chronicle

"Sonja's canny observations and mordant wit propel her into the heart of things. . . . Her voice is spot on and for the reader, a chance to become immersed in an unusual page turner."

—Norman Gorin
formerly of 60 minutes

"I don't usually read adult fiction. . .but the piecing together of their connection was sweet and intriguing, and quickly tragic. I look forward to Hillier's future work."

—Janice Carkner
The Gloss Book Club

"*Sonja & Carl* charges ahead like a Hollywood romantic comedy with entertaining characters that readers can easily root for."

—Winnipeg Review

Upcoming novels include:
The Pool in Myrna's Garden
The Salsa Dancer
War Boys (YA crossover)
Catherine Olsen's Truly Dreadful Taste in Men!
Dancing with the Bear, Volume 1
The Valley of the Shadow, Volume 2
Plus a book of novellas called *Killing of the Dear*